© Morgan Roberts

About the author

Dr Anita Heiss is an award-winning author of non-fiction, historical fiction, commercial women's fiction, books for children and blogs. She is a proud member of the Wiradyuri Nation of central New South Wales, and an Ambassador for the Indigenous Literacy Foundation, the GO Foundation and Worawa Aboriginal College. Anita is a board member of Aboriginal Art Co., the National Justice Project and Circa Contemporary Circus, and is a Professor of Communications at the University of Queensland. *Bila Yarrudhanggalangdhuray (River of Dreams),* Anita's epic historical novel about the 1852 Flood of Gundagai, received numerous awards, including the NSW Premier's Literary Award Indigenous Writer's prize, and was long-listed for the Stella Prize. Anita enjoys eating chocolate, running and being a 'creative disruptor'.

Paris
Dreaming

Anita HEISS

Paris Dreaming

**SIMON &
SCHUSTER**

London · New York · Sydney · Toronto · New Delhi

PARIS DREAMING
First published in Australia in 2010 by Bantam
This edition published in 2023 by
Simon & Schuster (Australia) Pty Limited
Suite 19A, Level 1, Building C, 450 Miller Street, Cammeray, NSW 2062

10 9 8 7 6 5 4 3 2 1

Sydney New York London Toronto New Delhi
Visit our website at www.simonandschuster.com.au

 A catalogue record for this
book is available from the
National Library of Australia

ISBN: 9781761109973

Cover image: Woman in sunglasses, Shutterstock/Bibadash; Paris skyline,
Shutterstock/Winner Creative
Cover design: Christa Moffitt, Christabella Designs
Printed and bound in Australia by Griffin Press

 The paper this book is printed on is certified against the
Forest Stewardship Council® Standards. Griffin Press holds
chain of custody certification SCS-COC-001185. FSC®
promotes environmentally responsible, socially beneficial
and economically viable management of the world's forests.

Contents

1	I'm on a man-fast	1
2	The One!	17
3	Cultural Canberra	27
4	I'm no Blackpacker	47
5	Festival du film français	58
6	The NAG, the P4P and the MQB	78
7	Monogamy bores me	92
8	Adieu, Canberra!	107
9	Bonjour, Paris!	121
10	The red béret	133
11	Man-fast to man-feast	146
12	Becoming Elizabeth	164
13	Champers on the Champs-Élysées	183
14	Feeling sexy in Paris	203
15	The Nude Poet	219
16	Le poet turns le prick	241
17	Embassy Bound	257
18	The Ancestors have a plan	275
19	It's on	300
20	This is not love, this is lust	314

21	*Oohlala*, it's Christmas in Paris	327
22	It happened again	340
23	The universe is a bitch	349
24	Au revoir, Jake	357
25	I'll be fine with or without him	378

Acknowledgements	387

Chapter 1

I'm on a man-fast

'I'm a born-again virgin!' I panted. 'Seriously, I can't remember the last time I had sex.'

'There's no man on the horizon?' Lauren asked, as we jogged around Lake Burley Griffin.

It was good to have her back from Manhattan. I'd missed my tidda when she'd left the National Aboriginal Gallery to work at the Smithsonian, and we were still catching up on basic goss and news.

'Oh, he's there on the horizon all right, I just never seem to reach it. And I can't even be bothered trying anymore.'

I was half-joking, but Lauren turned serious. 'You need to focus on what you really want, Libs. A fling or love?'

'I don't want either; the barman in New York was my last unintentional fling. And as for looking for love,' I said, jumping over a small puddle from some late-night rain, 'in my case, it's like jogging on a treadmill. You know, running and getting nowhere.'

1

I stopped and bent over, sweat dripping down my spine as the January sun stung my shoulders. I pulled the elastic on my ponytail tighter and was glad that nearly all the layers and my fringe had almost grown out. I breathed deeply, smelled the freshly cut grass and listened to the sounds of local birds chirping good morning to each other. Lauren did some stretches.

Our friendship was as strong as ever, but we didn't get to see each other much since she had returned with Wyatt, her Mohawk fiancé who adored her. I was worried she would become one of those women who dropped off the radar altogether when they meet a man, only available to their friends when the bloke was busy. But she wasn't like that.

'It's good to have you back, Loz,' I panted.

'I missed you too, Libs,' she said, as we started to run again. 'But you know you'd miss me less if you had someone to love.'

'Yeah, yeah, I've heard it all before.' I ran faster.

'I'm serious, you've become a loner.'

'I'm not a loner,' I protested, 'I'm just self-sufficient! I don't need a bloke or romance to be happy.'

I kept jogging, Lauren keeping up with my pace.

'Don't you want to fall in love?' she asked seriously.

'Love schmove, you know it's not my thing. I've been on a man-fast since I got back to Canberra. The way I see it: no love, no lust, *no dramas!*'

Lauren looked at me with a frown.

'I'm telling you now, Loz: I'm never having another boyfriend – EVER!' The words carried me back to my first heartbreak in Moree, when my first love, Peter, cheated on me. In my misguided youthful life, I'd had my share of loser boyfriends. I'd sworn then that I wouldn't date again, but this time I meant it.

'Never say never, Libs. Anyway, I really don't understand why you're on this man-fast as you call it. You used to like men; you used to have fun. You used to try and set me up with blokes, remember? And you didn't waste any time on that fella at the Australian bar in New York. You were like a bee to honey.'

'I was on holidays, and there was nothing really in that, no heart stuff anyway. Which was lucky because he was full of shit. Gonna send me emails and come visit: blah, blah, blah. He never did and he never will. I've just learned not to expect anything from men, they can't be trusted.'

Lauren stopped running and looked at me, concerned. 'I want the old Libs back, the fun Libs who perved on firemen and worried about her friends' dating dilemmas.'

I wondered if I really had changed that much over the past couple of years. Maybe Lauren was right. Maybe I needed to get back into the dating game. But why would what worked for Lauren work for me? She and I were different. She always wanted a man in her life, whereas to me a bloke was secondary to my happiness. 'I don't need you to look after me, Loz. I need this man-fast.

I need a bloody good detox of them, just like *you* needed with Full-of-himself.'

Lauren stopped still at the mention of Adam Fuller, her ex. She had spent months agonising over her first love – Canberra's bad-boy footballer otherwise known as Adam Full-of-himself – who had once crushed her self-esteem and her sense of logic.

'We don't talk about him anymore, remember?'

Lauren hadn't mentioned Adam's name since Wyatt declared his love for her atop the Empire State Building eighteen months ago, like all good men did in all good love stories, apparently.

'You've been away so long, you've forgotten what my love-life was like before you left or, indeed, while you were gone. Shall I remind you?'

I turned around and jogged backwards, aiming to work my postural muscles, ankles and hips. Lauren stayed forward-focused, guiding me with her hand so I didn't bump into anything or anyone.

'Ben, remember him? Scrawny, sickly white, shaved head?'

'That's mean. He seemed all right, just not right for you.' Lauren never really said harsh words about anyone, even ex-boyfriends.

'Mean? I'm being generous, trust me, he totally gaslighted me, only to tell me at our final meeting that he was gay.' I had really liked Ben and my tone softened at the thought of how devastating his revelation had been to me. 'I felt like I was just his litmus test, to see if he liked women or not. It hurt.'

'I can understand that. It's unfortunate he hadn't figured out his sexuality before he met you.' Lauren was trying to help but I knew she couldn't possibly have understood what it felt like for me.

'I should've known when he agreed so easily to watch *Bridgerton* with me. If it wasn't for the gorgeous costumes, it most definitely was for Regé-Jean Page. I mean that's why *I* was watching too.'

'Fair enough, Libs, he's hot!'

'Maybe it's all my own fault. I told him, "Look, if you love Regé-Jean so much maybe you should leave me for him." I mean, as if that would have even been possible. But you wouldn't read about it, he ended up dating a guy in Sydney who's a dead ringer for the Duke of Hastings. Lucky bastard.'

'Ouch!' Lauren screwed up her face. 'That had to hurt!'

I tried to jog off while Lauren keeled over laughing.

'Oh well, good on him for moving forward with his life, I guess. It's not good for you, but at least *he's* found his match, eh?' Lauren somehow remained the eternal romantic, even if it meant her best friend lost out.

'Yeah, I guess.'

I loved working *and* working out with Lauren. It was moments like these with her that made me feel like I had a sister, a real sister. It was hard sometimes being the baby of five brothers, with Mum – whom everyone else called Aunty Iris – living up in Moree. I missed having someone close to talk to about life and men. The girly conversations were important, and often I just wanted to yarn with Lauren. It was difficult while she was away; the time difference made it hard to FaceTime.

As for talking to my brothers about men issues, they simply refused to accept that their little sister was a fully-grown woman who could be sexually active. I was always just the baby of the family.

Lauren would not change the topic. 'And what was wrong with that John guy again? He didn't last long either. I don't think I met him more than half-a-dozen times. But he seemed really sweet.'

'Yes, really sweet, that was John the Fyshwick Freak!' I jogged on.

'That's right. Oh god, now I remember, Fyshwick. You can pick them.'

'How is it I find a bloke who every weekend wanted to invest in "marital aids" despite the fact we weren't even married? And swinging by Fyshwick wasn't the only swinging he wanted to do either.'

'No, seriously?' Lauren looked shocked.

'Seriously! And it's not like I'd been living under a rock, but it reached the point where I would've been grateful for some boring missionary sex.'

'Geez, I'm glad I've got Wyatt!' She slowed down. 'Not that I mean he's boring or anything, just that he's "normal", you know?'

'I know. And you should be grateful, because after Ben and Matt there was Richie. Remember him?'

Lauren started laughing. 'Yes, the one you called Hamlet behind his back.'

'Only because I am sure he was in love with his mother!' I said, looking Lauren directly in the eyes.

Lauren's tone changed dramatically. 'Now, there's some serious issues going on there.'

I shook my head. 'Tell me about it. How many times can you cancel dinner because you have to do things with your mother? And when he wasn't with her, he was talking about her.'

'That's too weird.'

'Then there was the bullshitting barman and, well, I threw him back in the sea and haven't really been interested in fishing since.' I made long sweeping brushstrokes with my hands. 'I've literally wiped my hands clean of men altogether.'

As I got ready for dinner with the girls that night, I looked in the mirror and noticed two small creases around my eyes. I wasn't game to see if there were any grey hairs. Mum didn't go grey until she was in her forties, so I knew I had good genes; the creases were simply 'laugh lines'.

I was in good nick for thirty-two: the running had toned my legs, the nightly crunches made me believe there was a sixpack there somewhere, a good bra made my D-cups sit right and the pigmentation in my skin was evening out after regular glycolic peels. I had big boobs and big hips, but everything was firm at least.

I was pleased I never got into women's magazines and all the propaganda that affects the self-esteem of female youth. Two legs, ten fingers and toes, a brain, teeth and all my senses meant I was doing okay in my books. I did want my fringe to finally be gone, but at least my hair was strong and shiny, and the new shade of burgundy really suited me.

'I love this place,' I said as we entered the busiest Vietnamese restaurant in Canberra, iconic to locals. I always enjoyed reading the walls covered in testimonials from pollies, locals and tourists.

'I wish they'd ask me to write one,' Lauren said, also scanning the newest additions.

'Lucky-dip dinner?' Bec enquired, only vaguely looking at the menu.

'Yes!' Lauren and I agreed.

It had been a while since we'd all been there together. When Bec and I shared a house we hung out all the time. Now she shared with a local lawyer, Caro, while Lauren shared with Wyatt and I lived with my cats Bonnie and Clyde. These days we had to schedule girly catch-ups in advance.

'We'd like three mystery dishes, thanks,' Bec instructed our waiter, who smiled at the opportunity to surprise us.

'I missed this when I was in New York,' Lauren said, pouring water for us all. 'My flatmates worked the weirdest hours so we didn't go out for dinner that much.'

'And you were clearly very busy.' Bec rolled Lauren's hand over to reveal a stunning emerald-cut diamond.

'Apparently,' she giggled, losing herself in the stone's brilliance as if it were just her and the ring in the restaurant. 'Wyatt is absolutely perfect for me.'

Lauren looked like she was the first woman to have ever fallen in love.

'I can't believe I ever dated He-who-shall-remain-nameless. We had nothing in common, but Wyatt – he and I were made for each other.'

I couldn't imagine ever being 'made' for someone. Were my previous boyfriends 'made' for other people?

Lauren continued, 'I always believed I would meet the love of my life up the Empire State Building and I did. Okay, so I didn't know it was going to be Wyatt, but half the premonition was correct.'

Lauren drifted off into a romantic headspace where only she and her sparkling rock could fit. I was happy for my friend but couldn't imagine wanting a man in my life like she did.

Although I hadn't known my dad for long – he abandoned me by dying from lung cancer when I was only six – I'd always been surrounded by men at home. My five older brothers were there all the time: working, brawling, causing Mum grief sometimes, making her laugh hysterically other days, and they were nearly always there at dinnertime.

Mum is a good cook, not like me. I hate cooking, always have, always will, and I certainly have no desire to cook for a man or men every night like Mum still does. I've always admired her ability to throw together a meal for the boys and all their mates at the last minute. Snags become a gourmet curry, and mince is never mince in Mum's kitchen.

I had decided I could probably do without living in the same house as a man ever again after leaving home, unless he could wash, cook and clean for himself. And definitely didn't smoke. God knows I was flat out getting myself organised in the morning and then working long hours at the gallery. I couldn't imagine having or wanting to coordinate daily meals and clothes for a man as well. Making sure Bonnie and Clyde were fed every day was a hard enough task for me.

And yet, somehow, meals had always been the cornerstone of maintaining my relationships – personal and professional. Now with Lauren glowing like a meteor across the table from me, and her diamond as blinding as a mirror hitting the sun, I wondered if the right man might make me glow like she did.

'Yummy calamari, yummy chicken and yummy vege hotpot for you ladies tonight.' The waiter placed the dishes on the table.

'Looks like you're going to have it all,' Bec said, smiling at Lauren as she served rice into her bowl. 'Career, great man and eventually kids, right?'

Lauren beamed in response, but I couldn't help myself.

'Do you really think you can have it all?' I asked gently, not wanting to rock the romance boat, but desperate to understand how it was possible.

'Of course you can, and *I* can.' Lauren sounded defensive. 'Don't you think so?'

'I'm not as confident as you are, Loz. I have a hundred per cent happiness at work; I don't think it's then reasonable to expect a hundred per cent with relationships as well.'

'What are you saying?' Lauren looked confused.

'I'm not convinced that we can have everything without some serious trade-offs. It's not possible.'

'But you think men can?' Bec asked.

'No, I don't think men can either.'

'Ploise explain?' Lauren said, in a perfect send-up of Pauline Hanson.

'Women complain that men have it all because they can have careers and families and lifestyles. But they only *appear* to have it all, because in reality they trade important things off.'

'I still don't follow,' Bec said, before putting a forkful of chicken in her mouth.

'Men trade-off time with their families to have careers and so it's the same trade-off women make to have careers. But women whinge about it, men don't.'

Bec nearly choked as she swallowed too fast in order to speak. 'God, the feminists will hate you.'

'I'm a feminist, it's just no-one ever talks about men and kids and so forth, they just say that *women* can't have families and careers. Well, they can't. No-one can. There are only so many hours in a day, so many hours to go round to so many different aspects of life. We all make choices on how the day is broken up.'

'Go on,' Lauren said, as both girls stopped eating and listened intently.

'Personally, I think it's because a lot of men don't actually *want* to be at home, and that's cool. If I met someone and chose to have kids and stay home, I wouldn't complain about not having a career. I'd be happy to be a full-time mum until the kids went to school. Or I'd marry someone who wanted to stay home and I'd go to work.'

'Everything, for everyone, is a trade-off though. You trade-off time with kids to go to work, or you trade-off going to work to stay home. And you trade-off time for yourself doing either or both. That's life. But don't say you lose time with your kids because you have to work to pay off the McMansion and the two cars and three TVs. People – men and women – don't have to have all that stuff; they trade-off staying home in order to have careers and *things*.'

Lauren finally spoke. 'It sounds like you've given this a lot of thought, Libs.'

'I grew up in a house where Mum did everything after Dad died. She had to. She didn't have a choice and we didn't have lots of toys or holidays like families we knew.'

Lauren and Bec didn't take their eyes off me as I spoke and yet somehow still managed to dish out the vege hotpot for themselves. I kept talking, 'She worked long shifts at Lillyman's Cordial Factory to feed us all, otherwise she would've stayed home like she did when Dad was alive. They had a good groove.'

I picked up my fork with the aim of eating something, but felt the need to keep explaining.

'Mum worked making our house a home and keeping us dressed and clean and our whole lives organised. Dad busted his guts labouring to give Mum the resources to do that. It worked for them and it worked for us kids, and someone was always home after school.'

'Yeah, I wasn't a latchkey kid back in Goulburn either,' Lauren said, and I wondered if it was a regional thing, mums always being there to mind the kids.

'Don't get me wrong, I loved that Mum stayed home when she could and I was grateful when she worked. She never complained about either, though.'

'To be fair, not *all* women complain, Libs,' Lauren said.

'Not all, no. But I work with mothers coming into the gallery with children and they seem to love their lives. I work with a few dads too. I also listen to the women in my book club who never stop complaining about how much of an effort it is to get to a meeting once a month because their kids are so much work, or they can't find a good babysitter or whatever. I'm over parents complaining about choices they make. Don't have babies if you're going to whinge about losing your figure or career, or about your lack of money or time for yourself.'

I suppose it seemed like I must've given the topic some thought now that I was providing social commentary on an issue I knew little about, not having kids and not being in a position to have them. I wasn't even sure I wanted them. I took a sip of my wine.

'That's what you think?' Bec asked, raising her eyebrows.

'I'm just saying that we all make sacrifices and compromises in life to have what we want.'

'So it's okay to trade off wages and working conditions for women then, is it?' Bec was the union rep at her school and always conscious of equity in the workplace.

Lauren raised her eyebrows as she looked at me, equally questioning and awaiting my response.

I got defensive. 'I didn't say that. You're talking about a different issue. Of course I support equality in the

13

workplace, but I'm talking about choices we make as individuals to have both work and home lives. I don't necessarily want or need to have the fabulous home with every gadget and heaps of living space; god knows I fall asleep as soon as I get home after work anyway.

'I made a choice to have a career in the arts – which we all know is crap money – and I love it. I love my life, and if Lauren takes maternity leave then I'm going to move up the ladder faster and be next in line to take Emma's job as director.'

I could see Lauren gasp with surprise and fear at the thought of me taking her holy grail. Bec smiled and gave me a wink, knowing I was joking.

'I'm kidding, Loz,' I said, to put my friend out of her unnecessary misery, 'but I know your priorities have changed now you're with Wyatt. You want to settle down and have a family, right?'

Lauren was calm but her tone was serious. 'Yes, I do. But I still want a career even if it's not as the director of the NAG. So that hasn't changed.'

I tried not to look sceptical but knew it was in my voice. 'We'll see how you feel about that once you hold little Wyatt junior or little Libby – yes, you will call your firstborn female child after me – because I bet you'll be thinking otherwise. I've seen it happen before: career women have babies, look at the kid they've just brought into the world and never want to go back to work again.'

Lauren nodded, half-conceding. 'That would be fine, but don't write me off, Libs. I'm still career-focused for the next few years. I've been toying with the idea of reviving the Aboriginal Arts Management Agency after my work at the National Museum of the American Indian was so successful. And if I do that, then Emma's directorship is all yours!'

'Gee, thanks for letting me have it in that case.' I laughed as I finally caught up on eating what was left of the hotpot. Bec had been devouring every dish.

As if as an afterthought, Lauren added, 'Anyway, I've got some time before my fertility is apparently going to drop and the biological clock starts ticking.'

'Jesus, a woman's got to think about fertility too! It's all too complicated for me,' I said sarcastically as I looked at my watch. 'My own clock says we should just eat, drink and be stunningly single!'

'Libby, sometimes you are so negative.' Bec poured me some more wine.

'I'm not negative: I'm a realist, as opposed to a romantic, that's all. That's why we all get on. There's a mix of Yin and Yang, up and down, in and out, black and white. It's called balance.' I looked at Lauren. 'As far as I'm concerned, life is a series of cycles. It's complicated and complex, and quite frankly, I'd like to keep mine as simple as possible. If that means no bloke, then so be it.'

Lauren shook her head. 'God, you're so depressing, do you really mean this? What happened when I went away?'

'Let's see, when you went away I kept working my butt off at the gallery, Emma promoted me to manager of educational programs, as you know, and Bec and I hung out as much as we could. She moved in with Caro, then she met David and I only saw her sporadically.' I looked at Bec. 'And that's cool, really. I don't need constant company or attention, and I'm comfortable with myself.'

'Oh, shut up!' Lauren said, laughing. 'I think you have just managed to depress us all.'

'Hypothetically speaking, Libs, if you were interested, what kind of man would you want?' Bec asked, determined not to let me off the potential-husband hook.

'Hypothetically speaking, I don't imagine a relationship ever happening again.'

'But you have to visualise it to make it happen.' Bec wiped some sauce from the corner of her mouth.

'Have you been listening to me at all?' I asked, pretending to pull hair out of my head. 'I actually like my solitude. I like being alone. I've never been happier since I got myself mortgaged to the eyeballs and bought my little place in Braddon. Bonnie and Clyde love it too. I have an exercise routine that keeps me relatively healthy despite my inability to cook much, and I can still hang with you girls. And you,' I poked Lauren in the arm, 'haven't dropped off the radar completely, yet.'

I was putting on a brave face. I knew that eventually our friendship would become like Emma often warned: 'When you're married with kids and everything is about the soccer and excursions and homework and so forth, you really don't keep up with the perils of single life.'

Chapter 2

The One!

In the city shortly after, we walked into Hippo Co. with the sounds of jazz as a backdrop as we met up with the latest member of our posse, Caro, a forty-year-old, brown-eyed, long-legged, thin-hipped, thin-lipped, wispy-haired, big-drinking, dry-humoured, highly-accomplished lawyer. She was waiting with cocktails for all of us – one of the many bonuses of the electronic message stick known as the iPhone.

'I'm so glad the live music is back after COVID, I missed these jazz nights,' I told Lauren as I sipped my Bellini and witnessed what looked like a very old-fashioned hen's night in full swing.

'I've never seen so many trashy hens in one city, on one night, ever!' Bec leant over the table and whispered so as not to offend anyone nearby. 'Last night, Dave and I went for dinner at Rebel Rebel and then went for a drink in the North Quarter and, I kid you not, we saw *four*' – she held up four fingers – 'hens and their entourages along the way.' She sipped her drink then added, 'I didn't even know hen's nights were still a thing.'

'That should give you some hope, Libs,' Lauren winked at me.

'Hope for what?' I shook my head in exasperation.

'Finding your soulmate, falling in love, getting married.' She had a glassy-eyed romantic look on her face.

'And having a trashy hen's night, it seems,' I threw a nod to a hen wearing devil's horns at the bar. 'Trust me, you'll be having yours first, my dear tidda. Let's talk about that.'

'Aha, so there was a hint! You do believe romance is possible then.' Lauren acted victorious.

'Of course I believe it's possible for some, but I don't believe in soulmates or love anymore,' I answered coldly. 'I believe in compatibility and companionship, real things – things that can be proven and tested and demonstrated.'

'What about the love of your life? The One? Do you believe in the One?' Lauren looked like she might start crying if I said I didn't believe in it like she did.

'For a fleeting, blink-of-the-eye moment, I believed. Years ago.' I remembered back to being a student. 'When I was studying at Melbourne Uni, I dated a guy, Andy, whom I'd met at a reconciliation event on campus.'

'Oh, the politics–science major who wanted to be President of the Republic of Australia one day?'

Lauren had been the only person I'd discussed Andy with. The experience had been so painful at the time, and for years after, that for my own emotional wellbeing

I didn't ever bring his name up, but tonight seemed an appropriate time to use him as justification for my defined 'negativity' in relation to love.

'Yes,' I sighed. 'Andy was so passionate about everything: his study, politics, cooking, singing, sex and me. He could've been in one of my firey calendars with his sixpack, huge biceps and steamy bedroom eyes.'

I found myself smiling about him now for the first time in eight years, but I also felt the pain beginning to form in my chest. I knew exactly where my story was going to end.

'You've never told me about him,' Bec said, almost disappointed that I hadn't shared my history. I gave her an apologetic look.

'Sorry,' she said, 'it's not about me, go on.'

'We were hot and heavy and everyone thought we were made for each other. I sure felt that way, and he said he did. We adored one another and couldn't get enough of our time together. He made me laugh all the time, even on the bad days. He inspired me to study more, live more. We went out for three years, the entire time of my undergrad degree, and we were inseparable.

'I found it easy to love him, even after teenage heart-ache in Moree. Andy insisted on coming up home because he wanted to see Gamilaroi country and meet Mum and my brothers. It was the only time the boys were on their best behaviour. I was amazed that Bazza didn't give him a hard time.' I smiled thinking about my protective brother.

The girls said nothing, just listened. It was the first time I'd talked about my past with men in a way that didn't involve me trying to turn it into a silly television sketch to hide the disappointment of another bad choice. Andy was different, and I could tell the girls knew it.

'When we went back to country it was the most important thing a man had ever done for me. He cared about my heritage. He wanted to see where I called home. I took him to meet all the aunties and uncles, most of the cousins and we hung out in Stanley Village and Mehi Crescent.

'He loved it. And I loved being back home with the mob. I took him to the library and we talked about the Freedom Rides in Moree. It was important for me, if I was going to be with a whitefella, that he understood my history.'

The girls nodded in agreement, understanding the issues involved with interracial relationships; Lauren had been in one with Adam, Caro had been married to a Frenchman, and Bec had witnessed the dramas both Loz and I had had over the years. I continued, 'Mum even shouted us a night in a motel with an artesian spa so we could have some privacy. We soaked up the energy from the underground minerals and talked for nine hours straight about politics, the future, how we were made for each other.'

'I always thought he sounded perfect – for you, that is, until . . .' Lauren said, putting her hand on mine, knowing the heartache I had been through.

'He was. Then out of the blue, a few months later when we were back at uni, some girl from over west showed up at a function at the Wilin Centre with a local student she was dating and everyone, including me, could see how Andy reacted to her. The way he looked at her was so intense you could almost grab his stare out of the air. I knew that look: it was the way that I looked at him. The way I'd thought he looked at me in return, but I knew then I had been wrong.'

'What happened next?' Caro, typically the listener of the group, spoke for the first time.

'The problem was that she looked at that other fella the way that Andy looked at her and I looked at him. And while he never said anything, I knew immediately that it was over between us. I knew that the one I thought was my One, now thought the other woman was his One, and she thought someone else was her One.'

I took a sip of my Bellini.

'Andy just faded out of my life then because he was focused on her and how to get her. I cried every day for a year, and swore I'd never fall in love again, never trust again. And so there's been no bar, no expectation. That's why I have the fucked-up relationships I've had. And I don't want any more. None, zero, nil.'

I took a deep breath of relief at getting the truth off my chest. I'd carried it all too long, too painfully long. At least now the girls might stop humbugging me about meeting a fella. Maybe I should've told them sooner.

'So,' I said, looking at Lauren, 'to answer your original question, I think if everyone is expected to end up with someone then there probably needs to be at least two or three Ones to choose from, if in fact there is such a thing.'

The women looked at me sympathetically. Even *I* felt a little sorry for myself.

21

'You still have to believe your soulmate is out there to make it happen,' Lauren said. 'You have to at least be open to it.'

'Assuming I believe – and I am not saying that I do – how will I know when I meet him? Or, more to the point, how will I know when he meets me?'

'That's easy,' Caro said. 'He takes you shopping at Tiffany's, would rather make love on Sunday afternoon than watch the rugby, and he thinks you look hot in your trackie dacks and a hoodie.'

She raised her glass in a toast and took a sip.

Caro was divorced with no kids and, although sometimes cynical and somewhat scarred, she was emotionally wise about love and how to negotiate the world generally. Caro wasn't particularly interested in meeting men at this stage in her life, although she believed everyone should get married at least once. 'My wedding was the best party I've ever been to,' she often told us.

She'd had more life experience than the rest of us and her friendship was a blessing for me. Ever since she moved in with Bec when Lauren was abroad, we had all started hanging out together and she often invited us to events and seminars being run by her office at the National Centre for Indigenous Studies at the Australian National University.

Her lawyerly way of viewing the world – everything was either right or wrong, fact or fiction – worked in my world too. We were similar in many ways, despite the eight-year age gap. Apart from being helpful with a whole range of legal advice, Caro's singledom meant that she and I hung out more now too, and we often 'observed' the married motherly women who'd let themselves go.

'Shoot me if I wear Crocs and leggings to the shops, ever!' she said to me one day.

'Absolutely. Having kids doesn't mean you can't dress properly.'

As I lay in bed that night, I thought about how different Lauren and I were when it came to men and relationships. I never sought love, ever. And I'd only been really close to two men, the first when I was eighteen and back in Moree. I hadn't wanted to mention that relationship to the girls earlier, because it still hurt too much.

His name was Peter, and he was known as the 'Dark Dreamboat' around town. He was the 'nice guy' and hotter than all the other Moree men put together. He was the only good-looking fella I wasn't related to, so I was lucky when he chose to take me as his woman to the National Aboriginal Islander Day Observance Committee barbecue at Chocker's house. It was a statement to the mob that we were together.

All the girls were jealous, especially Jodi Upton – who everyone called Uptown – the self-defined Princess of Moree who all the boys wanted and most eventually had. Everyone knew she fancied Peter, but even Jodi knew he was mine.

Peter and I did everything together – we played pool, we went to karaoke on Thursday nights at the Amaroo, dinner at the RSL, we went out for Chinese, watched the Moree Boomerangs play footy on Sunday, drove over to Walgett on weekends to see some of his family.

I was his woman and he was my man. He said we'd be together forever and I had no reason not to believe him. I was happy with Peter in Moree, just like my mum and dad had been at our age.

Peter told me he loved me all the time. But the last time he said it was when I loaned him fifty dollars for petrol to drive to Grafton to see Archie Roach play. I couldn't go because I worked Saturdays at Jeanswest. I missed him the minute his purple Commodore pulled out of my street, but he didn't get a chance to miss me because Jodi cadged a ride with him to Grafton and that was that. I didn't stand a chance.

Jodi had legs that went up to her armpits, and a pout that made even married men drool. I had the boobs and the blue eyes, but I also had the skinny ankles and flat bum. Jodi didn't have either. She had normal ankles and a booty to shake, which she did, all the time. She had no shame, and there were rumours that she had gone so far as to tease the local priest.

I heard about Peter and Jodi hooking up before the concert had even started in Grafton. The Koori grapevine is fast, especially when there's drama involved, and girls can be bitchy. I waited for Peter to come back to confront him. I didn't sleep that night, wondering if my Dark Dreamboat was really with Jodi Long-Legs and if so, how could he truly love me?

When he finally showed up at my place on Sunday night with hickeys on his neck, I threw up straight after I threw him out. We didn't even argue. I just told him to leave. I felt betrayed and that was it. No turning back. I felt absolutely gutted and couldn't breathe. I cried like a girl whose favourite doll had gone missing.

Mum cried with me. She wanted Dark Dreamboat grandkids. She used to brag to her friends at line dancing that I had scooped the best-looking fella in town. But I knew that wasn't why she was upset. She hated to see me suffering.

'I think I loved him,' I sobbed into her shoulder. 'He said we'd be together forever. Like you and Dad were.' I sniffed hard. 'Until he died, that is. Another man who didn't keep up his end of the deal.' Mum ignored the remark.

'Men don't think with their heads or their hearts, Libby, they think from down there.' Mum looked towards her lap. 'It doesn't mean he doesn't love you. It just means he's weak. But you know you can't be with him anymore. I didn't raise my daughter to be treated like that. That Jodi's mother is just like her daughter.'

Mum would say what needed to be said, or so she thought, to make me feel better.

'I don't want to be with him!' I yelled and stood up. 'I'm never having another boyfriend: ever, ever, ever.'

I blew my nose and Mum hugged me once more before going to get tea ready. I was determined I would never cry over a man again. Jodi Loose-Legs could have the Dark Dud.

The truth was I'd never really gotten over Peter. He was, after all, my first boyfriend. 'You never forget your first love,' Mum used to say, and she was just lucky that Dad was hers.

I couldn't imagine ever having a second love, even though Andy appeared some years later in Melbourne. But that experience was something better pushed to the darkest recesses of my mind as well.

I couldn't remember ever having true romance in my life. I'd never received roses or chocolates or celebrated anniversaries. None of it interested me. I didn't rate relationship props anyway. If you needed 'things' to show you loved someone, then to me it probably wasn't love.

Lauren was at the other end of the spectrum. She was the eternal romantic, preferring to suffer heartache than go without the possibility of love and all its trappings. I was prepared to avoid heartache at all costs and find my fulfilment and happiness in my work.

It was the one thing I had complete control over, and it never betrayed me.

Chapter 3

Cultural Canberra

The following week at work was hectic as I went through the draft of an educational program we were about to implement, including a new set of teachers' notes for school groups.

I met with the consultant for the package and compiled all the feedback from Emma, Lauren and the head of marketing. There were still some amendments to be made to the materials before we could sign-off and send them to the designer and printer. I was excited about the direction my job had taken while Lauren had been away and liked having much more authority and control.

However, come the weekend I was exhausted and grateful for a sleep-in before catching up with the girls. After my morning run around Lake Burley Griffin, I met Caro at the National Multicultural Festival in the city, strolled around Garema Place and checked out the stalls in City Walk and Petrie Plaza. The sun was so hot I wore the hemp hat I'd bought at the Heritage Festival, when we'd had a scorching day and I'd slathered 30+ on my face and shoulders.

It was cool seeing local Aboriginal performers in Civic, but I found new inspiration from the international acts: Brazilian, Bosnian, Celtic, Latin, Punjabi, Japanese and Spanish cultures in all forms filled the centre of the city with life from around the globe. I walked through, grooving to the music.

Caro had to leave at 1 pm to meet her mum but I hung around a little longer. 'You going to be okay?' she asked, acting like a big sister.

'Of course, I love my solitude, remember?'

'Anyway, you're not really alone, are you?' Caro scanned the space, acknowledging what we both recognised was an extraordinary number of good-looking men for the political city.

I hadn't been consumed by thoughts of meeting the love of my life or the One, but I didn't ignore the fact that handsome men made welcome eye-candy; particularly the flamenco dancers and the Greek guy serving souvlaki, as well as the Chinese drummer.

I may have been on a man-fast but I was still human. I would allow myself to at least look at the menu but I knew I'd worked myself into a corner with Bec and Lauren regarding my attitude of disinterest towards men. It wasn't so much a corner as a lifestyle choice.

My concerns over maintaining my stand against men were forgotten as my stomach grumbled. I was often so buried in work that I was only reminded to eat when my stomach spoke. It was another reason I was glad Lauren was home: meals and good food were never neglected when she was around.

I walked the stalls, tossing up between Indian, Vietnamese, Lebanese and Mongolian. I found myself lured to the French crêpe stall. I ordered a savoury crêpe and salad, sat down and indulged in fast food so delicious it took my mind off men altogether.

As I ate and watched people go by, I wondered how bastardised the foods, the dresses, the dances and music had become by the time they reached me in Canberra. I thought back to my time in New York with Lauren and the mix of cultures I experienced there just walking down the street in Chelsea and around Grand Central Station.

People from across the globe made their home in New York, New York. I could've too, it was such an amazingly welcoming city. I loved the energy there. Millions of people, millions more lights, thousands of yellow cabs, bars, cafés, tour guides, the smell of donuts and pretzels and bad American coffee.

I closed my eyes and remembered the pulse of Times Square, the freezing cold day walking through Central Park, partying at that Australian bar, the cocktail up at Monarch Rooftop, and shopping. I loved those few days in New York and the white Christmas. But the city dreams are made of was a galaxy away from Canberra, even if the festival was trying to bring some of the world to the ACT.

Before I knew it, it was 4 pm and I was meeting the girls in three hours for drinks and dinner. I usually had a nap on

Saturday afternoon following a massive working week, but for some reason the adrenaline was pumping from a day in the sun and my pseudo-world trip via my day at the fair.

Our newest meeting spot was an upmarket wine bar in Acton called The Parlour which was known for its extensive Spanish wine list and tapas and art deco interior. We sipped cocktails: a Paparazzi for Bec, a Garden Party for Lauren and my latest fave, a Bellini, for me. As we settled in for a night of catching up, I was inexplicably edgy on my seat as I scanned the boutique environs and older crowd.

'I think it's a bit odd to have a Victorian-style parlour in Canberra,' Lauren said, scanning the room.

'I'm just glad there's no smoking in the outdoor area anymore.' I watched as some smokers disappeared from view around a corner, taking their vaping mates with them.

I was also glad that none of my tiddas ever felt the need to light up. I never tried smoking as a teenager when all my friends were doing it after school and every chance they got. Dad dying of lung cancer had made me hate it, and almost anyone who did it. I had never kissed a man who smoked, because to me anyone who sucked on cancer sticks didn't respect their health.

I never understood why Dad smoked and, being a kid, I guess I wasn't expected to. Mum hated Dad's habit but didn't nag him too much, even though she never let him puff in the house. I remember he always went out onto the back porch. I used to sit there with him and wave the smoke away with my little hands. It was the only time I ever had him to myself.

And then watching him die was the worst thing I could ever imagine, and I cried for what seemed like forever as a child. When my brothers started smoking I cried more, because I thought they would die too.

As I got older, we'd just argue and have screaming matches. Two of my brothers, Keiran and Jackson, both vape. I'm sure they've got scars on their lungs already and they'll be abandoning their own kids soon enough. Idiots, both of them. And Dad.

Lauren's and Bec's phones beeped with messages almost simultaneously. They looked at their gadgets, smiled at each other and then looked at me.

'Sorry, rude, putting it on silent,' Bec said. As an experienced teacher, she knew what behaviour was acceptable in what forums. 'Phones are not allowed in classrooms either.'

'And you?' I asked Lauren.

'Sorry, it's Wyatt, he's out with Dave tonight,' she said, throwing a warm glance at Bec, 'just telling me all's cool, having an awesome time.'

'Great.'

I was happy for Wyatt and Dave and Lauren and Bec, but I felt slightly out of the loop with no simultaneous text messages or man to add to the boys' night out.

It never bothered me in the past but now it was the three amigas and their two amigos, and Caro when she wasn't travelling for work, which was almost more often than not. Being the Pacific representative for Indigenous Intellectual Property Rights meant in any week she could be in Samoa, Noumea or the Solomons. I loved her lifestyle. I joked about tagging along on her exotic island trips, but never did anything about it.

The voices in my head were taken over by loud rumblings in my stomach that everyone could hear.

'Oops!' I looked at my watch. 'We better head off, I booked for 7.30 pm. I'm starving,' I said as my stomach grumbled again.

'Me too, I haven't eaten much lately what with the stress of dealing with kids in the playground and some bullying that still has my mind in knots.'

Bec didn't talk about work much, but we knew that the rise of bullying, even at her Catholic primary school, was something to be concerned about.

'Do you want to talk about it?' Lauren asked.

'Thanks but no, we had a major staff meeting after school yesterday, and we're adopting some new strategies. It just makes me scared for kids who are fragile. And makes me think I don't want to have kids myself who will then go to school and get bullied. Oh god, I'm already talking about it, aren't I? Sorry, that's it.'

'Don't be sorry. Are you all right?' I was concerned.

'I'm good, let's go eat.' Bec was up and almost out the door before Lauren and I had a chance to get our frocks out of our undies.

We walked around the corner to Monster Kitchen and Bar, and took a selfie when we entered the groovy Ovolo

Nishi Hotel. We walked the few steps to the restaurant and amid conversation with our friendly waitress, we consumed cabbage and cottage cheese momos, roasted broccoli and butternut squash katsu, washed down with a rosé from a winery in Orange.

'I think I've been bitten by the travel bug,' I said.

'Really? When, how, where?' Lauren asked enthusiastically.

'I want to see more of what I got a taste of in Manhattan and then today at the festival. Culture, history, food, arts and crafts. Oh, and probably some shopping too, because I did have fun doing that in New York and I don't have enough pairs of shoes, not if I'm going to maintain my Carrie Bradshaw role in our group.'

'More like Koori Bradshaw,' Lauren said, and we all laughed.

'I'm thinking of ways I can weave in some professional development if I can. Or maybe do some volunteer work overseas.'

I did want to travel and I was inspired to see the world, but I increasingly felt the need to prove it was okay to be single and that a woman could still lead a complete life, in Canberra or abroad.

'I want my own international adventure. A journey of learning.' I continued to justify my new idea.

'And on the journey, you may just find your own Wyatt.' Lauren looked hopeful.

It was painfully and drunkenly clear that my friends were only going to be happy if I admitted that I too needed a Wyatt or a Dave. I felt somewhat defeated by my gorgeous girlfriends who both thought I was desperate for what *they* had, and that I needed a man to be completely happy.

'Okay, I might even find my own Wyatt' – I shook my head at having given in – 'but . . .'

'Because there is always a "but",' Bec said.

'But,' I glared at her, 'that's not why I'm going, remember?' I waved the waitress over and did the international sign for 'bill, please'.

The night was sultry and the sky was a blanket of stars as we walked into Civic to enjoy the carnival. Our arms were linked and our heels clicked on the bitumen.

'You need a plan,' Lauren said, 'a "how-to" thingy.'

'You know me, I'm the list lady. I've already got them in my head. I'll start writing them down tomorrow and do some research online.'

'What will you research, pacifically?' Bec said. When she'd been drinking she couldn't say 'specifically'. She was also wobbly on her feet and Lauren and I were keeping her steady.

'You should do some research about where the best lovers in the world are. There's whole surveys done on that stuff, apparently. I've never participated in one, but I heard something on the radio once.' Bec was rambling. 'I can dig something up for you if you like; actually, I'd be happy to do that.' She went over on her ankle.

'Ouch!' she squealed. 'I hate these shoes, you can have them for your collection, they're too high for me anyway.'

She took them both off and walked barefoot. I wanted to escape her ramblings, but she looked like she was losing her balance. As Lauren and I gripped our friend tighter around the waist, we all walked in time with each other – left, right, left, right – and I took control of the conversation.

'I want to blaze my own trail, so to speak. I want a challenge, a non-English-speaking country so I can really push myself and get immersed in a truly different culture. I loved New York, New York,' I said, trying to high kick while walking, 'but it was easy to get around on the subway and cabs, the food was similar – although not as good as here, of course – and we're so flooded with their media that it was like being on a movie set the whole time. I loved it, really, but it wasn't challenging to me at all. Not after multicultural Melbourne.'

'So where are you blazing to then? Which continent? Europe? Asia?' Lauren asked her questions in time with our steps.

'I want to do something useful – work if I can. But it's not like a fellowship is going to drop in my lap like it did for you, Loz.' I leaned forward, looked past Bec over to Lauren and smiled.

'I know what you mean. That was the greatest opportunity of my life, no doubt.'

It had taken some convincing for Lauren to finally realise that the chance to go to Manhattan and work at the Smithsonian was the best professional gift she was ever going to get. At the time, part of me had wanted her to go just so that I could visit her. We'd both won on that front.

'You can teach ESL for room and board in some countries,' Bec offered.

'That's a thought, and it would be challenging.' I liked the idea.

'You could do one of those volunteer abroad programs too,' Lauren suggested.

'Another good option, thanks. And if I can do something in the arts that'd be optimal. I'll get online and start researching tomorrow.'

We finally arrived at the heart of the festivities, where families, teenagers and even retired folk were out to enjoy the best cultural activities Canberra had to offer.

There was a buzz of summer excitement and communal happiness in the air at the carnival, and although I wasn't a fan of fireworks – they're bad for the environment and a waste of money – it was nice to see the Canberra sky light up with colour. I wondered what the carnival in Rio – where half-naked men did the samba – would be like, or the carnevale in Venice with all those burly gondoliers.

I started to feel like a fraud thinking about men and yet telling the girls I wasn't interested. But of course I was interested in men, I just wasn't keen on the effort, the inevitable heartache or the expectation that I would probably have to breed and then become one of those women who complained about losing my career and my figure. As far as I was concerned a man meant complications, and I wanted a satisfying, simplified life.

That night, with the smells of spices and incense in my nostrils and the sound of fireworks ringing in my ears, I thought about how I'd returned from New York with a form of postnatal depression, only without the natal.

Some of it had to do with coming home to a comparatively lifeless Canberra and some of it was related to the barman never coming good with his promises of staying in touch. But I'd been so busy with the evolving gallery that the thought of another trip abroad hadn't even crossed my mind. But now, as every minute passed, I became more consumed with thoughts of taking flight to somewhere new, lively, challenging.

The women I hung with were all world travellers. Aside from Lauren, Caro had been to numerous conferences in the US and Canada and to the UN in Geneva, and Bec was planning a trip to Bali with Dave.

I'd done my trip to New York, but it hadn't been long enough. I hadn't had enough time to immerse myself in the city. Rather, I'd played tourist. I wanted more now. I wanted time to explore a new country and its landscapes, and most importantly its cultural activities, its museums, galleries, libraries and coffee shops.

I went to bed imagining being a volunteer in Western Europe or South America. I'd done a beginner's course in Spanish at the Canberra Institute of Technology but never used it. What was I waiting for? I had accumulated leave that I needed to take anyway. I hoped that Emma would let me schedule in a decent break, especially with Nancia, the new education program assistant, about to start.

After a solid sleep, I met Caro the next morning at Interlude Espresso Bar for breakfast. I cycled over to Acton with the aim of burning off the cocktails from the night before.

I ordered the truffled eggs with herbed potato rosti and a turmeric latté and I was in breakfast heaven.

'Wow, that's something spesh,' Caro said, looking at the pile of deliciousness that arrived at the table.

'You know what they say, order the first thing that catches your eye.'

I filled Caro in on my revelations of the day before and she was immediately excited about my plans to travel, suggesting some volunteering opportunities in South America.

'I have contacts in Brazil and Peru if you like, and I know a few people in Chile and Venezuela as well. We had an international conference at the ANU last year and many of us have kept in contact. I'm sure some of my colleagues would love to help if they can.'

I was taking notes to add to my as-yet-unwritten lists as Caro spoke. I put another forkful of rosti in my mouth.

'Sounds good, thanks. I was also tossing around the idea of going to Western Europe or Africa.'

'Well, I know you'll love the food.' Caro raised her

eyebrows in surprise at my nearly empty plate.

'Yeah, I know, I had crêpes at the festival yesterday for lunch. I think it might be a sign, I should follow my stomach to my working holiday.'

After breakfast, Caro went to Dickson for a swim, preferring to do two kilometres of laps rather than run with me. She had weak knees for running, but the best toned arms on any woman I'd seen, Michelle Obama included.

I rode back to Braddon, changed out of my sports gear and into a summer dress, climbed into my silver Astra and cruised over to Paperchain in Manuka to check out some travel guides for ideas and inspiration. Even though nearly everything is online these days, I really like to able to bookmark and sticky-note pages when researching, so I grabbed Lonely Planet's *Western Europe* and a Western Europe planning map that could be spread out across my kitchen table.

I flicked through *501 Must-Take Journeys*, which included everything from the Sahara Desert to the famous Route 66 in America. Chuck Berry started singing in my head. I picked up, and put down immediately, a book titled *Places in Italy Every Woman Should Go*. I was glad Lauren and Bec weren't there – they would've made me buy it for sure.

I became aware of the music being piped through the shop: Edith Piaf singing 'Hymne à l'Amour'. The sound of her voice, rather than her melody, lured me to search out books on France. I picked up *101 Beautiful Towns in France* and admired the photographs and stunning countryside.

I looked at Julia Child's book, *My Life in France*, recalling her annoying voice as portrayed by Meryl Streep in the film *Julie and Julia*. And then I saw it, a book simply titled *Paris*, on the art and architecture of the city. It had gorgeous photos of the city's most acclaimed buildings including the Musée du Quai Branly.

Then it hit me, just as if a hardcover book had actually fallen on my head. I had to go to the Musée to see the Australian Indigenous Art Commission. I had to visit the space, learn about the other collections and maybe even do some work for the Musée. I had found my destination, at last.

I felt relief and an odd sense of achievement at reaching my conclusion in less than twenty-four hours. But it was typically me, processing ideas quickly and being decisive. No time for 'gonna do' or 'gonna be'.

I put the book down, knowing I had to get to the NAG, where there would be material in the staff resource library. I sped from Manuka to Parkes with determination, grateful that the gallery was open seven days a week.

'What are you doing here?' Terry on security asked. 'Can't stay away, eh?'

'Yeah, I know, it's a problem when your job becomes your entire life.'

I grabbed my bag off the conveyor belt and walked at pace to the resource room. There was an extensive non-borrowing library for the public, but I wanted to sit and read in peace.

In the staff library, the resources were divided up by regions across Australia and then the world. The European collection wasn't huge and generally contained a lot of catalogues from galleries that had run Indigenous exhibitions, both solo and group.

I put my hand almost immediately on a slim hardcover volume titled *Australian Indigenous Art Commission – Commande Publique d'Art Aborigène au Musée du Quai Branly*. One of Michael Riley's signature works graced the cover.

A now iconic image in Indigenous arts, it was a boomerang floating in the blue sky, from his cloud series. It was the same image used on the cover of *The Macquarie PEN Anthology of Aboriginal Literature*, and had become one of the more well-known works of the late artist, who died early in life. Emma was trying to acquire some of Riley's work for our permanent collection and I knew Lauren was aiming for a Riley exhibition in the next few years. I wasn't surprised that it was part of the Musée commission.

I'd heard a lot about the Musée du Quai Branly. The location on the romantic Seine was enough to woo any budding arts fan or tourist to visit. But it was the Australian commission – gifted as part of the original building and opening of the site – that was the pièce de résistance as far as we were all concerned. I ran my hands over the pages of the book, closing my eyes, wanting to feel the texture of the façade of the building, and the work of Lena Nyadbi that adorned it.

I imagined what it would be like to be a Blackfella in the heart of Europe in one of the most artistic cities in the world, seeing the work of a respected Aboriginal artist as part of the architecture of one of Europe's most important modern buildings. A shiver shot up my spine. I knew that was where I had to go.

Other staff came and went over the hours it took me to absorb the book cover to cover, but I didn't shift from my seat. My mind was ticking over as I took in every detail of the eight artists who were commissioned to have their work as part of the architecture and installations in the Musée.

I felt a special surge of pride and inspiration as I read a quote in the book from artist Gulumbu Yunupingu, whose work *Garak, the universe* was a massive ceiling installation that allowed the millions of visitors to the Musée to enter the artist's own universe over time. Yunupingu said of her contribution, 'This is my gift to you, to the French people, and to the people of world, this is my heart.'

And what a gift it was. I was overwhelmed by the extraordinary insight and skill of the artist, and I needed desperately to be one of those visitors to see the night sky as she did, at least through her installation.

I started to think of my role as a professional working in the arts, and how I wanted to be part of a process of bringing the extraordinary works of a few to the masses, to be part of a gallery that helped tell the stories of Indigenous Australia to an international audience.

I wanted to be part of a movement that took us to a new understanding of who we are as a people, the First Peoples. I wanted, like Yunupingu, to be able to gift something to the world also. The only way I could do it was to showcase some more of those who did, and teach their work as well. The decision had been made, at least in my head.

I went back to Braddon and spent the afternoon online reading about the Musée and looking at hundreds of images of the building and the collections within it. I didn't waste time looking at Bec's suggested 'research' on the world's best lovers, and I didn't care at all anymore about a decent kiss. I was totally focused on the task at hand – developing a proposal to get some more Aboriginal artwork and *myself* to Paris.

I needed my Sunday afternoon nap though. I was tired, my eyes were heavy and I knew that going without it was something my body wasn't used to. But my adrenaline was pumping and although I tried lying down for a few minutes with the ceiling fan on low, earplugs in and eye mask on, I couldn't get to sleep.

My mind was working overtime, knowing that I'd set myself the biggest professional goal to date. I liked to set myself challenges to test my own growth: it's what kept me motivated. But I always had a fallback plan, so I was sure to land on my feet in a way that left me dignified and still challenged.

I thought it was worth making lists of different countries and opportunities to travel, just in case my idea to go to the Musée as something more than a tourist was simply too ambitious – for me and Emma. After all, who was I to tell the director of the National Aboriginal Gallery that we should do a temporary exhibition in a space that already had one of the most significant commissions of Aboriginal artwork in the world? Was I mad?

My Sunday afternoon nap was calling me again, and I just wanted to lie down, rest my eyes and think, but I knew myself too well. I knew that it would be Paris that would appear in my thoughts. So I cracked a caffeine drink and continued to search for potential volunteer arts programs in Paris, but no opportunities presented themselves.

I needed to talk to someone, I needed my tiddas. Although I never got lonely, it was moments like these that made the downfall of living alone glaringly obvious: I had no-one at hand to bounce ideas off. Bonnie and Clyde didn't respond appropriately, choosing to scratch around in the kitty litter rather than listen to me rant.

But I knew my tiddas were always there. They always returned texts as soon as they received them. That's what my friends were like. Always there, always responsive, always supportive, just being the kind of friend that I was to them. Mum had always told me, 'You have to be a friend to have friends.'

I texted Lauren and Bec to see if they could meet for a quick coffee at about 5 pm. My trip had taken on a sense of urgency that I couldn't explain to myself, let alone them, but there was no stopping me now.

I was a strong believer in positive affirmations. I would take any luck that might come my way and I had faith in the universe, throwing my wishes up to her regularly before taking a deep breath and just waiting for what came back. Mostly the universe was kind to me, but she could be a bitch if she wanted and I knew not to take anything for granted. That's why faith had to be accompanied by tangible practicalities and strategies and, in my case, a lot of lists!

I sat in Silo in Kingston with the Musée in my mind and pages of notes spread across the table. I thought about my friends on the way to meet me, and how I never knew what the acceptable amount of time you could expect your girlfriends to gift you once they met men was. Was it unfair to ask to see them at all on the weekend? Was it especially unreasonable to call them out of relationship bliss on a Sunday afternoon to talk about your own one-woman trip?

Such ad hoc meetings were how it used to be for us before the men arrived. Coffees when we felt like it or needed it, that's what we all used to do. We'd hang out on weekends, we were a posse. In the last two years I hadn't changed at all; my relationship status hadn't changed enough to impact our friendships, nor had the way I viewed our friendship. The reality was that both Lauren and Bec had changed. That's what happens when you're 'in love', apparently.

But even with the pseudo-relationships I'd had, I'd always put my friends first, to the point of causing arguments with boyfriends who felt 'neglected', 'unloved', 'unimportant'. In hindsight, perhaps they were. I used to say *c'est la vie* when men would complain about my 'tidda time' with the girls. It was the only French I used regularly, which didn't bode well for me now wanting to go to Paris despite having no language skills whatsoever.

Before Caro joined our group, I had always been the serious one of the three – the strong one, the one who everyone came to for advice. I liked my role in my circle of friends and at work. It never bothered me that I was considered the 'bad cop'.

I was comfortable with being brutally honest if need be, and knew some of my co-workers probably thought I was blunt in meetings when, in fact, I was just passionate about my work. I didn't tolerate tardiness or sloppiness. Life was for living, not fluffing around, and I believed friends were always going to be around longer than any man. It made me feel like I had everything sorted.

Not that I thought I was better off or more in control than anyone else. My life was not without flaws, but I tried to sort through them quickly, and as painlessly as possible, and believed in just getting on with it. I guess I could've been considered to be cold in that way. Cold maybe, practical most definitely. Logical rather than emotional. And that's why we girls all balanced out well. But watching Lauren and Bec with Wyatt and Dave now made me rethink my mates-before-dates philosophy.

Chapter 4

I'm no Blackpacker

Lauren and Bec arrived within seconds of each other, sitting on either side of me at a table set for four.

'What's so urgent it couldn't wait till tomorrow?' Lauren asked, sounding slightly annoyed.

I felt a pang of guilt for dragging her out, but over the years I had been the least needy of the group, and I had been through a lot with Lauren and her emotional dramas with her cheating footballer ex, Adam.

'Tomorrow we'll both be buried in work, you'll be getting ready for Tassie on Tuesday and I've got a full program of lectures and tours.'

I always had my schedule – and sometimes even Lauren's – branded in my brain.

'Thanks for the reminder about Tassie on Tuesday, another trip I need to pack for. Lucky Wyatt's coming with me and is probably already onto it, or else there's no way I would've left him lying under the tree in the backyard without me. It's the one thing I really love doing on Sunday.'

'I'm sorry.' I felt selfish for taking her away from her perfect man and their tree. 'It's just that I am totally consumed now with the thought of going overseas. I can't think of anything else. I don't know why, but I feel like it needs to happen asap.'

I turned my lists around to face them.

'And I needed you both today.' I looked at my friends, knowing that I really did need them.

'This is so you,' Lauren said, having experienced my passionate ways before. 'Get an idea and don't rest, or let anyone else rest, until it's implemented. Show me.' She grabbed some pages off the table.

'Wow, you move fast all right, did you sleep at *all* last night?' Bec was leaning over the table to take a look, always impressed with my list-making ability.

'Hardly. My brain was working overtime. It was like when I had that idea for Saturday afternoon masterclasses at the gallery.'

'I remember. You couldn't sit still until we did the pitch to Emma and then you didn't stop until it was up and running.' Lauren spoke without taking her eyes off the page.

'And six months later, they're a raging success, thank you very much! Classes fully booked each week.' I was proud of the achievement.

'That's true,' Lauren said to Bec, in case she needed convincing.

'Well, *this*' – I pointed to the pages – 'is just like that project.'

'How many coffees have you had today?' Bec asked as she scanned the pages.

'One coffee this morning with Caro and a can of Red Bull to perk me up at lunchtime. But now I'm running on adrenaline.'

'Well, to be honest, I was also a little excited about your trip and . . .' Bec pulled some printed pages out of her orange handbag. She had been convinced, last winter, that orange was the new black. 'I did some research,' she said handing me the paper.

'Really? Wow, that's very cool, Bec, thanks.'

'No probs, I had to do some school work anyway and just did a little extra "qualitative research"' – she made air quotes – 'to see who the world's best lovers are.' She showed me highlighted sections of her printed pages.

I was trying not to look totally gobsmacked that she'd actually researched the world's best lovers. 'Oh no, that's not the research I need, sis, really.' I shook my head just slightly, trying not to offend my caring, generous, considerate yet misguided friend.

'Don't shake your head at me, I'm trying to help.' I could see that Bec was a little disappointed at my lack of gratitude for her man-hunting assistance.

'So, what did you find?' I sighed, scanning the pages and feigning interest in the topic when all I wanted to do was talk about Paris and my plan.

'Well, a general search found the best lovers to be the French, Spanish and Greek.'

Bec had said the magic word, French.

'Great!' I responded enthusiastically, to her surprise.

'Um, excuse me,' Lauren piped up. 'Can I please add Native American to that list?' Wyatt was Mohawk, after all, and Loz had alluded to how good he was in bed more than once.

We all laughed.

'All these foreign places could do with an Aboriginal cultural injection, I'm sure,' Bec said, running her fingers down the pages. 'But before you make a decision you may want to look at this.' She handed me a printout with pics of shirtless men.

'According to this online survey of fifteen thousand women internationally, German men were considered the worst in bed, the English came second on the shame list because they tended to let women do all the work, and the Spanish were considered the best, followed by Brazil and Italy.'

I was amazed by the number of photos she had collected. 'When did you actually do this? I only decided that I wanted to travel this morning.'

'I made a quick search before I left home. Caro told me you had brekky this morning and she recommended South America, so Brazil might be the go – look at the photo here under "Latin lovers".' Bec opened her eyes wide, nodding yes, anticipating my agreement.

'I guess I should look too, just to support you,' Lauren said cheekily peering over the page. 'I love Wyatt, but that doesn't mean the odd perve isn't allowed.'

'You are seriously crazy,' I said, looking at both of them.

'Where do you want to go then?' Lauren asked.

'Well, rest assured I'm not that interested in going to Germany or England, it's bad enough being in a colony as it is. Spain, Brazil and Italy do spark some interest though, but . . .'

Before I had a chance to say I wanted to go to Paris, Lauren cut in.

'You did a year of Spanish at CIT so it makes sense to go there.'

'That's true. I'm not fluent, but neither am I useless.' I looked at the pages again. 'I have to be honest with you. I've pretty much decided I want to go to Paris.'

'Ah, *Paris*,' Bec said. 'Who wouldn't be drawn to the architecture: the Eiffel Tower, the Arc de Triomphe, Notre-Dame Cathedral – even though it's still fenced off from the fire – and of course, you'd love the Louvre too.'

I didn't have time to respond to the list of iconic buildings or add a few of my own, because Lauren jumped in.

'Oh my god, the food! Endless pastries, croissants, French bread, cheese, oh, and the macarons! All to die for. Tell me you want to go for the food, please? We both know it's better than Canberra and definitely beats New York!'

Lauren was known as 'the palate of the posse' – more interested in dessert menus than the wine menu when we went out for dinner.

'Let's face it,' Lauren went on, 'a girl's gotta eat, and dress, and Paris is the fashion and foodie capital of the world. You do need some decent clothes to go with your fabulous shoe collection. You can't be Koori Bradshaw with only half the wardrobe.'

'Thanks,' I said, half-hurt, but Lauren didn't notice – she was too excited.

'And let's not forget it's the city of love, also, just as an aside,' Lauren added with a wink.

'A coincidence, as it were.' Bec embellished the moment.

'You know, you could do a few cities on a Contiki tour, so you could do Paris and go through Spain if you wanted and then onto Greece?' Lauren suggested.

'Or you could go backpacking,' Bec quickly added.

'I'm not going Blackpacking. And Contiki? Please. I like my creature comforts, and I am NOT prepared to share a dorm with strangers snoring and farting and peeing in the shower and having sex when they think everyone's asleep. God, how awful.' I screwed up my face. 'The only thing worse than not having sex yourself is having to listen to other people having it. The thought of that does not inspire me at all.'

I knew I sounded like a Bourgeois Black. I didn't like that label, and I wasn't the only one in our group who would get tagged with it. Lauren never said it, but she was a target also, as were Emma and Caro. It was a common practice in our community: any educated woman with an interest in fashion and world travel had to deal with the tall-poppy syndrome – oddly enough, the ones trying to cut us down were often other Black women.

Lauren and I often discussed the issue of Black-woman-on-Black-woman criticism, confused because we were supposed to get educated and get good jobs and have decent, healthy lifestyles, only to be condemned by some for 'selling out' when we did. Apparently, doing well meant we were 'living like whitefellas'.

Well, I didn't want to live like my Nanna did in Moree with no rights until the late '60s – not even allowed to go to the local pool or the club. Nor did I want to be like my Old People, who were poverty-stricken. My Elders wanted me to have all the creature comforts they never had, and that also meant seeing the world. I was sure they'd be happy for me not to Blackpack either.

'So, what's your plan then?' Lauren asked with heightened interest.

'If you look at this list,' I said, pulling a final page from my big black folder, 'you'll see that I've been trying to find ways of incorporating some professional development into the trip. I know travel is educational anyway, but I've decided I want to do something meaningful, like you did at the Smithsonian, Loz, and explore a new city and culture.'

'Or *cultures*, like in New York,' Lauren added.

I was about to unveil my grand plan when Bec cut in. 'Could you find something like the NAG in Spain? Their Indigenous population is the Basque people,' Bec was eager to help. 'The library has the entire school doing a project on the region this term.'

'Of course,' Lauren added. 'They're around the western end of the Pyrénées, near north-eastern Spain and south-western France. How gorgeous would that country be? They might have organisations you could work in.'

'Sounds like a good option, Libs: Spanish men, Frenchmen, wine, food and salsa. I'm almost jealous,' Bec was still trying to make sure my trip involved the UN of men.

'No!' I said, not able to contain myself any longer. 'I've got a better idea.'

'Well, what are you waiting for then? Fire away, sis, something better than working in the Pyrénées must be bloody amazing.'

'It is better than amazing, it is a MUST! Deadly exciting, cultural, challenging, even sexy,' I said, looking at Bec, 'seeing as you have made it clear that guys obviously need to be included in the mix.' I knew I'd have to pretend to have an interest in potential romance if I was to get complete support from Bec. Lauren, on the other hand, would understand the artistic importance of my idea.

'What is the big idea then?' They were both impatient.

'The Musée du Quai Branly in Paris!'

'Oh my god! Of course. The Musée du Crème Brûlée! Perfect, why didn't I think of it?' Lauren was so excited she stood up, gestured with her hands, sat down, slapped herself on the forehead in a rather dramatic fashion and said, 'Genius, Libs, genius!'

'What is this museum of custard that is such a genius idea?' Bec asked.

'It's an amazing cultural museum in Paris, the legacy of a former president of France, Jacques Chirac. There's a fantastic Aboriginal collection curated back then by Brenda L Croft and Hetti Perkins,' I said knowingly. 'The top curators, the pioneers in our space.'

'The collection was gifted by the Australian government and opened in 2006, and it's an incredible permanent exhibition.' Lauren and I were working in tandem.

I looked upwards. 'The ceiling in some parts of the building showcases the artwork of Gulumbu Yunupingu from north-east Arnhem Land.'

'Kind of like an Aboriginal Michelangelo!' Bec was impressed.

'I think there's an opportunity to develop a short-term project to take to them. The French, that is,' I said enthusiastically to Lauren, desperate for her support and good wishes. 'If I can come up with a concept and find some funding support, I think Emma would approve.'

'I know Emma, and I reckon she'd love the whole idea.'

'I can do this.' I was determined.

'What kind of exhibition do you want to do? We need to brainstorm. And then we can work out how we can massage it into something Crème Brûlée won't be able to say no to.' Lauren was getting even more excited than me about my potential trip abroad.

I thought hard. 'I love program managing, but I thrive doing the educational tours at the NAG. I enjoy giving lectures to uni students, the sessions I run with school-kids, even the mums-and-bubs days are growing. I'm good at the face-to-face work. I love the interaction with the public and seeing light bulbs go on when I talk about the warriors and activists hanging in Kings Hall, then walking them through the temporary exhibitions.'

'That's where you're on fire, sis,' Lauren said sincerely.

'And I'm just about to sign-off on the curriculum resources we developed for teachers with Shelley Ware and Culture is Life. With that in mind, I thought I could put together an educational package to go with whatever we planned to offer the Musée?'

'This is perfect.' Lauren rubbed her hands together as if the project was hers.

'Hey, why are you so excited? You're not getting this gig. You've had your Manhattan Dreaming; this Paris Dreaming is all mine.' I laughed at my own words but there was a noticeable tone of ownership in the claim. I was already obsessed with the project, which in my mind was always going to be way better than being obsessed with a bloke.

'Let's just say, with the Musée you might even be one-upping me and the Smithsonian.'

'Loz, you know I'm not trying to one-up you, don't you, sis? I just want to do something extraordinary, I need the challenge.'

'I know, I was kidding.' Lauren and I had always been a great team because we weren't competitive. It was good that we worked in different areas of the visual arts world, even though we collaborated together on projects. We'd seen good friendships lost due to vindictiveness and unnecessary rivalry, especially amongst the artists themselves. Lauren and I each gave our careers everything, but we'd both reached a point of maturity and wisdom and knew that we'd never put a job before our friendship. We were both highly employable and could work anywhere with our skills.

'Not to be the spoiler or anything,' Bec said cautiously. 'And even though I'm clearly jealous of both of you with your exciting international lives, but what about your boss, Emma? Do you reckon she'll be in on this? Won't she have to, you know, let you go?'

'Good point, Miss Bec!' Whenever Bec acted as a voice of reason amidst the passionate dreaming and scheming Lauren and I indulged in, we referred to her like a teacher.

'Emma is huge on the internationalisation of the NAG. It's something we discussed when she proposed my fellowship to the Smithsonian. We just need to build a case along those lines. You'll need to do a pitch, Libs.' Lauren was like me in many ways and knew how to strategise.

'I know, I've already been thinking about it. Emma is smart and savvy so we'll have to be strategic and work out what will not only be appealing to the Musée, but what will benefit the NAG most. Emma's big on our own growth,' I said, putting a pen behind my ear. 'And so am I!'

'This is good, Libs, I think you're right on the money here.'

I put my hand in the middle of the table and led the cry: 'Yes, I can.'

Lauren put her hand on top of mine and Bec put hers on Lauren's. My personal decision had been endorsed by my dearest friends. I was leaving for Paris to work at the Musée du Crème Brûlée. I just needed to let Emma know I was going, and the French know I was coming.

Chapter 5

Festival du film français

For the next week, I was flat out at work doing my usual lectures and tours for uni students, school groups and tourists visiting the gallery. Each talk aided my thinking and gave me ideas for what I had codenamed my 'Pitch 4 Paris' or P4P for short.

I always took on board feedback provided at the end of a tour via the gallery's app. I took special notice of the constructive comments from teachers and students to help improve the education program, but mostly the comments were about what visitors enjoyed most in their time at the NAG. I pulled out some quotes from international visitors to add to my P4P.

My working day had grown to include up to ninety minutes of 'answering' time each day, devoted solely to emails and phone calls to researchers, students and members of the public. Some were doing assignments on Australian history and politics, which included information on

First Nations Australians. Others were doing profiles on artists or wanting to know where to buy art direct from communities.

'Emma had told me all about how public interest in Aboriginal art had increased ever since Kevin Rudd's Apology to the Stolen Generations back in 2008. I remember watching that significant event with my entire school, and now I was reaping the benefits of the symbolic gesture – there was increased communication between Black and white Australians. It was as if Rudd had endorsed a greater interest in Aboriginal art and culture, or so it seemed from my desk anyway.

As I compiled all the positive feedback, I took a moment to reflect on the enormous job I was doing at the gallery and, in fact, how well I was doing it. Caro often said that overachievers didn't stop to recognise what they'd done because they're too busy just 'doing' it. She'd been seeing a life coach for some years to help reach her own professional goals – she was being headhunted by universities internationally, the latest offer coming from the Faculty of Law at the University of Barcelona.

The only thing keeping her in Canberra was an on-again off-again relationship with another lawyer. The life coach hadn't helped her with that issue, but all the other advice Caro had been given eventually trickled down to me. I started making monthly notes on what challenges I had faced and what I'd achieved. It was a worthwhile task and the records were going to be useful when doing my P4P to Emma.

On top of my usual duties, I also had to go through a draft report on a commissioned review of the NAG, which included a future marketing strategy. With my experience in programming, Emma knew I'd see any flaws or gaps in the report and I was the last set of eyes to look at it before she would sign-off and the implementation process would begin.

A draft catalogue also sat on my desk for proofing. I'd done a copyediting course as part of my professional development early on in the job, which now meant that everyone came to me with proofing work. Being competent and reliable could often translate into simply creating more work for myself. But now, all the times I had said yes to proofing were going to pay off, because I knew about every aspect of the gallery and what was going on where and with whom.

As I continued to draft up my P4P at home most nights, I worked in a draft schedule and budget and dissected all the possible benefits to the gallery, to me personally and professionally, and to the First Nations arts community at large. I was inspiring myself just by writing up the proposal and I knew that the idea had legs, and strong legs at that.

I wondered why I hadn't thought of it earlier but, like Lauren's fellowship to New York, the idea arrived when the timing was right – when I decided I wanted to go abroad. Perhaps the marketing strategy would've unravelled the project idea anyway, even if the multicultural festival in Civic hadn't inspired me.

I had the ability and experience on paper and in practice, but I needed to have faith in the universe; I'd just have to throw it up to her in my usual fashion and wait to see what she threw back. But if I could attach some practical research to that faith, then I knew it would give a good shove in the right direction.

I was flying solo for the week, Lauren having left for Tassie as planned on Tuesday. She was going to be there until Friday, meeting with local shell necklace makers about an exhibition we wanted to host at the NAG. She also had meetings with Arts Tasmania about some long-term partnerships. There was no time to talk about the P4P while Lauren was away because her days were scheduled tightly, and I knew her nights would be spent with Wyatt as she showed him some of the Apple Isle.

Apart from the marketing strategy and the P4P – which was taking up all my spare time – I was focusing on my own program budget and biographies of guest speakers for floor talks that would take place during the upcoming twelve months.

Emma had also asked me to help with a ministerial response to the level of funding the gallery received in the last federal budget. She highlighted the income we generated, measured it against the funding given to opera, and listed the extensive community benefit of our free public programs. We knew that the federal arts minister, who was the best advocate we'd had in decades, would also add his own comments to our facts.

I liked working with Emma on ministerials and was impressed with the level of professionalism and dignity she always displayed when she was stating the painfully obvious to ministers and government bean counters. Lauren wanted Emma's job one day, but I just wanted to be like Emma. The way she managed staff and made her visions for the gallery into realities meant I had a great role model and mentor.

My enthusiasm for the P4P was mounting internally and I was aiming to pitch to Emma as soon as all my research was finished. Late one night, I sat up in bed reading an essay by Hetti Perkins titled 'Seeing and Seaming: Contemporary Aboriginal Art' and tried to develop further the concept for a potential temporary exhibition the NAG could offer the Musée.

I closed my eyes momentarily, but then Lauren messaged the group chat. I stretched out and scrolled.

Having an awesome time in Tasmania, went over to Flinders Island today with Aunty Patsy Cameron and we collected shells. The plan for the exhibition is coming together; Aunty Lola Greeno has some great ideas.

Libs – Bec and I want to do for you what you and Bec did for me with the Manhattan Movie Marathon. Remember that weekend we sat and just watched movies, drank coffee and ate too much? Not only was it fun, it really helped me visualise life in New York and got me excited.

So, we've decided we're going to do our own French

film festival for you as part of your research. You're coming to my place for the weekend (don't worry, Dave's taking Wyatt fishing on the coast as soon as we get back from Tassie so we've got the place to ourselves).

When are you pitching to Emma, Libs? Do you want me to go with you? Apart from work, sis, you've got to get back in the game and what better way than to be in the city of love. Okay, city of lust or whatever you want to call it. City of good kissers and compatibility. Okay, now I'm raving. I'm tired. Wyatt wants me to get off my phone, but I'll see you Sunday, yeah? Come early.

On Saturday I was up and running before my body even had a chance to realise it was morning. I pounded the pavement around Braddon, seeing only a couple of other runners. I was listening to the soundtrack from *The Sapphires* on Spotify. The language song 'Ngarra Burra Ferra' travelled through my earphones and into my body, and a shiver went up my spine. Another aspect of our culture for the world to experience. And it motivated my own desire to share our visual arts cultures in Paris.

As I took each step, I mentally scripted the pitch I would deliver to Emma as soon as the opportunity presented itself.

I arrived at Lauren's at 10 am to a kitchen full of almond and chocolate croissants, éclairs, Brésiliennes, petits choux chantilly and even a bottle of French champagne. The smell of coffee wafted around my nose.

'Did you get a pay rise? I'm talking to Emma because I haven't seen one.' I picked up a tiny chocolate croissant.

'You won't believe this . . .' Lauren said, pouring bubbles into a flute.

'What?'

'It's all from Wyatt.'

'Are you kidding?' Bec and I said concurrently.

'No, I'm not kidding. I told him about how you threw me the Manhattan Movie Marathon and he was so grateful to you for making me go to New York – which meant meeting him, of course – that when I said I was going to get croissants this morning for your French film fest, he handed me some cash and said, "buy something".' She held up a bottle of Mumm. 'So I did.'

We all 'aahhed' with the knowledge of how truly thoughtful – and apparently cashed up – Wyatt was.

'He is wonderful, isn't he?' Lauren said, more as an acclamation than a question.

'And very generous,' I added, holding out my glass.

'With great taste,' Bec said, reading the label. 'This is even bougier than Moët. And sorry, but this is the best I could do.' She put a bottle of Australian sparkling on the table.

'This is great!' I hugged her. 'This is how *every* Saturday should be spent. Who said Canberra was boring?'

'Everyone!' Caro said, seriously.

'Hahaha, it's true everyone says Canberra's boring, but they don't know how to live, that's all.' I raised my glass and clinked it to Lauren's and Bec's, but Caro waved her hand at me.

'What's wrong?' I asked, having never seen Caro turn down a drink, even if it was 10 am on Saturday morning.

'I'm still seedy from last night. I'm sticking to café au lait,' she said, as Lauren fluffed around the shiny new coffee maker.

'This is the first appliance Wyatt and I bought together, and it's already earned itself out.'

'Gee, that sounds romantic,' Caro said, with raised eyebrows. 'Are you counting the cost of every cup?'

'Of course not. It *is* romantic because every morning I make the toast and he makes the coffee and we have breakfast together.'

'Well, you'll have to put up with me making the coffee today, Loz, and while I'll make it with love, there'll be no romance,' Caro said dryly.

As the machine coughed and spluttered and the milk frothed, Lauren and I carried trays of fattening pastries into the living room. Bec brought the bottle in with her.

With the curtains pulled and two red bucket chairs on either end of her sofa all lined up square in front of the television, it looked like a row of very comfortable seats at the cinema. Lauren put a side table at each end of the row for the bubbly and food, and there were two footstools for our feet to share.

'I may never go to the movies ever again. This is better than gold class,' Bec said.

'It's platinum class,' I replied.

'I've got a load of films lined up for us, ladies, and this one is an absolute must!' Bec fondled the remote like a prized trophy, navigating to Netflix. 'Most of the teachers at school have seen it and it comes highly recommended. Apparently, it's the French version of *Gone with the Wind*.' The screen showed a film called *Les Enfants du Paradis*.

'Oh god, is it going to be all soppy? You know I don't do soppy.' I was interested in seeing Parisian scenery and culture and even some comedy if that were possible, but I wasn't remotely interested in a weekend of French love stories.

'Libs, show a bit of respect, please. This was voted the best film ever by the French Film Academy.' Caro also seemed to know a little about it.

'I'm not good with foreign films,' I said.

'That's not a good start or a smart confession for someone wanting to work in Paris.'

'But,' I added, 'I am willing to learn. Now press play on *Les Enfants du Paradis*.' I did my best French accent as I read the title out loud.

'You just massacred that with your Aussie-fied French accent,' Caro said. She was almost fluent in the language.

'*The Children of Paradise*,' I read the translation. 'Is that better?'

'Much.' She raised her coffee in a toast to me.

We watched the classic three-hour black-and-white film and I was surprised by how much I loved it, even though it was about relationships. When it was over we dissected the script and characters.

'The line "Life is beautiful and so are you" shits me,' Caro said seriously. 'I can't tell you how many times I heard that when I was in Paris, it's a standard pick-up line. And it was all bullshit!'

No-one commented. Caro was clearly in a bad mood.

'I liked Garance, she's a flirt but she is so elegant and subtle,' Bec said.

'A lot like me,' I laughed.

'My favourite bloke was Baptiste, he loved Garance before he even met her.' Lauren looked all misty-eyed. 'He loved her all along, just like Wyatt loved me, even when I was dating Cash Brannigan and even when I got back with he-who-shall-remain-nameless.'

'I can't believe you dated a man called Cash Brannigan in New York. Still, all this *lurve* talk is making me more nauseous.' Caro picked up her empty coffee mug to refill. 'I wouldn't have trusted Baptiste at all.'

'Why not!?' Lauren was mortified.

'He kissed her with his eyes open,' Caro said, as if we should know what that meant.

'So?' I asked.

'You never, ever trust someone who kisses with their eyes open. And there was no tongue. What is French kissing without tongue?'

'Fair point, Caro.' I raised my eyebrows at the other girls.

'I have another movie lined up,' said Lauren. 'Libs, if you're not interested in Garance, perhaps you are . . . *Amélie*!' She flicked through the list and brought it up on the screen.

'Well, at least it was made this century.' I read the blurb, with attempted interest. 'It says she's introverted and obsessed, thanks heaps! I know I like solitude and I'm passionate about my work, but does that make me introverted and obsessed?' I could hear how defensive I sounded.

'Hang on, she also thinks she can control fate, and that, my dear tidda, is you down to a tee, it's one of your best qualities. And that's what you're doing with planning Paris – twisting fate to suit you.' I could tell Caro was channelling her life coach then, it was the kind of affirmation she'd no doubt heard before.

'Fate needs a bloody good kick up the butt sometimes.' I pushed my size nine foot into the air.

'Fate isn't going to help you with your fashion sense though, is it?' Lauren, the Queen of Fashion, said.

'Right, so I'm an obsessed, introverted bad dresser. I'll die in Paris, won't I?'

'Yes.' Caro tried not to smile.

'No, you won't.' Lauren attempted to defend me. 'You've got a fantastic shoe collection and that's the best place to start your wardrobe from.'

'See, it's just your fashion sense from the ankles up that is the problem.' Caro pressed 'play' on the remote.

'Truth be known, I often dress down to help make you girls look better.' I said it with a straight face so they had no idea if I was serious or joking.

My butt was growing numb from sitting down so much and I was glad that the day, although warm, had turned overcast and progressively darker. At least I wasn't missing out on beautiful sunshine. We needed rain desperately, so no-one in Canberra would ever complain about a storm brewing.

As we watched the film, I realised that I liked Amélie – the character – immediately. She was full of hope and belief in what was possible. That was definitely me, although I couldn't imagine trying to manipulate fate to meet a fella who collected discarded pics from a photo booth. After watching Lauren's desperate and stalker-like attempts to make foul footballer Adam want her a few years ago, I'd become less and less interested in trying to meet and/or manipulate men in any way. Perhaps that wisdom came through Lauren's mistakes, and perhaps it came through my own failed relationships, or maybe it was just something that came with age.

'I can tell you women now, I will never plot or strategise to meet a man or to try and win him over. No blue arrows on the ground giving them directions to find me, no batting of the eyelashes, no going to deportment classes.' I stood up as if giving a public speech. 'I am Libby Cutmore, I am a champagne-drinking Black woman, and if they don't like what they see, then they don't get it!'

I had no problem being me. At least I knew I was without obsessions or delusions, but I was also without Lauren's fashion flair and Garance's flirting tactics. By my standards though – and they were the only standards I cared about – I was still doing just fine.

'Now,' Caro said, ignoring the speech, 'I have one more on my hitlist, but I'm not sure if you'll be into it.' She searched for a second, and we all turned our noses up at *Last Tango in Paris*.

'Doesn't he shove cheese, you know . . .' Bec didn't make any hand gestures but we all knew what she meant.

'Yeah, I can pass on that one I think, really. I like my cheese,' I said adamantly.

'Actually, it was butter,' Caro clarified, 'and it was ground-breaking at the time, I just thought . . .'

'Look, I'm not going abroad to get dairy products shoved anywhere other than my mouth, thank you very much.' I took the remote from Caro's hand and pressed 'back'. She sighed, and reached for her bag, fishing out her phone. 'Nice bag by the way,' I said, stroking the black patent leather, 'I wouldn't mind one of these, or another cup of coffee.'

'Café au lait, café noir and café crème for you,' Caro listed our orders and went to the coffee machine again.

'You're the best barista in the 'Berra,' I said, grateful for another hit.

'You'll have to make your own mocha, Loz, it's not in my repertoire.' Caro shrugged her shoulders in apology.

'Your French is pretty good, Caro.' I was impressed with her accent as well.

'I was married to a Frenchman for a couple of years, remember?' Caro rarely made reference to her ex. 'That is, until I realised what everyone had tried to tell me all along, that Brunel was banging every other woman he could get his hands on.'

'Ouch.' I didn't want to look at Lauren in case it triggered something from the days of Adam.

'Brunel . . . I've never heard that name before,' Bec said.

I'd never heard Caro call her ex by his name before either. On the rare occasion she did refer to him, it was as 'scumbag', 'lowlife' or 'the Bastard', but never Brunel.

'The name's not common, even though he was. It means "little brown child", which he was. A real man-child.'

'I think you need some sugar in your coffee to deal with that bitterness.' Bec tried to lighten the moment.

'I'm good. I am.' Caro was trying to convince us as much as herself. 'I just think every woman should date a Frenchman because it can only go up from there!'

'That's very harsh, Caro,' Lauren said.

'And racist, I might add.' Bec gave Caro her stern-teacher face. 'And perhaps for an alternative experience to Caro's, Libs, you could read Sarah Turnbull's *Almost French*. She's an Australian who fell in love with a Frenchman named Frédéric and they're very happy. One of the older English teachers at school is always raving about that book.' Bec gave Caro another stern glare.

Caro looked suitably chastised. 'You're right, I apologise. Let me rephrase it. All women should just date *Brunel*, because everything can only go up from there. My memories of him make me appreciate my singledom and life without lies even more.'

The room was silent. Caro didn't talk about her past much, probably because she was older and wiser. Since Lauren and Wyatt were setting up home and planning a wedding, and Bec was thick with Dave, and I was working a million hours a week and now planning my French adventure, we girls were rarely all together at the one time, so serious conversations were scarce. Caro's words now were a stark reminder of how we had all moved on and our lives were now heading in different directions.

'What are we watching?' Caro changed the subject.

'We can't end the festival without . . .' Bec grabbed the remote again and clicked a few times. '*Moulin Rouge.*'

'I love Ewan McGregor!' Lauren exclaimed, and Bec and I 'mmmmed' in agreement.

'I could listen to him sing "Come What May" all day, I kid you not. He is so sexy when he's singing that.' Bec was almost drooling.

'I wouldn't mind vanishing inside his kiss.' The song's words rang in my head.

I thought I'd said it to myself, but realised I'd said it out loud when the girls looked at me, clearly surprised. My research on Paris had reawakened my interest, at least physically, in the opposite sex, but I was not going to admit it to anyone else.

'Let's just watch the movie.' I tried to move on from the moment.

As Nicole Kidman did her cancan striptease scene for the duke, we all cringed.

'Getting tips are you, Libs?' Bec joked.

'Yeah, my version would be the can't-can't, or should I say, won't-won't!'

'The most important tip from this movie, girls, is: *the*

greatest thing you'll ever learn is to love and to be loved in return,' Lauren said, finishing with a warm sigh.

I took out my pen and my everyday Moleskine for random notes and lists.

'What are you doing?' Bec asked.

'Making a list, of course.' I hadn't stopped making them since I decided I was going to Paris.

'On what? Tips on how to have affairs?' Caro continued to stare at the screen.

'No, tips on flirting, of course.' Lauren was hopeful.

'Neither. I'm actually making a list of commonly used French words that I can throw into my vocab on a daily basis quite easily to seem a little French-like. The movies reminded me of some I hadn't even thought about. I've got a bigger vocab than I imagined.'

'What have you got so far?' Lauren asked with genuine interest.

'Give me a minute, I'm doing something . . . with the words.' I was writing as fast as possible. I looked at my short list and read them out slowly to nods of recognition, making little sentences where I could.

'We had a weekend *rendezvous* at Lauren's, the food was *à la carte*, and she also provided us with an *apéritif.*'

'Nice,' Lauren said.

'*Apropos* the food, it wasn't *cordon bleu*, but the *crème caramel* smelled better than the *potpourri*,' I went on. 'It was *déjà vu*, because I realised I'd been in this *cul-de-sac* before and the *soup du jour* arrived long before the *femme fatale* found a fiancé in America.'

The girls were cheering me on, Lauren laughing the hardest.

'There were four of us, one too many for a *ménage à trois*, so we had a film *matinée*, and the curator wanted to talk about the *objet d'art*, which I thought was a tad *passé* but she was *petite* so I didn't hassle her.'

Now they were laughing hard.

'I have *RSVP*'d to a *soirée* tonight but I want to stay here and learn more before I become the perfect *protégé* and say *bon voyage* and go to Paris, the city of *amour*.'

By this stage I was wriggling in my seat, desperate to go to the bathroom.

'*Voilà*! I can't do any more; I need to go to the *toilette*.' I stood up. 'Here's the rest of my list, you can make your own sentences.'

As I left, I handed Caro the list of remaining words, which read:

- *au contraire*
- *avant-garde*
- *c'est la vie*
- *coup d'état*
- *décolletage*
- *encore*
- *laissez-faire*
- *maître d'*
- *mardi gras*
- *souvenir*
- *hors d'œuvre*

When I returned, Caro handed me back the sheet.

'We added a few more words to your list: *bistrot*, which means a bar in Paris, and *café*, which is where you go for your *café au lait* and *pain au chocolat*.'

Caro's French connection, albeit painful for her, was going to prove helpful to me. Her accent also made me realise how much work I had to do just to perfect the few words and phrases I did have.

Bec interrupted. 'Now, I've got one more movie for us to watch.' She clicked on *Haute Couture*.

'Do we really need to see this?' I sighed at the thought of another film. 'It's not like I can afford to buy haute couture, I mean, I don't even think I can pronounce in properly.'

'Come on, let's watch for fun, and maybe you'll get a few more Parisian fashion tips, because clearly watching the entire series of *Emily in Paris* did not influence you at all.'

I looked down at my standard black look. 'What? You don't like the shift-dress style?'

'The dress is fine, but your whole wardrobe is black and grey. You belong in Melbourne.'

'I like black and grey. It's simple and conservative, but not lacking style. And hypothetically speaking, if I *wanted* to change my style, I wouldn't be looking to Emily Cooper for direction. I'm already guessing that the streets of Paris will be filled with foreigners dressing like *Emily*.' I said the character's name with more sarcasm than intended, but I was set on my individual style and didn't want to be forced into being someone I wasn't.

I thought I always looked professional, tidy, clean. I didn't fuss with colours and accessories like Lauren did. I was raised in a house where style wasn't about your clothes. It was about how you carried yourself in public places. Dignity was style, that's what I learned from Mum. My whole life was about what I said, not what I wore.

'That's fine, but boring.' Lauren was gentle, never one to be the bitchy stylist. 'Maybe just watch the film and see if you get some ideas about how you can mix up the plain blacks and greys. Check out how they accessorise.'

'All right,' I said, frustrated. Lauren had it all going on in terms of how to look super hot and cool at the same time, despite shopping in department stores.

'Scarves, my dear sister, will save you, and colourful bags and a belt or two with detail.'

'Oh yes, trust me, French women have a million ways to tie scarves,' Caro chimed in. 'Pity I didn't learn to tie one tightly around the Bastard's neck,' she added.

'Can I go now? I feel like I've been at Sunday school.' I hoped I didn't sound ungrateful.

'Yes, you are dismissed, and we have a list of other films for you.' Lauren navigated to the list she'd made. 'We've got the original *Cyrano de Bergerac* with Gérard Depardieu, because I know you loved the Hollywood version of *Cyrano* starring Peter Dinklage. And I personally recommend *Marie Antoinette* with Kirsten Dunst, and have you seen *Mrs Harris Goes to Paris* yet?' Lauren finally paused to take a breath.

'No, I haven't, and that's a great list,' I said, staring at the screen and feeling overwhelmed by the generosity of my friends.

'Yes, my film taste is eclectic. I've been adding French films to my watch list ever since you said you wanted to go to Paris,' Bec said.

'This is really so considerate, thank you, girls. I'm overwhelmed and grateful for all the effort.' And I was.

'Wait, scroll down, Bec. Libs, if you don't mind passing time watching endless family dramas with various levels of infidelity, I've got you sorted.' She had chosen a film called *Inside Paris*. 'And my two favourites,' she said, clicking down again, '*The Man Who Loved Women* and *Le Divorce* with Kate Hudson and Naomi Watts.'

'Nothing better than hearing about other people's dysfunctional families and relationship woes. Perfect.'

Chapter 6

The NAG, the P4P
and the MQB

I had a typical Sunday night organising my standard tunic dress for the morning before sitting down to make some notes for the week ahead. I focused on Nancia, the new staffer starting under my watch. I double-checked her activities for the week and went through my own priorities.

I was a woman of routine: schedules, lists and lots of items to be checked off – that's how I liked to have my life sorted. I liked to be organised. I needed to be efficient. I wanted to be cost-effective, and I hoped that Nancia was the same, knowing that neither of us would cope if she wasn't.

I lay in bed drifting off to sleep and felt physically relaxed after the lazy weekend watching films. But although my body was completely rested, my mind was frantic with visuals, sounds, characters, history and French food.

As I sat at my computer at 8 am on Monday morning, I acknowledged that the effective education program I was running meant that the gallery was getting more and more requests for tours and lectures. This was the reason Emma had decided we needed to employ Nancia: so I could mentor her to take over the tours, and give myself time to focus on planning and further growth.

I was looking forward to working with our new employee after she had interviewed well in a competitive field. She was from Rockhampton but had lived in Melbourne for the past two years, working at the National Gallery of Victoria. She had a degree in teaching and some training with NAISDA, a contemporary Indigenous dance college, but she hadn't pursued a career in that area. At the interview, though, she had said her interest in the Aboriginal arts scene remained strong.

Emma and I thought that employing Nancia might help us realise our shared vision of using some of the NAG space not only for dance performances but workshops as well, an idea Nancia responded to with enthusiasm. I didn't imagine my mentoring role would last long, since she'd come to the NAG with plenty of experience and drive.

'The key to a successful business,' Emma once said, 'is to surround yourself with capable staff who share your vision.'

Emma was right: the NAG was thriving because of the people Emma had employed over the years. She led by example in terms of her work ethic, her manner of speaking to her team and even her dress code. Although she made us feel like we worked in a collective as opposed to a hierarchy, she didn't participate in mufti day on

Fridays with the junior staff, preferring to always dress professionally. Lauren and I tried to follow her lead, and judging by Nancia's outfit at the interview, it looked like she'd do the same.

From the moment Nancia started, the week promised to be intense. I walked her through every aspect of the education program and was thrilled when she picked up the specifics about the gallery and the collections quickly. By Friday, she began to run tour groups by herself. Emma was as pleased with our new recruit as I was when we shared a table at the café in OId Parliament House – a sleek, renovated space with white tables and chrome chairs and locally produced artwork on the walls – and debriefed.

'I hope you realise, Libby, that Nancia's ability to settle in so well and so quickly is due to your mentoring style.' Emma sounded impressed.

I was humbled by her words, and knew my way of working with staff simply mirrored hers. It was a rare occasion to sit and have coffee with Emma and it was too good an opportunity to miss, so I broached the P4P plan that had been consuming me for weeks. 'Emma, with that in mind, I'd like to talk to you about my professional development, if I may.'

'Of course. Now?' She looked at her watch, and as she did I registered my own surprise that my boss even had time to sit in the café. I'd only ever seen her drink coffee at her desk or in meetings or walking the corridor with a takeaway. She was undoubtedly the busiest woman I knew, with Lauren and me close seconds.

'No, we don't have to talk about it now, I can make an appointment through Veronica if you like.' Veronica was the most efficient executive assistant in Canberra. Emma had poached her from a government department, not through financial incentives, but rather through the NAG's reputation for being the organisation that everyone wanted to work for.

'Good, I'll tell Veronica to expect a call from you then.' She stood up. 'And Libby, I'm glad you're on top of it all. It means I don't have to monitor what you're doing. Lauren's back and staffing is steady. So it's time to get you to the next level. I'm actually glad you raised the issue of your development now.'

I couldn't believe Emma's words and I couldn't have scripted it better myself. It *was* time to take me to the next level, and that level was running an education program at Quai Branly! Those five minutes with the boss left me feeling more psyched than ever and I felt I was in the exact position needed to do the pitch.

As soon as I got back to my desk, I called Veronica and made an appointment for Thursday morning at 8.30 am. Emma had fifteen minutes free and they were all mine. I knew I could do the pitch in that time and answer any of the questions Emma might have about the proposal.

But I needed to practise it on Lauren to ensure I was slick on the day. She was at an off-site meeting at AIATSIS discussing the running of a series of temporary exhibitions in the Mabo Room there, so I texted her:

I'm pitching to Emma on Fri, need to practise on you. OK?

Absolutely, meet you at lunchtime.

Do I need a ppt for pitch?

NO! You're best when talking naturally, give Emma a written pitch, no more than 2pp, 3 tops. xx

I panicked as I culled my ten-page P4P, trying to maintain the concept and my case at the same time. But Lauren was right: be concise, be clear, be certain of what it was I wanted to achieve and how I was going to do it.

I structured my notes to include a summary of my career path at the NAG, my goals, my strengths and weaknesses in my current role, and detailed the proposed project at the Musée, including the temporary exhibition, human resources and budget. Finally, I listed the benefits of the project to me personally and professionally and to the NAG and the First Nations community generally.

As my P4P finished printing, I went back to the thirty-five emails that had come in overnight. They were mostly the usual research enquiries, although one was from a cheeky student asking me on a date, which I ignored. There were also requests from six primary schools for visits, and the usual enquiries about things unrelated to the NAG altogether: questions on land rights, native title, Closing the Gap statistics and my favourite, Aboriginal spirituality.

Sometimes they weren't even from students; sometimes they were enquiries from journalists who were just too lazy to do the research or find someone working in the appropriate field. I never fobbed anyone off though, always referring people to the right person or resource. On the odd occasion when I was really stuck for a diplomatic response, I'd forward the email to Emma, who would cc me in on her response to the enquiry so that I knew how to respond the next time.

At lunchtime, I met Lauren in the staff room. 'Let's eat,' she said, opening the lid on her salad.

'Can I just do my pitch first, please, and then I can relax.'

'Okay, you do the pitch and I'll do the salad,' Lauren compromised, taking one piece of tomato out of the box, biting into it as she sat at the kitchen table. 'I'll be Emma. You've walked into my office, we've done the pleasantries. I'm flat out with meetings all day and you know it. Go.'

'You've already made me nervous, and I don't get nervous at work.'

'Stop it, you know the job backwards, you know the pitch. Just do it.'

And so I did it. I recited the script I had written out word for word and memorised. It was how I prepared for all important meetings and presentations. Public speaking was where I felt the most comfortable, which was why I was glad to move out from behind the desk and into working with the public on the tours and lectures.

I was ready for a new challenge. I had to raise my own professional bar higher. All I needed to do was make sure it worked for the NAG as well.

At 8.30 am on Friday I walked nervously into Emma's office. What if she said no to my idea, my dream, my plan for my own and the gallery's internationalisation?

'Thank you for seeing me today, Emma.'

I sat down opposite her at her huge desk, which was incredibly tidy compared to mine. I had open books and loose paper scattered on my desk, and notes stuck on my pinboard in different colours denoting differing levels of urgency. And I always had a dirty coffee cup and at least one protein bar wrapper hanging around. Emma's desk was clear of papers except the one she appeared to be working on when I walked in.

'Don't thank me, Libby, I wanted to talk to you anyway, given Nancia started this week and so many new things are happening. I've just read the final draft of the proposed marketing strategy and there's quite a lot we need to move on in the next six months, especially in terms of the educational program.'

It was like Emma was reading my mind and all the planets had lined up at that moment, ready for me to do my pitch.

'I agree, and that's partly why I wanted to talk to you. In regards to marketing, I've thought about ways of further internationalising our education program and working on my own professional development at the same time.'

Emma pushed her chair back and crossed her trousered legs. She had a look of interest on her face. 'Go on,' she said.

'I've been employed here for four years now and love my job. When you promoted me to manager of educational programs I hit the ground running and even implemented the new masterclasses. Now I've got another initiative that I think will take us to another audience and another level.' I put my written document on the table.

'Go on,' Emma moved from interest to excitement.

'I'd like to propose a working relationship between the NAG and the Musée du Quai Branly in Paris, where we offer one of our more successful exhibitions to them for their temporary space and include an education program as well. We would pitch it as something to complement the permanent collection there, to be exhibited for three to six months.'

The tone at the end of my sentence was almost a question and I hoped Emma hadn't noticed. It sounded a little like I wasn't sure it would work, or I wasn't sure about the idea. I hated myself at that moment but didn't have time to backtrack and didn't want to draw attention to it.

'Go on,' Emma said again, shifting on her seat and moving forward to lean on her desk.

'As you know, the Musée has a temporary exhibition space on the third floor that has had numerous international exhibits, and they are currently showing Songlines: Tracking the Seven Sisters.'

'Yes, of course, I'd heard that. Brilliant collaboration there. I'll need to see what the reviews have been like.' Emma wrote a reminder to herself on a yellow post-it note.

'I think something that could act as a companion exhibition to the permanent exhibit would be sensational. As you know, in the permanent collection we have work by Paddy Nyunkuny Bedford, Tommy Watson and Lena Nyadbi from WA. Plus John Mawurndjul, Gulumbu Yunupingu from the NT, and Ningura Napurrula from the NT and WA. And of course there's the deadly Judy Watson from Queensland, and the late Michael Riley from New South Wales.'

'Such a stunning combination of work,' Emma said. 'Hetti and Brenda excelled in getting those commissions up. Their legacy is inspirational. Imagine if we could do the same here.'

Emma looked to the ceiling and I knew she was imagining the possibilities. She looked back to me. 'You have something in mind for the Musée then?'

'There are a couple of options. We could offer the permanent portrait collection we have hanging in Kings Hall to them for several months.'

I could see Emma take a breath and I wasn't sure if it was a gasp of disbelief at the suggestion or she just needed to breathe deeply.

'Go on,' was all she said.

'I think there are two benefits to doing that. Firstly, it demonstrates the absolute faith and desire we have in building a serious relationship with them, offering works that are part of our everyday existence here at the NAG. Secondly, each portrait tells a story of the civil rights movement in this country. It's the perfect springboard to talk about the history and consequences of colonisation and the political landscape we've existed in,' I said, taking a breath. 'In fact, we still exist in. It is a way to tell a different narrative of Australia, *our* story, through the stories of some of our own leaders and heroes.'

I could see Emma's mind ticking over but I couldn't tell if she liked the idea or not, so I continued. 'Or, we could offer to exhibit some of our esteemed winners of the NAG Art Awards, there's an impressive list now we're in our tenth year. Collectively, the pieces provide a great range of voice, style, stories. Tony Albert's 'Remark' is an important conversation around cultural appropriation, one that the French really need to hear.'

Emma nodded because she was often having to send copies of the Australia Council visual arts protocols out to her peers worldwide. She was busy scribbling down notes in the huge black diary that sat on her desk. I couldn't stop talking, my mouth just kept moving.

'Then, of course, the *pièce de résistance . . .*' I opened the NAG awards catalogue to page three. 'Alison Munti Riley, who was recently showcased in *Vogue* Australia!'

I turned the catalogue to face Emma and we both looked at the Pitjantjatjara artist's painting, *Seven Sisters Dreaming*, and the vibrant pigments that drew the viewer into the women's story.

'This work took my breath away the first time I saw it hanging, and I know it has the same impact on others,' I said without looking up.

Emma sighed. 'Well, Libby, this is rather a grand idea of yours.'

Was being 'grand' a good thing or a bad thing? *Damn!* I thought to myself. I'd been raving non-stop and probably big-noting myself ad nauseam. Emma probably thought I was grandstanding.

But then she spoke again. 'I'm impressed by the thought you've put into this.'

I still couldn't tell if she really was impressed or just prepping me for a gentle 'thanks but no thanks' speech. My self-esteem demons were playing havoc with my confidence in my professional track record, and I got on the defensive, believing that one last effort couldn't hurt if she was going to say no anyway.

'I won't lie to you, Emma, I am proposing this as much for me as for the gallery. I want another challenge. Lauren's fellowship really inspired me. And when I saw the work she did there, I was blown away. I want to contribute something to the internationalisation of the NAG, and I need some professional development beyond what I'm doing here right now. I want to learn more. And, to be absolutely honest, I think it's a great idea.'

There was a silence. Finally, Emma spoke. 'It *is* a great idea, Libby.'

I couldn't believe what I was hearing. 'You really think so?'

'Yes, I'm pleased that your thinking is in line with mine in terms of internationalisation and ways to benefit your own career. I like the sound of your proposal. We weren't around to support the original commission at the Musée, but the National Gallery of Australia and the Art Gallery of New South Wales were. We need to do something at that level now ourselves.'

I breathed a sigh of relief. Still, the battle wasn't won yet.

Emma frowned as she continued, 'It is time, but like everything, it's about the budget, the personnel, the politics that exist between all the major arts bodies. And, of course, funding. This all needs to be considered. And the mob at the Musée will have the final say. They may not have a space in their program for years, as you can imagine.'

I was conscious that Emma was the boss, she had the knowledge and the nous, and I didn't want to seem cocky, just keen. I pushed my three-pager towards her.

'I'll leave this with you, Emma. As you can see, I've done a rationale for the board, a timeline, and have written how I see the exhibition working. Lauren has been through this with me as the curator, of course. We came up with the complete plan together, just so you know that the curatorial expertise is covered.'

'You've certainly done your homework, haven't you?' Emma sounded suitably impressed.

'If you look over the page, you'll see a budget and potential funding sources, and I've done some preliminary research in terms of potential philanthropic support too,' I said, pointing to a table on the page. 'I've budgeted for freight, insurance, catalogues – if we print offshore it will be cheaper, and we'll still be able to hire a First Nations designer.'

I watched Emma speed read the pages. I imagined in her job – with all the policy papers, memos, ministerials, communications, staffing issues and so on – she'd be used to reading quickly for the quantity she'd have to get through each day.

'Libby, this is a fantastic proposal. I think it has legs. Leave it with me. Just by chance, I have a meeting with the French cultural attaché next week. The French embassy here in Canberra were also part of the process of the Australian commission at Quai Branly way back in 2006, so they should be in the loop as well. There'll be French dignitaries here in Australia in the next couple of weeks, and they'll be coming through the NAG at some stage.

'I will put this on the agenda and I'll send a preliminary email to my counterpart at the Musée to sound out how they feel about the concept. The timing is perfect for us, but it needs to be good for the French, too.' Emma looked at her watch. 'Now, I'm off to a meeting at the National Library about a proposed joint publication.'

'A book?'

'Still in embryonic stages, I'll let you know when we've fleshed it out more.' Emma grabbed her tan bag from beside her desk and her black suit-jacket off the back of her chair. We walked out of her office together.

'Thanks, Emma, for your time. And please say hello to the mob over there for me.'

'It's not my time, Libby, it's *our* time. We're all working to the same end,' she smiled. 'And I'll say hello for sure.'

I returned to my office, pleased with the way I had presented and Emma's positive reaction. Now I just had to wait, patiently, but a lack of patience was my one major flaw.

Chapter 7

Monogamy bores me

For the following week the P4P was constantly in the back of my mind, but I was so busy with tours I didn't even have time to dream about Paris. With ten of the country's latest innovative and emerging Aboriginal artists about to blow the arts world apart with an Australia-wide tour beginning at the NAG, every one of my waking moments – and some sleeping ones – was taken up with work.

The days in the office were long, with both Lauren and I arriving by 7 am and not leaving before 7 at night. I worked on contracts for guest speakers and Lauren finalised every detail of the upcoming opening. At least daylight saving meant it was still light when we got home. Managing events at the gallery was stressful but I loved the adrenaline rush, especially on the day of the actual event. Everything was fast paced, and I enjoyed checking things off my numerous lists.

I had been so focused on the priorities of each day I almost hadn't noticed when Emma came into one of my lectures with the visiting French ambassador and his colleagues. It could only bode well for me though, and I knew it.

'One day we'll run this show ourselves,' Lauren said over a late-night debrief while we were both feeling particularly strong in ourselves.

'You will definitely be the director of the NAG, Loz, you know that, when Emma finally goes.'

'Not that we want her to go just yet, of course.' Lauren was a big fan of Emma's as well. We both owed a lot to her in terms of our careers and the faith she had placed in us over the years.

'So, if I become director, what will you be doing? You've gone from working on programming exhibitions with me to talking about them, and now you're doing both all by yourself.'

'And soon,' I sighed, 'I hope to be doing it with the French.'

'Doing it? Was that pun intended?'

'I'm ignoring you,' I said, smiling. 'Anyhow, I'm hoping I might move into international relations, maybe, and become an ambassador for the arts or something.'

'Ambassador for the arts, I like it.' Lauren nodded her approval.

'The triple A: the Aboriginal Ambassador for the Arts,' I said, as I wrote it on Lauren's whiteboard.

'I like that even better.'

We toasted each other with cups of organic green tea and got back to work.

Two weeks later, as I stood in the gallery shop at 10 am, I was impressed with our latest catalogue. I picked one up and felt the smooth cover inspired by the design work of Iscariot Media – who were now handling most of the gallery publications and managed to highlight each piece of work and its creator brilliantly. Our team loved the objective of the design house: 'Walking Together: Place, create and leave a legacy.' It was exactly what I wanted to do with my work here at the NAG and hopefully abroad. I breathed in a sense of achievement, knowing that nearly every step of the process for the exhibition was in First Nations hands.

All we needed now were some rich whitefellas to come shopping at our place and commission some of our artists. The reality was, there were few Blackfellas buying at the higher end of the range we carried and many still shopped directly through the visual arts cooperatives around the country. The NAG was targeting a particular clientele and no-one denied it. International dignitaries, government agencies, local politicians all relied on our curatorial knowledge and experience to bring the best we could to the capital.

'Libby, Emma's been trying to call you.' It was Veronica, standing by my side with two coffees in her hand. 'She's in her office now, you should call her back asap.'

'I'm going to Paris!' I screamed down the phone to Lauren. I'd called her because I was too impatient to wait the three minutes it would take me to walk around to her office. I'd already waited too long since the pitch – twenty-one days and one hour to be exact – for Emma to contact me and give me the good news.

'I'm on my way over,' she screamed back. Within minutes she was at my desk, bouncing around like a schoolgirl, just like I had when she got the fellowship to New York.

'When? How? What did Emma say?'

'I just spoke to her and it's a green light and she's sorting out the details.' I took a deep breath. I was so excited I was frightened I might do that hyperventilating thing I'd only ever heard about before. 'Apparently, the meeting she had with the French embassy here went really well; they loved the idea and they got onto it immediately.' I clapped my hands. 'I'm going to Paris!'

'What else did she say?' Lauren was trying to quell my breathless excitement long enough for me to get my words out. It was as though I was six years old again and had just got my first bike for Christmas.

'She said the Musée were thrilled with the offer because they had an exhibition from Britain locked in, but some minister said something negative in the press recently about the French and the political fallout has been ongoing.'

'Shit!'

'Shit indeed, but FAN-FUCKING-TASTIC for me because, as it happens, both countries have apparently – and I'm sure aggressively – agreed to pull the exhibition they had locked in for July, so there's a gap for their temporary space. They need to fill the void but save face in the arts scene in Europe and stick it up the Poms.'

'Of course, and that stick is . . .'

'That stick is MINE!' I couldn't stop smiling, my jaw was aching, my heart was racing and my head was already making lists of what I needed to do: professionally and personally.

Lauren hugged me. 'I'm so proud of you and happy for you.'

'I know, thanks, sis. I'm only doing it because of you, your inspiration and your help. And of course I meant that stick is ours. Not just mine, we never do anything just for ourselves.'

I hugged Lauren back but it was hard to keep still. I wanted to run along the corridors of the NAG screaming. I wanted to grab the microphone at security and blast it over the internal sound system so all the staff and all the visitors knew that Libby Cutmore was going from Moree to the Musée and she was going to kick some serious French butt. I couldn't believe my luck and, in our meeting earlier, Emma had seemed just as pleased as I was that the project would be going ahead.

'It's about us putting something into the bucket of goodwill,' Emma had said. 'And somewhere down the track we'll be dipping into it and taking something out.' I wasn't sure what she had in mind, but she was very strategic and I knew she'd be calling in the 'goodwill favour' sometime in the future; if not from the Musée, then from someone else. Or perhaps just having the French take me on with the show was their goodwill in return.

'We need to celebrate, I'll call Bec and Caro,' Lauren said, heading towards the door.

'Can we do it tonight?'

'Today's Valentine's Day!!' I wasn't sure if Lauren was shocked that I hadn't known what day it was, or shocked that I'd suggested going out on the major romantic festival of the year. I'd never celebrated Valentine's Day, not since Andy in Melbourne, and that was nearly a decade ago. As far as I was concerned, my pending trip to Paris and my future career projection into the European arts scene was much more important than any thoughts of Valentine's Day.

'No worries.' I tried not to sound too disappointed. 'Tomorrow?'

'Absolutely. I'm so happy for you. I know this is going to be the highlight of your life.'

'I think you may be right.'

I sat down, caught my breath and focused my brain, knowing my whole world was about to change. I was leaving Canberra, the political capital of Australia, for Paris, the fashion capital of the world. I was going from the NAG to the MQB with my P4P to follow my professional dream of making a contribution to the international arts scene with my own exhibition concept and plan.

I started typing up lists on my computer. I knew if I didn't get them out of my head, I'd never have peace. I even contacted my counterpart at the MQB, thanks to Emma already making the introductions. By the end of the day, it was all too real.

I went to Leyla early the following night. I couldn't keep still at home after another agitated day at work, trying to concentrate on my usual tasks and already sorting out the plan for Paris. I sat on the rooftop overlooking the city I would soon be leaving behind and sipped a Bellini. I imagined doing the same overlooking the Seine at night with Parisian lights reflecting artistically off the river.

Taking in Parliament House and surrounds, it made me think of the suburban landscape of Moree, and my brothers playing pool on Friday nights. The last time I played with them, Bazza nearly got in a brawl because I was being stupid, not taking the game seriously enough.

'It's not a bloody Olympic event,' I'd argued, as I shifted the ball slightly to be where I wanted it on the table. One of our opponents went crazy, yelling at me and waving his pool cue, and Bazza went into protective brother mode. It was on, we were just lucky no punches were thrown. I'd never been back to that pub, not since I was told I was a liability as a pool partner.

I thought about Mum too – how different we were. She was patient; I wanted everything yesterday. I hadn't told her about Paris yet. Mum and I didn't talk all that much on the phone, not like other mothers and daughters. Lauren went home to Goulburn to see her folks all the time and she often called her mother just to say hello and get the local goss. I'd never really had that.

I was more independent than Lauren and my brothers – three still living at home – and I had been away from Moree for more than ten years already. Geography – and the distance between you and the people you cared about – had a lot to answer for in terms of homesickness.

I planned to call my mum in the morning though, because the Koori grapevine worked fast and she'd never forgive me if she heard it from someone else. I knew she'd be excited, and I wanted the joy of hearing it in her voice.

Mum is like lots of the women in her line-dancing group who meet at the local Moree Services Club. They are content with the simple things. She isn't a big traveller herself, but she is an Elder representative and attended the World Indigenous Peoples' Conference on Education in Aotearoa, the Māori name for New Zealand. Mum had been offered a trip to Hawaii for another conference but, 'Crossing the Tasman was enough overseas for me,' she'd said.

The real reason Mum didn't like to fly was that she preferred to walk around on the train or absorb the scenery on the bus ride while she knitted. She wasn't allowed to take her knitting needles on planes anymore.

I often wondered how life expectations had changed between Mum's generation and mine. When did the pace of life become so fast that no-one my age ever had the time to sit on a bus from Moree to Canberra because it took too long? Young people were always on the go: things to do, places to see, people to talk to, cocktails to drink, dresses to buy, French pastries to eat, plane tickets to book. And yet Mum was happier than anyone I knew, young or old.

Just as I realised how much I would miss Mum – even though I hardly ever saw her – Caro arrived.

'Congratulations!' she said, placing a bottle of bubbly on the table.

I was really pleased to see my friend at that moment, and got up to hug her.

'Thanks! Sorry about the twenty-five texts yesterday but I was so excited I needed to share.'

'God, don't be sorry, I thought you'd take out an ad in the *Canberra Times*. Actually, I think you should. It's great news, and so deserved. It's too bad we couldn't celebrate yesterday because of that "love" day.'

I rolled my eyes. 'I know, and how monogamy bores me.' I raised my glass in a toast.

'What?' Caro looked shocked. 'I didn't think you were seeing anyone, let alone more than one.'

'It's a famous quote from former French president Nicolas Sarkozy's wife, Carla Bruni.'

'Yes, well it would be, she's dated everyone including Mick Jagger and Eric Clapton. And wasn't she even linked to the former French prime minister Laurent Fabius?'

'I did read she was *rumoured* to be romantically linked to some high-fliers.' I was slightly impressed.

'Only in France could the leader's wife get away with having such a colourful past and saying something like that,' Caro said, no doubt reminded of her ex's infidelities. 'But my favourite quote of hers – I think it was hers – is something like, "love lasts a long time, but burning desire – two to three weeks".'

'That's gold.' I raised my glass in a toast.

Caro sipped her bubbles, closing her eyes in concentration, then opened them as if the penny had just dropped. 'Actually, that flippant attitude about sex and relationships is so damned French. That's how Brunel used to think too. Maybe we've got the whole dating thing wrong. Maybe the French have the right idea. They seem happy at least.'

Caro took a longer than normal sip of her champagne. 'Perhaps you should make it your mantra, Libs. I mean, if it's good enough for the first lady, then it should be good enough for you too.'

'Yeah right, I need a love mantra like I need more work.'

'Actually, Libby, I think you do need some kind of love mantra.'

Caro looked at me seriously, and I knew my confusion was reflected on my face. 'I know, I know. I don't say anything when Loz and Bec are going on about romance and the like, and I know you don't *need* a fella . . .'

'None of us do,' I said.

'Of course, I agree, but the reason I don't say anything is because I'm all bitter and twisted because of Brunel and the fucked-up lawyer I'm seeing on-off. But I do actually believe in love and I want a real relationship, eventually. It's just that I'm not open to either at the moment.'

'Fair enough.'

'And remember, I've had plenty more years of disappointing men than you have. I can take a break for a while and regroup. But you, my dear,' she pointed her glass at me, 'you're too young to be bitter. I think you should be more open to the idea of meeting someone, sometime, somewhere. At least more open than you currently appear to be.'

I was stunned. Caro had always been the one who was practical in love, not mushy or misty-eyed. When I'd been completely screwed over by men in the recent past, she'd been my drinking tidda, always happy to drown her sorrows with mine. And if she didn't have any sorrows, she was still happy to get sloshed. I'd always thought we'd shared indifference to men in our lives. It felt weird now realising that perhaps that commonality didn't exist.

Caro continued, 'I think for the sake of both of us, while you are away you should at least have some fun.' She winked at me as if to say, *you know what I mean*. 'My mantra for you is: "I'm going to become a magnet for love!"'

'How much did you drink before you arrived?' I asked the woman I didn't recognise sitting in front of me. 'Who are you?'

I could tell Caro felt uncomfortable at having opened herself up so emotionally to me. I'd never seen her vulnerable before. She immediately changed the subject, which I was thankful for.

'You should stay in the Marais area – it was hip when I was there last,' she said.

'Actually…' I pulled out my phone. I had already been looking at apartments and had made a list. 'I emailed this apartment to my counterpart at Quai Branly.'

I showed Caro my screen.

'Her name is Canelle and she reckons that the Marais area is also the place to stay, there's the Cité Internationale des Arts – with hundreds of artists around the world visiting at any one time.'

Caro flicked through the images and handed me back my phone.

'I like the look of this apartment too,' I said, showing her another and then pulling up a map of where it was located.

Caro studied the map. 'Right, well, this one is in the 5th arrondissement, which is an amazing place to stay.'

'I kind of like this place in the 20th.' I showed her yet another apartment. 'I think they call it the east of Paris between the 11th and 20th. Canelle reckons it's more up-and-coming.'

'What did she say, exactly?' Caro was so cynical she made me laugh.

'She said,' – I opened the email Canelle had sent – 'and I quote: "the 20th is bohemian, trendy and arty, very diverse, multicultural, and in some parts gentrified".'

'Gentrification, hah! Just what you need.' Caro topped up our glasses.

'It's not that. I want to be around young people who aren't tourists. I want to immerse myself in a community, a suburb . . .'

Caro cut me off. 'Firstly, they're called arrondissements. And secondly, they start in the centre of Paris with the 1st and they snail around, so the 20th is a long way out. Where does Canelle live?'

'She lives in Bastille on boulevard Voltaire, in the 11th, which is, according to Canelle, apparently a mix of hip journalists, actors, writers and working-class people. Canelle's between the apartment I like and Place de la Bastille, which has cafés and restaurants and is also close to the Cité.'

'Well,' Caro said, almost conceding defeat, 'that sounds okay, then. Why don't you go for the 11th instead of the 20th?'

'I don't want to live in her pocket. I think she probably already thinks I'm a freak for having emailed her about five times today. We've got to work together all day and she might think it's strange if I move in next door. She seems cool and happy to show me around, but I think it's good for me to be in a different area to my colleagues, it'll force me to explore a few different bars . . . I mean, galleries.'

'The 20th, hang on, that's right near the Père Lachaise Cemetery, yes?'

'That's right, you know it?'

'Of course. Anyone who goes to Paris knows it. Edith Piaf's buried there, with Morrison and Chopin.'

'And also the scientist Édouard Branly,' I added. 'Is that who the Musée is named after?'

'Actually no. The Quai Branly, the road that runs alongside the Seine, is named after him. And apparently it's the road that actually leads to the Musée itself.'

'So, it's indirectly named after him then?' I loved it when Caro was matter-of-fact and lawyerly.

'Yes, I guess it is.' I laughed. 'Anyway, I imagine I'll spend a lot of time at the cemetery when I'm homesick.'

'Why?'

'It will remind me of dead Canberra!'

'Oh god,' Caro groaned. 'It really *is* dead here compared to Paris.' And we both looked out at the city, which had far fewer lights than the one I was heading to.

'Anyone for a drink?' Bec asked, as she and Lauren arrived together.

'*Un verre de rooge sivouplay, mademoiselle*,' I said.

'What?' Caro couldn't understand my appalling accent.

'I thought I was saying one red wine please, chick.'

Caro shook her head in mock disgust at my poor effort. 'I think I might have to give you some lessons so you can at least get some fluids into you when you go to Paris. Can't have you dehydrating.'

She was right. I knew I'd have to get onto some language classes asap, even though Emma's email had confirmed my program could be delivered at the Musée in English and visitors could utilise recorded translations.

Bec was making a dramatic scan of the table, running her hands over it.

'What are you doing?'

'I'm looking for your lists,' she laughed.

'Hardy-har-har! Here,' I pulled out a brand-new red Moleskine notebook. 'Specially for my Paris lists. As you'll see, I've got only four months here in Canberra to get organised, write the education program, research for the lectures, oversee the freight of the works there . . .'

'Okay, Libs, we need a to-do list that also includes what other people will do as well. Some of that work you

mentioned is mine, so don't panic or get carried away.'
I could tell that I'd gently stepped on Lauren's work toes.

'You're right, Loz, I'm just thinking and writing a million miles an hour, you know what I'm like. But two things you can't do are go see Mum for me or learn French.'

'No, I can't do either but I can help you learn some fashion tips so you fit in better in Paris.' Lauren adjusted my collar.

'Don't forget to add scarves to your list for Paris,' Bec said. 'It's not buying them that's the problem, it's tying them.'

'I'll show you how to do that,' Lauren said, looking as elegant as ever in a black and white wrap-around jersey dress with hot-pink slingbacks.

As I sat there with my posse, I mentally pinched myself about the life I had in Canberra with wonderfully kind and generous tiddas, and about the life ahead of me where I'd grow professionally and even, with some help, fashionably.

Chapter 8

Adieu, Canberra!

Over the next four months I took on my Paris planning with gusto. I wanted to get into the Parisian/ French headspace. I wanted to hear the language, to see how much of the landscape of the city I could work out before I got there. I read countless articles about French culture online and trawled the international films section on Netflix for the best new French films. My favourite was *Portrait of a Lady on Fire,* which was a historical love story about an eighteenth-century woman painter who was tasked with doing a portrait of a rebellious young lady.

I watched a few classics that Caro and told me about too, including *Gigi,* which reminded me of social class and women having to marry upwards, and *Woman Times Seven* with Shirley MacLaine, which only managed to confuse me. Out of curiosity, I even watched *Last Tango in Paris,* which put me off Marlon Brando forever.

I also read the entire Musée website before moving onto learning about the current political climate in France. I was increasingly concerned and confused about the continued debate over banning the hijab in public spaces. I knew that France had banned the burqa back in 2010, but I'd thought that the 2020s would bring on more acceptance of other cultures, not less. The fact that far-right-winger Marine Le Pen had campaigned to be prime minister while also proposing to ban the wearing of headscarves in public almost broke my brain, and my heart. And it scared me. Although she lost the election, there was clearly a lot of support for her in the country.

I was starting to fear the intolerance that I might be challenged with in Paris. Not because I was Aboriginal – because I knew the French were still obsessed with the exotic indigenous other – but because I might witness intolerance towards Muslims and others.

As I counted down each day on my firey calendar in the kitchen, I continued working long hours and saw the seasons change from summer to autumn – from Mr February wearing only his fire-engine red briefs, holding his fire hose, to a colder Mr April wearing boots and helmet as well. Then the temperature dropped dramatically on Anzac Day, as it always did. You could mark the change of your wardrobe by 25 April every year. The days grew darker quicker and autumnal orange leaves lined Northbourne Avenue and the trees around the NAG. I had already started checking the weather in Paris and I was looking forward to escaping winter and having my first European summer.

It was harder to run in the morning as it grew colder, but I knew I had to keep up the exercise routine with all the gourmet food awaiting me in France, and I kidded myself that the sixpack was soon to emerge from under my skin. I also used my exercise time to listen to and recite my French language lessons on an app I'd downloaded. I tried to imagine words phonetically in my head, '*Zhemapelle* Libby, *Zhe swee oztraylienne. Parlayvoo onglay?*'

When the time arrived for me to leave, I was as ready as I was ever going to be. Although not completely fluent in French, I felt confident that I was prepared for the challenge of working at the Musée and starting my new short-term life in Paris. And I was more than ready to head to warmer climes.

I sat in the Library Bar at the Peppers Gallery Hotel waiting for the girls. It was a place I'd been to many times alone to think, read and chill out while drinking coffee or a cocktail. It was the perfect spot for a hot chocolate as well, especially on a cold weekend afternoon when Caro was away and Bec and Lauren were with their fellas.

As I waited for the girls to arrive to celebrate my final hurrah before leaving Canberra, I thought about my brothers. I had wanted to fly up to see the boys, touch the ground of my Gamilaroi country again before leaving, stroll through the Moree Plains Gallery, and go to the Moree on a Plate Festival that Mum had been raving about. The winner of *MasterChef* would be there this year. I wanted to go to the Moree Library and donate some art books to the Aboriginal collection.

On a more spiritual level, I wanted to spend time in the healing waters of Moree's artesian pool. I'd done it rarely since Andy I were there years before, but my body was in dire need of some therapeutic assistance from the percolating underground water. Aside from my family, relaxing at the pool – which only fifty years ago hadn't let Blackfellas in – was one thing I really missed about Moree. And it was one thing I knew I would truly appreciate physically before I boarded the long twenty-hour-plus flight to Europe. But Mum was adamant that she would come to Canberra to say goodbye.

'You know I visit twice a year, Libby, it's time for me to get on that bus. And anyway, Olga from line dancing is going to visit her daughter, so we can travel together,' she said down the line. I knew there was no arguing with Mum. At least I could walk her through our latest exhibition at the NAG. Mum was always so proud when she visited me at work, and everyone, from security to the café staff loved her, fussed over her, made her feel like a queen. I'm sure that's another reason she liked visiting too.

I sighed deeply at the thought of Mum arriving and me not seeing my brothers at all – I was annoyed that none of them could be bothered to come see me. But I was looking forward to the night ahead with the girls. I was excited about leaving Australia, but I already missed my friends. I felt strangely emotional, which wasn't like me. Lauren was the sooky one; I was the strong, sensible one. But I was overwhelmed by what lay ahead.

I took a deep breath as the girls walked into the bar carrying a bundle of gift bags.

'You're here already!' Caro said, motioning the waiter over.

'I just needed to chill a minute. Mum arrives on Sunday and I fly out Tuesday. I think I need another suitcase.' I was seeing visions of all the crap I had to pack into my two black cases swimming around in my head.

'Well, you better make some room for this too.' Bec handed me a gift: it was soft and wrapped in red cellophane.

'A book?' I joked.

'Yes, a book. Open the card first though.'

The card was in a hot-pink envelope and when I took it out it had three firemen just in their duds with braces, red helmets and no shirts.

'Perfect!' I held the image up for the others to see. 'You just reminded me I need to pack my firey calendar so I can keep track of the days in Paris.'

'Keeping track, that's what we call perving these days, is it?' Caro said dryly.

'Keeping track is my only vice, and you know it.'

I smiled as I unwrapped the present: it was a gorgeous purple, pink, black and white silk scarf by a local Aboriginal designer.

'I think warm colours suit your skin tone.' Bec draped it over my shoulders.

'I've been practising tying scarves already,' I said enthusiastically, remembering how my nanna used to wear one tied on the top of her head when she did the washing.

When she wore rollers in her hair, she had a scarf tied underneath at the nape of her neck.

'You know I didn't want gifts, I didn't expect them. I just wanted to have dinner and drinks, that's all.'

I don't know why I always got embarrassed when I received presents, especially since I loved giving them.

'Stop it,' Lauren said, handing me a signature Tiffany blue bag. 'What did you do? You better not have spent too much money – you've got a wedding to save for.'

'This is essential for you, for Paris. It should go in your survival kit.'

I opened the box within the bag, which revealed a silk, egg-shell blue Tiffany scarf, and we all laughed.

'Great minds,' Bec said.

'Your colours are warm colours, Libs, but this will set off your blue eyes, and you need more than one scarf. This is a different shape to Bec's, so you can tie it like this.'

Lauren expertly adjusted the scarf to look like a man's tie.

'See, it falls perfectly into that abundant cleavage,' Lauren said. 'You jealous?' Bec asked.

'Yes, I have to do the push-up bra thing.' Lauren squeezed her chest together. 'And our tidda here has it all without any assistance.'

I looked down at my assets. 'Let me tell you, my girls get in the way sometimes, especially when men talk to them rather than my eyes!'

'Very chic,' Caro said, referring to the scarf. 'You will fit in strolling down the Champs-Élysées for sure.'

I smiled, imagining myself actually looking glamorous with the new accessories I'd never have bought myself. I stood up and prepared to do a catwalk turn.

'And this is from me.' Caro handed me a big gift bag. Inside, I found a stunning black patent tote just like the one Caro owned.

'This is too much.' I was speechless with gratitude and had a lump in my throat which I tried hard to swallow quickly. I didn't want to make a scene in public.

'Shut up. I was worried you might pinch mine one day. You'll need a bag that size with all the freaking scarves you've got now.'

Lauren handed me yet another gift bag. 'And this is from Emma – she wanted to drop in but had kid issues to deal with.'

I undid the ribbon and saw that it was a Moleskine on the city of Paris. 'This is so cool, it's got maps and . . .' I flicked through it slowly, 'and most importantly it's got plenty of pages for all my lists!'

'It's from the Moleskine City range, I got myself one on Barcelona,' Caro said.

And then, against all efforts, I started to cry.

'What's wrong with you?' Caro filled up my glass.

'I feel all emotional,' I blubbered.

'Why? You got two scarves, a bag and a notebook so you don't show up at the very glamorous Musée looking less than you should. Don't be emotional, be happy we think so much of you that we have to dress you! Personally, I'd be offended.' Caro shrugged her shoulders and did her usual deflecting-the-emotional-to-the-funny.

'*Bon voyage*, my friend,' Bec said, holding up her glass in a toast.

'We'll miss you,' Lauren added, putting her glass up also. I cried some more and then so did Lauren and Bec.

'Oh for godsake, women, will you stop it!' Caro was embarrassed by the emotional scene in front of her. 'She's going to Paris, the most stunning city in the world. If you're crying it better be because you're jealous.'

'That's right,' I said, composing myself and wiping tears from my eyes, 'and just to get you even more jealous, here's my list of things to do, oh, I don't know, in the first week!'

I showed them my list, which included the Musée d'Orsay, the Louvre, Notre-Dame, the typically touristy Eiffel Tower and the Champs-Élysées. 'That's my goal, but seeing as I have nearly six months, I guess there's no rush, is there?'

'Stop bragging,' Bec said.

'Sorry,' I giggled. 'And Canelle said she'll walk the Champs-Élysées with me the first Saturday after I begin work and then we're heading to the fancy department stores. I can't wait.'

'Sounds like you've got a new best friend already,' Lauren said, pouting like a child.

'Never!' I put my arm around her, held my phone up above our heads and took a selfie of us both, smiling big and slightly red-eyed.

Me going to Paris was very different to when Lauren left for New York and her mum, dad and brother Max saw her off. I wasn't as needy as Lauren. I'd been self-sufficient and had lived away from home since I moved to Melbourne to do my degree at the Wilin Centre. I hadn't been coerced into leaving Canberra like Lauren had to be. And unlike Lauren, I wasn't so dependent on my mother.

Mum and I loved each other, but her life revolved around her sons mostly, especially the three who still lived at home. The two who lived five minutes away got extra-special treatment when they visited her. The boys appeared to need her more than I did. It was as if none of my brothers ever grew up. Even though two were married, they still went home to Mum every weekend and she pandered to them, always. God knows how their wives coped.

I had tension in my neck as I waited at the North-bourne Avenue bus terminal for Mum to arrive. As soon as she stepped off the bus, I felt oddly at peace. Maybe that was something that mums did for their children without even knowing.

'Libby!' she screamed above all the other newly arrived passengers standing with their families.

She waddled over with the Koori Radio backpack I'd given her on my last visit. I could see her knitting needles poking out of the top, ready to pierce anyone who got too close.

'Hi, Mum.' I leaned in and hugged her tightly. 'Let me get your bags and then I'll take you home for a hot cuppa, eh?'

'That sounds perfect, dear girl. It's so good to be here and we had the best time on the way down, didn't we, Olga?'

Olga, Mum's line-dancing friend, was standing by her side looking worried that her own daughter had forgotten to pick her up, but at that moment a lanky brown woman waved her arms frantically in the air and came flying towards us. Olga sighed so loudly everyone within close proximity turned around. I nodded to Olga's daughter, giving her the 'looking after Mum for a few days' look, and we headed to our respective cars and homes.

'You don't want to throw this out!' Mum said, holding an ugly blue vase one of Bazza's ex-girlfriends had given me for Christmas.

'Yes, I do.' I took it off Mum and put it back in the box marked 'Vinnies'.

'And you can't throw this cardi out, your Aunty Ann knitted it for you. She taught me how to knit, you know.'

I closed my eyes and gritted my teeth, frowning but not allowing my frustration to be verbalised too harshly at Mum.

'It doesn't go with anything I wear,' I said calmly. 'Dark bottle-green is not my colour.' Aunty Ann was colourblind but no-one ever said anything about it, and if Mum told me once more that Aunty Ann had taught her to knit, I would get her knitting needles and stab myself.

'Mum,' I said, taking the cardi from her and putting it back in the box, 'why don't you have a nap? We've got the Sorry Day march tomorrow, so don't wear yourself out today.'

'You're right, dear girl, my line-dancing legs are fine but the rest of me needs a spell.' With that, she took the green cardigan and the blue vase out of the Vinnies box yet again, and went into my room to lie down.

As I continued to pack the clothes I'd leave behind at Lauren's and cleaned the place for the tenants I'd let to, Bonnie and Clyde sat staring at me from their respective cat beds. I was getting increasingly upset about leaving them behind and enormously grateful that Lauren and Wyatt had agreed to take care of them. I couldn't imagine what kind of payback I was in for when I returned. Missing them was only going to be easier knowing they were with my favourite tidda.

The next morning, Mum and I headed into the city to be part of the Sorry Day Bridge Walk across Commonwealth Avenue Bridge, marking the beginning of Reconciliation Week in Canberra.

'Where are all the people?' Mum was somehow disappointed at the turnout.

'There's about a thousand people here, Mum. This a good turnout. It's Canberra, we're a small city and people are at work or doing other things today.'

'I reckon since the Apology, the pressure's off people to march so much, like it's all over now and we don't have to remember.'

Mum was probably right, but before I had a chance to answer her she was straining her neck, looking to the back of the crowd to see if she knew anyone. She spotted Olga, who was yarning up with a group of ladies they both knew. As we walked, there was chatter but mostly peace as we remembered the day Kevin Rudd apologised in the building we were heading for. I had only been fifteen at the time, but I could still remember the electrifying feeling in the air that day.

After we went through the NAG I took Mum to the National Gallery, and I was glad we didn't have to queue for tickets, since it was the end of the exhibition season. We had an enjoyable afternoon together, with lunch in the gallery's dining room, overlooking the sculpture garden, where we could see Fujiko Nakaya's fog sculpture. Mum loved it, and it was a good way for us to spend our last day together. Neither of us was worried about the five or so months apart because we were always geographically apart anyway.

As soon as we pulled up in Braddon, Lauren texted me to say she and Wyatt were on their way over to get the cats. I panicked. I wasn't ready to say goodbye to Bonnie and Clyde, and Mum hadn't stopped talking since the minute we left home that morning.

My head was aching. I still needed to finish packing and now my babies were leaving.

The doorbell rang and I felt a pang of sadness sweep over me. 'Hey.' I gave a fake Canberra smile as Wyatt and Lauren entered cheerily. 'You know how much I appreciate this, don't you?'

'It's our pleasure,' Lauren said, kissing me on the cheek. 'Actually, I thought it was a good opportunity for us to train to be parents. If we can manage cats, then maybe we can manage kids.'

'One day,' Wyatt added. 'It's going to take me some time to learn all the rules of all your football codes before I can be a father.'

Lauren just rolled her eyes.

I walked outside carrying Bonnie. Wyatt had Clyde, both seeming to take to each other quickly. I kissed both cats on their heads and gave them long, loving strokes along their silky coats.

I pushed my bottom lip out like a pouting child. 'Don't miss me too much.'

'We'll make sure they write often,' Wyatt joked, and then he hugged me. 'Have a great time, Libby, I'll look after Lauren for you.'

'I know you will, thanks.'

'I'll see you in the morning for the airport run, okay? And no tears, all right?' Lauren said, hugging me tight.

'Tears? Me? Never!' I shooed Lauren away and went inside. Mum had just made a pot of tea.

'Here you go, dear girl.' She put a mug of black tea in front of me and I burst into tears. 'There, there, you know they will be all right.'

'How did you know I was crying about B and C?'

'Because I am a mother, and those cats are like your kids. Of course I understand, but can you give me grand-kids one day, please? Cos I'm not taking photos of your cats and their kittens to line dancing.'

I laughed at that. Mum always knew how to make me feel better.

'Now, you are going to Paris and you will have fun, and do good work and you will make us all proud.' Mum pushed damp hair out of my face. 'Just don't tell me you're getting married to a Frenchman, okay? You know there's no way I'll fly that far for a wedding, not even my own daughter's.'

'I can assure you, Mum, there will be no French wedding for you to worry about. Trust me.'

As I lay on the couch that night I could hear the faintest of snores from Mum in the bedroom. There were only a few hours to go before I'd be putting her on a bus back to Moree and Lauren would be putting me on the plane to Paris.

Chapter 9

Bonjour, Paris!

The plane touched down at Charles de Gaulle and I thought I would explode with excitement. I took a photo of the tarmac like I was one of those tourists who wear 'I love [insert city]' t-shirts.

The captain spoke in French and then in English, welcoming us to Paris and informing us that some of the baggage had not been loaded onto our plane back in Singapore. There was no explanation as to why.

I looked around – no other passengers seemed to be moaning or complaining, so neither did I. Perhaps the first thing I would learn was that it was Parisian to be relaxed. I had arrived in Paris, even if my luggage may not have. So what? It was the fashion capital of the world; I could buy clothes if I needed to, but thankfully, on Caro's advice, I had packed three outfits in my hand luggage. I just wanted to get out and explore, and thaw out in the Parisian sun!

I went through security easily and straight to the baggage claim area hoping that my suitcases had miraculously arrived while others' hadn't. I chatted with an American girl who'd just flown in from Chicago, and it soon became clear that neither of our bags had made it. She was calm. I wondered if I would become less stressed and controlling in Paris. That couldn't be a bad thing.

I filled out the forms for the baggage mob so they could send my missing luggage on to me when it arrived. Although I was jet-lagged, I found it easy to navigate around the eighth busiest airport in the world. My Lonely Planet guide had recommended taking the RER rail network into the city but, not using public transport much back home, I wasn't keen on throwing myself onto it in a foreign country after a twenty-four-hour flight across the Indian Ocean.

I thought a cab would be easier than an Uber for my first commute, so I followed the signs to the cab rank, and soaked up the various accents of tourists and locals, businessmen and women, lovers and children. The airport seemed completely under control, even if no-one knew where my luggage was.

A late-model, roomy, clean black cab was my chariot heading towards the city and I couldn't stop smiling. The city was twenty-three kilometres away but the time flew by as I absorbed the moment of arrival in Gay Paree. I was bursting with excitement and wanted to shout at the top of my lungs, 'I'm in Paris!', as if I was Leonardo DiCaprio in *Titanic* screaming 'I'm the king of the world!'

It was early Wednesday morning but the sun already promised a stunning day, with not a cloud in the baby-blue sky. My sense of awe was only broken by the crazy way the driver sped in and out of lanes and beeped and yelled at other drivers. But he did it with such a delicious French accent, he didn't even sound angry.

I was struck by the traffic in the many chaotic roundabouts in Paris, which were so large they made the ones in Canberra look like silent cops. In Paris, the roundabouts had five or six lanes, and no-one seemed to stay in them. I was nervous for all the cyclists who rode amongst the traffic without helmets, and yet I didn't see any accidents.

There were an extraordinary number of French flags flying throughout the city and it reminded me of how the Aussie flag always came out a few days before January 26 and every bogan had them stuck to their cars and tattooed on their foreheads. Somehow the flag felt different in Paris. Maybe because the French had decent dress sense and didn't wear them as capes or bikinis.

I immediately fell in love with some of the tree-lined backstreets we took. They were a lush backdrop that made the well-dressed local people look even more elegant. Even the grungy-looking youth seemed fashionable and the local women were well-groomed. I felt suddenly grittier and more unkempt in the back of the cab.

I'd taken some leave to have a few days holidaying in Paris before I started work, but my apartment wouldn't be ready until Sunday, so I took Canelle's recommendation and checked into a hotel called Mama Shelter in the 20th, only steps away from rue Saint-Blaise. I looked forward to exploring the local area and city before moving to my studio apartment in the Marais and taking up the challenge that would be working at the Musée.

The hotel was slick, arty and famous for having been designed by Philippe Starck. I liked the lifts, which had trivia written on the walls in French and English. On my first ride to the third floor, I learned that it was impossible to lick my elbow, and upon attempting it found that it was true.

My room was incredibly dark even with ten lights in it, but it was modern and I liked that. Living in Canberra – especially in the city – you get used to almost everything being contemporary, new and clean. Mama Shelter was therefore a good way to ease me into the city, even though my hotel was a long way from the Parisian centre itself.

I was glad I'd packed those three frocks and my toiletries in my hand luggage; they would see me through until my suitcases showed up. I wasn't stressed at all, but I was exhausted. Although I was hungry, I just collapsed onto my double bed. One side of the bedhead was decorated with a polar bear plastic mask, with a tiger mask on the other. I thought to myself that Starck must be some kinky fella.

My phone rang at 1 am to tell me my bags had arrived at the hotel. A young man delivered them to my room five minutes later and I went straight back to sleep.

I woke up at 9 am groggy with jet lag but determined to get out and play tourist. I looked at my to-do list. It included scouting for coffee and pastries and checking out the local markets. I went down to the front desk where the young staff helped me work out the buses I needed to get round.

I turned right out of the hotel and the first thing I noticed again was the fresh morning and the warmth of the sun. Memories of frosty Canberra dissolved almost immediately. I found the bus stop for the #69 bus I needed to catch to the Louvre, which was in walking distance of the Musée. I also found the #76 I could catch to Bastille, where Canelle lived. I was grateful both stops were close to my hotel.

I walked to the corner and found what would become my temporary pâtisserie. My stomach grumbled as if to say *oohlala* loudly enough to be embarrassing and so I entered, ready for some social engagement although nervous about trying to speak the language. I had, until now, been lazy and had spoken only English to the hotel staff.

'*Un croissant au chocolat*, please,' I said, and then added, '*s'il vous plaît.*'

'You speak English?' the pastry chef asked, almost accusingly. My poor pronunciation with my Aussie accent had blown my cover in one sentence.

'I speak English, but I'm Australian.' I felt the need to distinguish myself from the supposed cultural enemy of the French and at least remain on semi-neutral ground.

'*Un café au lait, merci,*' I added to my order.

'Your French is good,' he said, with a look and sound of surprise.

'This is all I have. I can get a cake and coffee.'

'The best coffee in the world is in Paris,' he said proudly. 'And it is the same for the pastries.'

I loved his accent and the way he waved his hands over the gorgeous cakes, flans and croissants in front of us both. And I loved that he was making the experience easier than anticipated. 'So, what more could you want?' he asked, holding his palms to the sky, looking for answers.

I nodded in agreement. What more could I want, indeed? I was in Paris, ordering coffee and a chocolate croissant in French, and chatting with a nice guy as if I were a local.

'Are you new to Paris?' The shop was empty and the pastry chef seemed determined to keep talking. I didn't mind. I had nowhere to be, had no friends yet and I needed to practise my minimal language skills.

'I arrived yesterday, and I'm just showing myself around today.'

'Well, welcome, I am Michel.' He held his hand out for me to shake.

'And I am Libby,' I said, letting go of his noticeably soft hand. 'Your English is excellent,' I added.

'I have travelled a lot as a backpacker,' he responded. *And banged a few backpackers too,* I thought.

'*Au revoir.*'

I walked out of the shop, beaming with coffee and a croissant in my hands and a new friend already. I found a wooden bench to sit on and watched people pass by. One young man in his early twenties resembled an arts student from back home. He wore black jeans, a t-shirt and carried a canvas bag whilst listening to something on huge wireless headphones. As he sat down next to me, he tapped his foot gently. We were joined by a woman with a toddler whose ice-cream was melting down his little milky arm. It really was more suburban than touristy here. Most people looked like they were on their way to work as opposed to visiting the city. I finished the best coffee in the world, as defined by Michel, and started exploring the area.

I walked around the 20th trying to pronounce the names properly: rue des Orteaux, rue des Pyrénées, boulevard de Charonne. They really made Commonwealth Circle and Northbourne Avenue sound boring. Time passed easily as I discovered little parks, markets, and interesting people with sexy accents that sang in my ears.

Every corner I turned inspired me with its melding of authentically French cafés and modern-looking boulangeries. Women dressed in neutral-coloured linen dresses and pant suits rode old-fashioned pushbikes and looked elegant in their perfectly postured positions. Middle-aged men in suits drove expensive new cars. On rue des Vignoles, I followed a narrow pedestrian path that led into what I guessed was very modern public housing with enormous trellises and blooming wisteria plants climbing all over it.

I stumbled upon a tacky French souvenir shop and couldn't help myself. I acted like a tourist but told myself I needed to send something back to Mum in Moree and the aunties she went line dancing with. I got aprons with baguettes on them, an umbrella decorated with a picture of the Eiffel Tower, some postcards, gloves, keyrings and 'J'adore Paris' t-shirts to send to Lauren and Bec. They would probably only wear them to bed, but I didn't think Caro would wear one at all.

I found a nineteenth-century flea market – the Marché Aux Puces de Montreuil – not far away, with rows of homewares, including linen tablecloths and retro crockery and glasses. I wasn't sure what would work in the apartment I would move into soon, so I didn't buy anything. Still, I mentally photographed everything I liked on first sight.

I was mostly impressed by the stalls with vintage clothes and designer seconds. I knew Lauren and Bec would've loved them and I needed the girls there to help me dress myself. As I walked through, the men working in stalls looked me up and down and spoke to each other in French, what I thought was Arabic, Portuguese and Italian. Paris appeared to be multicultural, but was it the ultimate integrated society? I would find out soon enough.

I followed Google maps as I walked about twenty kilometres trying to get my bearings, checking out the laundromat, supermarket and pharmacy – the essential services I'd need to make my life actually a life here in Paris. I'd always believed that walking was the only way to get a real 'feel' for any place, even Canberra.

By 4 pm I was ready to collapse; I was so exhausted from jet lag and walking. It seemed I'd absorbed more culture in seven hours than was possible in weeks back in our capital. The contrast in everything was so stark. The sky was a different blue, but I couldn't imagine the air was cleaner with so many cars and such a densely populated city. Canelle had mentioned that sixty per cent of Parisienes didn't drive, which is a good thing because there really was no more room for cars to park in some of the tiny streets.

Just as I approached the corner of my street, my hotel looking like an oasis, a small trinket store beckoned me in. I didn't need to buy anything, I didn't want to buy anything, I wanted to sleep, but there was a silver ring in the window with a stone that matched the scarf Lauren had given me. I simply had to have it. I wasn't the accessory girl, I wasn't the shopper of the group, but for some reason I needed the ring.

'I love this. What stone is it?' I asked the girl behind the counter, who was wearing the most extraordinarily artistic skirt I had ever seen: a patchwork of linens, cotton and corduroys in a range of neutral colours.

'It is an apatite, the stone of acceptance.' The girl responded in English with a European accent that was not French, and in a sad voice, as if she didn't care whether I bought the ring or not.

'I'll take it, and I'll take one of these.' I took a business card from the counter as she wrapped my new gift to myself, and thought I'd do an Insta post later.

'And I really like your skirt,' I said, as I walked towards the door of the shop.

'Really?' Her tone improved. 'I made it myself. You really like it?'

'Yes, I think it's gorgeous. You don't see anything like that in Canberra, Australia, where I come from.'

'It is made from old pieces of material. I can make you one if you like?' she said enthusiastically.

I shook my head, as much to decline the offer as to keep myself awake. 'Oh, I just arrived yesterday, I don't even have anywhere to hang my clothes yet, but I will definitely come back. I have your card now.'

'This is not my shop. I am only a helper here. And I may not be here much longer.' She looked despondent.

'Well, hopefully I'll see you again.' I didn't want to pry, perhaps she had a better job to go to, but either way I was about to collapse as I left the shop.

I set my alarm and napped for two hours before taking myself to the hotel restaurant for dinner. Walking in, I saw businesspeople sitting at the rectangular island bar, which was lit from underneath. It was dark, just like my room. The hotel really could've been called Mama's Dark Shelter.

I propped myself up at the bar and immediately noticed a young, lean, lanky guy mixing cocktails. He was one of three guys and two girls, all in their early twenties, with sculpted faces. He was the only one who smiled warmly at the customers.

I read the menu and waited for him to approach me so I could massacre my French with an Aussie accent.

'*Un verre de* . . .' and I pointed to the Chinon, Val de Loire 2008 on the wine list.

'Of course, *madame*,' he said, finding and pouring the wine in front of me.

I couldn't take my eyes off him. I'd never seen a man like that in Canberra, nor Moree for that matter. I watched him work the bar.

'You are American?' he asked, when there was a quiet moment.

'Australian,' I answered, waiting to say I was Aboriginal until I'd determined how well we could communicate.

'Ah, kangaroos and koalas. I love Australia.'

At least he didn't say Skippy and Vegemite, I thought to myself, like many of the Americans had when I went to New York.

'You've been to Australia?' I was only slightly interested in his answer.

'No, but I will go one day, to Bondi Beach. It looks like summer all year round in your country. I want to surf. Why would you come to Paris?'

'Australia is beautiful, but I live in Canberra, which is not near the beach, and it's very cold there right now.'

'I like the Billabong surf wear, I buy it online.' he said, as he ran a cloth along the top of the bar. 'It's Australian.'

'It was created in Australia, but the Americans own it now,' I said, forcing myself not to roll my eyes at the takeover of one of our most iconic clothing brands, while picturing him on the beach next to me at Ulladulla or Mollymook on a Canberra long weekend.

'Oh, well it is very big with the surfers here. I buy a lot of Billabong, and so do my friends. They want to surf in Australia too.'

I watched Billabong man closely, imagining his sixpack, and felt a yearning desire until the waitress came and ushered me to my table, reminding me that while I was on my man-fast, the only cravings I could feed were related to food.

As I ate my rabbit with mustard sauce and tagliatelle at a table in the hotel restaurant, I felt like I was falling in love with food for the first time, imagining that this was how Lauren felt when she talked about certain sweets. The French really knew how to cook, and I almost wanted to lick my plate.

I sat back, ordered another wine and scanned the room. It was full of groups of co-workers, tables of women, a few couples, one table of eight men and one man dining alone. It wasn't hard to believe the restaurant was so very busy and popular, because the food was sensational and forty-five euros for three courses was good value by Parisian stand-ards, or so I imagined. By 8 pm my eyes were heavy again. I took my tiramisu to my room to enjoy before crashing.

Chapter 10

The red béret

Iboarded my Big Bus Paris Hop-On Hop-Off tour bus and felt like a different person in my new city. As in many major cities around the world where you hop-on, hop-off an open-topped double-decker bus, there was headphone commentary to tell me where I was, a bit of the history and so on. I knew this was the best way to get a good feel for the city, its size and the layout. Until now, I really hadn't grasped the enormity of Paris.

But on this tour bus I was immediately disappointed and slightly embarrassed by how pushy and rude an Aussie family were when boarding. I tried to act like I was not from the same land, and frowned at their behaviour. When I found it difficult to deal with obnoxious countrymen and Americans from then on, I'd just turn the headphones up louder.

I smiled as the sun hit my face and we cruised past construction sites that had designer-looking scaffolding and images strewn across them – ice-skaters, divers and, my favourite, firemen. Only in Paris, I thought to myself. It wasn't long before I came to fathom the incredible expanse of the city. It was massive and left me wondering whether I could possibly ever manage to see a tenth of it while I was working here.

I was astounded by the number of tourists, not just on the bus but everywhere. I lost track of how many people I saw dragging suitcases, wearing backpacks, taking photos. And there were so many young women obviously doing their *Emily in Paris* Instagram poses at every major site. I wondered how the French coped with such an invasion, and if the city would look empty without them – and me – there. It must have been a completely different place during the pandemic. It was hard to imagine this chaotic space completely barren during lockdown.

I didn't want to be a tourist, I didn't want to think like one or look like one. And I certainly didn't want to behave like one. Even as I sat there on the bus with my phone in my hand open to Google maps and the headphones on, I chose to only ever consider myself a newly arrived local from that day forth.

We looped around Place de la Bastille and past the Bibliothèque Nationale de France. At Notre-Dame, I got off even though it was still closed to the public. It was surrounded by high fencing that held panels that conveyed the story; I could still see the scaffolding that had been built for the restoration of the building, which was still standing, even though the spire had been warped by the heat of the fire.

Notre-Dame was still an iconic and revered space, not only for Catholics but for many international tourists who just had to see the most famous cathedral in the world. I often wondered about how you experienced spirituality in a man-made structure, but the number of people filing past reading the story of the fire and the rebuild told me that this was an incredibly significant sacred place to many people.

I boarded the bus again at the rue de la Cité on its way to the Musée d'Orsay. I got off at the musée and snapped a picture of two elephant statues out the front to send to the girls back home. I went into the museum and tried to imagine what it was like when the building was a train station with a never-ending flow of 200 trains coming and going each day.

The space was large, open, overwhelmingly filled with light. I wanted to scream, 'This is fantastic!' I wanted to share the experience of being there with someone else, and I felt my first pang of homesickness, with a hint of sadness about being alone in such an important art space. I knew Lauren would've loved it.

I walked slowly through the museum trying to absorb each moment as I watched French art students sketching sculptures. I smiled at tourists taking photos of each other in front of the artworks, just like they did back at the NAG. I glimpsed two lovers cuddling in a quiet corner, and I wanted to scream, 'Get a room!' in my usual cynical way. But I didn't. In my peripheral vision I noticed a man wearing a clichéd red béret, watching me observing others.

I figured Paris was a city of watching, some might even say voyeurism, and I wasn't going to complain because I was doing it too. Everyone was watching someone.

I weaved through the gallery, taking in my favourite Impressionist Monet, the Post-Impressionists Seurat, Renoir and Cézanne, and the great Symbolist Redon. I was in artistic heaven imagining what it might be like to give tours and lectures about the permanent collection there, or even their temporary exhibitions. I would need to return to hear some of the lectures at the d'Orsay and was glad to see their tours were also in English and Italian. The number of children's workshops were also impressive, and I knew Emma would want me to suss those out as well. I was writing frantically in my Moleskine, making more lists of things I needed to follow up while here.

I could feel the jet lag creeping up on me again and my legs and eyes were heavy. Even the adrenaline rush of being in Paris and lots of coffee weren't helping to keep me awake. Before I could leave though, I had to check out the gift shop: it was a tradition that Lauren and I participated in whenever we visited galleries. Always, always, always buy oneself a gift. And of course, a gift for one's best friend. And so I entered the shop with a sense of purpose and obligation.

It didn't take me long to find the one thing I knew I had to buy for Lauren: a silk stole created in homage to Gustav Klimt, inspired by several of his works. But then I remembered that the warm colours of pink and orange better suited me than her. So I did what any woman with a new found sense of style would – I decided to keep it for myself. I then chose a Van Gogh *Irises* scarf in soft blues and greens for my tidda. It would look great against her slick black bob. I knew she would adore it.

Although I was so tired that my vision was blurry, I took my time in the store, thinking of ways we might further improve our own space at the NAG. While I checked out their book collection, I noticed the same man with the red béret from inside the museum was looking at me again. I felt unnerved by his presence and piercing stare, so I paid for my items and made my way to the exit. I stood outside and breathed in the Parisian air deeply. I felt more awake almost immediately. I was in dire need of caffeine though, and was thinking about where to go and the best plan to get home when I noticed the man in the béret was next to me.

'You work in a gallery, don't you?' he asked in English, as if he knew me. His pale blue, wrinkled eyes squinted to focus on mine. I guessed he was in his fifties. 'I can tell by the way you observed the artwork, the sculptures.'

I felt a bit uncomfortable that he'd been watching me and yet impressed by his knowing. 'I'm an educator at the National Aboriginal Gallery in Australia. I'm going to work at the Musée du Quai Branly for five months.' I wasn't sure why I was so forthcoming with my CV, but I just sensed that we had something in common.

'I knew that you knew art. I watched the way you viewed each piece: with interest, with appreciation, with a sense of analysis. As an artist myself I appreciate that,' he said, with the same sexy French accent as Michel.

'So you paint?'

'Yes, and I want to paint you.' He stared directly into my eyes.

I laughed, embarrassed. I worked with artists all the time and no-one had ever wanted to paint me.

'Oh, I am sure there are far better subjects and models in this amazing city.'

'I want to paint you nude,' he said, as if it was a completely normal and natural statement to make to a total stranger on the street.

I half-choked and coughed at the same time, assuming he must've been on drugs. What would the aunties back in Moree think about this proposition? Oh my god, what would my *brothers* think? Barry would want to kill him, and that thought made me laugh out loud.

'What is so funny?' he asked, as if offended by my not taking him seriously. 'You are an arts educator, so you need to know about the artistic process from all angles, *oui*?' He was doing his best to persuade the one person who would never buy his crap.

I could hear Caro in my ear warning me, and every sleazy line I'd ever heard was playing itself out over and over again. The only difference being that this time it had that *oohlala* sound to it, and I was in Paris.

I was keen to change the subject and end the conversation. 'So you are a local painter, then?'

'I am not Parisian,' he said, almost distastefully. 'I am

provincial. I hardly ever come into Paris. I come just for the exhibitions, some supplies and always for inspiration,' he said, looking deep into my weary eyes, 'from beautiful women like you.'

He touched my arm as if to make more of a point. I flinched away.

'I am interested in how the human body is represented in the history of art. There are amazing French painters and paintings which have magnified and represented the human body in original ways through art. You might know Modigliani's paintings? He lived in France. I think they would be of interest to you.'

'I really must go now, I . . .' I didn't know what to say and before I had the chance to make up a lie, he spoke again.

'I am staying at the Hôtel du Quai Voltaire; I would like you to join me.'

'I have to go.' I felt like a nervous schoolgirl and rushed off.

I walked quickly to the pick-up point for the bus and boarded, still in shock at such a blunt offer from a complete stranger. I felt like I'd had my cultural awareness training in terms of Frenchmen, and that I had experienced what I'd seen portrayed in all the films. The men here were incredibly different: more forward, flirtatious, inviting and sleazy when compared to Aussie men and most definitely those in Canberra and any Koori fellas I'd ever met, in *and* out of the arts.

Most of the straight blokes who crossed my path only ever invited me for a drink of some description, not a naked arts session in a fancy hotel. I planned on googling the Voltaire when I returned to my hotel but, in the meantime, I was back to being in awe of the city, and remained open-mouthed as we cruised down the Champs-Élysées, around the Arc de Triomphe, the Trocadero and the Eiffel Tower. It was like being on the set of every travel show I'd ever watched as we passed consulates and embassies, countless buildings that looked like palaces, and so many statues.

As I had noticed when I caught my taxi from the airport, I couldn't believe the number of cars there were in Paris. Little cars – Renaults, Peugeots and Citroëns – all steered around the city by crazy drivers. If a light turned green and a car hadn't moved in two seconds, the horns would beep like mad. It was an aerobic activity just to cross the road without being hit or tooted at. I was shocked and a little amused that bumping into a car when you were parking was completely normal. I saw numerous drivers rocking their cars back and forth into other cars until they were happy with the park.

The commentary told me that we were approaching rue Royale, which I'd read was a very luxurious street with shops selling caviar and truffles and other delicacies. Although I was tired, I forced myself to get off the bus because I had spotted Maxim's de Paris, and Caro had told me that not only was it *the* most famous restaurant in the mid-twentieth century but it also had Art Nouveau interior decor that I needed to check out.

I drank an espresso in the famous café to keep me going and headed into the museum section, which had two floors of Art Nouveau furniture and objects collected by Pierre Cardin over sixty years. I dreamt about dining on the French gastronomy there and I salivated, realising I hadn't eaten since earlier that day. When I looked at my watch and could hardly make out the time, I knew I had to head back to the hotel. Acknowledging my inability to take public transport in my delirious state, I ordered my first Uber to rue de Bagnolet.

The next morning, I went to spend the day at the Louvre. As I stood outside the entrance, I noticed a swarm of paparazzi following someone I soon recognised as Zendaya, looking absolutely stunning in wild animal-print shorts and jacket. Apparently, she was here for Paris Fashion Week. I hadn't even realised the event was on – the night before I had been too busy watching the BBC World News commentating on the attempt to ban the hijab.

As I stood gazing at the French glass icon of art and architecture, I wondered if they had anti-discrimination laws in France like we had back home. Not that it mattered because our own government had suspended the Anti-Discrimination Act back in 2007 in order to pass the racist Northern Territory 'intervention' legislation which claimed control over land and monies in targeted Aboriginal communities. Even now we were still asking for recognition, including in the Constitution – a referendum on the Voice to Parliament was slated to be held soon.

Clearly the government of any country can just play with legislation to suit its own needs at any time. Just as I thought about it, a skinhead with a swastika on his t-shirt walked past. I wondered why the French didn't ban racist slogans on clothes as well as the burqa.

I walked into the entrance lobby of the Louvre and fell in love. It was huge and full of light: the gateway to a place filled with artwork, stories and people. Weaving through the gallery would turn out to be one of the most amazing professional development, personal and spiritual experiences I could imagine. With eight curatorial departments covering everything from sculpture to decorative arts and Eastern antiquities, I had to sit and read a map of the museum before I started my tour.

I took my time going through one of the temporary exhibitions, Naples in Paris: The Louvre Hosts the Museo de Capodimonte. As a powerful collaboration between the Musée du Louvre and the Museo di Capodimonte, I was overwhelmed by the scope of the partnership. Over seventy pieces from Capodimonte were being exhibited in three sites in the Louvre, and it put my P4P to shame. But it also inspired to me to achieve greater outcomes in my own work.

I then made my way slowly around the permanent collections looking for 'the masterpieces' like Leonardo da Vinci's *Mona Lisa*, which I found to be breathtaking and to my utter surprise, much smaller than I would ever have imagined. There was a corralling of visitors like check-in at the airport, and as we wove our way towards the painting, excitement grew ahead of me. Was everyone else thinking the same thing? What was she smiling at? I loved the mystery of her grin and wondered if she was thinking about sexy men or fabulous food or perhaps just some new clothes. Unlike the many others looking on, I didn't take a photo.

I remained silent as I stood and viewed *Man reading* by Muhammad Sharif Musavvir. The gouache with gold highlights on paper was so different to anything we had at the NAG, but it touched me emotionally as much as anything else I had seen in my own country.

I was overwhelmed by the size of the Louvre, and got lost a couple of times, unintentionally retracing my steps, which wasn't surprising given it is one of the largest galleries in the world. The experience was truly a challenge in map reading. With over 3,500 objects from prehistory to the nineteenth century exhibited over an area of 60,600 square metres, I was bound to get lost at least once or twice.

Before I crashed for the night I sent a long message to Lauren, Bec and Caro in the group chat:

STOP PRESS!! My god! You will never believe the first few days here, really. Everything they say about Frenchmen is true. They leave Canberra men for dead – and buried – in the female-appreciation stakes. I've never felt more attractive in my life. They smile at you with a hint of oohlala on their lips and they proposition you straight-up. It's like all those movies we watched.

Some are sexy and flirty, others are just downright sleazy. Either way, it's clear that men here like women, and the approaches are almost business-like, without exchanging money. Caro, I know what you're thinking so keep it to yourself! ☺

Nothing's changed my end though, I'm still not interested in the weaker sex, but it's hard not to notice them here.

All I'll tell you is that from the minute I left my hotel on day one to explore the local area, flirtatious conversations with complete strangers were possible anywhere. I kid you not. I met this guy in the pâtisserie near my place. He – Michel – likes to chat and is very friendly. And just today, some sleazy, eccentric past-his-use-by-date artist wearing a béret tried to pick me up in the gift shop of the Musée d'Orsay – which I might add is possibly one of the most amazing galleries in the world. And yes, Lauren, I stuck to our tradition. ☺

Anyway, the Red Béret wanted to take me to his hotel – the Hôtel du Quai Voltaire – which, I've read, has stunning views of the Seine River and of the Louvre. People like Oscar Wilde and Pissarro stayed there. I'd never have gone with him, but I might go back for a drink and a stickybeak one day.

Check the hotel out online, the rooms aren't really any more expensive than a decent hotel in Canberra and let's face it, a view of the Seine is always going to be better than a view of Lake Burley Griffin. Oh, I can't believe it, have I said that already? I'm here only a few days and I'm in love – with the city that is and especially the Louvre!

I've just let out a deep sigh, my tiddas, because I wish you were all here to enjoy it with me. But I know you're having a great time back there without me.

Don't miss me too much! Love yas xxx

Chapter 11

Man-fast to man-feast

On Friday, I visited Michel again. It'd become a routine to get my coffee and have a quick chat with him, and I enjoyed starting my day that way. He was my only pseudo-friend in Paris and I was glad he hadn't been sleazy like the guys Caro had talked about, or the Red Béret bloke.

'*Bonjour,* Libby, it is good to see you. And where are you going today?'

'I might go to the Père Lachaise Cemetery later. It's nearby and I'm a bit over getting on and off buses.'

Michel's eyes widened and his face lit up excitedly. '*Oui,* it is not so far. I can come with you if you like, give you a tour if you can wait until tomorrow. I have been many times. It is a landmark for us and my favourite place in Paris.'

'Oh, no, I don't want to be a bother, really.' I couldn't believe the hospitality of the French.

'It is no bother for a Frenchman to show a beautiful woman around his city.' Michel wasn't sleazy, but he was a damned good flirt. 'I will meet you at the main entrance on boulevard de Ménilmontant.' He wrote it down on a tiny piece of paper. 'Do you think you can find it by yourself?'

'Well, I got myself across the world to your pâtisserie, I think I can get myself a few more streets away to the cemetery,' I said, trying to sound funny rather than sarcastic.

'So, I will see you at ten o'clock tomorrow, *oui*?'

'*Oui*.'

The next morning I went to the nominated entrance to the cemetery. The guard at the gate didn't speak English but tried to keep me company by smiling and laughing until Michel arrived and greeted me with the double-cheeked French kiss, just like we were old friends.

Our tour began immediately as Michel linked his arm through mine as if we were a couple. As if we had known each other forever, as if it were completely normal for him to assume such intimacy with me. I didn't fight it – I mightn't want a boyfriend, but that didn't mean I couldn't enjoy some attention and male company. In fact, I liked it. I liked being in Paris with my Pâtisserie Parisian guide. I liked that Libby Cutmore was seemingly desirable to men in this city. I may have been there to work magic at the Musée, but until that began, I reminded myself I was a newly arrived local.

'The basics,' Michel said, looking me directly in the eyes. 'Napoléon opened the cemetery back in 1804, and it has been expanded in size five times. They say there are between 300,000 and one million bodies buried here in 69,000 tombs, 250 famous people and fifteen kilometres of pathways.'

The idea of so many dead people – souls, stories, sadness – hit me hard and I automatically thought the area needed one massive Aboriginal smoking ceremony to cleanse the negative or evil spirits.

'Is there anything in particular you want to see?' Michel asked. 'Because it would take days, maybe weeks, to go through here properly.'

'If it's not too much trouble, I'd like to see the gravesites of Edith Piaf, Jim Morrison, Chopin, Pissarro and Oscar Wilde.' There were more, but I'd be happy just seeing those. '*S'il vous plaît*,' I added as an afterthought.

Michel walked me through what seemed like endless paths with the occasional canopy of trees overhead. It was interesting to see the way that changes in concrete and landscaping made additions to the cemetery over time look obvious. Tourists and locals alike roamed the grounds like it was a public park, rather than a place where parents, children, friends and yes, even famous people, were laid to rest. I watched school groups file through, some with guides, others seemingly alone. There were couples holding hands and strolling, as if a cemetery was perfect for a romantic rendezvous.

Suddenly I became conscious of how close Michel was standing to me. Was this meant to be a romantic rendezvous for him? I didn't even know if he had a girlfriend. *He's got a girlfriend all right*, I heard Caro in my head.

'This is the Garden of Memories where the ashes of people cremated are kept,' he said. 'Between twenty and twenty-five people get cremated a day here. It may be the only crematorium in Paris.'

We stopped so I could respectfully observe the space.

'This is like a museum, not a cemetery. People come here to look and learn a little.' He pointed to a site. 'This is Maria Callas – Aristotle Onassis left her for Jackie Kennedy.'

As we walked, Michel pointed out more graves.

'Max Ernst was a prolific German artist, a Surrealist. He died in 1976,' he said matter-of-factly. 'And over here is Achille Zavatta, he joined the circus at three and was one of our most famous pantomimes. He committed suicide in 1993. Very sad.'

We kept walking. 'And over there is Simone Signoret, one of our greatest movie stars.'

I looked at her grave and the fresh flowers on it.

'She was the first French person to win an Academy Award, for her role in *Room at the Top*.' Michel paused as if to give a moment's silence.

'Her husband, Yves Montand,' he continued, 'was an actor too, but also a singer. The songs he crooned about Paris became instant classics.'

The cemetery was extraordinary, so many stories, so much history, and yet I was too engaged with the man on my arm to truly appreciate the moment. No-one would believe me when I told them about this tour with a hot local French guy. I felt a sense of sacrilege – I should have been paying my respects to the dead but it was hard to focus. I couldn't remember the last time I'd had sex, and here was this man holding me close to him, knowledgeable in history, taking time to show me around. How generous. *How obviously sleazy*, I heard Caro again in my ear.

Michel rattled off more trivia. 'Sarah Bernhardt slept in a coffin as she prepared herself for death.'

Then some commentary: 'See the trees planted on the graves here, it is like they are eating the dead.'

He waited for my reaction but I hadn't been listening fully and was too embarrassed to admit it. I smiled stupidly. He sighed and continued with the tour.

'This is Victor Noir.' He pointed to a horizontal statue of a man. 'It is a long story, but he was a journalist, murdered when trying to organise a duel between Pierre Bonaparte, Napoléon's nephew, and another journalist. History has it that when Noir informed Bonaparte of the duel, Bonaparte slapped him in the face and then shot him. Over a hundred thousand people attended the funeral and this statue is meant to represent him having been shot.'

The statue was stretched out on the tombstone, looking as if it had just fallen dead. I put my hand over my mouth, slightly shocked.

Michel gave me a flirtatious smile. 'There is a myth that claims rubbing his crotch will enhance fertility, bring a better sex life, or even a husband within the year. There are many stories about people kissing his crotch also, and that,' he pointed to Victor Noir's bulge, 'is his erection.'

I looked at the statue closely and could see where many women had rubbed. I frowned at the thought of anyone kissing the statue, especially since COVID meant we were often elbow-bumping even those we knew and loved. There was not enough sanitiser in the world to entice me to do either. Not only did I have no desire to rub the crotch of the statue of a dead man, I wasn't remotely interested in being fertile or fertilised while in Paris, or meeting a husband.

We continued to walk and I strained not to take my phone out to take photos for the girls. I didn't want to treat such a sacred place as a tourist attraction . . .

'And here is Oscar Wilde.'

But then I couldn't help myself – I had to take a photo, even though the tomb was surrounded by Perspex, you could see where lipstick marks once were. Moving closer I snapped a few shots and exclaimed, 'There's lipstick marks all over his tomb!'

'Yes, would you have kissed it too, if you could?'

I thought it was an odd question and responded frankly.

'Absolutely not! His tomb is sacred and, hopefully, heritage listed.'

'It is heritage listed, *oui*. He is the greatest man to ever live. And the kisses were a desecration of his grave.' Michel was suitably angry as he spoke.

'I agree!' I knew how to show respect without defacing property. Working in the arts you learn to admire without touching. It was something I tried to teach the schoolkids who came into the NAG on tours.

Michel became more serious than angry. 'Most people think I'm being dramatic when I say that, but I think it's disrespectful. Would you go and kiss any other stranger's gravesite? Someone who wasn't in your family?'

I looked more closely at the tomb. 'I can understand the need people might feel to pay homage, that makes sense to me, but . . .' I didn't get to finish my sentence before he cut me off.

'I am a man who knows how to pay homage, to demonstrate my love, even for a great man like Oscar Wilde. But I think there needs to be boundaries.' Michel was waving his arms in fury, but I understood the passion he was expressing.

We continued to walk and Michel eventually went back to being my friendly, knowledgeable tour guide.

'And here is Frédéric Chopin, the great composer. A mask was taken of him on his deathbed. Many buses with Polish people come here to pray and sing at his grave all the time.'

I was amazed at how much Michel knew about the people buried there.

'Why don't you do this professionally?' I asked. 'Be a tour guide?'

'I like to just come here and think, to get ideas, to dream, to be at peace. It is not work for me. I like to share the stories with my friends, and other people I like.' And there it was, the flirtatious French style that Caro had warned me about one minute and told me to enjoy the next. I got immediately nervous. It was only day four, I couldn't be getting excited – momentarily or otherwise –about a bloke in Paris, and certainly not while I was walking through a cemetery with the spirits of dead people.

Wanting to break Michel's gaze, I said, 'Someone told me Jim Morrison's grave is the most visited site here. Is that true?'

'Yes,' he said, leading me in the direction of the spot where the legendary American rock star had been laid to rest.

'See the fence?' He pointed and I looked accordingly. 'It has to be bordered off because of security. There are even cameras on his grave because people steal items from it.'

I took another sly photo quickly.

'And the second most visited gravesite is Edith Piaf.' He ushered me further. 'She was known as the woman who sounded like a little bird singing in the streets of Paris.'

'You are a fan too?' I asked him.

'*Oui.* Her life was singing and men, not money. I write songs and I like women, and I am not motivated by money, so we are kind of alike, Piaf and me.'

I wondered what kind of songs Michel wrote and what his singing voice sounded like as he continued to talk.

'The story goes that she gave a watch to a man to tell him it was time to go. Then one night she invited all her exes to a restaurant and they all had the same watch on.'

I laughed. 'Is that true?'

'I don't know, but it's a great story.'

'It sure is. I'll have to tell my girlfriends back home.'

'Will you tell your boyfriend that story too?' he asked with a sly smile.

'There's no boyfriend,' I offered, before realising I should've lied to save the next thing from happening.

'No boyfriend for such a beautiful, intelligent woman? This is surely a crime.'

He pulled me close to him, his hands firmly on my waist.

'We shall solve this mystery by going back to the pâtisserie where I will make you the best baguette in Paris and we will sit on my balcony in the sun.'

'Oh, Michel, thank you so much for the offer, but I have to do some work this afternoon.' I wasn't going to go back to Michel's house. I didn't even know him, but I knew he wanted more than lunch.

'Ma chérie,' he said as he pulled me closer, and I could feel his own baguette growing against me.

It made me weak, it had been a long time since I'd been that close to any fella, let alone one with a grasp of history who wrote songs and served the best coffee in the world. But there was no way anything was happening.

'Really, Michel.' I pulled myself away. 'I am so grateful, merci beaucoup for the wonderful tour, but I do have to do some work today.'

I had to lie. What else could I say that would make sense to him? He walked me back to Mama Shelter and when I got back to my room I stood under the cold running water in my tiny shower and wondered if this was what life in Paris was going to be like when I wasn't working.

I thought it would be uncomfortable going to the pâtisserie the next day, so I found a new one on the corner to the left of Mama Shelter and closer to my own apartment. The one thing I didn't want, having just arrived in Paris, was drama with a bloke. I didn't leave Canberra and my life of man-fasting to come to Paris for a man-feast. Michel was a blessing in some ways, it reminded me of what it was like to be desired by a man, but I wasn't interested in a repeat of my dramatic and destructive past.

I woke on Sunday still tired. I lay in bed for a few minutes, thinking about moving into my apartment. But with only two suitcases it wasn't going to be that difficult. I packed everything and checked out of the hotel but couldn't check into my apartment until the afternoon, so I left my cases at reception and walked to the Métro at Alexandre Dumas and got the #2 train to Nation. Then I took the #6 to Bir-Hakeim in the 15th arrondissement and made my way to quai Branly. I walked past the Australian embassy on rue Jean Rey and then the Eiffel Tower. I envied the view the Australian diplomats must have from their offices.

As I faced what was to be my new office for the next five months, I couldn't believe my own life and how lucky I was. I stood in awe of Aboriginal artist Lena Nyadbi's creation on the Musée's façade. The size of the work – *Jimbirla and gemerre* (spearheads and cicatrice) – rendered into the wall expressed the vastness of the creator's own country. I looked forward to starting my day, every day, with such inspiration. I thought about the first time I had seen that image on the page back at the NAG. I was momentarily breathless.

I looked at my watch. It had taken me only forty-five minutes in total. I boarded a #76 bus back to rue de Bagnolet and sat marvelling at the ability of the driver to manoeuvre the huge tank through small streets, often only an inch away from parked cars. I was glad for the air-conditioning on the bus, and guessed that it would be better to be above ground than below it on the subway on a hot day in the heart of summer.

As we turned corners, I looked at different businesses along the way. From the window I gazed at the boucheries and considered becoming a vegetarian, but the French even made the word 'butcher' sound sexy. I saw motor-cycles on the streets – Yamahas, Kawasakis, Harleys – but I'd never heard of the Motul brand.

I was grateful there was an announcement of each stop accompanied by a rolling red electronic sign at the front of the bus. I read and listened at the same time, hoping it would improve my French, even slightly.

I looked at the Juliet Monument at Bastille, which commemorated the July 1830 revolution, before spotting L'Opéra Bastille – the modern opera house – that I had first seen on my 'touristy' days. I was pleased I was getting my bearings. I was becoming a local.

I squeezed close in my seat as if it would make a differ-ence as the bus sat within three lanes of traffic with only two lanes marked on the road. *The French really are crazy drivers*, I mumbled under my breath. I stared out the window and saw young people peddling their bikes alongside the bus and thought them incredibly brave.

I got off before Mama Shelter and treated myself to lunch at L'Abribus. I'd walked past it so many times in the last few days and each time was inspired by the locals eating and drinking, although I wasn't so inspired by the smoking. Lots of people still smoked in Paris and that disturbed me. Perhaps they didn't have massive anti-smoking campaigns like we did.

I went inside the restaurant and ordered the penne au fromage, the crème brûlée à l'orange and a glass of red. The space had wooden chairs and tables and benches with red paper placemats. There was a funky wine bottle display and the ceiling was two shades of blue with yellow circles. The service was average, but I liked that I could sit in a cool place that was close to my soon-to-be new home.

The lunch crowd finally found its way inside and in no time at all there was a father and baby, a lone traveller reading a guidebook and two businessmen. I finished my meal and walked past *the* pâtisserie – pretending not to but most definitely looking to see Michel. I couldn't. I headed back to the hotel.

I called an Uber and was excited about the drive to my new temporary home in the Marais. I loved it the first time I saw photos of it online, and now I was finally moving in.

'Welcome, Mademoiselle Cutmore,' the old man said. 'Cutmore' had never sounded more elegant than it did when he pronounced it, more like *Cootmurrrre*.

'I am Dominic Robert.'

I shook Monsieur Robert's hand before he carried my cases up to the second floor to my tiny studio apartment. I knew it was going to be small but it was more obvious when the two of us and my two huge cases tried to enter at the same time. Nevertheless, it was modern and clean and I loved it. There was a double bed with European square pillows and a blue doona cover. I'd googled IKEA and discovered I could walk to it, so I would change that as soon as I got the chance.

The apartment walls were stark white, in contrast to the dark of Mama Shelter, and I could smell the fresh paint with the slightest of breaths. There was a two-seater sofa, and two black leather chairs, a bookcase, hanging robe, a desk and a dining table with chrome chairs. All in one room. A small kitchen for meal prep and the bathroom both led off the main room.

'Is it okay?' Monsieur Robert asked. 'I repainted the front door and the bathroom door because the last tenant made many marks when they moved out. It is not toxic paint, there is no more lead in paint,' he reassured me, even though I hadn't even considered the toxicity of paint.

'It's perfect. You did a good job,' I said, knowing the need to praise the work of a handyman. Monsieur Robert puffed his chest out with pride.

The kitchen cabinets were designer red, the appliances stainless steel and there was a microwave, so I knew I'd be fine. The bathroom had been renovated and the white walls and vanity matched the tiny, blue-tiled shower recess. There was no bath, but I knew I could manage. Having lived in a full house with five brothers growing up, I'd become used to having really quick showers anyway.

Monsieur Robert was talking me through the wi-fi and the garbage collection days, but I was already thinking about where I would put my books and clothes and other bits and pieces that I had in my case. I was planning on heading back to the markets for the linen tablecloths I'd seen. I liked the flat-screen TV, although I didn't imagine spending much time watching it.

'I love this place, Monsieur Robert, it feels like home already,' I said.

'Please call me Dom, everybody does.'

'Thank you, Dom, please call me Libs, everyone back home calls me that.'

Dom smiled like a father, the father I hadn't had for most of my life. I had a fleeting moment of homesickness and missing my dad, and wondered what he would have thought of his only daughter moving to Paris, even for a short time. I couldn't even imagine him saying 'arrondissement' without a cigarette stuck to his bottom lip.

'I will let you settle in now. I will leave these forms for you to sign, please, and you can bring to me. I live in apartment four on the first floor.' He put the papers on the kitchen table.

'And when you are ready, just down the street to the left is my favourite boulangerie and café, Salon Marie Antoinette on Rue François Miron. Ask for Monica, she will take care of you. Tell her I sent you. They make the best coffee in Paris.'

I wondered what Michel might've thought about that.

I spent the afternoon unpacking and placing the few items I brought with me to make it *my* place. I placed a Delvene Cockatoo-Collins runner across my desk and placed a tiny Tony Albert painting on the shelf. I rinsed my favourite NAG coffee mug, and organied my clothes, while listening to the soothing sounds of Archie Roach, saddened that his haunting vocals would never be heard live again. I perked up when 'Love In the Morning' came on, and sang a few lines before I paused a moment to remember him and his partner, the late Ruby Hunter – two special lives lost too soon.

The only place I could find to hang my firey calendar was inside a kitchen cupboard door. Hidden but not out of reach. I just needed to put some food in there as well.

By the time I had everything out of my cases, the place was full and already looked lived in. I was about to head to the supermarket when there was a knock at the door.

'I am sorry to bother you, Mademoiselle Libs.' It was Dom holding a black poodle.

'Not at all, was my bad singing bothering you? The music too loud?'

'Not at all. My wife, Catherine, she made me come here to say she really likes the man singing and could she perhaps have the name of the musician?'

'Oh, of course,' I said. 'It's Archie Roach, I'll write it down for her.'

Dom smiled enthusiastically. 'Oh, Catherine will be very happy and will want to cook you something and ask questions about him. And she will be very happy with me also.'

'Well then, we will *all* be happy, won't we?' I smiled. 'And I'm extra happy your English is so good.'

'That is because I have only English-speaking people in this flat for twenty years. I had to learn and so did Catherine, and we get to practise with our grandchildren who learn it at school. Perhaps you will come have coffee and speak to us in English so we can practise more?' Dom looked hopeful.

'Of course, I'd love to.' I couldn't believe how I'd lucked out with the apartment and Dom.

My landlord left content that he could make his wife happy and I headed to the supermarket, turning left outside the building, seeing Salon Marie Antoinette at the end of the street and making a note to stop there for my morning coffee from now on.

The supermarket was smaller than ours back home, but I just needed some basics to tide me over. I grabbed what I wanted, including a bottle of wine for under ten euros, and I was the happiest newly arrived visitor in the city. On the way back I passed a small artisan market and got a bit carried away, buying a hand-sewn tablecloth and an art deco vase plus matching bowl. They were housewarming gifts for myself and a small attempt to Paris-ify my apartment.

I struggled up my stairs, carrying the gifts as well as all
the essentials, including five of the most popular cheeses
as recommended by Caro – Brie de Meaux, Roquefort,
Camembert, Cantal and Bleu d'Auvergne. I'd also picked
up some cheap roses to give some life to the place.

I struggled with getting over the jet lag and planned on
an early night. I had bread and cheese for dinner, washed
down with a housewarming toast to myself. I ironed my
clothes for work, organised my papers and NAG promo-
tional kit to take into the Musée, and sat down to message
the girls before I went to bed.

My dear tiddas,
I can't believe I am still so tired. I have been non-stop
trying to get a grasp of the city and moved into my flat
today so I really haven't had a good rest.

Walking and watching is helping me immerse myself
in Paris. Strolling the streets each day has helped me
experience the people, the buildings, the businesses
and the traffic. So many cars! I am truly thrilled to
be here. It is the best thing I have ever done, and
I haven't even begun working on the purpose of the
trip yet!

They have the best bread and cheese in the world
here, true. I may eat a wheel of brie every day. I'm
really hoping I develop a wheat allergy because the
bread here is the best in the world, I'm sure. We really
don't know how to make bread back home. In fact, I'm
never eating bread again when I go back to Canberra, it

just couldn't compare. You might have to remind me of that vow though. 😉

I don't know how the women aren't all fat here. What with brioches, croissants, baguettes, pastries, bubbly. It never ends. And sure enough, there's Subway and McDonald's between cafés and bistros. They look so out of place here, it's almost sacrilege, but they're full of American tourists anyway.

I did 18,000 steps today, so I'm extra tired, so I'll sign-off now, day one at work starts in less than twelve hours!

Sending love and hugs from Paris. Don't miss me too much! 😊

Chapter 12

Becoming Elizabeth

I woke up at 5 am after a solid night's sleep, eager to start work. I decided to catch the bus rather than the Métro and waited nervously for the #72 from Pont Marie.

There was an air of friendliness amongst the locals at the bus stop, but no real conversation going on. I was trying to take in every action, smell and sound. I watched the road workers fixing a pothole, runners on the opposite side of the road tracing their steps along the Seine. Well-coiffeured women with beautiful skin strolled by looking effortlessly glamorous, while shops opened their shutters and doors.

I boarded the spacious, air-conditioned bus, said *bonjour* to the driver, who only nodded a reply, and tapped my Navigo travel card and I was on my way to the Musée, to my new job, only fourteen stops away. I was excited and only a little nervous. My Paris working life was about to begin.

As the bus cruised along, I stared out the window at couples, groups of teenagers and businesspeople all sitting on sidewalks having their morning coffees and croissants. *What a life!*

When we stopped to let people off, I saw a young girl hug and kiss her father goodbye before he ran off to work and the girl and mother walked away in another direction. I momentarily pondered whether my own life would be like that one day, but my thoughts were broken when the bus stopped for an inordinate amount of time. I strained my neck and saw the driver had been stopped by police to let a protest pass by. There were hundreds of Iranian flags and thousands of women and men, marching, some on loud-speakers. I had to ask the young woman next to me if she could translate the placards for me. *Femme. Vie. Liberté.*

Woman. Life. Freedom. I recognised the words. The young woman next to me saw me staring at the placards, so I asked her what had provoked the protest.

'The protest is about the rights of women in Iran, where it is still mandatory for women to wear the hijab.'

The freedom to choose was denied in Iran, and potentially it soon would be denied in France as well.

'Wow.' It was all I could say to express myself.

'But it is about more than that, this is about democracy for Iranians, and the resistance movement is here too.'

'This is a big protest,' I said, as the line of people just kept coming.

'Oh, this is nothing,' she said, and proceeded to tell me about the ongoing action that closed down the city of

Paris on a regular basis, where public transport ceased and roads were blocked as French citizens exercised their right to protest against the government's pension reform bill. The French didn't want to see the retirement age increased from sixty-two to sixty-four years of age.

'But that is so young,' I said. 'Our retirement age is sixty-seven and likely to go up.'

The young woman just shrugged and continued.

'The police presence at these protests is like nothing you will see anywhere else in the world.'

'Trust me,' I said, 'I have seen a lot of police at protests back home, especially at our land rights marches, and our Black Lives Matter marches – they're are always out in force.'

She pulled out her phone, scrolled through her photos and played a video for me. 'This is from a recent protest. Look, that's a water-canon truck, and see how many police vans are coming around that bend?' The video played and the sirens and vans continued for what seemed like minutes. I lost count of vehicles, and the foot soldiers too. She was right, I had not seen anything like it in my life. All I could say was 'Wow!'

The bell to stop the bus rang, and as she walked towards the door to exit at the next stop, my head was in a spin. There was so much I needed to learn about the politics of the city, but I already loved the passion the French had for enacting their democratic right to protest. That would never get lost on this Wiradyuri-yinaa.

I finally got off the bus at the Musée d'Art Moderne – Palais de Tokyo, and had plenty of time to eat before the walk to the Musée, so I popped into one of the few places where food looked healthy and tasty, without the deliciously buttery, creamy or fattening extras that French cuisine was famous for.

I had a fresh fruit juice, yoghurt and Bircher muesli, and checked out the fashionable looking space, set in an old building. White laminated tables and benches, grey and chocolate-brown leather and chrome stools, massive silver ball lights. I felt like I was having breakfast in a nightclub. The salads and baguettes looked so good, I was already imagining what I'd order next time. I'd found a new interest in food since landing in the city and every mouthful of my muesli made me think of Lauren and how she'd love the French cuisine.

I strolled along the Seine, crossed over the Passerelle Debily, turned right on the other side, and walked along quai Branly. I followed the directions I'd been given by Canelle to the staff entrance at the back of the building. I climbed up the stairs to the reception desk and while I waited for Canelle to collect me, watched couriers come and go, two people manning one phone on the front desk, visitors waiting to be served. No-one appeared to be stressing out except me, because after I had asked at the reception desk no-one had seemed to be able to find Canelle.

I calmed down when I saw Judy Watson's *two halves with bailer shell* (2002) reflected above me. I couldn't believe I would be greeted each morning by the rich Prussian blue of her canvas made into an enormous installation. She had won the Moët & Chandon Prize and numerous others for a reason. Watson was the perfect example of why I wanted to bring more First Nations artists to the world stage. There was so much talent in our community, and it was easily measured when you saw such stunning works. I took a deep breath, lost in a moment of awe as I considered the journey of just one woman from Waanyi country becoming part of the interior of this extraordinary institution.

'Hello.' A soft voice only just broke my thoughts. A gorgeous black woman stood before me, smiling. She had black hair slicked to her head, full lips coated in sheer lip gloss, dark brown eyes and fingers covered with bling. She was shorter than me and was wearing black pants and a black top with flat red shoes.

'*Bonjour,* Elizabeth,' she said warmly. '*Je suis* Canelle. It is so wonderful to have you here. Everyone is very excited.' She kissed both my cheeks.

'*Bonjour, je suis* Libby Cutmore,' I said in response, emphasising the 'Libby', concerned that perhaps she had confused me with someone else.

'Of course you are, but Libby comes from Elizabeth, *oui*?'

'*Oui,*' I said, although no-one had ever called me Elizabeth. Not since kindergarten and only when I was in trouble.

'Elizabeth is so much more elegant, don't you think?' She raised her eyebrows, seeking my agreement, and her red scarf was so perfectly tied around her neck, I couldn't argue.

'*Oui.*' I'd just agreed to change my name, what the hell was I doing? I was thrown off balance but gathered my senses quickly. 'I am very excited to be here too.'

'I love your shoes,' Canelle said, looking at the black Kenneth Cole sandals I'd picked up when I'd been in New York visiting Lauren. But my feet were already killing me.

'*Merci beaucoup.*' I wished Lauren could've heard the compliment about my fashion style. She would've been impressed.

Canelle smiled. 'I need a coffee first, and you?'

'*Oui.*' Hell, I'd need to say more than '*oui*' or she'd think I would need to be called boring Libby and not elegant Elizabeth.

I followed Canelle to a coffee machine downstairs below the staff entrance, which turned out to be a hub of activity with people catching up on their caffeine hits. Senior staff, curators, administrative staff and labourers were all chatter and laughter.

'I need a cigarette,' she said, taking me to the smoking area – which I was surprised to find also had artwork near it. I laughed to myself at how the French could make any place look cultured and artistic, even the smoking room. My distaste for smoke remained though.

'This is a great place to catch up and get all the news or share news, it's still all work here,' Canelle advised on exhaling. 'That's what we call the musicology tower,' she pointed behind me, 'it goes up every floor and has instruments from all over the world.' I turned to see the massive glass edifice rising from one floor through to the next.

After her cigarette, we continued our tour of the building and Canelle briefed me on the basics of the organisation. We went up a lift, along corridors lined with what looked

like average offices. We made our way back via the staff
entrance again to the museum entrance, where patrons were
going through security and into the main exhibitions. All
the while, Canelle kept talking. She was from Guadeloupe,
so at least we had something in common in terms of being
people 'of colour' in a colonising country.

'There's around two hundred and seventy staff here,
including trainers, cleaners, caterers, security and electri-
cians. I'm in charge of the Oceania collection and I work
alongside the curator who worked with Hetti and Brenda
on the original commission, as you would know.' We
turned a corner. 'I secured the job because my English is
good. You have to be bilingual to work here.'

I took a deep breath, knowing my French still wasn't that
great. It was far from great. We walked past the bookshop
and when I turned from the window display, I looked ahead
to see Jean Nouvel's architecture from a different angle.

Canelle continued, 'We have shows at the Musée in
the springtime and the summertime. We recently had a
Hawaiian dance show, and a South African choreographer
with musical instruments made of bamboo. It's a wonderful space for a whole range of international work. That's
why I love it here.'

We went back inside the Musée and she directed me
forward.

'This is the school groups and workshops reception.
You'll be speaking mainly to French students, mostly from
around Paris. You can do it in English, of course, but you
must talk slowly.'

'I thought perhaps there would be a large international audience?' I said, hoping I didn't sound disappointed.

'Actually, about eighty per cent of our visitors are French, and mainly from Paris. Which is opposite to the Louvre, where I understand only forty per cent are French.'

'That's interesting.' I was surprised.

'Well, we have items in our collection that are international, that the local French population haven't seen. And we are relatively new, compared to the Louvre, which was built around 1793.' I nodded with understanding.

'I get it. The Louvre is what the rest of the world wants to see, and the rest of the world is what the French want to see. Sounds like a good balance really.'

'Exactly.'

Canelle took me to meet the head of human resources to get my paperwork sorted, and as we walked I tried to remember every turn, lift and stairwell and the names of various staff we met along the way. There were five floors and three office buildings in the Musée. It made the NAG look like a cubby house. I was trying to recall which lift went to what floor as we met the curators of each section. All the while, I waited patiently to see the artwork-adorned ceilings.

In yet another lift Canelle introduced me to the marketing manager, Adrien: short, balding, lean, round face, bushy eyebrows, piercing grey eyes and cigarette-stained teeth.

'*Bonjour,* Elizabeth, we are very pleased to have you here,' he said, looking me up and down, 'and so young to be working on such an important project.'

I wasn't sure if he was being sarcastic and questioning my credentials or actually flirting with me.

'I am well-qualified to do the job, Adrien, and I am very excited about being here. I'm looking forward to the opening of Authentication.'

He put his hand on my shoulder. 'Of course, we are looking forward to the exhibition as well.' I looked at his hand on my shoulder and he removed it. 'And we need to talk about the marketing and publicity. I have some journalists lined up to speak to you. We have a release ready to go out.'

'Excellent! May I see it first, please?'

Adrien used the same hand from my shoulder to almost shoo me away with a flick of his wrist.

'What for? It is a media release, we do them all the time.'

With a hint of confusion and some frustration in my voice I said, 'It's just that back home we always have the relevant curator read the copy before it is released, it's a process we follow. We generally have a quote by the curator as well. Would you like me to write something? I mean, I would have done it earlier, but it's only my first day.' I was feeling like a few decisions I should have been part of had already been made. I was a bit cranky and annoyed but trying not to sound it.

'Elizabeth, it is my job to know the language to use with French media.' Adrien was clearly pissed off.

'I'm sure Elizabeth understands your role, Adrien.' Canelle came to my aid.

'Of course,' I said. 'Adrien, I don't question your knowledge of the media at all, but I don't think you could possibly know what I would say. If you could please send me the draft I will insert my own quote.'

The lift door opened just in time to prevent a major argument and he exited. I felt hot with embarrassment and anger that already I had a white man wanting to write my words. I understood that organisations everywhere worked differently, but this was just plain wrong. I was worried what Canelle might think. I really didn't want to get anyone off-side in my first hour on the job.

'Do not take it personally, he is like that with everyone,' she said, before I had a chance to ask. 'He is very good with the media, but sometimes thinks he is the one that runs this place. He is only on contract here while our head of marketing is on leave. I think he likes flexing his male muscle while his very strong female boss is away. I will make sure you get the draft release.'

My blood stopped simmering towards a boil when we reached Michael Riley's *cloud* series along the ramp wall on the ground floor. It was what I had waited and wanted to see more than anything since reading about it back at the NAG. Such an incredible legacy left by the Wiradjuri/ Gamilaroi photographer. It took my breath away to see his iconic images – particularly the boomerang and the feather – so large and so dominant in this amazing institution. It was a beautiful vision and I knew that no matter whether viewers got the intended messages of the artist or interpreted it their own way, everyone would walk away having felt an emotional reaction to the work. At that moment, I had never been prouder of being a Blackfella working in the arts.

The tour continued into the Claude Lévi-Strauss Theater, the cinema and the range of venues for cultural education activities. We finished at the café and I was already overwhelmed with what I had seen and heard.

'I must go to another meeting. You should have a coffee now and then read this.' Canelle handed me a press kit titled *Arts and Civilisation of Africa, Asia, Oceania and the Americas*. 'Spend the rest of the day going through the collections slowly, getting to know the layout. There is much to see.'

Canelle walked off and I sat at an outside table with a perfect view of the Eiffel Tower. I couldn't believe this would be my life for the next five months. I vowed to sit there every day for coffee and then looked at the prices on the menu. It was equivalent to $9 for a cappuccino, $8 for a Diet Coke, and the same price for a rosé! I may as well have a wine for that. I decided that breakfast once a week at Café Jacques would be my indulgence, my working gift to myself.

I ordered a café crème and the corbeille de viennoise-ries – an assortment of three mini-pastries. I felt particularly French and very, very lucky – much like a Very Important Indigenous Person, or VIIP, as Emma would say. I took my phone out of my bag and snapped my coffee, the cakes and the tower to send to Lauren. I knew she would be green with envy, especially when I told her about the coffee and chocolate special they had there. I'd try that next time.

As Canelle had recommended, I spent the rest of the day weaving in and out of the exhibitions, acquainting myself with the space and the collections. I knew it would take me weeks, probably months to look at the displays fully. But I took the time needed to walk through the Black Indians of New Orleans exhibit. It was the most vibrant space I'd seen in many years, with works by Darryl Montana, Victor Harris, and Michael Ray Charles. Many of the pieces were incredibly powerful – particularly the work on the KKK – and expressed the impact of entrenched racism, from childhood and across every part of society.

I liked the peacefulness of the MQB. The NAG had more energy and was more brightly lit throughout, but the Musée was enjoyable in a different way. It was almost sombre. It was dimly lit, which I thought was a slight contradiction given the whole point was to 'showcase' and 'see' things. But the lighting, layout and design worked for the various collections.

Visitors to the Musée took in all the exhibitions by following one long, winding ramp as opposed to stairs. The space was contemporary, although it held materials, artefacts, objects and artwork that belonged to lands and times far more traditional and ancient.

I was immediately struck by many of the unique design features of the museum. It had small video screens inlaid in the leather-covered walls, complementing the engravings and images. Exhibition text was also in braille. There were tiny alcoves with benches to sit on, so I did. I imagined I was the typical audience. I listened to the audio, and then drifted back home, wondering how everyone was, before mentally slapping myself for wasting time daydreaming – I could save that for when I was back in Canberra. But the darkness of the space made me want to lie down, close my eyes and nap. I couldn't believe I was still jet-lagged.

I went to the multimedia mezzanine, where there were more video screens and benches. I immediately started thinking of ways we could incorporate something similar into the NAG. In the mezzanine there was an emphasis on anthropology in the traditional sense and I felt slightly unnerved, especially when I read on one of the plaques that 'Anthropology builds the other – gives a different perspective'. Another quote said that anthropology was 'seeing others with others' eyes'.

I'd always been a firm believer of supporting Aboriginal people so we could have greater opportunities to put forth our own perspectives on ourselves, as we frequently had to dispel myths and inaccuracies concerning who we are. Myths are often created by looking at us through the observers' gaze. But it was day one. I wouldn't get on my soapbox straightaway, but with my exchange with Adrien in my thoughts I knew I would be on it sooner or later.

I made my way to the Australian exhibit and read the introduction: 'The age-old cultural practices existing in this vast territory were handed down by semi-nomadic Aboriginal peoples.' The words carried me back home to country.

I thought of Moree and my Gamilaroi ancestors, and imagined what life might have been like for them before colonisation, before life allowed us to visit other lands like France to then read about ourselves and our heritage. In some ways, it felt odd to be sitting a hemisphere away, reading about my people back home. I remembered when I was only a few years old, before Dad died and we'd sit on the porch with my grandad, who'd tell us stories about the first time his grandfather saw a whitefella and thought the man was a ghost. I remember laughing but being a bit scared at the time.

I moved into the Bark Room, which exhibited about fifty examples of bark paintings collected in Arnhem Land in the 1960s by Karel Kupka. The area also had shields and spear-throwers as well as funeral poles from Bathurst Island and contemporary acrylic paintings.

I was anxious to see the space where my own exhibition would hang, so I went to the West Mezzanine, the temporary exhibition space. I gently moved through the many Japanese tourists interested in the kimono exhibition curated by Anna Jackson and Josephine Rout, curators of the Asia Department at the Victoria and Albert Museum in London. I had no idea there were so many variations of the traditional dress and that it was being transformed into a completely modern garment by some designers.

I looked around the space and started imagining where my own pieces would be hung: where the commissioned dhouri (the traditional ceremonial headdress of the western Torres Strait) would fit, where Emily McDaniel's soundscape would best work, and where the mannequin with Michael McDaniel's possum-skin cloak would have the greatest impact.

'This exhibition has been very popular.' Adrien was by my side. 'With all the discussion about banning the hijab, I think the interest in cultural costumes and fashion has grown. I feel like we've got extra marketing at no extra cost. Maybe we should think about banning other things – like the Americans – to get more interest in our collections.' Adrien laughed but I wasn't convinced he was joking.

'Yes, but that's not really the kind of marketing that's good for the country, is it?' I phrased it as a question simply because I didn't want to have a second disagreement on my first day at work.

'Professionally, the publicity and marketing for us is a good thing. We want people to come to our museum. But personally, I agree with Marine Le Pen. She should have won the election.' He leant over and whispered in my ear. 'The Muslims are going to take over Europe.'

I was gobsmacked but contained my physical reaction. 'Do you really think it's possible for five per cent of the population to take over the whole of Europe? It doesn't seem probable to me.' I was thinking Pauline Hanson, xenophobia and racism. This man was ticking all the wrong boxes *and* pressing all my bad buttons at the same time.

'So you think the hijab is okay? A woman of such fine fashion as you?' Adrien said, running his sleazy old eyes over my body from my painted toenails to the trimmed tips of my hair.

I looked at what I was wearing quickly then answered. 'I share the same views as Obama: you can't tell people what to wear, especially if it's going to stigmatise Islam.'

'Why would you support Obama, you're not even American? And you want religious freedom when your country is not even free from British rule? Australia is still a Commonwealth country, no?'

That stung me but I didn't bite.

'Well,' he went on, 'my feelings are more aligned with our ex-president, Sarkozy, who once said "the Republic must live with an open face".'

The universe jumped in and saved me as Adrien's phone rang and I was unbelievably grateful.

'Pardon,' he said. 'I must take this call, but as requested I will email you the press release tomorrow.' He walked off.

I was exhausted by the mental strain of understanding the level of intolerance in the 'Republic' and felt challenged by trying to remain composed in my new workplace when talking about an issue that had incensed me back home. I still lived in an intolerant, fear-driven society, but at least the discussions on the burqa and the hijab didn't last more than a few days in the media, and hopefully we would never see it legislated against in our parliament.

It was 4 pm and I needed some air. More importantly, I needed some light. I headed to the gift shop and admired the work of Bernard Naube, sculptures made out of recycled goods such as Coke cans. I picked up a book called *Boomerang Collection* by Serge d'Ignazio, which was positioned next to mass-produced Kenyan beads.

There were a few 'Aboriginal-inspired' items such as wallaby-decorated boomerangs, called 'bamboorangs'. I was at first sceptical, but when I googled the company I saw that they were affiliated with the Keringke Aboriginal Arts Centre eighty kilometres from Alice Springs within the Aboriginal community of Ltyentye Apurte, also know as Santa Teresa.

I spent the rest of the day filling out paperwork and going through the works that were waiting to be hung in the temporary space. I got the Métro home at 6 pm and was exhausted and brain-fried, but I found the glamorous people along the way home lifted my spirits. I felt crappy having not touched up my makeup all day, too busy with details and learning.

I sat on the couch with a baguette and cheese and a glass of wine – my now regular dinner – and messaged the girls.

Dear tiddas,

Day one on the job is OVER! Wow, what a space! What a collection! What a view from Café Jacques – see attached photo of my regular morning break, and sorry I'm really not trying to brag it's just too easy. 😛 No kidding, slightly better than the view of Parliament House from the café at the NAG.

Anyway, Canelle is great, very friendly, but insists on calling me Elizabeth – it sounds more elegant, apparently. And yet, I didn't feel very elegant coming home all sweaty on the metro this evening, squashed in with all the beautiful people. Please msg me a quick beauty fix for end of day public transport schmoozing! I'm working with a marketing manager (acting, phew) who doesn't really want to show me drafts of the media release. Oh, and he wants to ban the hijab. How's that for Frenchmen? Clearly I don't need one, because biting my tongue isn't one of my strong points, as you girls would know.

I'm sorry this message isn't longer. The truth is it's hard to express what I felt in that space today – but basically all the feels. You'll just have to come visit and experience it yourselves! 🩶

Miss you,

Libs aka Elizabeth xxx

Lauren replied:

Firstly, I'm sending you the pages we sent the MQB for the catalogue. We pulled it all together here. The final copy should be the same. Ask for their first pages and check for consistency. It is *your* exhibition. And yes, we always sign-off the press releases. You have a quote in there, right?

Secondly, you might have to get lots of 'blowtox' and wear massive amounts of fat red lippy to compete.

Miss you too, Loz aka Lauren

Bec joined in:

If you're getting the blowtox then best you get some super-high four-inch heels, but try not to trip while getting on the train, that wouldn't be very elegant, Elizabeth.

Chapter 13

Champers on
the Champs-Élysées

The week flew by quickly. I was flat out at work and it wasn't without drama. Adrien had emailed me a press release with 'aboriginal' in lower-case throughout. It was an exercise in grammar and diplomacy to finally have him accept the need to capitalise it to 'Aboriginal'.

I printed out the style guide from the NAG for him and highlighted the bits relevant to our current disagreement so he would understand the need to use initial capitals for Aboriginal as an adjective and noun in relation to the First Peoples of Australia but, where possible, to use First Nations instead. And that he should only use the word 'aborigine' as a generic term referring generally to indigenous people from anywhere in the world. I still hated the Latin term for who we are, and I always heard that anthropological tone no matter who said or wrote it.

Adrien also wanted to amend my quote on the exhibition that I had finally managed to convince him to include. I wasn't sure if he genuinely didn't like my style of writing and voice or just felt the need to know more than his female colleague twenty years younger than him. The main problem, though, was that in the collection of images he sent to the media, he included a photograph of a local French model wearing Michael McDaniel's possum-skin cloak as a fashion statement. Worn over a barely-there black silk slip with no bra, it totally demeaned the cultural value of the fur.

'It's a cultural artefact and not for *fashion* purposes,' I stressed down the phone. 'Unlike Andrea Fisher's work, which is body adornment or wearable art. Please, please don't allow anyone else to put it on. The artist will be here, as you know, and he will expect it to be handled with respect by staff.'

'Of course, Elizabeth, please don't question my professionalism.' Adrien sounded annoyed. 'In case you didn't know, women here *like* fur coats – I thought it was a good marketing hook.'

'These are not fashion statements, Adrien.' I gritted my teeth. 'They represent culture and history. And in case *you* didn't know, fur coats aren't seen as a fashion statement in Australia, more an animal rights issue.' I really was on the wrong foot with this man or, more so, he was on mine.

Despite all the strained communications via phone and email, Adrien did line up some useful media. A crew from the French cultural television channel ARTE interviewed me under Yunupingu's installation and I truly felt her galaxy and universe were looking over me with a blessing of support. Print and TV media from across Paris and French Polynesia interviewed me in the amphitheatre outside the building, and interest in the exhibition was gaining momentum.

Life at the Musée immediately replicated my fulfilling and frantic life back home. My fashionable feet hardly touched the ground as I raced around the building, getting lost more often than not, and making new acquaintances.

Canelle asked me to do a briefing for the other curators on the artwork in the exhibition for their own knowledge base, and then I signed off on the printing for the catalogues, which were already at proof stage. I was glad we'd done a lot of work by email before I arrived.

The last step before the opening was supervising the hanging of the works. When I was still in Canberra, Lauren and Canelle discussed how it looked at the NAG, but at the end of the day the Musée mob would place the artwork and set up the installations with their own vision and flair.

There was a buzz around the Musée about 'my exhibition', as I'd taken to calling it in my head, and I was anxious about everyone's expectations – including those of my colleagues back home. By the end of the week I was exhausted and ready for the weekend – not to sleep, but to get amongst it again as a 'recently arrived local'.

As I stood in the shower one evening after work, my skinny Koori ankles ached from walking so much and my feet were scarred with blisters from not wearing the correct shoes in this city of cobblestone streets. There was a choice to be made. Be comfortable or be fashionable. I had clearly made the wrong choice trying desperately to fit in with the Paris glamour. I couldn't keep the fabulous shoe thing up any longer. It was time to throw away the self-imposed need to look chic 24/7, and so I decided from then on to wear my running shoes to the Métro and change at the other end.

As I headed downstairs, I bumped into Dom on his way to take his jet-black poodle, Romeo, for a walk. I hadn't seen him all week but had heard the dog bark on occasion. Each time it made me think of my own pets back home.

'Mademoiselle Libs, you are hardly ever home. Catherine wants to know: are you eating enough?'

I felt strangely loved by that one question of concern from Dom, but laughed as well because I'd not stopped eating since I'd arrived.

'Dom, how kind, please tell Catherine that I am eating far more than I ever would at home. The food here is too good. I should really run up and down these stairs twenty times a day!'

'No running on these stairs, mademoiselle, please, I would hate for you to fall. You can take Romeo for a walk any time you like if you want to exercise.'

I liked that Dom was such a caring old man, and I was glad that of all the places I could've ended up in Paris,

I was in *his* apartment block. The sense of community in his building and the 4th was the very reason I moved there.

'I have to go, Dom, I promise I'll drop in for coffee soon, but this morning I am going to see Monica at Salon Marie Antoinette.' He smiled as I kissed him on the cheek instinctively and remembered I used to kiss Dad on the cheek all the time as a child. Before school, before bed, before he died.

'The French do two cheeks,' Dom reminded me, so I corrected myself, kissed his other cheek, patted Romeo on the head and felt a pang of homesickness, missing Bonnie and Clyde.

I walked to Dom's recommended café and when I was greeted with a warm smile by a woman in a black dress, I knew she was Monica. When I told her I was from Australia *and* Dom had sent me, she introduced me to the staff and the other patrons there. I had planned on a takeaway coffee, but the chandeliers and velvet sofas enticed me to stay.

'An americano?' I asked. 'And a macaron fraise, please.' Their macarons looked yummy, but I was only going to have one strawberry one for today. I had five months to get through the entire selection of treats.

Monica fussed around and delivered my coffee and treat with enthusiasm.

'*Ma cherie*,' she said, 'from me,' she added, pointing to what was a large heart-shaped strawberry macaron with cream and fresh strawberry on the top. This was not one of the ones from the window, this was something special.

I was overwhelmed with the welcome, and the generosity. I think I may have even blushed.

I took a sip of my coffee as Monica served another customer, and I knew then that this was going to be mine *and* Dom's favourite hangout.

The Métro was packed at peak hour but I loved it. The efficiency of travelling so fast and far and most of the time underground made me wish we had something similar in Canberra. Maybe then I'd visit Tuggeranong more often.

People didn't generally talk on the train or even look at each other. And yet the seats were so close I was forced to touch knees with strangers. I liked it, in an odd kind of way. There was a whole new sense of intimacy in my life with using public transport and standing or sitting so close to people, as well as asking people for directions so they then knew where you were going. These are things I never did back home: random conversations, and even accidental brushing up against strangers every day.

I watched a young couple in business suits smiling and holding hands, pushing hair out of the other's eyes and removing lint from the other's shoulders. Who would've thought that romance was to be had on the train?

As the elbow of the man next to me kissed mine, I could see how small accidental moments of touching, even on public transport, could be romantic and even sexually arousing. I could feel how Paris was already impacting my own thoughts about intimacy and the opposite sex.

I was slowly becoming influenced by the romance of the city and thought that perhaps the Libby Cutmore that never existed in Canberra might emerge in Paris. I was even beginning to feel a little desirable as strangers smiled at me. I knew the difference between sexy and sleazy: the little winks and nods of the head were sexy, the Red Béret was sleazy.

I found myself smiling at my musings and saw my reflection in the window as we went through another tunnel. I felt good. I looked fresh and happy and even somewhat attractive. I certainly never considered myself 'pretty' at home. Did anyone think of themselves that way? I thought I was fit and firm, even with my big bust and wide hips, but never did I think I was pretty, or even very girly for that matter. I never did the frills and flimsy frocks: conservative, clean, simple lines – that was me.

And here I was in Paris, on the train to work, looking more feminine than ever before. I turned to catch a smile from a man in a grey suit and knew it was a reflection of my own. 'We get back what we give out,' Mum had always told me.

My thought pattern was broken a woman with a pink electric ukulele singing an interesting rendition of a song I recognised from the Disney movie *Mulan*. She was popular and passengers were happily handing over notes as she walked by, stopping at the end of the carriage and lunging into a song by Radiohead. I frantically googled and found that there were professional buskers with permits to perform on the Métro. She must've been one of them. I found myself grinning with the musical start to the morning – I wanted to sing along and I really had to restrain myself. Other commuters just continued to read their papers or their novels or sat with their AirPods in. It was the coolest possible way to go to work, being serenaded by a French busker before 9am. It was so European and so un-Canberran.

There was a homeless man asleep on the footpath across the road when I arrived at work. I asked a bloke in a café nearby if we should call someone.

He frowned as if I was being ridiculous. 'No! He is always there. He drinks more coffee than I do. Have you not noticed that this is a city of homeless people?'

I shook my head, embarrassed and shocked at how easy it seemed for him to say it. I bought a coffee and took it over to the man, leaving it next to his swag. I wondered what his story was, and I felt a pang of sadness and sorrow, and even some guilt for the extraordinary life that I had. It reminded me of the homeless people I sometimes saw in Canberra, whose numbers were increasing with the cost of living crisis, and I wondered how in such wealthy countries like my own, people still went without basic living standards.

I was still disturbed by the coffee shop conversation when I got to the office.

'I saw a homeless man across the road this morning,' I said to Canelle at the coffee machine.

Canelle shook her head and tut-tutted in disgust and disappointment. 'Yes, he is there often, most of the staff know him. It's not the same in Australia?'

'Of course, but it's less obvious in Canberra. I imagine all the politicians don't want to see homeless people on their way to work,' I said sarcastically, reminding myself I needed to get back into working for the night patrol when I returned. Sometimes I forgot what was going on outside the NAG and Braddon.

'He's a gypsy,' Canelle said, walking away from the coffee machine, 'the government deported many of them ten years ago. You have heard of this?'

I nodded. I had read about the gypsies from Romania and Bulgaria that France had deported under the Roma crackdown.

'The government gave people a one-off payment of three hundred euros and a so-called "voluntary" return flight home.' Canelle sounded sympathetic. 'They deported over one thousand Roma and dozens of "non-authorised" Roma camps were broken up.'

I knew the ruling party at the time had been very conservative but it was still hard to fathom how and why the French government would execute such a policy. And indeed, why hadn't it been more vigorously condemned by other European nations and countries internationally? But then again, there was our own unchecked treatment of refugees back home.

'It sounds a little like Australians with asylum seekers. We have a huge landscape, we're a rich country, we have resources and space, but not the spirit, it seems.'

'Elizabeth, I cannot tell you how embarrassed I am that men and women were hunted down in this country just because they are of a certain ethnicity and not because they had committed crimes. That man you saw this morning – his name is Petru – he used to live in a camp, but I think he feels it's safer to be alone than in a group, and so survival for him means being without friends also. Some of us, we invite him out for lunch and bring him food, at least he has that.'

Adrien walked past at that moment. 'You're talking about Petru?' he asked Canelle, who nodded yes.

'He probably eats better than I do, and drinks more coffee. He just takes from other people who work hard. Send them all back, I say.'

'My boss Emma has always said that some of the best artwork comes from the oppressed and the politically voiceless,' I said angrily, staring directly at Adrien, who just sneered in response.

I couldn't let him get away with that. 'The arts are our political platform in Australia. Our plays, novels, poetry and paintings give voice to the truth of our history, give voice to the oppressed. What would the artistic voices say about the Roma crackdown?'

Adrien shrugged his shoulders and walked off. Canelle had some words of support.

'It is the same here, Elizabeth, soon I will take you to *les banlieues* – the housing estates on the outskirts of the city – where you will see the work of the oppressed. But first, we must take you shopping for a new *parisienne* look.'

'I'm under the Arc de Triomphe,' I squealed down the phone with excitement on Saturday morning. 'And I'm wearing Chanel No. 5. Me! All French-fancy, and I feel at home, really. I want to live here. I mean I *do* live here.' I could hear the joy in my voice.

'Homesick, I see,' Lauren laughed down the line.

'Of course! But only when I have time. Say hello to Wyatt and the girls, and Bonnie and Clyde. I'm off to the Champs-Elysées now. *Au revoir.*'

I hit 'end' on my iPhone and looked at the arc – a monument that honoured those who fought for France, particularly in the Napoleonic Wars. I considered the size and design of the structure, in awe of its presence, and wondered what our equivalent would be back home. The Australian War Memorial perhaps?

Canelle met me at 11 am.

'Elizabeth, it is good to see you,' she said, kissing both cheeks. 'I do not come here so much, it is for the tourists, but you are a tourist so I will walk with you. But we will go to other places to shop for your wardrobe.' She looked me up and down smiling and I felt immediately self-conscious. 'It is okay, I know Canberra is not Paris, but you are here now.'

And so I was. I wished Lauren was here too. She and Canelle would've got on perfectly in terms of fashion and certainly in terms of re-fashioning me.

As we walked along the Champs-Elysées, I saw huge posters of *Vogue* magazine covers in glass boxes lining the street. All the major designers had stores along the stretch: Valentino, Gucci, Christian Dior, Chanel, YSL, Lacoste,

Louis Vuitton, and there was the signature egg-shell blue, Tiffany & Co.

Canelle resisted but I forced her to stop at Café George V on the Champs-Elysées, a canopied café with an interesting mix of people. Four German men sat next to us, and threw the odd lengthy look our way.

The menu had a special 'drink of the day', champagne and crushed strawberries, which I didn't think was that special but I ordered one anyway because it was Saturday in Paris and I needed to celebrate that.

Canelle ordered a mineral water and I hoped that she wasn't going to be a teetotaller; I needed a buddy to do the bubbly with in Paris. It was the *real* champagne here, not the sparkling wine we called bubbly back home. So I *had* to drink it in Paris.

Canelle made a phone call while I watched tourists file past. I looked to my right and saw Frenchmen in designer suits standing in a shop doorway smoking cigarettes as they perved on stylish European women strolling by. While I watched the street traffic, the café filled up with American tourists, families and couples at tiny, tiny tables. Tiny tables, tiny cars, tiny hotel rooms and tiny-waisted women. And yet, the city was so bloody enormous!

'The tables in Paris are all so small,' I stated to Canelle as she put her phone back in her bag.

'Just enough room for a coffee and resting your hands,' she said, placing hers elegantly on the table. I could learn a lot from Canelle about local art, culture, fashion and, apparently, table manners.

We walked the back lanes for thirty minutes. I loved strolling the old streets, which felt safe and somehow authentically French, with trees lining them, couples holding hands, tiny cars and horns beeping.

It was hard to ignore how romance played itself out in Paris, and it served to make my own city of Canberra appear romantically sterile. Lovers everywhere cuddled and gazed at each other in the street. I hardly ever saw that in Canberra, except with the younger, drunk crowd in Civic on Friday nights.

I watched with interest and an unusual and unwanted pang of envy as I saw a couple kissing passionately as if enjoying their first and last kisses rolled into one. It was bizarre experiencing other people's romance. Then I heard Caro in my ear whispering, *It's someone else's wife he's kissing!* I suddenly felt a little less interested and envious.

When we arrived at the Printemps Haussmann, the first thing I noticed was how the sheer size of the department store made ours back home pale into insignificance. It was like a sexy, more elegant, high-class Macy's, which I'd visited in Manhattan with Lauren.

When Canelle and I began to shop, I decided that if I never fell in love with another man it didn't matter, because I had fallen in love with Paris. More specifically, I'd become besotted with buildings like the Galeries Lafayette, which dated back to the nineteenth century and made the Canberra Hyperdome look like a school fête.

I wished I were rich so I didn't have to look at the price tags of anything and could just buy something stunning.

'Just buy one quality "item piece" for your wardrobe,' Lauren advised when I was packing to leave.

'I need a new scarf,' Canelle said, directing me to the accessories.

I wanted to say I was a scarf wearer also, but didn't want her to think I was mimicking her like some Single Black Female stalker or something.

As Canelle looked at scarves, I was drawn to the designer handbags showcased on much of the ground floor. I held on tightly to my one and only decent tote, which Caro had given me as a farewell gift.

'Accessorise,' had been the general advice from all the girls for my new look in Paris and I decided I needed a new bag: a bag to congratulate myself for doing the pitch, selling the idea and landing in the fashion capital of the world.

I was overwhelmed by the choices and the price tags and guessed that French wages must be very high if people could shop here. I was drawn to a red Lancel bucket-bag, totally impractical but ever so classy, and I knew it would go with all my black, grey and white outfits. This would become my 'item piece' for the time being.

'What do you think?' I asked Canelle, who was by my side as I checked myself out in the mirror.

'You must have it!'

I started to think that everything about Canelle was a 'must have' or 'must do' and I liked that about her. Definite about things immediately, no mucking around, no wasting time. I already felt as if we could easily be good friends and colleagues while I was in Paris, and I was grateful on so many levels, given I knew no-one else there.

On Sunday, I walked to the station feeling grateful for my new life and for how incredibly friendly and hospitable Canelle had been, giving me tips on where to go and how to get there. She told me to head out that morning to check out some famous markets.

I took the Métro to Porte de Clignancourt and, as per Canelle's advice, I followed the crowds to where it was impossible not to shop. I bought a gorgeous pink and cream wool pashmina and an orange scarf. I could see my accessory collection growing quickly and was proud of my new-found ability to be fashionable, even by Paris stand-ards. Lauren would be very impressed. And I was already thinking about what shoes would go with the pieces.

I walked aisle after aisle and saw rows and rows of imported jeans, boots, bags, and cheap costume jewel-lery – for five euros, I could buy some pretty glam pendants. There were hoodies, running shoes, sunglasses and dress shoes from China, jewellery from Africa, clothes from India. The place reminded me of Paddy's Markets in Sydney, and the items were nowhere near the quality of locally produced jewellery at the Kingston Bus Depot Markets back home.

I grabbed a coffee in a Turkish café across the road and watched what looked like deals being done: money exchanging hands between men, then money offered to what looked like wives and daughters.

That afternoon the pièce de résistance was sitting under the Eiffel Tower, the symbol of Paris. It was overwhelming to be in its presence. I assumed this must have been how visitors to Australia felt about the Sydney Harbour Bridge or the Opera House. I sat below it reading my guide, which told me it was the tallest building in the city, built in 1889 for the Paris International Exhibition.

I took the lift to the top of the iconic structure so I could get a view across Paris and as I did so I thought about a terrible argument I'd had with Lauren when I was in New York. I'd wanted to go up the Empire State Building and she hadn't.

I wasn't aware at the time that my dear friend was prone to anxiety attacks triggered by confined spaces like lifts. The memories made me homesick for the girls and as the lift ascended I felt guilty again. I took a photo when I got to the top to send to Loz.

As I stood there amongst hundreds of tourists, the sky was clear and I wondered if I was actually seeing as far as sixty-seven kilometres into the distance, as my guidebook had promised. Unlike Lauren, I wasn't afraid of heights and so had no problems peering down below, wondering if there had been any suicides from the tower.

The commentary on the tour bus I had taken when I first arrived had told me that an Austrian tailor who was experimenting with a new form of parachute had jumped from the Eiffel Tower back in 1912, but his experiment didn't work and he died instantly. I shook my head, remembering the story.

Back on the ground, I looked at all the buskers and sellers of everything: mini-tower keyrings, bottles of water, postcards, Slinkys, every piece of touristy crap you could imagine.

Then I spotted a lone girl sitting on a piece of material on the ground selling handbags. She looked familiar and as she started talking I realised it was the girl I'd bought my blue-stone ring from back in the 20th.

'You sold me this ring,' I said, excited about reconnecting somehow.

'Oh yes, that's right.' She looked surprised that I actually remembered her.

'Don't you work there anymore?'

'Yes,' she said cautiously.

'And you work here too?' I asked, picking up a black canvas bag the shape of a teardrop with pink handles.

I looked at all of her handiwork: well-sewn bags, some practical, some more stylish than others.

'These are fantastic, where did you get the materials from?'

'Why are you asking all these questions?' She sounded slightly annoyed and scared.

'Oh, I didn't mean to pry, I just like the work and making small talk,' I said, hating myself for obviously upsetting her. Even *I* knew that street vendors like her were usually operating illegally, desperate for money.

Her tone softened. 'I'm sorry, I thought maybe you were the government.'

'Me? No, I'm a tourist, well, kind of. I'm working here for five months.'

'I'm working too, but I only have a few days' work and it is not enough money to feed my family,' she said as a whisper. 'And I am scared to be selling here as I do not have a permit.'

'My name is Libby,' I extended my hand, thinking of Petru at the same time, wondering stupidly if she knew him. Or maybe it wasn't that stupid. Maybe it was a really close-knit community, like Blackfellas back home where everyone knew everyone. Maybe they had a Roma grape-vine like the Koori grapevine.

'I am Sorina,' she said, shaking my hand while looking over my shoulder. 'I have to go now,' she added with urgency, grabbing her bags.

'What's the rush? I'd like to look at what you're selling, if I may.'

'I have to go,' she repeated desperately, putting her wares into a huge red cotton sack. 'I am what they call one of the visible minority. But I want to stay here, and I work hard, I speak French and English well because I practise every day. I just need to sell some more bags. I make these myself.'

She started to walk off and I walked alongside her. The black teardrop bag was poking out of her sack and I grabbed it.

'I'll take this one, Sorina. It will go with all my black dresses.'

'Thank you. Are you sure you don't want two?'

Sorina was a great seamstress, good with languages and a damn good businesswoman too. I handed her twenty euros as we walked and she looked around nervously at the police in uniforms who watched us both.

'I'm going this way,' she said, disappearing into the Métro before I had a chance to say anything else.

I continued along the Seine, thinking about what I'd just experienced with Sorina after a morning feeling blessed about being in such an amazing city full of culture and sites I'd only ever read about or seen on telly.

I felt emotionally mangled as I wrote a quick message to the girls before crashing that night:

Tiddas, I went up the Eiffel Tower today, finally. It was the clearest blue day and I didn't care if I looked like a tourist. I think it was better than the Empire State Building, Lauren; although there was no Wyatt, there was plenty of room to move!

Hey, I eavesdropped on someone else's tour guide and heard the best story ever about when Hitler visited Paris in 1940. Urban myth says that the lift to the tower wasn't working so he had to walk 1792 steps to the top. Apparently the repairman determined what the fault was and fixed it as soon as Hitler reached the top.

The saying here is that Hitler conquered France but he didn't conquer the Eiffel Tower. Don't you love it? I do.

I've also met an amazing designer, a woman from Romania making the most gorgeous handbags just to survive. They are stunning quality and interesting designs made from old clothes, curtains, etc. When I see her again I'll buy you one each. She's one of the Roma gypsies they were tossing out of France ten years ago, but she's multilingual and hard-working, she deserves a better life than being on the run like she was today. She is seriously scared of the police. It's really sad. And yet, understandable, we know all too well how mob at home fear the police because of the track record.

Anyhoo, I'm exhausted, will write more later. Until then, loads of love to you, don't miss me too much!

Lauren replied:

Gotta love that handyman, eh? Some might think they're not political, but what a political act. And I bet he looked good in his overalls too! I'm off to buy Wyatt a pair tomorrow. Or maybe just a tool belt! 😉

When I went to bed I couldn't stop thinking about Sorina being one of the 'visible minority'. I wanted to help her sell her bags and maybe have some security here, but how?

Chapter 14

Feeling sexy in Paris

The next day, Monday, I realised that I'd never really considered myself attractive until coming to Paris. And when you're not having sex it's hard to feel sexy, or so I thought. But I sauntered down quai Branly on my way to work, rather than walking with purpose like I usually did. I noticed my hips swinging ever so slightly, which they didn't do before. The man sweeping the street noticed as well, as he winked and said, '*Bonjour, mademoiselle.*'

'*Bonjour,*' I replied politely.

The sun was already hot by 10 am but there was a slight breeze which took the sting out of it, unlike back in Canberra. I wondered how much of the ozone layer still existed over Paris. I noticed women in shorts riding bikes and I thought of Lauren immediately, wondering how she would comment on the fashions each day. Some locals were more casual than I'd imagined they would be, but still they looked stylish. I'd been warned that it would get very humid in July and August and I knew it would be difficult to remain elegant in the humidity.

A small European car with its roof down stopped at the traffic lights next to me. There was a middle-aged man and a gorgeous young woman with him. They looked healthy, brown and happy. Everyone in Paris did. I wasn't sure if they had sun cancer campaigns here like we did back home. I still put 30+ on my face every day from fear of getting melanoma, knowing the Canberra sun could be harsh. I didn't want anything other than laugh lines on my face. Bazza always made fun of me back in Moree when I talked about sun cancer.

'Have you ever heard of a Blackfella with melanoma?' he used to say.

'No, but there's no ozone and cancer doesn't discrim-inate by race like people do.' Privately, I almost wished a Koori did get it, not that I wanted them to die, just to make my point that no-one was safe.

The best part of my second working week was when Canelle took me and some of her friends from her building to an after-work picnic at Champ de Mars, the park at the base of the Eiffel Tower.

In the French summer it's twilight till after ten and people walk in the street and enter restaurants for dinner then. I was blown away at the lifestyle. Canberra is asleep at that time of night in summer, even earlier in winter. The Parisians and those who visit this city really did know how to milk the most out of each day.

'It's what the French do in summer: late-night picnics as people wait for the tower to light up,' Canelle said, as we ate and waited for the first light to appear on the tower at 10.30 pm.

Young people kicked balls, families were laughing, kids were playing with frisbees. It was extraordinary, especially for me, who had nothing similar to compare it with back in Moree or even Canberra.

Before I left, I went and spoke to Sorina at her stall and took Canelle with me. I ended up buying three handbags from Sorina, telling her I'd send them back to Australia. One was made from maroon velvet with a tortoiseshell handle, another was made of pink silk from an old kimono that someone had given her. The third was made from a pair of old jeans and reminiscent of the styles from the seventies. Sorina's own addition to it was a white dove with a red rose in its beak. It was her logo: peace and romance, she said.

'The poor need both also.'

At work on Wednesday I was busy preparing for the opening that night and the space was now mine. The carpenters had built new walls and plinths and painters had turned everything stark white. I'd supervised most of it and checked on all the artwork. I was glad Emma and Lauren had decided just before I left to include a video installation of the Ikuntji Artists collection at Australian

Fashion Week, and a portrait of Australia's first Aboriginal model, Elaine George, wearing Kalinpinpa fabric in silk by Mavis Marks. The French would love the fashion element of our exhibition.

'How are you coping, Elizabeth?' Canelle asked as we both stood in the busy space.

'Actually, good. I'm pretty much just ticking the boxes now and of course waiting for one or two disasters to present themselves,' I half-joked, but knew it was almost a given that something would go wrong, however minor.

I looked at my list:

- Check and email final speech notes to Adrien.
- Send final running order and guest list for opening to Adrien and Canelle and security.
- Media follow-up.
- Check catalogues in the Musée shop.
- Brief welcoming committee, photographer and front of house.
- Confirm with audio/visual staff that technology has been double-checked.

By 3 pm everything was coordinated and ready to go. I changed into a black dress, patent black slingbacks and my Tiffany scarf. I took my GHD into work and Canelle fixed my hair, making it poker straight because I loved the sleek look. You couldn't even notice the remnants of the layers that were still there. For a woman with little hair herself, Canelle was certainly good at doing other people's.

At 6 pm I was nervous when few people had arrived. But I had learned that the French were sometimes on Koori time. It wasn't glamorous to rush or panic or get flustered. When I had first arrived in Paris, I noticed how long it sometimes took for people to respond to an email. Canelle was the exception to the rule in terms of a quick turnaround. Normally replies would only arrive after they had been crafted properly, and that took time, unlike back home, where a quick slapdash email would suffice. It was one of the things I had to get used to.

Adrien had organised local arts television coverage and some print press for the opening. I was proud to be talking on behalf of the NAG and the artists being shown in the exhibition.

By 6.30 pm nearly all the guests had arrived and Canelle was introducing me to local artists and curators, academics, staff from the Australian embassy and the ambassador himself, who was opening it. There were apologies from the President of France and his wife and from the Australian first secretary, who was apparently a Blackfella. I made a mental note to be in touch with him, just to connect.

I met the cultural attaché, Judith, who was born in Melbourne to Greek parents and was, I guessed, in her mid-forties. She had clearly brought her sense of Melbourne style with her and added a dash of Paris as well. She had a blonde bob with tiny chocolate streaks in her hair and chocolate-rimmed glasses with a patent dark brown leather bag to match. *What an effort to coordinate one's accessories with one's hair*, I thought to myself.

I was pleased that the Wiradyuri artist Emily McDaniel had been flown in by her university. She brought life to the exhibition and would run multimedia arts workshops on how to create ephemeral soundscapes, channelling sonic spirituality, bending and sculpting sounds into shape. Emily wore a black lace dress with white cropped jacket and flat black ballet shoes. She had blood-red lips and a stylish chocolate-brown bob. I knew straightaway Canelle would love her dress sense as well as her work.

'And what I want to share here with you,' Emily's approach to her audience was warm and inclusive, 'is called *You just keep going.*'

A woman in a black linen pant suit was signing for the audience, something I had asked for in order to cater for those with hearing impairments.

'It's about resilience and the oral history of my Elders. If you really focus on listening and watching, I promise I can take you back to nature and to the wilderness of my country.'

'The hairs on my arms just stood up,' one woman whispered in a thick French accent to an Englishman next to her, doing a dramatic shiver.

The reactions from those engaging with Emily and her new medium were positive.

'*Je n'ai jamais rien vu de tel avant,*' a woman in her sixties wearing sleek black glasses said to her male counterpart.

'*Je n'ai jamais vu une femme comme* ça *avant!*' the man responded and his wife rolled her eyes.

I knew enough French by now to work out that she had appreciated the art and he had appreciated the artist.

A uni student put his hand in the air. 'I would like to sign up for your workshop, Miss McDaniel.'

'Great,' Emily said, 'there is a table near the ramp that has all the details.'

Viewers were intrigued. Emily's work and presence helped to complement all the other works, demonstrating the range and modes of storytelling employed by visual artists. Having her at the Musée for the opening added a whole new dimension to the exhibition and also gave it a sense of 'the real'; of the 'authentication' the exhibition was about.

My mouth was dry and my palms sweaty with nerves because I knew this was possibly the most significant exhibition I would work on in my career, especially if I never got another gig in Europe. It wasn't like these opportunities presented themselves to me often. Furthermore, I'd actually created this opportunity myself.

I was looking at what I wanted my future to be, what I'd put in long days and weekends for years to have: something that made me stand out from the rest. I wanted to be the tall poppy, just so I could shake off those bastards trying to pull me back down. I'd worked hard for everything I'd ever had, including getting to Paris, and tonight the opening vindicated me.

But as I scanned the room looking for someone to share my achievement with, I felt a pang of homesickness: for Moree, for Mum, for Bazza and the boys. And I missed my tiddas and Emma. I wished they could all be here to see how much our effort was being appreciated and valued by so many at the Musée.

I walked through the exhibition, watching the guests engage with the artwork. I could hear the whispers of academics talking in English about Tony Albert's two canvases in the series *Welcome to Australia* and how they played into notions of discovery, invasion and colonisation. Albert's point was being made and the artwork was, indeed, working.

Another major talking point was the bark painting *Incident at Mutpi, 1975* by Nyapanyapa Yunupingu, a Yolngu artist. It chillingly depicted the true story of the artist being gored by a water buffalo. It was accompanied by video footage of the event, which was shown on a massive screen beside the painting. There was a crowd around it listening intently. It was a true drawcard wherever it was exhibited and here at the Musée was no different. I got goosebumps watching the level of interest in the story. I couldn't believe the buzz in the room and the level of intellectual conversation and critiquing happening. It was far more powerful than I had anticipated and my expectations had been high.

The spotlight for much of the evening was on Michael McDaniel, who walked into the exhibition space looking respectfully regal in his possum-skin cloak. He took his time during the evening to talk to guests about the painstaking effort of his three thousand stitches used to sew the possum skins together, and the process of using cold tea to stain the skin and burn his designs into it. I could see a desire to have one in the eyes of some of the women, which cooled my excitement, as I began to fear they would use the skin as a fashion accessory. I'd have to ask Michael what he thought about it.

Before I had a chance to see the other artwork, Canelle was at my side.

'Congratulations, Elizabeth, this is a success for you, and for the Musée, I think everybody loves the work you have brought with you.'

Canelle's appreciation meant everything to me right then. I wished Emma and Lauren and all the other NAG staff could've heard her, because the moment was as much for them as for me.

'*Merci beaucoup*, Canelle. I wish all the artists could see the impact their work is having here.' We both looked around the gallery.

'I think Emily might never be allowed to leave, so many people have signed up for her workshops already.'

I looked over at her and she was glowing with pride at the attention she was receiving from an adoring crowd. This is what I loved about my job: showcasing First Nations artists and their artwork to the world. I was overwhelmed with the emotion of it all.

The rest of the night was a blur of introductions, French/English small talk, thankyous, congratulations, empty pleasantries, business-card swapping and too much air kissing. But I loved it. The Musée had put on a fine spread too: loads of bubbly and hors d'oeuvres.

'Come, I'm taking you for the best mojito in Paris, Elizabeth,' Canelle instructed me. 'And we're taking young Emily, I think she needs chaperoning in this big city.'

I appreciated Canelle's zest for life, and the time she took to include me in her social engagements.

'You really are a social butterfly, Canelle,' I said, as we walked towards the artist who was handing business cards out to eager hands.

'Well, Guadeloupe is known as the "Butterfly Island" so I am just living up to its expectations.' Canelle threw her signature sparkling white smile at me. 'I am glad you are here, that you like to shop, to drink champagne and to party. And you stand up to Adrien, and for that I am most grateful,' she whispered.

'Oh, we have plenty of Adriens back home. Trust me, he is a breeze compared to some others, but thanks.'

'And now we celebrate and Emily is coming with us,' Canelle announced as Emily appeared at my side.

'Are you sure it's okay for me to tag along?' Emily asked, retouching her blood-red lipstick as she walked enthusiastically along with us.

'*Oui*, of course, it is my pleasure that you are here also,' Canelle said adamantly. 'You are also exotic as an Australian, so I think the men will be drawn to you. I am actually tagging – as you say – along with you!'

Soon we were in one of Canelle's favourite watering holes, and as I sipped my mojito I scanned the luxurious club where everyone looked like a model or actor or wealthy banker. I was glad I had my best 'opening night' dress on. The carpet was plush, the seats leather, and most people were drinking champagne. We were served by handsome men in uniforms and I couldn't imagine any place in Australia, let alone Canberra, as flash as this one.

'Let's take our drinks out to the terrace garden; it is a clear night so we can see the stars.'

'It's very busy, will we get in?' I asked.

'I called today, we have a table. I often bring guests here – you could say that I am a preferred customer.'

I couldn't believe my luck in meeting Canelle, an acclaimed curator, a fashionista, a preferred customer and my new tidda.

By midnight, Emily had reluctantly gone to her hotel. Although she wanted to stay, she was desperately fighting jet lag, but I was on such a high from the opening that I couldn't imagine sleeping ever again. On the way back from the ladies, Canelle bumped into a group of friends and brought them to our table; two friends from her neighbourhood and a friend of theirs.

'My name is Libby Cutmore, *je suis Australienne*,' I said, extending my hand to a man in a navy linen jacket and jeans. He kissed my hand instead of shaking it.

'*Mon nom est Ames et je suis originaire de Bourgogne.*' He had a deep yet warm voice that I wanted to hear more of.

I was immediately attracted to Ames from Burgundy – my heart started to race with excitement and I felt a hot flush at the sight of the classically handsome man who looked like he was in his late twenties. My body was trying to adjust to his presence while my head was reciting: *I'm on a man-fast, I don't need a man.*

He didn't say anything as he sat opposite me. I imagined myself looking at him like a lovesick fool. Or lust-sick fool, because my loins were fluttering more than my heart. *It's just the opening adrenaline and the mojitos*, I told myself.

But I knew it was chemistry. I could feel the love drugs rushing through my body: the pleasure chemical dopamine gave that blissful feeling and norepinephrine was causing my heart to race. I'd read about them in a *BuzzFeed* article.

I was excited being physically near Ames and was ready to get high on the cocktails swirling through my body. Then voices started in my head: *He is too young for you, Libby. And he is too criminally good-looking for you as well. And he is French, so he will be sleazy.*

Ames was not much taller than me. Funnily enough, that didn't seem to matter, even though I've always liked tall men because short men somehow made me feel huge, especially since I have broad shoulders myself. I was concentrating more on analysing his features than the conversation going on around me. Canelle kept trying to include me.

'Elizabeth?' she asked, as if for the umpteenth time.

'Sorry, yes?' I turned to her, dragging my gaze from Ames's three-day growth, green-green eyes and chiselled face.

I couldn't remember the small talk I'd made with the other two nondescript friends because I spoke as fast as I could, then allowed my eyes to travel across to Ames's pointy nose and high cheekbones. I wanted to touch his skin. I wanted to touch his face. I just wanted to touch him, anywhere.

'We need a photo together.' Canelle pulled me to one side of her.

I also wanted a photo with Ames, just to have him close by my side. He took both Canelle's phone and my own and we posed like Black models used to the camera. I didn't know if I closed my eyes in the photos trying to picture his arse in his jeans, but I was snapped out of my perving daze when Canelle said, 'Now you two.'

I couldn't believe my luck as she pushed me towards Ames and he put his arm around my waist.

'Say *ouistiti*!' Canelle said.

I assumed it was the equivalent of 'say cheese' but as my eyes were misty with lust I didn't care or say anything. The smile itself was involuntary.

She took the photo and handed me my phone to look at it. Ames also wanted to see and as both our hands held the phone and his touched mine, a flame shot through my thighs. He had entranced me without any effort. That's when I decided: I deserved a reward for a sensational opening, and Ames was going to be that reward.

'I must go, Elizabeth, it is late and I have a very early meeting,' Canelle said, standing up on wobbly legs.

'How early?' I asked, disbelievingly.

'Nine,' she said, as if appalled. The 7 am starts Lauren and I used to have seemed a universe away from Paris. 'So, you know, I must get my beauty sleep.'

Canelle left with her neighbours, and Ames and I had one more drink.

As we walked into the night air I knew that if not my heart, then most definitely my loins had finally been won over by sexy Paris. We walked a few streets not talking. Ames held my hand firmly but gently. I felt blinded by his intensity and attention.

I wondered if this is what Lauren felt when she finally got together with Wyatt. Surely Ames wasn't my Wyatt? He couldn't be. We had just met, and I was indifferent to men. I wasn't interested in a relationship. I was never going to have another boyfriend and I couldn't fall for a French guy anyway, Mum would never stand for it. And Caro had warned me against it. But she *did* say have some fun.

I began a dialogue in my head about whether this was some kind of sick joke the universe was playing on me. My thoughts were scripted with cynicism: *Look what happened to Caro, Libby. Remember all those movies, Libby. Ames might be Bertrand from* The Man Who Loved Women. *Perhaps he follows women all over town seducing them, just like he's doing to you. How did I end up here?*

The laughter in the street was loud and the night sky had even more stars than usual, or so it seemed. Despite my negative thoughts, I couldn't stop smiling at meeting this handsome local man whose hand was in mine and who just spent an hour looking at me. I didn't care that he was probably looking at the lines around my eyes.

I was ready to explode with too many months of untapped lust, but I wasn't without my wits and texted Canelle to let her know I was going home with Ames, in case he turned out to be a murderer; one reason I rarely had one-night stands was the fear of being murdered.

'They don't want to murder you, they want to shag you,' Caro had said through a fit of laughter when I revealed my secret to her once. Still, I was always cautious, so going to a strange man's house wasn't a normal thing for me to do, and my safety needed to be considered.

I could feel the tension building as we climbed the stairs to his apartment and he held my hand tighter. His hands were soft, like they'd never cleaned or washed dishes and certainly never done hard labour.

'Who do you live with?' I asked, as he opened the door.

'I live alone,' he said, putting his hand around my neck and pulling my head and mouth to his, closing the door behind us and pushing me up against it.

We kissed passionately with a gentle grind of his crotch against mine and his hands on my face. He slow-danced me across the small room while softly moving his tongue in my mouth. I was moaning involuntarily, which made him pull me closer. He lay me down on his couch in a move so smooth he'd clearly done it before.

'What does the name "Ames" mean?' I felt like I should know a little more about the man I was going to make love to.

'It means "friend". And I want to be your friend,' he said, running his tongue down my cleavage.

I left his place at dawn. I hadn't done the walk of shame for years, and wasn't proud of myself, but no-one except Canelle would know unless I told them. I didn't expect to see Ames again, even though he asked for my number. He was French after all and, according to Caro, they were all players.

But before I reached the 4th, Ames had sent me a text asking to see me again. It made me smile. *He* made me smile. I wanted to see him again too, but I was tired and couldn't think straight.

Chapter 15

The Nude Poet

Bonjour, Canberrans!

I'm just checking in to let you know all is good here. The opening went off beautifully and without a hitch. We had a lot of media and I'll send you the links when things are posted. The mob here are all very pleased and I'm sure Emma will get a formal note soon enough. I'm on such a high with it all, I'm almost out of emotional control!

But it's not just that. I love everything about the culture of Paris. I should say cultures, because there are so many here. It really does make Canberra seem very vanilla. Sorry, but you could name any culture and there'll be a film festival or exhibition or something going on here in Paris to honour it. And lucky for me, there's plenty to see and do that you don't need money for, because I tell you, things are expensive here. Thank god there are free concerts and exhibitions every day, and you can even get a cheap ticket to the opera. Plus there's going to be plenty of 'work' related events to go to as well. Canelle is literally my social secretary.

Ne me manquez trop!!! Elizabeth 😃

It was Thursday, the day after my night with Ames, and it felt like a honeymoon for me, but I wasn't going to say anything to the girls just yet. The last thing I needed was a long-distance interrogation from them. I didn't even know what was going on myself so I wasn't ready to translate the experience to someone else. It was just a one-night stand, not something I'd normally brag about anyway. It was more important to report back on work than anything else.

Although I was enjoying the glow from the success of the opening and my night of pleasure, I had little time to stop and think about Ames and the fun we'd had. I did send a short text, just to keep me on his mind.

Looking forward to seeing you again 😃

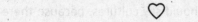

Emily was back at the Musée preparing workshops which I was helping out with, and emails and phone calls were coming in from all directions: artists, collectors, universities, the media – which of course meant I had to deal with Adrien, who was at least becoming less controlling. I think the success of the exhibition had really put him in his box about my abilities, and although our communication was never warm, it wasn't always a conflict now either.

'Are you ready to party again tonight, Elizabeth?' Canelle asked down the line. It was only because of the second wind I had found via a 4 pm café crème that allowed Canelle to psych me up into a frenzy talking about Nomad's. It was one of her favourite places to dine because it always had some kind of exhibition or window display going on.

'There are often events here: book launches, award nights and so on, Elizabeth. I think you will like it.'

I was mostly excited because that night we were going to the launch of a novel by a Torres Strait Islander woman. Terri Janke's latest book had been translated into French and was being launched by the Australian ambassador, so many Australians working in Paris were invited, as were many Musée staff because of the relationship being nurtured between the two bodies.

Canelle and I left work together and invited Emily along, but she already had plans with her father. I was glad she was comfortable and enjoying her trip.

'Douze rue du Marché Saint-Honoré.' Canelle gave the driver the address as we climbed into a cab. Even instructions to cabbies had a flair about them. And the destination sounded so much more glamorous than Northbourne Avenue.

'I'm starving,' I said, as my stomach grumbled softly.

'Me too, and there'll be very good food there, Elizabeth. I eat at Nomad's a lot because of the menu. I like food, Elizabeth.' Canelle put her hands on her thighs, laughing. 'Nomad's is not a treat for someone who likes to eat. It is almost essential.'

There was that definitive statement. Canelle and I were very similar, but I wondered if there was anything she ever ummed and ahhed over.

'You go just for the food?'

'I like the atmosphere there, and the design. It is not a fake place, how you say . . .'

'Put on,' I said. 'And Blackfellas would say gammon.'

'*Gammon*,' she said, which sounded much sexier in a French accent.

Canelle was right about Nomad's and I joined the appreciation society before we even walked in, stopping to take photos of the window display. One window had surfboards and surfing photographs shot along the coast of Australia. The next window had musical instruments: didgeridoos and clap sticks, all propped up against the Aboriginal and Torres Strait Islander flags.

'Wow,' I said, impressed with the Aboriginal presence there. 'It is very cool, *oui*?' Canelle asked.

'*Oui*, too deadly, we'd say.'

Canelle waved her hands as if on a game show presenting a prize. 'Every month they have a different theme in the windows, this month it is Australian, of course. And that is why the launch is here.'

'I love it.'

Inside, the atmosphere was electric even though the lighting was dim. There were solid wood tables which kept their original tree shapes and were merely sanded and varnished, without the need to craft them into exact squares. There were Friesian cowhide-covered chairs and a huge labrador making its way through the crowd.

'This is Fanny and Benoît.' Canelle introduced me to the owners of the restaurant, who were keen to meet me.

'We were at the Musée opening, it was superb,' Benoît said, Fanny nodding in agreement. 'We would love to have some Aboriginal artwork here as well one day, and tonight we are glad for Terri's book launch.'

We all looked in the direction of the author, who was in a teal-blue strapless dress that resembled the waters around the Torres Strait Islands. She was flanked by fans already requesting autographs although the official launch hadn't even happened. I wanted to meet and congratulate her and see what connections we could make, but I'd wait until she was finished working.

Canelle, Fanny and Benoît were talking too fast in French for me to keep up, so I made small talk, introducing myself to every staff member at Nomad's, aiming to maintain my look as the 'newly arrived local'. The staff were as multicultural as the city, with Croatian, Brazilian and Jamaican waiters serving prawns, ostrich and rabbit terrine.

'What's this?' I asked Canelle quietly when the restaurateurs walked off, not wanting to look like the country bumpkin I had always accused Lauren of being.

'*Foie gras* with chutney. Try it, it's delicious!' She kissed her fingers like a chef might.

The speeches started and the ambassador talked about how many First Nations authors had been translated into French: Doris Pilkington, Alexis Wright, Melissa Lucashenko and others. I thought to myself that the French probably liked the fact they could publish stories about what bastards the Brits had been to Blackfellas in Australia, without considering how colonisation had impacted on the Tahitians in Polynesia or the Mohawks in Quebec.

Afterwards, when the signing queue died down, I introduced myself to Terri, who was grateful to have another Blackfella there.

'There's also a fella from home here too, somewhere, in a black suit, red tie,' she said, scanning the room. 'He's the first secretary at the embassy, and helped coordinate getting me here. I've been so busy we haven't had time to talk properly.'

I started looking too. I hadn't seen a Blackfella yet at the launch, even though I had already spoken with some embassy staff, including Judith, the cultural attaché. I was disappointed in myself for having been there so long and not having met him. This was not the protocol I would normally follow. I searched out the red tie almost frantically but couldn't see it. Canelle was on her way over as the room was emptying.

'I have to go, sis,' Terri said, touching my arm, 'the publisher is taking me to dinner somewhere with some booksellers. Gawd, this is all new to me. But it's fun.'

'Live it up, sis,' I said. 'We need more people with more books like yours. Thanks for signing my copy, when do you leave?' I ran my hand over the blue cover, grateful for a piece of home.

'Tomorrow, I'm doing a tour through France. And my French is *merde*.'

I nearly spat my drink out and we both laughed, knowing everyone learns the rude slang words first.

'Have a great trip.' I hugged her, knowing she might be the only sista from home I'd see for some time. She hugged me back hard, as if she felt the same way. Neither of us said anything else.

Terri was whisked away by her publicist so Canelle and I called it a night at 11 pm and headed outside, looking for a cab.

'The whole night was delicious,' I said. 'Everything and everyone.

I loved it.'

'I knew you enjoyed yourself, I saw you taking photos like a tourist,' Canelle said.

'For my friends and family back home only.' I defended myself laughing.

At the taxi stand, we bumped into a group of people from the launch who were saying goodnight to each other. Canelle knew a lot of them and was speaking French and giving farewell kisses. I felt warm and comfortably relaxed from the Australian wine that was served.

I looked to my left and saw a red tie. It was on a Blackfella. The first secretary. He was one of the tallest men I'd seen in Paris. He had a round face framed by masses of brown curls and titanium-rimmed glasses. His eyes were too close together, making him look shifty, I thought. He had a big smile but thin lips. Broad shoulders, small waist and the same golden-brown complexion as me. He wore a black suit and white shirt and expensive-looking black shoes with his red tie. I couldn't believe it, but I was now becoming more conscious of men's fashion as well.

He spotted me at the same time.

'*Bonsoir, mademoiselle*,' he said, extending his hand before I had a chance to say anything.

I took his hand and said, 'Hi.'

'You're Libby Cutmore.'

I nodded and smiled.

'And you're absolutely beautiful.'

'Yes, I am,' was all I could say, embarrassed and yet cheekily self-assured.

I immediately thought of the Red Béret outside the Musée d'Orsay and how sleazy he was with his lines. Now it appeared that Blackfellas from home were using them too. I didn't want to be rude, because he was the first secretary, so I attempted an appropriate level of diplomacy.

'Yes, I am!' I said again. 'I mean, I'm Libby Cutmore, not yes, I'm beautiful. You know what I mean.'

'But you are beautiful, and I am Jake Ross.' He handed me his card.

I gave him my card in return. 'I'm here for five months working at the Musée doing educational lectures and tours.'

'Yes, I know, and you're Gamilaroi, from Moree,' he said, smiling so wide I thought his thin lips would split and his round face would crack. 'I am sorry I missed the opening of your exhibition, I had to deliver a speech in Cannes and couldn't get back in time. I heard it was a huge success though. AusTrade have called me about enquiries they've had regarding some of the artists involved. We should have a meeting.'

'Of course,' I said politely, but I was sure he was just using the business talk as an excuse. You don't start a work discussion by telling someone they're beautiful. Not in my world. Even though I did look rather special with my orange scarf, black pinstripe tunic and black pumps.

'*Bonsoir*, Jake,' another suited man was at Jake's side. Jake turned and shook his hand and Canelle appeared at my side to usher me into a taxi without an opportunity to say goodbye.

Minutes later, my mobile rang, but I didn't answer it in time. There was a short voicemail message that I played out loud for Canelle to translate in case it was in French.

'Libby, it's Jake Ross.' Although we had just met it took me a few seconds to register who it was. 'I'm sorry we didn't say goodbye properly. I'm with some staff and we're going back to a bar near the embassy. I'd like you to join us for a nightcap. Perhaps you could call me back.'

'*Oohlala*, Elizabeth, I think he is interested in you. And he was very, very handsome. And very important.' Canelle was more impressed with the call than I was.

I pressed 'return call' on my phone and got his voicemail. I imagined his phone was tied up because he was calling the next in a long line of women to have a drink with. After the beep, I left a short message: 'Hello, Jake, it's Libby Cutmore. Thanks for the offer of drinks, but I am almost home now. I will call your office to arrange a meeting to discuss the AusTrade interest you mentioned. Nice meeting you. Goodnight.' I hung up the phone only to hear Canelle laughing like a teenage girl.

'What?' I asked, confused.

'Why did you say that? You should've gone to meet him.'

'It's late, Canelle. I'm not travelling across any city for any man this late at night, not even if he is the first secretary and looks good in a red tie.'

I sounded arrogant, but it was what I'd become thanks to my previous disasters and disappointments, and with Ames on my mind I didn't need to think about anyone else either. Now that I was starting to feel better about myself and felt attractive being around Frenchmen, well, someone could chase me for once.

'Anyway, why would I want to meet him this late at night? That doesn't send a good signal for either party, professionally or personally.'

'This is France, it is not late for us to eat and drink. And anyway you are both professionals. Why are you being a . . . how you say?'

'A bitch?'

'Yes, a bitch, *merci*.'

'You're welcome.' I stared out the cab window.

'Elizabeth, only some men like bitches, trust me, and some men, well, they like life to be less complicated than it

228

sometimes is. You are being too serious and you are already
complicating this situation.'

'What situation, Canelle? Even if I was interested i
him, he's a Blackfella from Australia and I certainly didn
come to Paris to meet a guy I could meet back hom
Apart from that, we're probably related, stranger thing
have happened in more unlikely places, believe me. No
that doesn't make me a complicated bitch, does it?' I was
even sure myself.

'Maybe not,' Canelle said unconvincingly.

'The thing is, Canelle, I came here to work. It's s
flirting with someone who lives in another count
because there's no chance of being hurt flirting w
someone on the train who you'll never see again. But Ja
is Australian – I just don't want to get involved. Anyw
I'm going home in a few months.' I said all that with An
still occupying my thoughts.

'I just don't think it is a very smart move to t
down the first secretary of your home country, Elizabe
Canelle was almost chastising me. 'Do you not wan
make more contacts?'

'Of course I do.' I could hear the annoyance in my vo
'But I don't think a work meeting is going to happen a
too many drinks, late at night. I know enough of me
know that. I'll arrange a meeting with him to discuss w
during business hours.'

'Whatever you think, my friend, but you know in
arts, every hour is a business hour. Pull over here, dri
she said, handing me some euros before getting out o

cab. 'I think he had a very nice *derrière*. I'll see you in the morning.'

I hadn't looked at Jake's arse and didn't know when Canelle had had the chance to either, but it wasn't something I was going to consider. The last thing I needed while building my reputation in the arts in Paris was building a reputation for following Australian men's arses in France.

After organising my clothes for the next day, I was grateful to crawl into bed at midnight, feeling my calves in pain from standing in heels all night. I soon swapped thoughts of sore feet for vivid images of how Ames had kissed my ankles and each of my toes the night before.

I woke in the morning to find a text message.

> You are the most astonishingly beautiful woman I have seen since I arrived in Paris, and most certainly on any cab rank anywhere in the world. I would be honoured to take you to dinner. We also need to talk about the artists. Jake.

My head was flooded with questions, looking for justifications. This must be a joke. Blackfellas don't talk like that at home or in Paris. He must've had one of his French staff write that. Or he was charged up. Or he was just a sleazebag using his position to his own advantage, and that wasn't a game I was going to play. I had earned every stripe I had through hard work and was happy to keep doing it.

I didn't respond to his text. I wanted to talk about it with Canelle first after work.

'I think he sounds like a stalker,' I said over coffee at Café Jacques.

'You are being ridiculous. He is your countryman, he is a good-looking man, and he is an influential man.' Canelle sipped her espresso.

I shook my head at Canelle's naivety. 'I think the common factor he shares with the guys back home is that he is a *man*. And anyway, who says those kinds of things to someone they've just met?'

'This is Paris, this is romance. If it is not Aboriginal, then it is very French. I like it. Give him my number, and I will sext him back.'

'Don't you mean text?'

I couldn't believe Canelle had her phone out as if she was going to text him right then.

'*Non, Cherie*, I meant what I said. Did I mention he had a nice *derrière*?'

'Yes, you did.'

I liked Canelle's sense of humour. She reminded me of me before I became bitter and twisted over the men who'd burned me. And although I had been seduced by Ames and the romance that envelops even single people on trains in Paris, I really wanted to focus on why I was here: my work.

Back at my desk, I got Jake's card out of my wallet and emailed him about a meeting, completely ignoring the text he had sent me. I received a response later in the day from the cultural attaché, Judith Marks – with Jake cc'd in. It said that Judith would meet with me in the next few weeks. I was relieved that Jake wouldn't be there.

'Thanks for meeting me here, Sorina,' I said, as we sat in Salon Marie Antoinette on Saturday afternoon.

Sorina had a big smile. 'It is wonderful to see you, Libby. You are not just my best customer ever, but you are a positive face to see in my day.'

'I have an idea,' I said, hoping she wouldn't think I was imposing. 'Yes?'

'I think we can get more people to buy your bags if we can get you some more promotion and perhaps a proper place to sell.'

Sorina's eyes widened with interest, then her face became sad. 'Libby, it is kind of you to think about that and I wish it were possible, but I cannot make any more bags than I currently sell. I only have access to a sewing machine one night a week at a friend's place. She is already doing me a huge favour. Anyway, I would have to have more materials to produce more bags.'

I thought hard while I looked at Sorina's dark brown eyes and the dark circles under them. It was time to tell her my other idea.

'What if I got you your own machine and your own materials, do you think you could make more bags, even on order?'

'Of course, it is my love, designing these bags.' She pulled something out of her red sack. 'This is my latest, do you like it?'

She handed me a brown and gold corduroy bag with sequins and beads. A press-stud closed it and it fitted snugly under my arm.

'I must have this.' I reached for my wallet.

Sorina put her hand on mine to stop me. 'It is yours then, a gift.'

I was shocked and embarrassed. My plan was to help Sorina *sell* bags, not take them from her for free.

'Absolutely not! I will pay you for it, and when you sell your first hundred if you want to make me one then, fine. But I am going to help you start a little business, okay? And I have worked out a plan.' I pulled out my folder and what I had coordinated already, explaining the whole setup to my new friend. I had told my landlords about Sorina's problem and they were eager to help. Dom was getting a second-hand sewing machine for me, and his wife Catherine was rallying materials from all her friends and family and already had three bag orders waiting. Back in Australia, Lauren had asked someone at the NAG to design a simple business card that I could print out on cardboard at work. Bec had offered to set up an Etsy store and an Instagram page for Sorina.

At this point, Canelle arrived, carrying one of Sorina's bags. I'd invited her to meet us.

'Perfect timing,' I said, as she sat down. 'I'm just telling Sorina about my idea to grow her talent and her business and I'm just up to the part about needing to find someone to be her patron of sorts.'

'You would know about *les banlieues*, Sorina. Yes?' Canelle asked.

'Of course,' Sorina said knowingly. 'Some of my friends are desperate to be discovered by the wealthy people visiting there.'

Canelle turned to me. 'Most of the people in these outskirts are "people of colour", often disenfranchised, but they contribute to French culture as a whole through hip-hop culture, graphic arts, music publishing and other artistic activities like fashion design, and many others.'

Canelle leaned in towards Sorina. 'Many "mainstream" French personalities have been digging for artistic novelty in the *banlieues*, hoping to stumble upon the next brilliant fringe artist like Jean-Michel Basquiat. Now,' Canelle turned her attention back to Sorina, 'one of the fastest growing designers in the last few years is Agnes B, and she has put her Parisian facilities at the disposal of several artists from the *banlieues* and regularly sponsors art exhibitions. She is a fabulous patron for emerging designers.'

'She sounds great.' I looked at Sorina, who nodded. 'And this is the kind of support we want long-term. Do you know her?' I asked Canelle.

'I know someone who knows her. I think we can at least get an introduction. Do you have some bags with you today?' Canelle looked at Sorina.

Sorina tipped her collection of bags out on the table, and Monica came over and picked one up with interest. We were all excited about what Canelle had just said.

Canelle looked impressed at the different styles in front of her. 'Then, today we will go to the non-tourist *banlieue* art scene in La Seine-Saint-Denis, which is also the most impoverished *banlieue*. They have set up an association in order to offer a platform to local artists and help them display their creations. I think this is where we shall start.'

At La Seine-Saint-Denis, I was impressed by the arts and crafts being created as part of employment programs, but the sight of burnt-out vehicles and people living in poverty made me sad. It reminded me of communities back home and I was uncomfortable about my own privilege in the life I had in Canberra and even in Paris.

By the time we left the area, Sorina had been granted a space for three months to sell her bags. It was all systems go.

As we caught the Métro back later that afternoon, I think we all felt a sense of relief and hope. I was making lists in my head regarding messaging the girls about setting up an Instagram, designing business cards and coordinating the machine and materials. Canelle listened to music on her AirPods while Sorina sketched new bags in a notebook.

'Libby, next weekend is *Nuit Blanche*,' Sorina said, without looking up.

'*Nuit Blanche*?' I asked, with less of the accent than it really required.

'It is a celebration where museums, art galleries and other cultural institutions are opened to the public, free of charge.' Sorina seemed proud of the city that wanted to kick her out. 'It's good for families especially.'

'What a great idea!' I got my Moleskine and made a note to check it out. It would be even more professional development I could write up in my report when I went back. And more to make the girls envious about.

Canelle watched me writing in my book and took her AirPods out.

'Ah, you know the best thing about *Nuit Blanche* is that the city becomes a de facto art gallery with designated space for installations and a whole range of performances across art forms,' Canelle said, her voice sounding excited as she spoke.

'Most of our museums and galleries are already free in Australia, but a joint effort across art forms over one weekend is something that we could do in Canberra for sure, and perhaps the NAG could coordinate it.' I'd add it to my debrief when I got back home.

I thought about Ames over the next few days, as I waited for him to respond to my text. I assumed he was a player, so I had relaxed into waiting. I thought about the sex and I reminded myself it was just about fun, and good health, because it wasn't natural to go for lengths of time without sex – or so I'd read once in a glossy magazine.

I started to think about my health and how I should be considering the benefits of sex to me physically, beyond the pleasure of orgasms. I knew sex helped to relieve stress and I was finding the language barrier at work somewhat stressful. It also helped burn calories and I'd been consuming far more carbs in Paris than I ever did back home. Sex also helped build up the immune system and although I had travel insurance, I really couldn't afford to get sick, so sex was also preventative medicine.

After five days of internal debate, I decided that sex with Ames again was absolutely necessary for my health and wellbeing. It was Thursday, and with *Nuit Blanche* approaching, I had the perfect excuse for asking Ames to be my guide.

I sent him a text:

I am looking for a guide. What are you doing for Nuit Blanche?

Ames texted back:

I am showing you my city xo

Ames's text made me smile, and made me hot. I was keen to get naked with him again, and being in Paris had slightly altered my view of men over the past weeks. The Ancestors had a plan for me it seemed, and after my mistakes in recent years I was grateful.

I met Ames at his flat on Saturday evening to explore 'his city'. But all we did was explore each other, beginning with a long soak in his deep cast-iron bath with clawed feet.

He then read me poetry in French and English while he sat in his living room in the nude. I didn't understand most of what he recited but I loved the sound of his voice. When he read to me it reminded me of Linda in the movie *Woman Times Seven*.

He propped himself up against the black bedhead in the bedroom and I just listened for hours. He wanted me nude as well, but I couldn't bring myself to be completely naked, although I liked the feeling of freedom in being without clothes just for the sake of it. I was more modest though, and draped a pashmina across my shoulders, explaining that there was a chill coming in from under the door.

I had a copy of Kath Walker's *We Are Going* in my bag to read on the train, and I asked him to read it to me as well. I made him dress for that reading, out of respect for the late activist.

Ames wrote a lot of his own poetry: love poems, environmental poems, poems about social responsibility and disadvantage. But when he didn't find his own words adequate enough, he told me he recited the words of Maximilien de Robespierre.

'We need another revolution. We need another Robespierre,' Ames said, standing to attention as if he was the incorruptible revolutionary himself. He was naked, his penis standing to attention too, and he looked serious and sexy at the same time.

I knew he wasn't the One – thanks to Andy I no longer believed in the One – and I certainly hadn't gone to Paris to meet someone I didn't believe even existed, but I was happy to just sit and watch and enjoy Ames' nude oration.

'Society is obliged to secure the subsistence of all its members!' he proclaimed. 'Providing the necessary help against poverty is a duty of the rich towards the poor.' He walked across the room as if he was on a stage and I was the crowd. 'The wretchedness of citizens is nothing other than the crime of government.'

He stood still, and I wasn't sure if he was waiting for me to applaud or not, so I did. Then I stood up, took off my pashmina and stood naked with him. We were revealed revolutionaries. It felt wonderful. Maybe he *could* be the One.

The euphoria of feeling desired by Ames and being in tune with him politically, while also feeling sexually liberated in the city of Paris, fed me emotionally and physically, although I knew I was nowhere near ever falling in love again, not after my bad luck.

I was excited about my new sex life when I messaged the group chat, sending the photo of Ames and me from our first meeting.

Hey tiddas,

What's happening? Warming up there yet? Are you planning on going to the coast at all? How was Bali, Bec? Good shopping and food? Did you try surfing? Send me some pics, please. And what about my Bonnie and Clyde? Can you ask them to call sometime, please!

It's getting colder now and you won't believe it but women still wear fur here. It's normal. Not sure where the animal rights activists are, but the women are quite comfortable wearing skinned foxes, rabbits and minks as coats, wraps, shawls and hats. At least most men manage to be stylish, whether simply in a suit or jeans with a knit and scarf. Or even in the nude!

Okay, so that's a story for FaceTime because I'm not putting anything in writing. Let's just say . . . I've met someone. His name is Ames, he likes poetry and nudity and sometimes both at the same time. He is very political and into social justice. I like hanging with him. And no I am NOT in love, but I AM in lust!

He makes me feel less like a 'newly arrived local' and more like a potential permanent fixture.

Send me some news from work, from your lives, from your shopping trips.

Love you all xxx

Lauren replied first:

Forget shopping; tell us more about the nude poet!

Bec wrote:

Who cares about my photos of Bali? Send pics of the nude poet.

Caro chimed in:

Have fun but remember what I said . . . 😉

Chapter 16

Le poet turns le prick

'Coffee, mademoiselle.' Dom presented me with a cup at his kitchen table while Romeo sniffed around my ankles.

To appease both Dom and Catherine, I had a cuppa with them once a week before work. Sometimes at their place, and sometimes with Monica down the road. That way I could assure them that I was not only alive, but happy and healthy and eating properly.

And they often asked for an update on Sorina and her business. Catherine almost always had some more material – deep coloured satins, a variety of crushed velvets and linen. She once even had some electric-blue lurex and black spandex for me, and when I enquired where she got them, she just laughed. I was convinced she went out and bought it.

'You are smiling a lot more these days, Libby,' Catherine said, with a cheeky glint in her eye. 'I used to smile like that when I first met my Dom.'

'Don't you still smile like that, my love?' Dom pretended to be hurt.

'Of course I do, darling.'

Catherine and Dom had the most romantic vibe I'd ever seen. As a child, I was too young to notice the looks that Mum and Dad threw each other, and being around Catherine and Dom made me appreciate the real love and respect between two people who share a life and almost a lifetime together.

'We are already sad that you are going to be leaving us, Libby, we like having you in our building,' Dom said, putting his arm around my shoulder in an awkward half-hug.

'I like being here, and already know I will be sad to leave. I've spent more time with you both drinking coffee than I've spent with my own mother in the past few years. It's because of you that I don't feel homesick.'

'Oh, I think there is someone else who stops you being homesick also,' Catherine smiled.

They could sense that there was a particular spring in my step and that I dodged any romance-related question. I imagined that being without a daughter themselves, they would be happy for me to marry locally and fill the daughterly void in their lives. Of course, my own mother would have something to say about that.

Over the next few weeks I enjoyed hanging out with Ames. We walked around the Place de la Concorde and the Tuileries Garden and it was so cold I had to buy a hat made in Taiwan sold to me by an African. We also checked out the Latin Quarter on the Left Bank, the academic hub of the city. We took our time going through bookshops and record stores and drinking coffee among students and professors.

We walked hand-in-hand along rue de la Huchette in the heart of the Latin Quarter to a royal palace built in the thirteenth century, and the Exchange Bridge built in the fourteenth century. In whitefella terms, Paris was old.

Ames took me to the house where Ernest Hemingway lived in the 1930s and I just relished all the culture I was absorbing with a hot Frenchman wrapped around me the whole time.

This was my new life. On top of the romantic strolls, I was enjoying my routine of *un Americano et un pain au chocolat* with Monica most mornings on the way to work. The nights I didn't see Ames, I'd go to the fromagerie and have a selection of cheeses, a baguette and wine for dinner. Sometimes I'd just grab my favourite trois-fromage quiche, ganache and Coca-Cola Light to balance the diet. It was my standard, especially if I was in a rush and couldn't be bothered cooking.

I was getting more and more acquainted with the city and the language every day. I started to feel like a true local with my fabulous job in the arts, ongoing lessons in history and culture and the best diet in the world. Then there was Ames: who needed love when you could just have intelligent conversation and great sex?

One night in August, Canelle and I were on our way to the opening of an exhibition of photographs of Australia by French photographers. It was a collaboration between the Musée and the Australian embassy.

As we walked down quai Branly, I realised it was the first time I'd been invited there since the flirty call from Jake a month before. In fact, it dawned on me as we arrived that Jake and I never did speak after that night because all my official embassy contact had been with Judith Marks.

My mind wandered back to the embassy itself. I was looking forward to checking out the interior of the building, having seen it from the outside numerous times. The architect was Harry Seidler, well-known back home for designing Australia Square in Sydney and QV1 in Perth.

We entered the front doors on rue Jean Rey and were met by an Australian security guard as we put our bags on the conveyor belt. It was such an unassuming entrance to an important place. I liked the guard's friendliness and his Australian accent; it reminded me of life back at the NAG.

We had our names checked off by the staff at the desk and were directed into the large exhibition space. Men wore suits and women wore designer shoes and looked effortlessly glamorous. Even the Aussie women dressed with a sense of Parisian glam.

The opening was different to exhibitions back home – it wasn't necessarily more cultured or 'civilised', but the crowd were definitely more self-controlled than at some of the openings we had at the NAG and other galleries around Australia. There were no cheers of excitement at the reunion of artists or families or past colleagues, like we often saw when Blackfellas from across the country would attend our openings, where the joy of reconnection added to the success of the event.

The French may have been more refined but I wasn't convinced they were actually more fun than we were. I wondered how many of those attending were embassy staff and expats.

'I feel a little strange here,' I whispered to Canelle. 'Why? These are your people.'

'Actually, they're not my people. My people are Black-fellas. It's just a little staid for me,' I said, to the disgust of a snooty French woman, who looked at me disapprovingly.

Canelle saw her and smiled. 'I'll get us a drink,' she said, 'and then people will seem much more fun to you, *oui*?'

'*Oui*,' I laughed, loving Canelle's approach to the world even more.

She walked off, leaving me alone.

My feet were aching from the blinged slingbacks I'd raced out to buy in Montparnasse at lunchtime to feel more glamorous at the event. I spotted a free seat and walked over as elegantly as possible and sat down.

As Canelle chatted to other Musée staff who had just arrived, I watched and tried to guess who everyone was. One man looked like a diplomat. I watched him greet a woman I assumed was his wife. They kissed the French way – a light kiss barely touching each cheek – and then they smooched on the mouth. I felt like a smooch on the mouth too. Ames came to mind and I got a tingle in my knickers. I breathed in deeply.

'Hi, Libby.' Judith Marks caught me off guard.

'Judith, hello, how are you?' I stood up, noticing immediately her chocolate streaks had gone burgundy and were quite striking in her now slightly longer blonde bob.

'Didn't mean to startle you,' Judith said matter-of-factly, 'but I just want to let you know that my boss Jake Ross is keen to meet with you.' She grabbed a prawn from a passing platter, also matter-of-factly. 'Do you mind giving me a bell to line up a time for a meeting?'

'Sure thing,' I said. 'I'll give you a call tomorrow.'

'Thanks,' Judith was already one foot out of the conversation circle. 'I've just spotted a regular being annoying to one of our visitors, I better go save them. Speak soon,' she said, and walked off with purpose in her stride.

'Here you go.' Canelle had finally returned from the bar and handed me a glass of bubbly. 'Stand there,' she said, positioning me so she could see something on the other side of the room.

'What are you doing?' I asked with a wriggle.

'There is a tall, very handsome man in a dark jacket, wearing thin dark-framed glasses, behind you.'

'You are outrageous, Canelle. You're worse than a Frenchman in terms of flirting and perving.'

'Worse than?' Canelle sounded offended. 'That makes it sound bad. Flirting and perving, as you summarise it, is a good thing, so I would consider myself to be, let's say, as good as a Frenchman.'

I laughed. She certainly was as good as any Frenchman, and five times better at it than any Aussie bloke I'd met.

'He has dimples, and a warm smile.' Canelle was perving, grinning and talking to me at the same time.

'Let me look.' I tried to turn but she stopped me aggressively. 'You don't need to see him: it is the man with the nice *derrière* from Nomad's. The one you don't want to talk to, remember? Never mind anyway, you will not get a chance to talk: he is surrounded by hot young women.'

'He is the first secretary and I have to work with him,' I said dismissively. My mind was on Ames – Jake Ross could have all the young women he wanted to for all I cared.

'Is this a big crowd, do you think? I mean for a city of eleven million people?' I was desperate to change the topic from men to almost anything else.

'It's big enough, why?' Canelle was confused.

'We've had bigger openings for solo exhibitions at the NAG, that's all.'

'Yes, Elizabeth, but there are dozens of openings in Paris tonight and film *premières* and so on.'

Canelle was making the point that in Canberra there wasn't a lot to compete with. She was right, so I didn't argue.

I continued to scan the room. 'Everyone is dressed incredibly well, expensively well.'

'So are you,' Canelle said, affirming me. 'This is new, *oui*?' She touched the fabric of my frock. I had on an uncharacteristically soft knee-length pink-and-black spiral print dress and a black glass heart choker I'd bought in the Marais.

'*Oui*, it's from a small boutique on rue du Bosquet. I am branching out from my block colours,' I said, proud of the evolution of my wardrobe since arriving. 'Anyhow, let's see the exhibition before the speeches start.' I motioned Canelle into the main area.

We walked through the space of winding white walls with colour photographs that moved from landscapes to portraits of people from all walks of life in Australia. I was getting increasingly homesick as I took in photo after photo, including some shots of Koori kids in Sydney. I passed small groups of people discussing each print: the sunrise at Bondi, the sunset in Broome, the drought-stricken countryside, the busy harbour and the Sydney Opera House brightly lit up during VIVID, as well as a photo of the Summernats car show in Canberra, the life that I had left in Australia.

I spotted Jake as I was looking at the photographs. This time, I was about to go over when I saw him shaking hands with what I assumed were dignitaries. I watched him sweep them gently through the room, introducing them to guests. I found myself staring. He looked very professional and there were no young women in sight, and no other Blackfellas. I suddenly found myself missing Lauren. I got my phone out to text her:

Am at the Oz embassy, not enough Blackfellas, wish you were here. XO

It was time for the Australian ambassador to open the exhibition. He introduced some of the photographers in attendance and talked about the relationship between the embassy and the Musée. I struggled to hear him as the crowd around me spoke the whole time. I couldn't believe the level of disrespect for a speaker, let alone the Australian ambassador.

'People are so rude,' I whispered to Canelle, motioning to a group talking in front of us.

'This is normal,' she said flippantly.

I thought back to my own opening at the Musée but couldn't remember the same background murmurs during our presentation.

After the speeches were over, Canelle insisted I have dinner with her in Bastille. I was starving and needed to eat, so I agreed without much thought.

'Un rue Delambre,' she told the driver, as I climbed into the cab seat behind her.

'This is . . . how you say . . . my local. You must have the calamari and ravioli,' she advised. Seeing as her advice was usually spot on, I knew to take it.

Sitting in Bistrot du Dôme with Canelle, I joked with the waiters in their funny ties with pictures of Donald Duck and pigs on them. Canelle and I talked fashion. She suggested I could get some of Paris's best and most afford-able bling from a store at the Métro station Châtelet-Les

Halles; I could walk there from my place. While she wrote down the exact location of the store I should check out, I became anxious about going to see Ames. I'd become more than interested in the great sex we'd been having. I needed to see him.

As I waved Canelle goodbye, I booked an Uber and headed towards his apartment. I felt a sense of adventure in my plan to surprise him with a print I'd had Lauren send me. I wanted Ames to have some Aboriginal art in his flat for inspiration, so Lauren had selected one of Gordon Hookey's more controversial works: *Sacred nation, scared nation, indoctrination*. I knew that Ames would appreciate the politics behind it. I'd been carrying the cylinder it was packed in around with me with all night and had almost forgotten it twice: once at the embassy coat check and then in the restaurant.

I climbed two steps at a time to his apartment. It wasn't ladylike, but rather demonstrative of my eagerness to get to his door and eventually into his bed. When I arrived, the glossy grey door was ajar – unusual but not alarming. I felt even more adventurous as I pushed it gently, hoping not to make any sound for maximum surprise impact.

Ames's sound system was blaring out Yannick Noah – he'd played me one of his albums after a long walk in the Latin Quarter. Ames liked the ex-tennis-player, who now worked to improve the lives of underprivileged children. I liked the reggae sounds myself, but the player was louder than usual and the only light came from a lamp in one corner of his living room. Ames wasn't to be seen though. I imagined he'd raced home and into the shower.

Kicking off my shoes and peeling off my dress, I made my way towards the bathroom, ready to join him immediately. I pushed open the door wearing only my bra and French knickers and yelled, 'Surprise!'

But the surprise was on me. Ames was in the bath with another woman. Not really a woman. Rather, a female who looked so young and thin it was hard to believe she'd even reached puberty. My thoughts were like short sentences. Flashes of what my eyes didn't want to see. Ames. Teenager. Bubbles. Bath. *My* Ames in the bath with a teenager! The man who I had let into my heart and my bed, who was supposed to be into me, was now into someone else, literally.

I felt an immediate shiver of shock and cold as I stood there, half-naked with the cylinder in my hand. I imagined bludgeoning them both into a coma with it, but dropped it instead as a hot rush came over me – the kind of hot-flush Mum had told me happened during menopause.

'Libby,' Ames said, eventually. 'This is not what you think it is.' My head was screaming, *WHAT THE FUUUCCCKKK!!!*

'Are you naked?' I accused.

'*Oui*,' he said, without hesitation.

'Are you in the bath with another woman, I mean female?' I felt like Caro in a court of law cross-examining a defendant.

'Um, *oui*.'

'Are you cheating on me?'

'This is not cheating,' he said, looking at the girl then me. 'This is . . . this is what we do. We make love because it is good for our bodies and our minds and our creativity.'

I stood stunned for a minute, trying to comprehend what I was seeing and hearing. They both looked back, stunned too, probably because I hadn't left immediately. But I was stuck, my feet would not move and time had stood still while I tried to fathom how I had met yet another man with the cheating gene.

I stared down at them. While there were masses of bubbles, I assumed she was fully attached to his baguette. She looked familiar and it annoyed me trying to recognise that face, and then it hit me. She had lips like Jodi Uptown and memories of Peter and Moree came flooding back. Andy and his eyes on the woman at the Wilin Centre flashed before me. It had happened again. Whenever I trusted and I believed, I got fucked over.

I was furious and couldn't think of the French translation of bastard to shout at him. I didn't think imbecile was strong enough, so I just said, with as much venom as I could muster, '*Le prick!*'

I threw my dress on quickly and stormed out of the flat as Ames struggled to get out of the bath, and the pre-pubescent was squealing something I couldn't decipher. I was determined Ames would not see me cry. I had cried my fair share with the last two bastards and I was determined that I would not cry over another man again. Caro was right. What *had* I been thinking?

I headed to the nearest bar, already planning my demise through too many glasses of wine. I called Canelle but got her voicemail and didn't leave a message. I tried as hard as I could not to weep but a lone, dignified tear ran down my cheek.

I sculled my first glass of wine and took a few minutes to stare into the second glass. I thought about Maria Teresa from *Woman Times Seven*. Was my life becoming that of Shirley MacLaine? Was I now supposed to have revenge-sex like Maria Teresa did when she found her husband in bed with another woman?

I sat at the bar scribbling in my Moleskine, trying to write through what had happened. I wrote about Ames and called him every single name I could think of in English and French and the odd Spanish word I'd learnt when studying at the CIT. I ordered another wine and another and got progressively drunker as my disappointment and anger turned into homesickness. I missed Lauren, Bec and Caro. I looked at my watch and it was almost midnight, making it 8 am in Canberra. I was drunk enough not to care about the fact that Loz was likely on her way to work.

'Libs!' she answered. The tears fell unwillingly at the mere sound of my tidda's voice. 'Oh my god, Libs, how are you? It's so good to hear from you. What are you doing right now? Where are you?' Lauren rattled off enough questions to give me time to compose myself.

'I'm in a bar. I'm a bit drunk.' I looked around to see if anyone was listening, but no-one seemed to notice I was even there.

'Good girl. I'm glad you're having fun.' Lauren sounded genuinely happy for me.

I couldn't speak.

'Libs? What's wrong? Are you okay?' Lauren's happy voice turned quickly to concern.

I still couldn't speak. I forced a lump down my throat.

'Libby, please, you're making me worry. What's wrong?' Lauren's voice was gentle, nurturing.

'I hate men,' I said through gritted teeth, trying to contain my anger and remain dignified in a public place. 'All they ever do is hurt me.'

'What happened? Where's that nude writer dude?' I could hear Lauren become more protective of her tidda a long way away.

'He's in the bath . . . with someone else.' I said, as if it were normal.

'What? What are you talking about?'

'I just walked in and found him with someone else.' I took another mouthful of wine. 'I've never been so humiliated in my life. I don't know what to do.'

'Sis, I'm so sorry, I wish I were there. Do you want me to get on a plane? I can be there in twenty-four hours. Tell me, I can do it.'

'No, don't be silly, you can't do that.' I noticed a couple walk into the bar cuddling and it felt like someone punched me in the stomach again.

'Libs, I know the pain, I've been there. And I only got through it because of you. I'm a plane ride away. I have leave. Emma won't mind.'

'Don't tell Emma. Don't tell anyone,' I said half-aggressively. 'I'm embarrassed.'

The last thing I wanted was everyone back home knowing I'd managed to geographically relocate my inability to have a normal relationship.

'Why are you embarrassed? You didn't do anything, he's the idiot, moron, loser, dropkick who should be embarrassed for letting you go. And so cruelly.'

Just hearing Lauren's words made me feel better. Friends always knew the right things to say, and in situations like these it meant saying as much horrible and nasty stuff about the offender as possible.

'You are a strong, capable, intelligent, gorgeous woman. You are too good to be treated so poorly.'

And of course, the positive words in relation to myself also helped.

'Is there anything I can do?'

'Actually, just talking to you has made me feel much better, but I better go now, people are starting to stare at the sad lonely girl crying into her phone.'

Lauren laughed. 'Okay, sis. Message me if you need anything and we can always FaceTime when you get home tonight.'

'Okay, gotta go, keep this to yourself but say hello to everyone, okay, and Wyatt.'

I pressed 'end' and put the phone back in my bag.

I was still in shock. I hardly knew Ames and I had told myself that I didn't want a relationship, that I never wanted another boyfriend. And this was the reason why. I had let myself get swept up into the bullshit around romantic

Paris and poetry and Frenchmen with accents and good politics. I should've known better.

Why hadn't I learned and accepted that I was never going to be happy with a man or have any decent, normal sense of romance? I hated the universe at that moment: she was a fucking bitch and I didn't deserve what she was doing to me.

My mobile buzzed.

My Libby, I am sorry that you are upset. She does not mean anything to me but I have known her since before I met you.

There were more words but I didn't want to read them. I deleted the message before it could do any more damage to my head, my self-esteem or my heart. I blocked his number and then deleted it from my phone. There were never going to be any more second chances with me. No man was worth that: French, Black, nude, revolutionary or otherwise.

I pushed any thought of Ames to the darkest recesses of my memory with the other losers and hoped they all had fun keeping each other company.

Chapter 17

Embassy Bound

Weeks later I was still angry and sad about Ames. My low moments were compounded by the fact that October was around the corner and the countdown to returning home had started. My love-life only added to the depressing thoughts I had about leaving Paris and heading back to a comparatively boring Canberra.

I knew I would never be the same after my life in France. Although I'd felt lonely at times, I loved the way I lived in the French capital. I knew it would be hard to go back to the NAG, although I remained committed to the work I did there. And I missed the girls terribly.

All in all, though, my life was amazing in Paris. I had grown so much as a woman since arriving. I had met my French-Caribbean soul-twin in Canelle. I'd seen Sorina shine in her craft really quickly and I was proud to have been part of a community effort to help her cement her life and feel secure in this somewhat insecure country. She was blossoming as a woman with new-found self-esteem and also as a designer, busy filling orders for her bags.

I had learned a lesson from my experience with Ames, but I had no intention of forgiving him, *ever*. Until one morning over coffee when Canelle gave me a dose of her worldly wisdom.

'Unforgiveness,' she said, 'according to the writer Debbie Ford, "is the poison you drink every day hoping that the other person will die".'

I didn't want Ames to die, but clearly the toxic feeling of carrying bitterness would only kill me emotionally.

'I like that quote,' was all I said as I burned it into my brain.

'Yes, it is a good one, but it does not help the pain, for that we must shop. After work, I will take you to one of my favourite areas. It is a surprise!' Canelle got up, kissed me on both cheeks and added, 'This is not a dress rehearsal, Elizabeth, this is life. We must move on quickly from the misery and find happiness again.'

I spent the afternoon keeping myself extraordinarily busy doing an audit of the Musée library with the aim of building up the First Nations collection and keeping Ames out of my thoughts. The library space was dark – mirroring the rest of the museum – and I had convinced myself that I was going to need glasses by the end of my placement.

Nevertheless, I liked how it looked and it was a peaceful place to work. There were five massive lampshades atop one length of bookcase. A huge square table sat about three metres square with three wooden sculptures in the middle of it. I imagined a great feast of French food on the table as I thought about what I might eat for dinner that night.

The collections were divided into permanent exhibition resources, temporary exhibition resources and so on. There was a substantial collection of art magazines from across the world and I started getting ideas of how we could develop our library space and catalogue back at the NAG.

I spoke to the librarian about helping to build up the Musée's Australian library collection, adding to the exhibition catalogues from across Europe. I made a list of some of our more popular art journals that the library could subscribe to. I emailed the Aboriginal Studies Press within the Australian Institute of Aboriginal and Torres Strait Islander Studies to get an update on any art-related publications.

Then I began trawling through the Musée's own collection of First Nations material, and found numerous French translations of art books and related works, some authored by Aboriginal writers, others by Europeans. I tried not to get bogged down in the 'typical' looking books they had, but rather focused on what was missing. I started my own inventory so I could fill in the gaps and cull anything in the present collection that was inappropriate or outdated if necessary.

The Musée's catalogue included *Yirribana* (AGNSW), *Culture Warriors* (NGA), *Peinture Aborigène Contemporaire, L'Art Indigène de l'Australie Catalogue, Musée du Quai*

Branly: Le Temps du Rêve, Wati: Les Hommes de Loi (The Law Men) and *Problematic*. Their catalogue was missing some current publications so I would need to send the list back to Emma and Lauren so I could update it.

At 6 pm I met Canelle at the staff entrance and we headed towards one of her favourite areas: Les Halles. We boarded the Métro to do my much-needed retail therapy and help my continually evolving wardrobe.

As we sat down, we saw two women at the end of the carriage wearing hijabs, fussing over three children. An elderly couple sitting opposite the women were tut-tutting and shaking their heads in disapproval of the attire. I could make out enough of their French to know what they were saying: we were in France, people don't approve of hijabs here, they should go home if they wanted to dress like that. I shook my head in disgust. I had to ask Canelle what she thought about the Islamophobia in France and other parts of Europe, and the banning of the religious item. She was onto the issue without much provocation at all.

'As a feminist, in defence of women's rights, I always thought the French were progressive and that we didn't live behind or support awful traditions like slavery but wanted to make people's lives better. People come first. This is what I thought. But I cannot believe we have banned the burqa, and people are still agitating for hijabs to be banned as well.' She seemed as bewildered and upset as I was about the issue.

'This wouldn't happen in Australia – or maybe it would,' I said. 'Only two years ago, when Switzerland banned the burqa, Australians fiercely debated the issue in the media – and not everyone felt the same way about the issue as I did.'

'Really?' Canelle was surprised.

I was desperate to defend the most banal level of rights in Australia. 'Yes, and there's no real logic to it in a rational society. Nuns used to wear full tunics they could hide guns under. And while feminists argue that the veil is oppressive to women and a symbol of men's power over us, what about women who *choose* to wear the veil?'

Canelle agreed. 'Yes, women who live in supposedly free countries and choose to wear the burqa or hijab to announce their faith or identity and so forth, where are their rights?'

'Exactly! Civilisations grow and change, or they are supposed to, but today I think France has demonstrated its archaic values. And if they were going to legislate on fashion related to ideology or religion, then why not on offensive t-shirts with swastikas and so forth? The Nazis were one of the most destructive ideological cults in history!'

'I know. They banned the swastika in Germany, so why not across Europe or the world even?' Canelle looked shattered to be living in a country that had such narrow views of the world. 'And if we thought about all the things that women do to please men, we'd ban high heels, v-neck tops, backless dresses. Women may choose to wear those things for themselves, but at the end of the day, we all know much of it is about appealing to men. And that's okay, because we are allowed to exercise our rights to do it.

And we assert our right to dress to make a statement about our identity as a woman by choosing what we wear.'

'To me it's just like how footy fans wear the colours of their club: it asserts their identity in that area.'

'I couldn't agree more,' Canelle was nodding as she spoke. 'Personally though, I think there's a health issue. I can't imagine that it's good, I mean, that black polyester in the heat. I don't know if my normal deodorant could cope with that.'

Canelle stood up suddenly, laughing. 'This is our stop. We will be happy now, Elizabeth, okay? It is time to put politics aside and shop for a while.'

'*Oui*,' I said, as she led me through the crowd of people up to the street.

'This is my favourite place to shop.' Canelle's eyes were sparkling as they scanned the area. 'It is very much a Black hip-hop area and used to be a red-light district. It is not so much now because it is being gentrified.'

I looked around at all the people and shops with sales and waited for the rest of her commentary.

'This is what we know as the heart of Paris.'

'What do you mean exactly? Is it because it is really exciting and pumping?' I studied the crowds and music flowing out from various shops.

'No, this is the point from where they measure distances to other parts of the city. Les Halles is known as the heart of Paris and Île Saint-Louis is the oldest part of the city.'

Canelle took me to some of her favourite shops and I bought a pair of tan boots, a red cashmere bolero and a slinky black dress for going out. Retail therapy really did work: cheering me up by making me feel physically beautiful and then emotionally happy. I felt uplifted when I got on the train back to the Marais.

I picked up a quiche and tarte à l'orange from Salon Marie Antoinette and ate them both in front of the telly. But as I sat there I suddenly felt totally alone. Perhaps my ability to be self-sufficient was beginning to disappear.

As I drifted into a deep sleep that night, I thought about how my relationship with Canelle mirrored my friendship with Lauren back home, where we could talk for hours about politics, and then shop for hours too.

At the end of September, I received an invitation from the Australian embassy to celebrate the Prix Nomad – an annual prize that resulted in the publication of an artist's work. It reminded me that I hadn't called Judith to arrange a meeting with Jake Ross. The Ames situation had knocked me around a bit and the call slipped through the cracks. I rsvp'd to Judith and said I'd see them both at Nomad's.

A local photographer had won the award for his photos, taken travelling around Italy, and I was looking forward to the prize-giving. I was thinking about the network-ing opportunities that might present themselves. Time was running out for me in France, as I knew my contract with the Musée would not be renewed: a new exhibition was locked in for the temporary space when mine ended.

I really wanted to find a way to stay longer if possible. I was homesick and had moments of loneliness, but I wasn't ready to leave just yet.

As I approached Nomad's, I looked forward to what the window display might be, since the restaurant changed it regularly. This time, it reflected the theme of the month – Italy – and the winner's work. There was an Italian-made car in one window – a logistical feat if nothing else – and Italian films running on a loop in another window. I was impressed by the installation and it gave me ideas about what might be possible when I got back to the NAG.

I saw Jake the minute I walked in. We locked eyes. We walked towards each other immediately, his thin lips smiling the entire time. I wanted to be able to smile the same way, but I was still suffering from Ames's betrayal and was not in the mood for flirting. But I had to try to at least be professional; I knew this was the perfect opportunity to let Jake know my contract was just about up.

'*Bonsoir*, Libby, it's good to see you.' Jake was friendly. 'I'm glad you came.'

'Oh well, you never know who you might meet in a big city like Paris, and I love this place.' I was making small talk but hoped the effort wasn't noticeable. 'It's funky, and the food's great.'

He was looking at me but I sensed he wasn't listening.

'I'm sorry I haven't lined up that meeting Judith asked for – I've been buried.' I felt guilty that I may have offended him and was worried I'd been unprofessional at the same time.

'I know, everyone's in the same boat,' Jake smiled warmly, 'it's important but not urgent. Can we have a quick chat now, before the speeches begin?' His voice had a definite diplomatic tone to it.

We sat at a table in the corner as people milled around the winner, looked at the photos on the walls, bought books and had them signed.

I looked directly into his thin-framed glasses. 'I should've asked you when we first met, who's your mob?'

'I'm a Ross from Deniliquin,' he responded proudly.

'Oh, I thought we might be related; there's a running joke where I'm from that all the good-looking people are related.'

I couldn't believe I'd just said it, but it was true. Especially with my mob, it was hard to find someone attractive to date who wasn't a Cutmore. Jake didn't seem to mind, he was grinning with his thin lips because I had unintentionally told him he was good-looking. And I had just realised that I thought he was.

'Sorry, what did you want to meet about?' I was desperate to change the subject.

He put his hands palms down on the table. 'Are you interested in some work?'

'I have a job,' I said, frowning with confusion.

'I heard your contract is up soon,' he said, taking a sip of his wine.

'How?' I nervously took a sip of my water and wondered where the conversation was heading.

'I am the first secretary at the Australian embassy, and I'm a Blackfella.' He sounded slightly defensive and offended that I was answering his questions with my own questions. 'So, aside from being the ambassador's right-hand man, fostering links with key French decision-makers in government and industry, managing the major policy advocacy and reporting requirements of the embassy *and* overseeing high-level visits to France, I also make it my business to know what contracts Blackfellas have here, when they end, et cetera. I'd like to keep more of us employed here if I can. And, we have a relationship with the Musée, as you know.'

'Of course, I'm sorry, I'm a little vague tonight,' I said apologetically, feeling like a complete fool. Of course he knew what was going on with me, it was his job. 'You'd know then that I met with Judith and we set the wheels in motion for two of the Musée's featured artists to be represented by two small galleries here.'

'Yes, I know. I asked Judith to take control of the issue, because . . .' He paused and took a deep breath. 'Because I was attracted to you the night I met you and I didn't know if I could separate my personal interest in seeing you again and my responsibility to work with you professionally in the arts. And I was embarrassed when you didn't respond to the text so I got Judith to respond to your email.'

Jake had just vomited the whole speech in one breath and I was so shocked that I wasn't able to interrupt. I couldn't believe it. He was behaving seriously inappropriately, I thought, if he was sober. And if he was drunk, then he should really stay off the juice, for everyone's sake.

'Oh,' was all I could say, and the surprise must've shown on my face, as he looked equally and suitably embarrassed.

'But for the record, I wasn't trying to sleaze onto you or anything. It was strictly a professional invitation. Can we move on from that now?'

'Yes, please. I'm sorry too, and I appreciate your honesty, there's not a lot of it around these days.'

Jake didn't respond at all and it was awkward.

'It's funny, you know?'

'What is?' he asked, almost nervously.

'Sometimes I have to remind myself I'm just a Koori girl in Paris. It's easy to get lost in the sea of other Black faces here.' We both looked around the restaurant. 'I can't believe how many people I've met here from Senegal, Mali, the Ivory Coast.'

'Not to mention the Black Caribbeans from Haiti, Guadeloupe and Martinique,' he added to my list.

'I know. Canelle is from Guadeloupe, so it was like meeting up with another tidda here in so many ways. I feel like I'm at home. I think I might've struggled if I'd chosen to go to a Nordic country.'

'If you really do feel comfortable and want to stay, there is a job on offer when your contract is up.' He sounded impatient as he stood up. 'I have to talk to some guests now, but it's a genuine offer, and we'd love to have you on staff. I've only had good reports about the work you've done at the Musée.'

He touched my elbow gently, obviously not wanting to cross any more lines. I smiled and nodded.

When I arrived at 10 am at the embassy a few weeks later, it was quiet. I signed in, helped myself to the antiseptic gel on the counter and wondered how many germs I may have picked up on the train journey.

I looked at the photos of Julia Gillard and Quentin Bryce and a bust of Nicolas Thomas Baudin – a French-born mariner, explorer and botanist – in the foyer. There were also Aboriginal and Torres Strait Islander flags in the uncluttered space, which was noticeably quiet for somewhere so close to the street.

I sat and waited nervously for Jake to collect me. I had no idea what the job was, just that I wanted to stay. Jake was warm but in diplomatic mode when he collected me from reception.

We got the lift to the first floor and went to the café. I liked the space, with its orange-and-brown leather bucket chairs and plenty of light.

'There's sixty embassy staff here, made up of the Australian delegation to France, a delegate to UNESCO and another to the OECD. These are all Australian-based staff: diplomatic, fixed-term and employed by DFAT.'

Jake was very formal, so I followed his lead. 'Where and how exactly would I fit into that structure, given my very specific background in visual arts?' I couldn't imagine what I might do.

'We're just about to begin a short-term contract to look at developing Indigenous arts and culture in Western

Europe, and the position will be based in Paris. Here at the embassy.'

'Who's funding it?' I asked, more out of curiosity than anything else.

'First Nations Tourism and a silent philanthropist,' he advised.

The job sounded perfect. 'Will the position be advertised? I mean, what's the process of appointment?'

Jake leaned forward in his chair. 'I have the authority to appoint, and professionally I can't think of anyone more suited. Judith gave you a good reference, as did the Musée, and I have had some email communication with your boss Emma at the NAG. She gave you a glowing reference as well.'

I couldn't believe this had been discussed behind my back. I was not only surprised but a little annoyed that I hadn't been included in the conversations. 'All of that without me even knowing?'

'You must understand that a range of security and employment criteria are always sorted out before an appointment can even be flagged with a potential staff member, Libby.' I was starting to realise the important role Jake had at the embassy and hated myself for not paying him more respect that first night.

I had one major doubt screaming in my mind. 'Is my French good enough?'

'You'll probably need some more language training as there will be meetings with foreign ministry people in French, and the protocol is that you should speak their language.'

'Of course, I don't know how I've gotten away with it for so long here. Or should I say: *Je ne sais pas comment je m'évade depuis si longtemps ici.*'

Jake smiled politely and then looked at his watch. 'I have a teleconference in ten minutes so I'll have to go. Here's a copy of the job description and selection criteria.'

He handed me the document and our hands brushed awkwardly.

We looked at each other and then the paper.

'The position reports to Judith and you'll need to send her an up-to-date CV and application addressing the criteria if you're interested. If you could do it by the end of the week, it would be good to get the paperwork sorted sooner rather than later.'

He stood up, so I did as well.

'I'm flattered that you think I am capable of the role. I really do need to speak to my colleagues back at the NAG to make sure I'm not leaving the team in the lurch. I also need to talk to my family.' I was grateful to the point of wanting to explode with excitement and just hoped there was no tone of arrogance in my voice.

'Of course, I completely understand.'

He shook my hand gently but firmly and smiled with his thin lips. He had dimples that I hadn't noticed before. I smiled back and thought how sexy some influential, authoritative men could appear, even to those no longer interested in men.

I called Mum as soon as I got home that night. 'Hi Mum,' I said excitedly. 'It's me, Libby.'

'Hi there, it's Mum,' she said.

I had to laugh: of course it was Mum.

'How are you?' she asked first, and without giving me the chance to answer she added, 'Your brothers ask about you all the time, and wonder if you speak with a French accent now.'

'*Oui, Maman*, tell my brothers *c'est vrai*,' I said, turning the accent on as severely as I could.

I could hear her giggling like a schoolgirl down the line. 'Mum, I'm having a great time, working hard, meeting amazing people and even other Blackfellas here. One's just offered me a job at the Australian Embassy. I think I should take it.' It was an affirmation to make the statement out loud.

'Dear girl, a job at the Australian embassy! I can't wait to tell the ladies at line dancing. Can you send me a letter with the details so I can read it out to them, please? Don't send me an email, I can't get the printer to work.'

'Yes, I'll send a letter. I also bought you a nice scarf from a fella near the Eiffel Tower to keep you warm in winter. I'll post it this week.'

'You know, Libby, if you didn't give me a present I'd never get one, your brothers are hopeless. Your father never missed a birthday or anniversary and I always got a present, and a card.'

'Dad never wrote on the cards though, Mum.'

'No, he didn't, but he went to the paper shop and bought them. You know he couldn't write very well, it was the thought and effort that counted.'

I could hear some racket in the faraway background.

'Okay, the grannies have just arrived, I better go and make something to eat for them.'

'Hug and kiss everyone for me, please, and I'll write you this week with all the details and my dates, okay?'

'Okay.'

Mum was gone before I was ready to hang up, but I could just picture the chaos that was unfolding back at her place right now.

Before going to sleep that night I emailed the girls about the proposed new job and Jake:

Tiddas, I have EXCITING NEWS – yes, I am yelling it. I've been offered the potential to stay another six months and set up a new project based at the embassy. There's a Blackfella who's first secretary, his name is Jake Ross. Do any of you know him? Can we all FaceTime Friday night? I miss your voices and your daggy Aussie accents.

On Friday night Caro, Lauren and I all got on WhatsApp. Bec was away on school camp. It was great to see the girls on my screen.

'Well, I've got some details on Mr Jake Ross,' said Caro. He's thirty-eight and there's a wife somewhere in country New South Wales, but no-one seems to know what she does. He's from Deniliquin. Background in international relations and used to be deputy director general of Aboriginal Affairs, New South Wales.'

'Really? He's married up, eh?' I said. 'That's interesting. I didn't see a ring on any finger of either hand, and he was pretty good at mentioning how beautiful I happened to be.'

'Do you need a comment from me here, Libs?' Caro raised an eyebrow.

'No, I'm good, got it all sorted myself, thanks.'

'Does he look like a firey?' Lauren wanted to know. 'What's he look like anyway?'

'Glasses, thin lips, eyes too close together. Bit of a nerd actually. But Canelle reckons he's got a nice arse. I haven't looked. And clearly don't care.' I tried not to think about noticing his dimples.

'When's the job start?' asked Caro, all business.

'As soon as I finish at the Musée, which is perfect. But is everything cool at the NAG, Lauren? I don't want to leave you in the lurch.'

'Are you kidding? Nancia is all over your job, we'll be fine,' said Lauren, waving a hand lazily to show she had everything under control.

'Thanks for making me feel missed.' I frowned.

'I'm kidding. I'm just so glad you nailed the Musée. I extended my contract too, remember? This is good news for everyone, sis.' I could tell Lauren really meant it.

'I'm really happy, really. The feedback has been great from the staff and the visitors and I've got masses of ideas for when I get back, but seriously, five months wasn't long enough. There's still so much to see here. But right now I've gotta go, loads of love. Tell Bec I'm still waiting for photos from Bali, she hasn't sent any!'

'Hey, we haven't seen them either,' said Caro. 'We reckon they just banged the whole time.'

'Nice. See you girls, love you to bits. But can you please send me some pics of Bonnie and Clyde so I have proof they're still alive?'

Lauren aimed her camera down at Bonnie, sleeping on her lap. 'Say bye bye, Bonnie!'

'Oh my god! Bye, beautiful!'

'I'm out of here,' said Caro, laughing.

Caro was gone and then Lauren and then me. I hadn't told them how much I truly missed them. I should have.

Chapter 18

The Ancestors have a plan

Four weeks later at the end of November, winter had settled in Paris and I had settled into my new embassy workspace overlooking the Eiffel Tower.

I had easily coordinated the logistics of staying on in France. I realised the Ancestors were looking over me, and they were being kind again. Even Adrien had come around by the time I left the Musée, making a speech at my farewell afternoon tea, commenting on how much he'd learned about Indigenous protocols through working with me. Resolution and reconciliation was a good way to go out.

Dom and Catherine were thrilled to have me stay and cooked a special meal to celebrate. Extending my lease was no problem at all, and they didn't even want to put an expiry date on it. There were a couple of things that needed doing in the flat, including hanging new curtains, so Catherine bought some material and I paid Sorina – whose business continued to flourish – to sew them for me. Catherine liked Sorina's work so much she recommended her to another tenant on the fourth floor.

Dom hung a new framed print I'd bought from *les banlieues* and suggested he put track lighting over it. I was worried they thought I'd never leave. I don't think they wanted me to. Dom felt like the father I'd never had growing up. I wanted to take him back to Canberra to do all the 'fatherly duties' around my flat in Braddon. Romeo the poodle had started coming up to my apartment to keep me company on occasion as well.

Bec had messaged to say she and Dave were moving in together and that they'd love to take my flat and the cats and would mind both for the rest of the time I was away. It all fell into place quickly and when it happened without too much effort, I knew it was all meant to be.

With my new ability to 'forgive', I had gotten over Ames, sort of, and I was back to thriving in Paris. I couldn't believe that my life had become even more amazing and monumentally better with the job opportunity at the embassy.

I was building the new position from the ground up and was both challenged and inspired by the opportunity it presented to me, as well as the potential the role had to showcase even more First Nations artists across Europe. I had ideas about interdisciplinary exhibitions with writers and visual artists, collaborations between Aboriginal and Basque artists. There was potential for a touring arts market. I felt like anything was possible, and that I had this new sense of professional invincibility. I was back to being happy with the only relationship that ever truly satisfied me: my career.

I worked directly with Judith. With her super-efficient working methods and appreciation of a glass of wine, we quickly became friends. She had a background in languages and her dry wit and worldliness reminded me of Caro. She only had a few months left in her job though, and was taking a post in Barcelona. It made me wonder how my new job might also springboard me somewhere else.

'Libby, the ambassador is going to Australia next week and is keen to meet with some First Nations curators and artists, given your new role here. Can you draft up a brief for me on the key players, with relevant contacts?' Judith was at my desk holding a cup of coffee.

'Of course, I'll get it to you by COB. Sounds great.'

'Here are some names that have come through from the Australia Council and others already.'

She handed me a sheet with a list of appropriate people from the NAG, the MCA, AGNSW, Queensland Art Gallery and two regional galleries.

'This is my ultimate dream job, Judith. I'm getting paid to do what I love. I'm all over this.' I waved the page.

'I'm pleased on both fronts,' she said, turning. 'Oh, are you coming for a drink at Matilda's tonight?'

'Where is it?' I'd never heard of Matilda's and hoped it wasn't 'Waltzing'. I had fairly strict rules about not visiting Australian bars overseas.

'It's the embassy social club bar, it's in-house. It's only open to embassy staff, and our friends.'

'Sounds *très* deadly,' I said.

'I'll come get you about sixish.'

At 6.15 pm we headed down to the makeshift bar where staff, their family and friends were already mingling. I was proud to hear Thelma Plum playing in the background and there was an end-of-week buzz of relief in the air.

'This is great!' I whispered to Judith. 'Is it every Friday?'

'Every second Friday,' she said, as we weaved through the crowd towards the bar, 'and it's staffed by volunteer social club members. There's usually music, or a special theme, sometimes there's karaoke or trivia nights.'

'What's tonight?' I asked, before realising everyone was wearing a hat.

'Hat night.' She passed me a fire warden's helmet from the table of hats.

I laughed as I put it on my head. 'You have no idea how apt this choice of headwear is for me. I collect firey calendars.'

'So do I,' she said, high-fiving me. 'But don't tell anyone here. I have them sent in brown-paper wrapping to a friend's place in the 15th and pick them up from there. Can't hang them at work, but it's one of my small pleasures from home.'

'Ah, but tidda, it's all in the name of fundraising, isn't it?' Those like Judith and I always found ways to legitimise our calendar fetish.

'Of course, or fun-raising, as my friend calls it.'

I liked Judith. She had done incredibly well to get where she was at the embassy, and was super intelligent. I respected her ability to be professional but also to be able to enjoy herself, but I daresay that was a skill she honed in Paris.

'Can you order me a calendar when you next order yours, please?' I smiled but was completely serious.

'Consider it done.'

As I looked around the room at all the staff I was still to meet – some in beanies, others in baseball caps, one in a top hat – I couldn't believe this was where I now worked.

'So, why do they do this so often?'

'It's just a good opportunity to meet staff in a casual atmosphere,' Judith said. 'You can be my wing-woman tonight, if you like.'

'Thanks,' I said, spotting Jake across the room.

He waved me over, and I was glad to see him. I wanted to thank him for one of the best working weeks of my life.

'Just going to say hello to first sec,' I said, heading in his direction. 'I'll catch up with you.'

'Okay, I'll be around.' She winked at me as I walked off. I felt bad leaving her, but she knew everyone anyway, and wing-woman or not, I'm sure she didn't want to have to entertain me all night.

Jake shook hands with a man wearing a similar navy suit to his and walked towards me. He was wearing an Australian cricket cap.

'How's the first week been?' he asked, toasting my glass of Australian wine.

'Challenging, interesting, inspiring!' I answered in all honesty, but the first drink had immediately made me woozy and I hoped it didn't affect my speech.

The Australian wine hit me much harder than the local stuff did. I rarely ever got drunk in Paris. Wine was for appreciation when dining here, not quaffing like we used to do on our girls' nights out. And the champagne was the good stuff, so you never got a hangover, regardless of how much you drank. Paris had already been a good detox for me, although on this occasion I was well on my way to getting legless if I kept up my current pace.

Jake and I made small talk about my first week at work and I told him about how I'd moved on the strategy. It was good to debrief with him, and he seemed happy with the progress I'd made so far. We chatted for about twenty minutes, never straying from work-related topics.

Soon enough, *dernières boissons* were called, and the booze was being put away. People started moving quickly out of the building. I really wanted to sit somewhere quiet and eat something, and could easily have gone home.

'Come to Au Dernier Métro,' Judith said, 'it's where we always go after Matilda's.'

Judith was like the embassy's Canelle in terms of organising people and social events. Perhaps that's why I got on with them both so well. In many ways they were like me when I was back home.

'Where?' My ears were ringing from the music and I was slightly disoriented.

'Au Dernier Métro, it's a bistro on boulevard de Grenelle at Métro Dupleix. It opens late, it doesn't cost an arm and a leg for a drink, and we usually go there because the diplomats and their families live in the apartments above the bar here, and noise can be a problem. That's why last drinks were called just now.'

'Fair enough.' I was finding the noise a bit of a problem myself.

'Just come for a drink,' Judith said, slightly flushed. I loved her energy.

I was starting to feel really out of it. 'I don't think I can drink any more. I've got things I need to do tomorrow.'

'Come for the best steak then. Trust me, you won't be disappointed.'

Judith had me by the arm and led me out of the building. Jake and eight others were in tow also. The thought of a steak inspired me along, as did the opportunity to hang with my new embassy friends.

We walked into Au Dernier Métro and it was bustling with a whole array of characters: locals, tourists, and Australian embassy staff. The space was vibrant, cultured, busy and I imagined it was the classic French bar. The music in the bar mirrored what was being played across Paris: Arya Starr's 'Rush' which I listened to on rotation some days when commuting to work.

'The best steaks this side of Wagga,' Judith said, as she made her way to a table up the back of the bar near the kitchen. 'That's the only other place I've tasted steak this good.'

'Really?' I screamed over the noise.

'I always have the Landes duck confit, always.'

The waiters and waitresses were in red sports shirts and spoke in French too fast for me to translate over the noise, but Judith was onto it.

'There's ten of us and only room for six at the table,' she said, as two fellas I didn't know immediately squeezed their way back to the bar.

'I'm not coping with the noise, I might head somewhere else for dinner and come back,' Jake said.

I was hating the loud conversation and with Arya still singing over it all I thought my head would explode. I was immediately tempted when Jake asked, 'Do you want to join me?'

But I was recalling the night we met, the fact that I knew he was married and he was still my boss. And I knew that Paris could turn anyone from being decent and faithful to dirty and flirty. Then someone pushed hard into my back as more partygoers arrived and I had to get out of there.

'Yes, thanks.'

We slipped out and no-one even noticed, let alone cared, that we were gone.

Jake took me to Café Procope in the 6th arrondissement. 'This is the oldest café in Paris,' he said as we were seated.

'Monsieur, I believe it may be the oldest café in the world,' the waiter politely corrected Jake.

'I have heard that too,' Jake agreed, knowing the importance of not getting your waiter offside.

I had French onion soup for an entrée, which was nothing like what I'd ever had back home in Moree, where it usually came out of a foil pack that you added boiling water to. Rather, the real deal had a lid of cheese across the top which made it sufficient for a whole meal. I didn't need the beef burgundy pie that followed, but was glad to have had it. I knew, like the bread I could never eat back in Australia, a standard pie would never touch my lips again either.

All the while I was appreciating the food and the extraordinary surroundings, I felt Jake staring at me. I didn't want to acknowledge to myself or to anyone else that there was chemistry, but it was there. And so was he. And so was I. I knew he was married but there was no ring to be seen. *Maybe you really are a sleazebag*, I thought to myself.

I broke the awkward silence. 'So, how did you end up here, all the way from Deniliquin?'

Jake counted the steps of his career trajectory on his fingers. 'I did International Relations at UNSW, went straight to DFAT as a cadet, got my first posting to Vietnam, went back to Canberra briefly, was seconded to the Department of Aboriginal Affairs in Sydney for two years and when this post came up I was headhunted for it. And that's how I got here, in a nutshell.'

With a level of restrained pride on his face, I could see that he was trying to impress me.

'Wow, how do you leave your family for so long?' I noticed the absence of any mention of wife and kids.

With a hint of I-don't-miss-people machismo, he said, 'My family are scattered around Australia doing all kinds of things and so we hardly see each other anyway. I don't have kids so it wasn't that hard to make the choice.'

'No partner?' I was prying, I knew, but there had to be more to his story than he was letting on. 'Sorry, that's personal.'

'No, it's fine. Most of the staff here have families so it's a fair question.' He looked me straight in the eye. 'I had a partner for a long time. I married my high school sweetheart in Deni when I was twenty, she was eighteen, but she never wanted to leave the Riverina, so married life was hard. I had to leave to study and then to work. The constant commute was hard but worth it.'

I could almost feel my eyes pop out of my head. 'Wow.'

'What? You think I'm selfish?'

'No, not at all. I was actually wondering what might keep someone in Deni as opposed to going to Paris.'

Jake got immediately defensive. 'Deni's great, it's my home. Some days I'd kill for Saturday morning brekky at The Crossing Café, or just to listen to 2QN, the local radio station. God, I miss community radio and country music too. Mostly I miss the red river gums I used to lie under to read the paper on weekends. I had peace in Deni, it's something you can never really have in Paris because there's so much going on all the time.'

It was like Jake was in a world of his own, thinking back to his life in New South Wales.

'And there was *no* work there for you?'

'There hasn't been, but if the CEO job comes up at the Yarkuwa Indigenous Knowledge Centre then I'll throw my hat in the ring. It would be the perfect opportunity to work with the local mob again, but until then I'm here.'

'Here's not that bad, eh?' I turned my palms to the ceiling as if to say, *look at the gift the Ancestors placed in our hands.*

'The truth, Libby, is that I'm here doing all this to pay tribute to my folks. They had nothing.' Jake was still justifying himself to me. 'They worked hard to put me through Catholic school. I was smart, I wanted to go to uni. I wanted to make some social change, make a mark in the world, make something of my life. The life that they had given me through their own sacrifice.'

'And your wife?'

'I wanted her by my side, but she didn't want the big city. She came to Vietnam but only lasted a couple of months. And there were no opportunities for me in Australia,' he said sadly. 'She wanted to be a yoga instructor in Deni and I supported her desire for that – emotionally and financially – and we tried to make it work. But it didn't.'

'Wanting your own business is admirable,' I said. I wasn't impressed with the easy way in which he seemed to have written his wife off.

'Of course, it's admirable. But it wasn't feasible. I bankrolled it for years, sent her to Byron, Melbourne and even India to train and network. I bought every video and book possible and endorsed her going to Mind, Body Spirit festivals so she could find her *chakras*,' he said with a roll of his eyes and a tone of sarcasm. 'And you know what she did with all that training and reading and festival-ing?'

I was almost too frightened to ask. 'She set up her own yoga studio?' I asked with trepidation.

'I wish. She did a few pathetic stretches with her friends each morning in our living room and then they spent the day drinking coffee and eating sticky-date pudding. It pissed me off.' He sighed deeply.

I was sure it wasn't as straightforward as he claimed but who was I to protest: I hated yoga.

'Look, I didn't care if she ate cake all day, it's just,' he paused, 'there was always something missing.'

I couldn't wait to hear what was missing, I felt like I was sitting through the rural Australian version of *The Bold and the Beautiful*.

'What?'

'She liked yoga but she wasn't passionate about it, or business. She didn't do anything to grow it. She didn't learn about how to market it or do any business courses. She didn't get what being in a business meant.

'I realise now that her view of the whole thing was symbolic of how she viewed our relationship. How she viewed me. She didn't get me either. Or what I stood for in the cause. She wasn't passionate about anything. Just happy to go along, exist, rather than love and live passionately.'

I couldn't believe how harsh Jake was about his ex's lack of business skills. And he must be really superficial to leave a woman who preferred sticky-date pudding to doing bookwork – even I, with no sweet-tooth, could relate to that. Our conversation was heavy for a work-related dinner, but I chose not to say anything about it.

'And so you left your wife and came to Paris?' I was still hardly impressed with his behaviour.

Jake looked shocked at my question. 'No, I didn't leave, she left. She had an affair with a frigger who came to Deni for the ute muster.'

'A what at the what?'

'A bloke at the ute muster. You haven't heard of the muster?' I shook my head.

'Deni's the "ute capital of the world",' he said, making air quotes, 'and every year about twenty-five thousand-plus friggers – station workers – come from around the world for a parade and festival. I never went, Suzanne always did. Now I know why.'

I had visions of his ex trying to show ute drivers how to do the downward-facing dog pose at the muster. I felt sorry for Jake, I felt the raw pain of being cheated on myself; the humiliation of it and the lingering question of 'why?'.

Jake went on as if he needed the chance to explain himself. 'I tried to get her back, but we both knew there was no point. She basically said she never loved me the way she loved him.

'A week later, the post to Paris was offered and there was no reason for me not to take it. The Ancestors had spoken and provided both a practical and emotional escape for me. So here I am.'

I liked that he acknowledged the Ancestors' role in his journey as I did in mine.

'Here you are, but hearing you talking about her now, it doesn't sound like you're completely over her.'

He shrugged. 'I'm over her. I've just never talked to anyone about it. Men don't. Well, not the men I know anyway, and I only have one real mate here in Paris. At my level, junior staff don't make friends with you and I'm also on the road a lot so the social life is contained to nights like tonight.

'And trust me, even this dinner is a rare thing. Since I've arrived I've been completely immersed in my work, and my days include extraordinarily long hours. It was the easiest way to move on.' He paused. 'I'm sorry, I'm raving.'

I felt the need to comfort him. 'No, don't apologise. I have five brothers, and I'm sure they would never sit down and talk like that, even though they probably should.' I imagined my poor mother having to sit through and deal with all the emotional fallout that my brothers brought with them for Sunday dinner.

'It's a bloke thing.'

'Do you still love her?' I don't know why I asked, but I did.

Jake looked up from his wineglass momentarily, then spoke. 'I thought I would never stop loving her. I thought I could never love anyone else. I felt like I was in the same place emotionally for a long time, and then I just turned a corner and found the capacity to move on, to even love again one day. It's only natural. Does that make sense?'

'Not really.'

He looked disappointed.

'I don't think it's only natural to love again if you've been shattered. Or if it is, it's only natural for some, but not me.'

He looked at me oddly. 'How can that be?'

'What?'

'That love's not possible for you?' He sounded confused.

'Track record, I guess, and the universe, or the Ancestors, or both in cahoots making me jump hurdles all the time. I'm over it.'

'You're single then?' Jake said, more as a confirmation than a question.

'Yes, I wouldn't be in Paris if I was married up – white-fella or Blackfella way.'

Jake winced slightly, then said, 'I can't believe you haven't been snapped up.'

'Apparently it's the sixty-million-dollar question.' I could hear the sarcasm in my voice, and the girls back home nagging me about love, romance and the One.

'Can I be honest with you?' Jake leant forwards over the table. I smiled. 'Haven't you been honest all along?'

'Yes,' he laughed. 'Of course. It's just that . . .' He paused, took a sip of his wine, and went on. 'I've had too much to drink now and really shouldn't be saying this,' he said, taking another sip of wine, 'but when I saw you at Nomad's, I thought you were the most beautiful woman I'd ever seen, I even told you as much on the night.'

I thought back to the comment that seemed sleazy at the time.

Jake continued, looking directly into my eyes.

'You had a presence that made me nervous. And clearly it made me stupid as well, because I sent that text to you the next morning.'

I was embarrassed, not only because Jake was flattering me and I didn't know how to cope with it, but because I could also feel my attraction to him. It wasn't just physical – he seemed like an honest man who was a go-getter professionally. He'd left Deni – like I'd left Moree – to do the things our parents had wanted for us.

His thin lips and narrowly-placed eyes began to look attractive across the table. And I liked his laugh. But I wasn't going to like him. I didn't want to like him. I could still feel the humiliation of Ames's infidelity every time I thought about it. And the disappointment, the pain of the disappointment. There was no way I could like Jake. I shifted uncomfortably in my seat.

He finally broke the silence. 'I'm sorry, I didn't mean to embarrass you.'

'It's all good.'

I wasn't going to tell him of my disasters back home, or walking in to find Ames in the bath with a skeleton. I didn't want to keep talking about his relationship either, but curiosity got the better of me. I wanted to know how men simply moved on from one woman to the next.

'Do you still talk? To your ex?'

'She sends the odd email and by that I mean the emails are "odd".' He shook his head. 'She talks about dreams for her yoga retreat and the next festival she'll attend to network, but she still hasn't done much more than that. There's been opportunities for her to do things, and in hindsight I think I was the goose that made her life too easy, which enabled her to be lazy and just fluff around. It's funny what we realise when the love-goggles are off.'

'Tell me about it!' I raised my glass in the air.

'Libby, can I ask you to keep this conversation between us? No-one knew me when I arrived, so I didn't have to answer questions about my marriage and so forth. And although I've just blabbered on to you, I'd rather keep my private life private. Especially in the diplomatic world. Anyway, there's far more interesting things to talk about than my disastrous love-life.'

'Oh, I don't know, I think there might be a musical in that story somewhere.' It was getting easier to share with Jake as we relaxed with coffees.

'Just sitting here with you . . .' Jake smiled. 'I actually miss just sitting and yarning with Blackfellas about anything. We have artists and academics pass through but it's fleeting, and discussions are usually short and always about work and community politics back home and . . .'

'And what?'

He gave me a look that made me feel uneasy. 'None of them are anywhere near as pretty as you are.'

My mouth opened in utter disbelief and I put my hand up in the STOP pose. 'Hang on, you've just been raving about the love of your life for the past half-hour, it's not really timely for you to be trying to flatter another woman.'

I couldn't believe how men would have a crack any chance they got. Jake was just as sleazy as I'd thought he was the first night we met.

'She wasn't the love of my life,' he said defensively.

I raised my eyebrows. 'I think my friends back home might argue that with you.'

'Fine, I'll argue it.' He sounded angry. 'The one lesson I learned from that experience was that your soulmate or the love of your life is the one who feels the same way about you. She didn't. Granted, she was the woman I loved for a lot of my life. I've never loved another one. But I tell you what, if you haven't noticed it, Paris is the perfect place to start believing in love again.'

Of course I had noticed it. It had ended up causing me heartache with Ames.

'As long as you don't want monogamous love,' I said sarcastically. 'Is anyone faithful here?'

'I'd be faithful,' he said, as if I had accused him.

'I was talking about the French, Jake,' I snapped. 'I wasn't hitting on you, if that's what you were thinking. There would be so many things wrong with that, if I was. I wasn't.'

'Geez, you know how to wound a man, thanks.' Jake feigned being shot in the heart. 'But that aside, what things would be wrong exactly?'

'You're my boss, for starters. I thought this was just two Blackfellas having dinner like we should've done as soon as I arrived. Secondly, aren't there protocols for social behaviour in your job? And finally, and most importantly, it's clear you're still in love with whatever her name is.'

I sounded like I was a little jealous, but I wasn't, I was more annoyed at how stupid men were most of the time.

'To respond to your accusations, or whatever they are,' Jake said in his diplomatic voice. 'Firstly, I am not your "boss" as such. Judith is your boss. Secondly, this *is* a dinner between Blackfellas and yes, we should've done it earlier but to be completely honest, I was so nervous about you I couldn't organise it after I sent that text message. I thought you'd think I was a lunatic. And this dinner, well, I kind of planned it, hoping you would join me this evening.'

I was shocked and must have looked it.

'That's right. I asked Judith to make sure you knew about the drinks event so that I could see you there – I didn't tell her that of course. Judith has worked with me since I arrived. She probably thinks I'm asexual, she's never seen me with anyone, and would never ask. She's a consummate professional, that's why I like working with her.'

I just sat listening, fury building up at his sleaziness.

'I come here quite a bit, so it was easy to have a table on hold for me tonight. I hoped that you would have dinner with me.'

Could this guy get any more arrogant? Who did he think he was, aside from being the first secretary? He was just another fella from New South Wales. Bazza would put him on his arse in two seconds flat if he had too many assumptions or expectations of me. And then I reminded myself that no man in the history of men in my life had ever pre-booked a table in the hope of eating with me. Still, that hardly made up for the presumptuousness.

He wasn't finished. 'And thank you for being concerned about my ability to adhere to policies of behaviour in my position. I am aware of my professional responsibilities and how to behave in my role but, for godsake, and this might surprise you, even *I* am allowed to have a private life. Having dinner with you is included in that.'

He took a breath as I felt appropriately chastised and, against my better judgement, mildly impressed by his diplomatic tone and mature outlook.

'Finally, I am not still in love with her. I did love her. Past tense. There's no need for me to be anything but honest with you. She was my first love. She's the only woman I've ever loved. And quite frankly, with such heartache it was hard to imagine I'd ever be swept away again. And then I saw you outside Nomad's after Terri Janke's launch and I was immediately captivated. But you never gave me the chance to even talk to you.'

'I thought maybe you'd had too much to drink,' I said flippantly.

'I'd had three wines all evening, Libby, so I wasn't drunk.' He stared into my eyes. 'I know everyone thinks diplomats are notorious drunks, but contrary to what you've seen here tonight, I'm not one of them. And I certainly wasn't drunk when I woke up the next morning and you were the first thing on my mind. I haven't been drunk every day since, when I've wanted to see you and speak to you.'

'So you created the job to keep me here?' I was beginning to think Jake had used his power and position to do something completely unethical and it made me feel incredibly uneasy.

He shook his head. 'No, I didn't. The position was in the pipeline long before you even arrived in Paris. It was only finalised weeks ago, as you know. And I didn't even put your name up for it. Your boss Emma did. There was some headhunting done and some proposals put up, and that's how you got the job. I really had no say in it.'

'Fair enough.' I was glad he hadn't been involved, and yet strangely disappointed at the same time.

'It just felt like the universe was finally on my side. You mightn't agree, but she can be a bitch sometimes.'

I couldn't believe that Jake thought the same way. All I could say was, 'Yes, she can. But the Ancestors will always have our backs.'

He smiled and nodded. 'The truth is, Libby, that I've stood back these past months and just followed your work at the Musée from a distance.'

This guy really is a stalker!

'And I've heard nothing but good reports this past week about people you've dealt with and it's not that I'm watching your every move, because I'm not. God knows I haven't got time.'

Of course he's not a stalker, he's the first secretary.

'But what I like about you, Libby, aside from your eyes and your hair and the way you walk, is that you're a doer. You get things done. You're young and passionate and an inspiration to other Black women. That's the kind of woman I want on my team, and in my life.' He blushed as much as a Blackfella could blush. 'You know what I mean.'

'So that's it then?' I wasn't quite sure what else I expected him to say but I didn't have anything else to contribute and I was torn between his sleaziness and his extreme attractiveness in being a Black diplomat who was impressed with my own work ethic. I needed to sober up fast.

'No, that's not it. I think you're gorgeous and I like that about you too. But mostly I find you have a positive energy that's infectious. I feel like I want to smile around you. There are few people in life who touch us so deeply, so quickly. I know I hardly know you, but you've done it.'

At that point I thought he was a complete crackpot. Why was he telling me all this stuff? He had to be more drunk than I was. I had to get out of there, but before I could get the message from my brain to my body to move, he put his hand on mine.

I felt a bolt of electricity go through me, right up my arms and into my belly and down to my loins. It took my breath away but I didn't want it to. Not after everything I'd been through. I'd been cheated on and lied to and disappointed, and now this thin-lipped, titanium-framed, curly haired bloke from Deniliquin was making me want to feel from the heart again.

But I liked his hand on mine. It felt right. Perhaps Jake was correct about the Ancestors leading us to this city. But the whole underdeveloped notion went against my plan for Paris – if indeed I were to meet a man, he was supposed to be exotically European: a bum-pinching Italian, a salsa-dancing Spaniard, a flirtatious Frenchman. Not a Blackfella from Deniliquin, the ute-muster capital of the world!

I needed to get back to my flat and make a list: pros and cons. My lists always gave me the answers, clarified the situation. At the top of my cons list was the fact that Jake appeared to be an emotionally unbalanced man having just passed a whole heap of very intimate information onto a woman on a *not* first date. If a man falls for a woman that quickly, he's likely to fall out of love quickly as well. I was really starting to freak out at his behaviour.

'I have to go,' I said. 'I'll walk you to a cab.'

As he stood and turned to take his coat from the maître d', I finally saw what Canelle meant about his nice arse. For a fleeting moment, I imagined him naked: the broad-shouldered, thin-lipped, taut-bummed Mr Universe from Deniliquin.

I'd had too much to drink and followed him carefully to the front of the restaurant and onto the street. The night air was cold and hit my face hard enough to sober me slightly, for which I was glad. I needed my wits about me. Jake mightn't be my boss, but he was Judith's and I needed to keep focused on the job and not add any unnecessary hurdles.

Jake fidgeted with his keys and looked at the footpath while I looked to the street for a cab.

He moved closer to me, then said, 'I'm a little embarrassed now, Libby, and I'm sorry for putting you on the spot like that. But I know what I feel inside. I've only felt it once before, and I know enough from my experience that it's best to be honest and straightforward up-front.'

I felt sorry for Jake, and I didn't want it to be awkward between us at the embassy, so I just said, 'Don't be embarrassed. I'm flattered, but I really don't want to start something. We have to work together.'

He put his hands around my waist and laughed softly. 'God, you make it sound like we have to abide by a code of ethics to have a drink. I can't control my heart, Libby. Maybe you can.'

My own heart raced as he pulled me towards him. He

didn't say anything. I didn't say anything. We just stood pinned to each other.

I could feel the muscles in his torso through his shirt. They felt the way I'd imagined every fireman's in every calendar I had ever bought would feel. I tried to ignore how his hardness made me weak and his heartbeat caused my own to race.

Time seemed to stand still as he leant in closer and I reluctantly met him halfway. He kissed me softly, warmly, and he tasted sweet after the dessert wine. My head began to spin with desire and I wanted to pull him even closer. Even though I still wanted his thin lips on mine, I pushed him away.

I was determined but inwardly disappointed, because on paper he was almost perfect for me. 'No. I don't want this.'

'I'm sorry,' he said, as if being chastised by a parent.

'Whatever this is, I don't want it.' I looked to the street for a cab and also to avoid his eyes.

'I'm sorry if you feel I disrespected you.' Jake sounded contrite as he tried to catch my gaze. 'I don't want you to think I took advantage.'

My body was aching with desire in a way I'd never experienced before and I wanted to be taken advantage of, but I didn't want to ruin my whole professional life by falling into a passionate heap for one night. It was disrespectful, he should've known better. He was the first secretary. I was a contractor. It could only end up as another disaster for me.

'Let's just stay colleagues, all right?' I was annoyed that Jake had put me in that position, but I didn't want to rock the work boat so I told myself to remain pleasant and just get home.

He looked crestfallen but didn't say anything.

'Jake, I didn't come to Paris to meet a man,' I said gently. 'Especially not a Blackfella I could meet back home.'

'The thing is, Libby,' Jake mirrored my tone. 'We didn't meet back home. And we were working in Canberra at the same time. We've probably been in the same meetings, at the same openings at the same time. We didn't meet because I was married and you were busy being beautiful.'

I sighed internally. I loved that he thought I was beautiful, and I was glad I had my red bucket-bag and red shoes on to help me. But there was no way I was getting involved with a Black man in Paris after the disaster I'd already had with Ames, and the three-strikes-you're-out back home.

He was still talking. 'Don't you think there's something serendipitous about us meeting on the other side of the world?'

'No, I don't!' I said, flagging down a cab. 'I'll see you at work.'

'Wait!' He grabbed my arm.

'No!' I was almost yelling as I climbed into the taxi. I slammed the door in his face.

Chapter 19

It's on

I was stressed out about that dinner with Jake, but life was hectic with work and helping out with Sorina's new business. She'd named her label 'Roma Designs', had a growing Instagram following, and had her own pages on Etsy and an artists' collective website where people could order online.

I'd sent promo flyers to anyone and everyone I knew, and her business had grown so much that she left the shop she was working in because she was sewing all day, seven days a week, and loving it. She was supplying bags to a store nearby called Shopping for Happiness, and had orders coming in from women at the Musée who wanted to be part of the fashionable political statement. My girls and their friends back home were making orders on Etsy and Catherine even hosted a 'handbag party' in her apartment one Saturday where eight bags were sold. Sorina had now begun to make bags from material that customers brought with them to match their own dresses and shoes.

Canelle and I were delighted to see how well Sorina was doing. She was even looking better, with a new hairstyle thanks to a friend of Monica's who ran a salon on Rue Francois Miron: bartering a balayage do for a custom-made bag. Sorina had also started wearing bold lipsticks to match her creations.

We decided to take our friend out to celebrate. We sat in the very cool Le 1905 having a cocktail. It was a cosy bar with a vintage vibe and a great tapas menu.

'I'm making skirts for myself and clients now too,' Sorina said, standing up and modelling the one she was wearing. 'I have one a-line pattern, but with so many different materials they all fall differently and look different and sometimes I wear them with my black boots and sometimes flat shoes and the look is always different.'

She had become her own walking mannequin and I was inspired to do something more with my wardrobe too.

'The girls back home are so impressed that I have my own designer here in Paris,' I said, smiling at Sorina. 'Actually, I'll need to take them all a skirt when I leave.'

It felt good being able to buy fashion and support an artist at the same time, it was like buying Aboriginal art direct from cooperatives back home.

'Here's cheers to Roma Designs.' We raised our glasses.

'I have something to celebrate a little also,' Canelle said, smiling widely.

'Oh, what is it?' Both Sorina and I were excited.

'I have met a wonderful man,' she exclaimed. 'His name is Pierre and we are crazy about each other.'

'That's so wonderful!' I gave her a seated hug. 'What's he like?'

Canelle spoke non-stop for thirty minutes, describing Pierre physically and adding all his wonderful attributes and their shared values. She was clearly in love.

'Cheers to Canelle and Pierre,' I said, making a toast.

'Now you need to meet someone, Elizabeth,' Canelle said, sipping her Ricard. 'It is time. It is not normal to be in Paris this long and be alone.'

I looked at her. She'd obviously forgotten about Ames. I didn't want to bring it up again, but I did tell both the girls about the dinner I had with Jake, playing down how weird and sleazy I thought he was. The last thing I wanted to do was defame the first secretary of my country while I was on his payroll. Anyway, his politics were all right, and in that job, that's all that mattered. I told them I had enjoyed the kiss though, and then wished I hadn't, because without the backstory, it looked like *I* was the weird one.

'What are you going to do, Elizabeth? That man is around for a higher reason: *destinée* – I remember him from Nomad's. He has the great *derrière*, *oui*?'

I giggled at Canelle's obsession with Jake's arse, but had to put her straight. 'Canelle. The reality is I'm here to work. I've only ever been screwed by men, and not just in the good way. He is my boss and, most importantly, what kind of person pours their heart out to you when they hardly know you and you're not even on a date?'

'You are sometimes a hard woman,' Sorina said, to my surprise.

Canelle smiled as if she'd been vindicated.

Sorina continued, passionately, 'Sometimes time has nothing to do with how much you know someone. My parents were married within months of meeting each other. My mother said she knew my father was the one when he waltzed with her in a little restaurant in their village, the first night they met. He didn't care what all his friends thought about it. He just wanted to make her happy, and that's what he's been doing ever since.'

Sorina made me think about my own parents and the true love they knew. I momentarily wanted to believe in it, but I couldn't.

'There are no rules, Elizabeth, only the ones you seem to make up for yourself that somehow stop you from having fun,' Canelle added. 'You know what I know, Elizabeth?'

'What do you know, Canelle?' I felt under fire and was getting annoyed. It was like being harassed by Bec and Lauren back home.

'I know that when you talked about this Jake man just now, your eyes lit up and they haven't lit up like that at all since I met you. This Jake man makes your eyes sparkle. This I know.'

I felt like I'd been sprung telling lies to my parents about something I didn't really do.

'Well, I've hardly seen him at work anyway, he's probably avoiding me now.' I just wanted the conversation to be over.

'So, now we toast to Sorina,' Canelle said, raising her glass towards my talented friend, 'and her future on the European catwalks and in French fashion houses. And we toast to my new man, who is the sexiest man on the planet. And you, Elizabeth, we toast to your eyes sparkling more often.'

I was looking forward to attending the embassy's First Nations Film Festival, curated by an expat from Victoria. Greta Morton Elangué was one of the deadliest expats I'd met in Paris, and had pulled together her seventh festival program, this year featuring *The Drover's Wife: The Legend of Molly Johnson*. There was also much excitement around the Noongar language version of Bruce Lee's *Fist of Fury*, with Noongar voiceovers done by Clint and Kylie Bracknell and Kyle J Morrison. I was hoping to meet them all, but in her speech, Greta made their apologies, as other commitments back home kept them in Australia.

Judith had arranged invitations for Canelle and a few others from the Musée, and Sorina to attend as well.

On Tuesday, the embassy bustled with energy and people eager to see Leah Purcell's latest triumph, and Judith was on fire introducing everyone to everyone and coordinating the dignitaries. I could see she was coordinating Jake as well.

I helped by ushering the VIPs to their seats. When it was time for me to take my seat, I realised there was only one left: in the front row, next to Jake.

'The universe has a sense of humour,' I said, as the lights went down and our knees touched.

'Or the Ancestors have a plan,' he said, facing forward.

I was so aroused I couldn't imagine how I was going to sit through the film without at least holding his hand. As soon as it started though, the storyline took me to another place: a reminder of the resilience of our women and the need for us to tell stories. I almost forgot Jake was there, but I could smell his aftershave wafting into my nostrils, down my cleavage and into my lap. Knowing we were watching the film through the same lens – both being Blackfellas – made me feel closer to him.

At the end of the evening, the audience was buzzing with conversation about the talent of the actors in the film, the issues raised and the international impact the film was already having.

When the last guest had left the building, I went back up to my office, grabbed my bag from my desk and headed to the lift. As I entered it, my phone rang. It was Canelle.

I answered with an apology – I'd been so busy making sure the VIPs were well looked after that I hadn't said goodbye to her before she left.

'*Je suis désolee*. I'm only just leaving work now.'

'Elizabeth, *de rien*, it is fine,' Canelle was her cruisy French self. 'We are, how you say, tiddas now, no need for apologies when you are working so hard like that. I know you well enough.'

I was relieved. After all the hospitality and fun Canelle

had shared with me, she really was my tidda, as if the universe had brought her to me.

'I lost my glove, my left one,' she said down the line. 'I think I may have dropped it in the theatrette. Can you check tomorrow?'

'I'm still here, I'll look now and I'll text you if I find it. I can give it to you on the weekend, *à bientôt*.'

'Goodnight.' The phone went dead.

By the time I got back to the ground floor, everyone had left except the security guards. I didn't think I needed to tell them I had to race back into the theatrette, expecting to be only a few minutes. So I upped my pace and opened the huge doors, only to find Jake up the front of the room.

'What are you doing here?' I asked, surprised to see him.

'I might ask you the same thing,' he laughed.

'Canelle lost a glove.'

'I lost my favourite pen.' He had a pathetic little-boy look on his face, as if he'd lost his favourite football.

'Canelle was sitting almost behind us,' I said, conscious of staying on-topic and getting out fast. 'You check the front row, I'll check behind. Your pen may have fallen down here.'

We searched the rows and just as I found Canelle's glove, the lights went out and the theatre was pitch-black.

'What the . . .' Jake exclaimed.

'Hey!' I said.

'Are you okay?' Jake sounded concerned.

'Of course, but why did the lights go out?'

I was worried about security getting angry that we were there. I pushed a seat down and sat on it, not sure what else to do.

'Did you tell anyone you were here?' Jake asked.

'No, I was only going to be a minute, did you?' I asked.

'No. Same. Can you get to the aisle? I'll meet you there.' Jake was in professional mode.

I stood up carefully and felt my way along the backs of the seats with my right hand. It was the blackest space I could recall ever being in. I couldn't see anything other than 'SORTIE' signs to guide my escape.

'Are you here yet?' Jake asked.

'Shit!' I growled as I arrived at the end of the row.

'What?'

'I dropped the glove. Hang on.' I bent down to rummage for it, and so did Jake. We bumped heads on the way down.

'Shit!' he said.

'Sorry.' I fumbled, trying to rub my head.

'Here.'

Jake grabbed my forearm, pulling me towards him. He ran his hand around the side of my face, like a blind man might, and then kissed my forehead better.

In an instant, the lust of every teenager in the city had made its way into our bodies. With a sense of urgency, we kissed like we'd never kissed anyone else before and never would again. Jake's mouth was devouring mine and then he was on my neck, nibbling my ear. I ran my hands down his chest and then pushed him away.

'We can't do this.'

I finally found my phone and turned it's light on and ran up the aisle as fast as was possible, hearing only, 'Libby, please!' from Jake behind me.

I quickly walked out of the embassy, nodding to the security, and ran to a cab.

As I lay in bed that night, I was confused. I didn't want to get involved with someone I worked with, and I was still bruised from the recent trauma of Ames, and yet I couldn't help but smile about the kiss that was the most passionate I'd ever had. I was strong enough to stay away from Jake, but I couldn't deny my growing attraction to him.

I busied myself without effort over the following days, working through the tasks that had been originally set for the strategy of getting more exposure for Indigenous artists in Europe, and following up new contacts I'd created already.

On Friday I went to the Bibliothèque Nationale de France to meet with their events people and librarians about coordinating some visiting First Nations authors, and to assist them in building a collection of their books. I aimed to broker a relationship between the head librarian and the national coordinator of the Black Words research of Austlit, and with the librarian at AIATSIS in Canberra.

The French national library was extraordinary. There were four towers representing four open books, which I thought was pretty cool. The NLA back home was so bland by comparison. The whole Paris Rive Gauche district where the library was located was an exciting, still-developing urban area that extended from the Gare d'Austerlitz to boulevard du Général-Jean-Simon, running along the Seine on one side and rue du Chevaleret on the other. The library was the flagship building of the area, but there were also new housing, offices, commercial outlets, services, schools, universities and public and cultural amenities gradually being built in the area.

But it was the Richelieu site of the Bibliothèque national de France that took my breath away. It was possibly the most beautiful library I had ever entered. At the public library of the BNF I did a few laps around the oval room, speechless at the beauty and design, trying to mentally steal ideas for how we might present material in the research area of the NAG.

I was glad for the distraction of the library. It took my mind off the few fleeting but memorable moments with Jake: the dinner, the conversation, the attraction and especially the kiss in the theatrette. The intensity of my confusion over Jake was nothing I'd known before and certainly far beyond what I felt for Ames.

I wasn't sure how I was going to manage the project if I was going to see Jake often, because I knew how strong my physical attraction to him was now. I'd even come to find his thin lips inviting and I wanted to kiss him again.

I hadn't spoken to or seen him since the movie night three days before, but as I walked out of the library he texted me.

If you're free for lunch, meet me on the steps of the old opera house.

I was nervous with excitement but knew I was going against the rules I had set down: not to see each other socially, and definitely not romantically. But I couldn't help but walk faster to get to the venue.

I'm close by so will head there soonish. 2 pm?

Perfect.

I arrived early, taking a few minutes to stroll around Place de la Madeleine and all the shops I'd fallen in love with when I'd first arrived.

I saw Jake standing at the base of the steps of the Palais Garnier – the grand old opera house where *Phantom of the Opera* was set – wearing a black coat and grey scarf. The December weather was the coldest it'd been since I arrived.

I crossed the street carefully, having learned some lessons over time on how to negotiate the crazy traffic.

'Hey,' Jake said, holding two baguettes.

'Hey yourself.' I tried to sound casual, but I knew there was a nervous quiver in my voice. Jake was the first man to ever make me feel that way. 'I didn't know it was a picnic.'

'I grabbed these on the way. I thought we could sit and get some sun, it's been days since I've had any.' He motioned me to his left. 'If we get a spot out of the wind, it's really pleasant here.'

'Great idea.'

I wondered if he too was thinking about the kiss from the other day and if, like me, he wanted to do it again.

'I like it here,' he said, as we sat and looked out onto bustling traffic.

'It's got a good feel. The sun's great too. God, it's hot in Canberra now, and I seriously want to thaw out!'

I looked at the huge Lancel shop windows across the way to the left and smiled at my gorgeous red bucket-bag resting at my feet. 'Sometimes I sit here and think about what's going on back home. I really do miss Deni, and Albury where Mum lives.' I knew exactly what Jake meant. 'I write cards to Mum and my nieces and nephews. It's kind of like my "homesickness spot".'

'Is it okay to be here with someone else then?' I felt like I could be intruding on his sacred place in Paris.

'It feels good to share the place with someone from home.'

He was right, and suddenly the nervousness subsided and a feeling of comfort took over. I felt honoured that he wanted to share it with me.

We bit into our baguettes as a fire truck drove past, sirens blaring. It was a natural instinct for me to check the fireys out, and they didn't disappoint. I wanted to be near a fire on such a chilly Paris day.

'Libby,' Jake said cautiously.

'Jake,' I said, almost mocking his tone.

'I want to see you.'

He looked directly into my eyes and I hoped I didn't have food on my face or in my teeth. I didn't answer.

'And when I say that, I mean I want to see only you. I've wanted to see you socially since we met at Nomad's and I know now that I probably freaked you out that night at Procope, but please understand I am a novice at this.'

I still said nothing, waiting to see what else he would expose about himself. I didn't want to look, but I couldn't take my eyes from his face. His smile somehow warmed me.

'I'm just a lad from the country,' he said nervously. 'And I thought being honest with you straight-up was the best thing but maybe not.'

'You freaked me out a bit,' I said. 'I'm sorry. This is all new to me.'

'In many ways it's new to me too.' I could hear the vulnerability in my voice.

'I'd like it if you would go on a date with me. Dinner or a movie or whatever. Just give me a chance as a bloke and not the first secretary.' He looked at me with a raised eyebrow. 'I know you're worried about that, but don't be. We're grown-ups, we're both single. We are allowed some happiness outside of work.'

'I don't think it's a good idea.'

Oh god, I thought to myself. I did want to go out with this man, but I didn't want to fuck up my heart again, or my job.

He pulled me close to him, our bulky coats only slightly getting in the way.

He kissed me tenderly and it made me melt. If I never kissed another man, it wouldn't matter.

'I think it's a great idea,' he said.

Chapter 20

This is not love, this is lust

This is not love, it's just lust, I need to break the man-fast, I told myself over and over during the following weeks as I was challenged by the exercise in discretion and diplomacy that confronted both of us.

I was paranoid about people at work finding out about Jake and me dating and that my project would be pulled out from under me. Worse still, Jake would be accused of doing favours by appointing me. I was sure something would go wrong, it always did.

As far as I was concerned, the universe had spoken in terms of my love-life and the Ancestors seemed to be in cahoots – clearly romance was a bad idea for me – but there was no turning back as neither of us could get enough of the other. When we were apart, we wanted to be together. When we were together, we wanted to be touching each other. The physical attraction was only heightened by the respect that grew between us every day.

Nevertheless, I had decided that, unlike the way I'd jumped in headfirst with Ames, I'd wait to have sex with Jake. He was as polite as possible, but I knew it was difficult for him. I just wasn't prepared to sleep with the boss until I was absolutely certain it wasn't going to affect my job.

When we were together, we talked about every Black issue possible: the politics of identity, how native title rights were the only rights Blackfellas had and how few understood that though there were two groups of Indigenous Australians – Aboriginal and Torres Strait Islanders – Australia was Aboriginal land.

We laughed at the same things. We both liked the colour red – his tie, my shoes and bucket-bag. We both liked walking. We were both workaholics. We believed we had a choice to be happy rather than sad. It was uncanny how alike we were. We were perfect for each other in every way. Did the Ancestors bring us together in Paris on purpose, so the eyes of our mob weren't dissecting our every move? There'd be plenty of time for that when we eventually got home.

I couldn't believe my luck in meeting Jake. Maybe it was like Lauren meeting Wyatt, maybe it wasn't. I knew he wasn't like Ames: Jake was honest. He liked a bit of flesh anyway, so no skeletons for him either.

We hung out on weekends as much as we could but we never disclosed our relationship at work. I only told Canelle, and Jake told his mate Joseph, a lawyer friend across town. We remained formal and professional in front of our colleagues, but when we were alone in the office it was hot.

I was waiting to tell Lauren, Bec and Caro because I wanted to be sure before they all got excited as well. I didn't want to have to explain anything after the Ames disaster. I knew they'd only worry if it happened again. Although the one thing about Jake I believed to be true was that he would never intentionally hurt me.

When I was with Jake, I couldn't fathom why his ex would ever have let him go. If nothing else, he was drop-dead sexy: thin lips, eyes too close together and all. There was only one thing that really bothered me about him: he was so affectionate – a little too much for my liking.

On our first weekend outing, we strolled around the Marais and visited the Musée Carnavalet, learning more about the history of Paris. When we met at the Métro stop first thing in the morning, he went to hold my hand and I shied away.

'What's wrong?' Jake asked, confused. 'It's highly unlikely that we'll bump into anyone from work.'

'I don't do handholding.' I put my hands in my coat pockets.

'What?' He stopped still in his tracks. He was clearly annoyed. 'Libby, let me get this clear, you'll let me kiss you passionately for hours, but you won't let me hold your hand?'

'That's right.'

Jake looked at me confused.

'Oh, don't worry, we can bang *eventually*,' I joked.

'Please don't say it like that, Libby.'

Jake was conservative when it came to talking about

sex. It was something that I liked about him, that he wasn't throwing it around back home or across Paris. Since he'd been with his ex for so long, there wasn't a lot of sexual history I had to worry about.

Jake was shaking his head. 'I'm just trying to get this clear: you'll let me sleep with you *eventually* but you don't want to hold my hand *today*?'

'I'm just not big on public displays of affection is all.' I couldn't understand what the drama was. 'I thought men would choose sex over handholding any day.'

'What a load of crap.' He took control of the situation. 'I've kissed you in public, now give me your hand.' He held out his left hand and smiled.

'I guess I shouldn't cross the road without holding someone's hand anyway,' I said, reluctantly taking it.

Jake laughed. 'You are the funniest woman I've ever met.'

'Yes, I am,' I said seriously.

He squeezed my hand, still laughing.

'Do you think you could walk faster, please? Now you're just holding me back with your handholding exercise.' I laughed.

Later that day, we cruised the Seine. It was incredibly romantic to see the city from a different perspective, even though the skies were grey. The cold weather just made us cuddle more.

As Christmas fast approached, it was getting increasingly difficult to keep our relationship a secret at work, but I convinced Jake it was still for the best.

I'd helped to organise Judith's farewell party and we were going to the Moulin Rouge before she took off for a new job in Barcelona. I would miss working with her. She was a fair boss, allowing me time to duck out to check on Sorina occasionally, as long as all my tasks were completed. Judith had also come to appreciate Roma Designs and wanted to support the struggling artist.

I organised the tickets for the Moulin Rouge, and on Friday night Judith, Jake and I and a few other staff went off to the boulevard de Clichy in Montmartre.

We queued for forty minutes to get into the show, but I passed the time taking photos of the crowds, the lights around the venue and the busloads of tourists arriving. I watched the bouncers trying to keep the masses on the footpath and deal with cheeky people trying to push in.

I liked the crush of the crowds, though: it forced Jake and me to stand closer together and we both smiled, looking in different directions as I felt him hard against me. I'd already decided that tonight was the night we'd get down and dirty for the first time.

Jake slipped his hand with mine into my jacket pocket and squeezed. We were in the heart of the red-light district and the street was lined with sex shops and peep shows. I wasn't sure if I was turning Jake on or if what was going on around us was.

Seediness aside, I was excited to see the nightclub that was so famous. I knew the girls would expect me to keep clicking photos to send back to them, especially since we'd all watched *Moulin Rouge* before I left Canberra. As we finally reached the entrance, I took a photo of the signage inside.

'*Photographie interdite,*' a doorman said.

'No photos allowed,' Jake whispered to me.

I begrudgingly put my phone away. We hurried into the venue and took a table right near the stage.

'So, this is Moulin Rouge,' I said excitedly to Jake, who was sitting next to me, looking everywhere but in my direction, acting like we'd never had a personal conversation before. It was the first time I really resented not being able to just 'be' the couple we were when alone.

Our waiter Antoine arrived with champagne and the show began soon after. In the first routine, the men were completely covered in white sequinned long pants and jackets and the women were all half-naked.

The show was spectacular, but it bothered me that the men were almost always fully-clothed and the women were nearly always mostly naked. And there was only one Black woman among them.

'It's hard to believe the first complete striptease was performed at the Moulin Rouge in 1936,' Jake said. 'It seems like they've been doing it forever!'

'Stripping is the national dance,' Judith laughed. 'You do know many of the girls are Australian, don't you?'

'No, I didn't,' Jake said, not taking his eyes from the stage. His stare hit me like a bolt of jealousy.

'I knew,' I answered, remembering Bec, Lauren, Caro and me watching the film back in Canberra.

The acts in between the dance routines were incredible: magicians, acrobats and jugglers, all blew my mind with their skill and talent.

'What did you like breast?' Dan, an admin officer from the embassy asked at the end of the show, having enjoyed the dancing *and* the drinking.

'Well, clearly I know what you liked best!' Jake responded. 'I actually liked the juggler. God he was impressive with those batons, what was it, six?'

'Seven,' I said. 'I liked the ventriloquist. How did he actually make it look like that puppet was talking?'

'And what about when it looked like he was singing "Feelings"?' Jake added.

'I know.' Judith too was impressed with the singing puppet.

'I actually think the men were far better dancers than the women,' I said, being honest and, I thought, objective.

'How do you figure that?' Dan asked.

'Let's face it: no-one's actually watching the women dance, are they?' I eyeballed Jake. 'And the men, if they're fully clothed, then we are forced to just watch their moves, not their bodies, as such.'

'Ouch, are you jealous?' Dan accused me, and then gulped his beer.

'Jealous of what?' I could hear how defensive I sounded. 'I wouldn't dance around naked in public anyway, even if I did have a body like those girls.'

I got up and went to the toilet. I *was* jealous. It was crazy. I just didn't want Jake fantasising about those women, who had beautiful faces and great bodies. I'd not been worried about my body with Jake, but it certainly wasn't good enough for public display.

After the show we all went for a drink. Jake and I sat at the bar trying to look like colleagues and hiding any sense of electricity that sparked when our legs brushed. We made the most inane conversation in case the other staff listened in.

'I like walking,' I said.

'Me too, can't get enough of walking,' Jake joked, having walked miles with me around Paris. 'I walk as much as possible because there is so much to discover in this city by foot.'

'Oh, I know, little mini-markets, little parks tucked away.' I winked and we both laughed at how ridiculous the conversation was getting.

'What are you two talking about?' Dan asked.

'Walking.' We echoed each other.

'As if. I know you were talking about some poor bastard in the office. I don't care if it's me,' he slurred. 'I'm outta here.'

He sculled the last of his drink and walked off with a wobble. 'Wait up,' Judith said, 'I'll split a cab back to the residence with you.'

And she left too.

In our own cab on the way back to my place, Jake and I were all over each other and could barely manage to keep it publicly decent. I tried to temper the situation with conversation but Jake kept sticking his tongue in my mouth whenever I opened it.

Fumbling up the stairwell, we ended up writhing enthusiastically on the stairs with the edges of the carpeted-yet-still-painful steps hard against my back.

'I can't wait any longer,' Jake said.

'Can we get into the flat, do you think?'

'Okay,' he breathed heavily into my ear, ushering me with determination to my door.

Inside he started peeling my layers off straightaway.

'Wait,' I said. 'I have to get organised. I'll call you in when I'm ready.'

He pulled me against him hard and kissed me passionately.

I didn't want to stop but I had a plan.

'Wait in the bathroom. I'll be one minute, I promise.' He walked the few steps to the bathroom.

'And don't start without me,' I said, cheekily.

I grabbed the premeditated sexy-underwear-for-the-first-time outfit I had prepared earlier that day: a black satin bustier and the tiniest of black lace panties with red roses on them.

I carefully slipped on some black lace-top stay-ups and hoped they stayed up long enough for Jake to appreciate them. My thighs were thin and I'd had a number of embarrassing experiences where my stockings had fallen down in public places. They were not sexy moments.

I slipped my feet into my killer black patent heels and looked quickly in the mirror. I looked okay, but as soon as I threw a red scarf over my bedroom lamp, I looked better.

'You can come out now,' I called to Jake, hitting play on my most seductive Spotify playlist.

I sat with my legs crossed in attempted elegance on the edge of my bed. I wasn't quite sure what I was doing, or should be doing, but I was trying to look seductive. Piaf's 'Les Amants de Paris' came on. It wasn't a classic burlesque or striptease song but it didn't matter.

'Wow,' is all Jake said as he came towards me.

I was grateful that no high-kicks were required as he was all over me immediately. He used his mouth to pull down my stay-ups, which, for the first time in my life, didn't want to move, and we both giggled.

'Shall I help you?' I asked, with a smile in my voice.

'I think I can manage,' he said, using his hands and his mouth. 'You are sexier than all those women combined, Libby.'

'You're just saying that because I'm here and they're not.' I pretended I wasn't grateful for his words.

'You should learn to trust,' he said seriously, 'and take a compliment.'

He kissed my ankles.

'I'm sorry,' I whispered.

'You are sexy because you are dignified and smart. And that is sexy,' he said, as he kissed his way up my legs.

'And this underwear is sexy,' he mumbled as he slid off my knickers. 'This is sexy,' he whispered as he kissed me.

Jake and I spent much of the next day in bed and Sunday at Montmartre, taking the stairs to the top to work off some of the buttery pastries we'd had for breakfast.

There was a busker sitting on the steps leading up to the Basilique du Sacré-Coeur, the Roman Catholic Church housing one of the largest mosaics in the world and the place for one of the best panoramic views in Paris. Hundreds of people sat and stood, clapping along to the English songs. Then the busker sang 'Happy Birthday' to a backpacker in French, English and German.

As he started singing his next tune – Eric Clapton's 'Layla' – Jake and I turned to face the city. It was an unusually warm day for December. Paris, it seemed, hadn't escaped the evils of global warming, and the climate crisis was obvious from where we stood.

Jake placed his arm over my shoulder and I couldn't have been happier. I thought briefly about life back in Canberra and watching *Amélie* with the girls and seeing Montmartre for the first time in the film. I was conscious that I didn't feel homesick at all. But I wasn't a traitor to my family, my friends or my country, because I was keeping it all alive with Jake and my work.

'Lunch?' Jake asked, always ready to eat.

'Absolutely,' I said, hesitating to suggest Café des 2 Moulins from *Amélie*, because he was already leading me in a specific direction.

'I know a spot where we can sit and just watch people walk by, how does that sound?' Jake smiled enthusiastically.

'Sounds great!'

We sat with dozens of others at Au Cadet de Gascogne on La Place du Tertre, enjoying soupe à l'oignon gratinée and more bread. I seemed to appreciate the flirty waiters more than Jake did, and I liked that he looked a tad jealous when they said how beautiful I was.

After lunch, we strolled the markets, admiring the travelling artists showcasing their wares: many did portraits, others did caricatures. I wondered if Sorina would end up here also one day. We weaved our way through the tourists, the families and kids, and the gendarmerie – the French military police.

The first time Jake told me he loved me, I panicked. We were walking across the Pont des Arts bridge at night. It had been raining and the streets had a sheen as the light from the antique streetlamps bounced off them. We stopped in the middle of the bridge.

He kissed me and said, '*Je t'aime.*'

I froze, kissed him to buy time and then whispered in his ear, 'Thank you.'

Even *I* knew how lame it sounded but I couldn't offer anything else. Although I believed I was in love with Jake, I couldn't say it back. There was still some fear of possible abandonment, rejection and humiliation because of the past. What if I told him I loved him, and then he changed his mind, like Peter or Andy or Ames? I believed I had met my soulmate, but it was something I wanted to keep pure and to myself a little while longer. I believed Jake's proclamations, and I appreciated all his good qualities that I'd been saturated with. But there was time, wasn't there?

I wanted to be absolutely sure. I would wait until it was the right time for me.

Chapter 21

Oohlala, it's Christmas in Paris

I was loving my life in all its *oohlala* glory. Everything made me smile, especially the surprises Jake would give me regularly: the French macarons from Ladurée were apparently the best in the city, the chocolates from Maxim's reminded me of home, a glass of champagne on the fifty-ninth floor of Montparnasse Tower at dusk was so romantic it left me weak in awe.

Everything he did to express his appreciation and affection for me, I loved. Everything we did together, I loved even more. Mostly, I loved being around Jake because he respected me and he made me laugh at simple things, at him, at myself. I never knew that a man could be respectful and romantic.

The week before Christmas, he texted me.

I have a surprise for you tonight. Meet me outside La Chapelle Métro station. Line two. 8 pm.

I left work early as most of the contacts I'd been dealing with were already on holiday leave. Jake and I were having Christmas in my apartment and we were going to kill ourselves with laughter trying to cook a turkey.

I raced home and changed into a black skirt and red and gold top, black stockings and a new pair of black boots. I wrapped myself in my black coat and a red cashmere scarf Jake had given me. And I carried a Roma Designs bag. I looked like a million dollars, just like I belonged in Paris with my new style. How proud Lauren would've been of me.

I met Jake at La Chapelle, where he was waiting with six red roses. He kissed my cheeks: left, right, left; one, two, three. I couldn't stop smiling at how my life had become so romantic, so peaceful, so fulfilling, so wonderful in Paris.

'Where are we going?' I asked, as we strolled arm-in-arm through Paris's biggest Indian neighbourhood.

'I read about this designer hotel and I wanted to take you there,' Jake said, holding my hand as we walked. 'You know what today is, don't you?'

'Friday,' I said dryly.

'You're hilarious,' he responded with a hint of sarcasm.

'Why? Isn't it Friday?' I asked, childlike.

'Yes, it's Friday, smartarse. It's also nearly six months since we met outside Nomad's. That's why I gave you six roses.'

'Right.' I was trying to calculate backwards in my head.

'You already know I fell for you that night.'

'I know, I know,' I said, trying to take the seriousness

out of the moment for fear he would declare his love again and all I would be able to do was pat the lovesick puppy on the head.

I pulled him close and kissed him passionately, not only because he was so sexy at that moment but because I wanted the subject changed.

'Happy anniversary of the night we met,' he whispered as he hugged me afterwards.

We walked on, closely pressed together without speaking. True happiness, it seemed, could come in simple forms. Holding hands, six flowers, a warm smile, an honest disclosure. But I still couldn't tell Jake I loved him. I just wanted things to stay as they were.

The air was chilly but my heart was warm as we entered the bare courtyard of the hotel, with its white moulded designer lounges positioned like installation art. I went and propped myself up on one immediately.

'You're crazy,' Jake said, trying to get me up. 'Come on, my nuts are freezing.'

'Charming,' I said, conscious that Jake was rarely crude, but funny when he was.

Inside the restaurant at the base of the hotel we found photos of burlesque girls lining the walls, fibre-optic lamps from the '70s barely lighting the space, huge wineglasses hanging above the bar and long velvet curtains falling against the windows, making it very dark.

'It's like a *boudoir* in here,' I whispered to Jake, who squeezed my hand tight.

'Welcome to Le Kube,' a young waiter greeted us.

'Table for Ross, please,' Jake said to the waiter, who looked disturbingly boyish to be working in such an adult venue.

'Is he even the legal age to wait?' I whispered to Jake.

'This way.'

The boy ushered us to a table with black bench seats.

'What's your name?' I asked him.

'Frédéric, *mademoiselle*.'

Jake just looked at me and laughed. 'Must you always ask the waiter's name?'

'I must. Because I'm counting how many Frédérics I can meet in Paris.'

Jake and I decided on the tasting plate for dinner and while we waited for the food, we commented on all the glamorous people filing in and out of the bar and restaurant, imagining they were models and politicians and actors.

'I bet the models from Fashion Week don't eat this well,' I said as Jake and I shared our meal by the glow of tea-light candles and music being played by a DJ that we barely noticed above us on the mezzanine.

After we'd finished eating Jake got his trademark thin-lipped sexy grin on his face, one I had grown to like seeing on him.

'I booked us a room here tonight,' he said coyly.

'Really?' I replied seductively, uncrossing my legs, kicking off one shoe and pushing my stockinged foot into his crotch. He jumped.

'Libby, this is a public place.' Jake was embarrassed but smiling.

'Well, where's the room then?' I said, trying not to sound impatient.

As soon as the bill was paid, we were in a colourful lift with orange and black carpet on its walls, both giddy with love and liquor. I ran my hands over the carpet and Jake ran his hands over my body.

Christmas in Paris was enchanting. The city was adorned with festive lights and colour and the French knew how to celebrate with food, wine and decorations. Canelle invited Jake and me to her place for a pre-Christmas dinner and to meet her new man Pierre.

'This is Pierre.' Canelle introduced us as we entered her first floor apartment.

His broad white smile matched hers and together they lit up the room.

'*Bonsoir*,' he said, laughing and doing the double French air-kiss thing.

Canelle had already warned me that Pierre didn't speak much English, but he was interested in Aboriginal Australia and was pleased to cook for us. I could smell the meal already, spices lingering in the air of her flat, which by Parisian standards was quite large, with a string of fairy lights running along the hall and around the doorframes.

'Pierre has prepared a French Caribbean curry for us. Lamb with vegetables and Colombo curry powder from Guadeloupe,' Canelle said, proud of her man's cooking accomplishments, while my stomach rumbled at the thought. My mouth was already watering.

'It is not traditional French Christmas fare, but we wanted to give you something authentically ours.'

'It smells delicious,' Jake said as he unpacked some Australian beers – Coopers, Hahn and Foster's – onto the table. 'And we wanted to give you something authentically ours.'

Pierre laughed. Clearly both men thought the beer a hysterical gesture.

'This is *punch d'amour*,' Canelle said, handing me a small glass. 'It is love potion punch from the French West Indies – Guadeloupe, in fact. It has ginseng and other secret spices.'

As I sipped the cocktail made of white rum, fruit and cane sugar, I smiled at Jake and then watched my friend and her man organise our meal in the small kitchen.

There were art-deco type Coca-Cola signs above the stove, and I saw a different side to Canelle. My bling-covered, elegant Canelle loved soft-drink paraphernalia, who would've known? She caught me looking at the signs.

'I collect them. I like the suggestive way she sits and says, "Are you ready?"' Canelle pointed at a sign with a particularly glamorous woman on it, then she and Pierre looked at each other lovingly and laughed.

We all sat in Canelle's lounge with the television on in the background, eating the meals off plates in our laps. I studied the room. I loved what she had done with her plants to give the place the feeling of an oasis under the windows facing the street. I needed some more greenery in my apartment, I thought.

I saw the Aboriginal flag I'd given her in a pot near her fireplace.

I wanted to acknowledge that it looked perfect there but didn't say anything because I was too busy enjoying the most amazing flavours of coriander, turmeric, cumin, mustard, cloves, pepper and fennel seeds. I thought about trying to make a Colombo kangaroo curry for Lauren, Caro and Bec when I finally got back to Canberra. Hopefully Jake would be there too.

'What is Christmas like in Australia?' Pierre asked us enthusiastically.

'Hot and dry in Canberra,' I said, remembering the last heat-wave Christmas I'd had with Bec and Caro because I didn't go home.

'We have barbecues and seafood platters and legs of ham and cold beer,' Jake added, as if he'd said the same line a million times since he'd arrived in Paris.

I was less excited about the food aspect than Jake was. 'Mainly family and friends get together, but I'm not really big on it anymore. A lot of expense and trouble preparing food for one day. And I can't cook, so it's even more trouble for me.' I cleared what was left on my plate.

'What are you doing this Christmas?' Pierre asked.

'We're spending it together,' Jake said, claiming the day as his, as ours.

In the kitchen Canelle and I washed the dishes.

'I like to see your eyes sparkling, Elizabeth. This Jake man is good for you.'

Jake and I spent Christmas Eve doing a tour of the city, gasping in awe at how beautiful it looked lit up. Braddon was another universe away from the Champs-Elysées, which had been turned into a wonderland of frosty blue lights like snowflakes draped over the bare branches of trees lining the street.

We walked over to the Christmas markets in St Germaine and looked at all the festive arts and crafts and drank some mulled wine to keep warm. A choir sang carols in French and I swooned when Jake joined it. I didn't know that he could also sing.

'You have perfect pitch,' I said with amazement and awe.

'Trained as a baritone in the school choir.' He puffed his chest out with pride.

'My baritone Blackfella, is *le sexy*.' I pulled him in for a kiss.

Before heading home, we went to the Cité International des Arts, where the artists in residence from around the world had organised a Christmas meal for the homeless people who slept rough along Rue de l'Hôtel de ville every night of the year. We picked up some pre-ordered hot meals that Monica prepared and the three of us helped serve them up, alongside the creatives. At 8.30 pm we walked the 400 metres to my place.

'Wait!' Jake said as I went to enter my apartment.

'Here.' He pinned some mistletoe on the arch of the doorway.

'Oh, I see.'

I pulled him to me and we kissed under the traditional sprig.

I didn't care if I was never kissed by another man ever again.

When I stepped out of the shower into my now crowded apartment, I found Jake putting candles on my windowsill and trying to dress up my less than healthy plant.

'What are you doing?' I giggled, unsure of what he was attempting.

'It's traditional to have candles and a *sapin de Noël*, aka Christmas tree. Following the French way, we should decorate it with apples, paper flowers and ribbons, but this is the best I can do.'

He continued to tie little pieces of red ribbon on the fragile twigs. 'Anyway, one apple would snap this poor, neglected plant in half.'

'Where did you get the ribbon?' I started to help.

'I picked it up at the markets, you like?'

'I love it.' I almost wanted to say that I loved him, but I didn't. Rather, I continued to smile at his considerateness for making our Christmas like a real Christmas.

'There's not much room for anything else.' We scanned the tiny space.

I looked adoringly at the extraordinary man in front of me. A Blackfella full of traditions and who could sing Christmas carols in French. How lucky was I?

'I like seeing you smile,' he said, pulling me to him.

'I like seeing *you* smile.' I looked into his eyes.

'You make me smile.'

'I'm glad.'

I kissed him gently.

We spent the evening preparing some of our menu for Christmas Day and listening to Bob Dylan – something else that Jake and I had in common.

'I'm going to make something very traditional for dessert,' Jake informed me, as he looked at the ingredients.

'Oh yes. You look convincing.'

'A *bûche de Noël*,' he said with flair, before breaking into a broad Aussie bush accent. 'It is a yule log, my love.'

I flinched at the term 'love' and chose to ignore it. 'What the hell is a yule log?'

'It is a log-shaped cake made of chocolate and chestnuts, and it's meant to be representative of the special wood log burned from Christmas Eve to New Year's Day in the Périgord province of France. The ceremony is a holdover from a pagan Gaulish celebration,' he said in one warm, knowing breath.

'Stop. You had me at chocolate and chestnuts.'

On Christmas morning, I woke to feather-like kisses on my face and Jake desperate to give me his gift: a vintage Chanel rhinestone and pearl flower brooch. It was the most exquisite piece of jewellery I had ever seen and all

I wanted to do was show the girls back home. I now had my final 'accessory'.

'It is stunning,' I said, pinning it to my cami.

'It is befitting my Gamilaroi Princess, I think.' Jake kissed me on the forehead.

'I have something for you too.' I climbed over him and reached into my bag near the bed. 'I hope you like it – them.'

He ripped the paper off like a five-year-old. I was feeling anxious, praying that he would appreciate his gift as much as I did mine.

'I know this blue box. What did you do?'

He gave me a cheeky smile as he untied the signature white ribbon.

'If you don't like them, you can change them, I don't mind.'

Of course I would mind, I walked the length and breadth of the city to find cufflinks with red on them somewhere. It turned out they were waiting for me in Tiffany's; Paloma Picasso had made a set in sterling silver with red enamel.

I couldn't believe the size of the smile on Jake's face and I knew he loved his gift immediately.

'Red is my favourite colour, they'll look great with my tie.'

'I know, I know, that's what I thought. And they match my bag and shoes.' I was excited that Jake was excited.

'We'll be the flashest Blacks in town,' he said, looking at the box and then at me.

'Not hard when we're the only ones.'

We both had gifts from home to open. Mum and the boys sent me a small photo album with pics of everyone and some shots from around town. It was the best gift.

Lauren sent me a thin white belt for my growing wardrobe. 'Be daring', she wrote on the card. Bec sent me some red glitter, heart-shaped earrings from Hauz of Dizzy. I put them on straight away. And Caro sent me a silver cork stopper in case I ever left anything in the bottle once opened.

Dom and Catherine popped in briefly before going to visit their son and grandchildren. Catherine gave me some beautiful red woollen material and said she had spoken to Sorina, who was going to make me a skirt. I cried and hugged her.

Dom gave me a lavender plant. 'This one should survive, Libby, it is sturdy and can stay indoors. But maybe water it occasionally.'

We all laughed when we looked at the plant, and what was left of my original one.

'And for you . . .' I handed them a gift I'd ordered from the Archie Roach Foundation. Inside was his memoir, the kids picture book version, the CD of his story, stickers, and a cap, all wrapped up in a tote. I saw a tear fall down Catherine's left cheek, and I hugged her. 'And here's a little something for Romeo,' I whispered in her ear.

I'd had Sorina make a little red, black and yellow dog collar for the cheeky poodle, and matching collars for Bonnie and Clyde back home.

After Dom and Catherine left, Jake and I spent the day inside, entertaining ourselves as snow uncharacteristically swept across the city. The blizzard outside mirrored the storm of happiness inside as we danced around the apartment in our underwear and jewellery listening to music, eating our divine menu of foie gras, stuffed turkey and our yule log. We even amazed ourselves with our ability to cook an above-average Christmas lunch.

Chapter 22

It happened again

I woke up on New Year's Day with memories of Jake and I making love in the fifth floor conference room the night before. Along with other staff, we'd enjoyed the stunning view from the embassy overlooking the Eiffel Tower. There had been a huge crowd present, lots of belly laughs, wild dance-floor antics, incredible food and an endless stream of champers.

I couldn't believe that not only had we not got caught but we'd managed to ignore the fact that ministers met around that table we made love on, and that staff meetings were held in that room. How would we ever sit through another briefing again?

I was glad to be back in my apartment to deal with the hangover from lack of sleep and to do something about the state of my own home. It looked like a bomb had hit, and I had a long list of domestic duties to attend to and some shopping to do. I'd managed to run low on all the basics: detergent, soap, loo paper, juice.

I smiled when my phone rang, knowing it would be Jake.

'Have you seen *Bienvenue chez les Ch'tis*?' he asked.

I tried to translate quickly. '*Welcome to the Sticks*? Is it a movie about Deni?'

'You're hilarious, but no. It translates to *Welcome to the North of France*. It's a contemporary classic.'

'Well, I haven't seen any movie about the northern sticks of France.' I laughed at my own attempted humour.

'Then put on your little Moulin Rouge outfit,' Jake said in a cheeky voice, 'and I'll bring over a bottle and we'll have a night in.'

He arrived at about seven and we were both still in a state of recovery from the previous night's party. We ate and drank very little before settling on the bed to watch the movie.

'The people in the north don't have the sun, but they have the sun in their heart,' Jake mused, as the movie drew to a close.

'I like that.' I cuddled in closer to him.

'And you're the sun in my heart,' he said, as the credits rolled and his moves began.

As I watched Jake from my window the next morning, I was privately glad he was going away to Prague for a few days to join the prime minister's tour, so I could catch up on emails and FaceTime the girls. I still hadn't shown them my Chanel brooch. I felt secure with Jake, though I missed him the minute he turned the corner at the end of the street.

I worked ten-hour days while he was gone, because I was filled with inspiration and adrenaline. I tried not to pine for him but I surprised myself with how much I felt the loss. I saw him everywhere I looked and could still smell him in my flat. He was in every waking – and most of my sleeping – thoughts.

By day three, I couldn't wait for him to get back to Paris. Prague seemed a hemisphere away. I really needed my man nearby, in the same city, preferably the same building and more so the same bed.

On the night Jake was due back in Paris, I stayed awake as long as possible, desperate just to hear his voice and know he was safe. I'd never craved another person like I craved him. I knew I'd only be at peace fully when he was back in my arms.

By 9 pm my eyes were heavy and I crashed on top of the covers, fully clothed. The phone rang at 11 pm and woke me, startled, but I knew it could only be him and smiled before I even answered.

'It's me,' Jake said down the line. 'I'm downstairs, I need to see you.'

'I missed you!' I buzzed him in and raced to the bathroom to squeeze toothpaste into my mouth quickly. I wanted a long pash as soon as he got in the door.

'I missed you,' I repeated, wrapping myself around him as soon as I opened the door, planting a kiss on his now sexier-than-ever thin lips.

I wanted to tell him I loved him but he kissed me again gently before I had the chance.

'We need to talk,' he said softly.

'You must be tired, we can talk tomorrow.' I kissed his neck and started to peel off his jacket. 'I missed you so much.'

'I missed you too, but we need to talk tonight.'

He was serious and I started to panic. It was never a good thing when a woman said those words, but when a man did it was always going to be bad.

'Suzanne is coming to Paris.'

There was silence. I stepped back confused. 'Who?'

'Suzanne, my ex.' He looked as confused as I did. 'She called me when I was in Prague and said she's coming to Paris.'

'What for? Why? And who cares? She's with the friggin' frigger, isn't she? She left you. You're with me now.'

I moved towards him, trying to claim the man I had missed the past few days. The man who maybe I had fallen in love with and who made me happy.

'She wants to make a go of it,' he blurted out.

'What do you mean she wants to make a go of it? She left you. You moved here. You're with me, right?'

I stepped back flabbergasted, getting angrier by the second over the fact that instead of falling into a passionate heap we were talking about his ex who was too lazy to keep her marriage or business going.

I was careful not to run her down though; I knew it was important to keep the higher ground, remain dignified, and be in control. She was the bitch. I was the wonderful, kind, caring one.

Stay calm, I told myself. *Be reasonable*. I searched for the right thing to say to end the conversation.

'You're not married anymore. So there's nothing to make a go of anyway.'

'Actually, technically I still am,' he said softly, with a strained look on his face.

'What do you mean you're *technically still married*? You told me you were single!' I could hear my voice getting louder and I felt a hot rush. I was losing control.

'We never actually got divorced.' He said the words softly as if he didn't want to hear them himself either.

'What? Are you crazy? You've been doing all this with me and you're still fucking married? You're a fucking liar and a bastard!'

I threw one of the candles from the windowsill at him. There was no point in telling myself to be calm now, it was too late. I started to breathe quickly as my mind raced and the room became blurry. I could hear him mumbling but I couldn't decipher what was happening. I sat down on the bed.

Jake sat next to me. 'I'm only married on paper, I haven't been in a marriage, so to speak, for over two years. I told you that.'

'So why is she calling you in Prague then?' Nothing was adding up. 'I didn't think you kept in contact.'

'I sent her divorce papers last week and told her I'd met you, that I loved you and my future was with you.'

I felt the walls in my already tiny room closing in on me. Despite all my efforts not to cry, I couldn't help it. I started to sob uncontrollably, as if years of crying had been waiting for release.

Jake put his arm around me, but I felt betrayed and pushed him away hard. My tears were burning my face, I was getting hotter and hotter and I felt dizzy.

'Libby, stop, please,' his voice was shaky. 'I didn't lie to you. I never got around to getting a divorce is all. Meeting you and realising that I never wanted to be apart from you is what set the legal process in motion.'

'You're a fucking liar, you all are,' I screamed. 'And you're an idiot. Which makes you a perfect match for her. You deserve each other.' I punched him hard in the arm. 'Get off my bed.'

I felt like Jake had completely deceived me. I felt like the past months had been a lie. That there was no real connection, no love, no honesty, no future at all.

She was coming back to claim what she should never have let go. She was the one he had loved all those years. How could I compete with all that history? Why did I fool myself into believing that it would be different this time, that the universe had been kind to me out of pity for all the misery of the past?

The room was silent except for my deep sobs.

'Libby, please say something.' There was a quiver in his voice.

'She wants you back after all this time? Why?'

He sat silently with his head in his hands. 'I don't know why.'

'I'll tell you why.' If I had to spell it out like a school-teacher I would. 'She only wants you back because you're happy with someone else. Classic. *I don't want you but I don't want anyone else to have you* – nice woman indeed.'

'Libby, please.'

'Don't defend her.' I put my hand up to his face. 'She cheated on you. Or have you forgotten about the ute root? What happened to him? Let me guess, he couldn't bankroll the business she doesn't know how to run?'

'Libby, stop it, sarcasm doesn't suit you. You are better than that.'

'Yes, I am!' I shook my head. 'At least tell me you are smart enough to realise what she's doing. Or maybe you're not. Maybe you want her back. Is that what you want? What about how happy we've been?'

He was silent.

I felt a sudden pain in my heart. I didn't want to argue. I wanted him. I wanted to tell him how much he meant to me. But there was no way I could tell him I loved him now, not if he was thinking of going back to *her*.

'It's the honeymoon period, that's what we were supposed to feel.'

I was furious again. 'What the fuck? You've had one girlfriend your entire life, and by the sounds of it she walked all over you and then left you for a bloke she knew for five minutes in the back of a ute. What the hell would *you* know about the freaking honeymoon period?'

He looked sheepish.

Then it dawned on me. 'Oh, I get it. Let me guess. She

said something like: *you can't compare a few months with her with all those years with me*, is that right? Because we're just in the honeymoon period?'

He tilted his head to one side, looking apologetic.

'Jake, you know in the end she was using you for your money, don't you?'

'She did love me. She says she still does.'

I started to yell. I found a lung capacity I didn't know I had, and all the years of betrayal, infidelity, emotional and psychological abuse by men who were not good enough found a place in my vocal cords.

'So, what was I? Just one of those 5-to-7-pm affairs everyone talks about in Paris? Is that what I was?'

We were both standing up and he walked towards me. He reached for my hand.

'No, you know that's not what we had. I love you.'

'If you love me, why are we having this conversation?' I looked him directly in the eye. 'Because you don't love me enough, clearly.'

I turned to face the window and stared into the night sky.

'I'm pretty sure it's you who doesn't love me,' he said behind me.

I didn't turn around, rather stood there silently looking down at a lone woman on the street.

'Do you think that when the honeymoon period is over, we'll have nothing left to feel, or share or even like about each other? Is that it?'

'That's not it,' he said, stumbling over his words as if he'd forgotten his script or, worse, didn't have one. 'It's just that she was my first love. The only love I had until I came here, until I met you.'

'She wants to reconcile so you're just going to do it?' I could hardly breathe I was so angry. 'You are pissweak.'

I walked towards the door, while he just stood looking as useless as he was.

'*And* you're a monumental fool. Get out.' I opened the door.

'Libby, please,' he mumbled, on the verge of tears.

'I need a man with a high IQ and a high EQ, and certainly one who knows right from wrong. And clearly that's not you. Get out, and don't ever speak to me again.'

He didn't move.

'LEEEAAAAVVVVE!!!' I yelled.

He walked past me, head hung low.

I slammed the door behind him.

Chapter 23

The universe is a bitch

Tears flooded my cheeks for the rest of the night as I cried out a lifetime of disappointment. I had never felt such heartache before. I couldn't sleep and lay awake analysing and over-analysing Jake's actions, his irrational thinking. How he could just decide to walk away and go back to a woman he had admitted didn't love him.

It dawned on me that this was the very reason why I had never believed in love or the One: because, inevitably – unless the universe was in a really good mood – chances were things like this happened. They always happened to me. I'd had the final humiliation: yet another man had left me for another woman, even though I loved him more than she ever could.

I saw Peter's hickeys and Andy's loving look at another woman and Ames in the bath with the skeleton and my world came crashing down around me. But even with those memories burned into my mind and my heart, nothing had prepared me for the pain I felt at that moment, or hurt me as much.

I went to work the next morning but the entire day was a blur. I walked to and from the bus and Métro stations on autopilot, with my legs feeling like they were full of lead. I had no appetite at all, and was terrified of bumping into Jake. I made my way through security, up the lift and to my desk as quickly as possible, looking at the ground most of the time.

I was paranoid that my eyes were red and puffy from crying. My new boss, Bronwyn, was still on Christmas leave, and an email to all staff detailed the movements of the ambassador and the first secretary. They were out of the office for three days. I sighed with relief when I read the message, and I realised Jake and I hadn't discussed the week beyond the night of his return.

I was glad I had no meetings to attend. I wasn't up to making small talk or serious talk. I'd received messages from the girls back home and one from Canelle, who wanted to catch up for a drink, but I didn't even have the capacity to chat online.

Sorina also messaged me to say she'd reached 1000 fans on Instagram and had orders for fifteen skirts and twenty-five handbags and that business was booming. I could read the happiness in her words. She wasn't sleeping either, it seemed, but for much more positive reasons. I smiled for her, but it was all I could muster.

I went through the processes of a job that for the first time was a grind. By bedtime I couldn't remember the conversations I'd had or the ground that I had travelled. I fell into an exhausted sleep after spending more time beating myself up for falling so hard for Jake, only to be humiliated all over again.

'What's wrong?' Canelle said down the line as I trudged across the road the next morning. 'I texted you last night. You usually get back straightaway. I know you're in love and all, but please don't lose your manners like those other women you don't like.'

'I went to bed early,' I said pathetically.

'Are you sick, Elizabeth?'

'Yes,' I said softly, exhausted.

'What is it? COVID? Or this terrible flu sweeping across Paris? I am still fighting it off.'

'No, I'm sick of men.' I burst into tears.

Embarrassed but still holding the phone to my ear, I turned from the footpath to face a wall, but it was a salon window and in it I saw my reflection. I hardly recognised myself. I looked so sad it scared me. This was not who I was. This was not who I wanted to be and it certainly wasn't someone that anyone else would want to be around.

'Meet me at Ladurée Bonaparte now, I am on my way.' Canelle had given the directive and I was without the strength to argue.

I was ahead in my duties from working overtime while Jake had been away, and I didn't feel like I could be productive at the embassy. I made my way to the Ladurée tearoom in the heart of the Saint-Germain-des-Prés district. The décor was elegant and looking at the sweets on offer cheered me up and upset me at the same time because I was reminded of the macarons Jake had given me.

'He dumped me,' I cried into my green tea. I'd lessened my caffeine intake after noticing it made my already sensitive state of mind more hyper.

Canelle didn't ask for details, and I didn't want to go through it, it was too painful.

'Go away for the weekend. Go for a week. How much leave do you have?' Canelle was concerned and practical.

'I have eight days, I think. I'd have to check.'

'Then go for eight days, at least. You need to be away from where the memories are, and out of that office.' She put her hand on mine, caringly.

'But where to?' I asked, not being able to think clearly.

'Go to Barcelona. It is warmer there, the men are nicer, trust me, they are not so stupid as your Jake man. He is, how you say, a jerk. Go see Judith – she is a good friend, another tidda, *oui*?'

'A tidda, *oui*.'

I started to think Canelle might be right, just as she took my phone from the table.

'What are you doing?'

'I am calling Judith, I will organise it. This is what friends do.'

I put in for leave and Bronwyn, while not having become a close friend of mine, knew that I'd worked hard over Christmas and approved my eight days owing.

I hadn't heard from or contacted Jake. As I prepared for Barcelona, I went through the motions of life as much as possible, although every minute it felt as if someone was standing on my chest, squashing my heart. I knew it was pumping blood around my body, but that was all the good it was.

I was an emotional wreck and didn't want to share my misery with anyone back home, so I didn't contact the girls. I didn't want to lie to them, and I knew my silence would suggest I was busy being happy. They would only worry if they knew the truth.

I went to Mama Shelter – where I'd stayed in my first days in Paris – for a drink after work on the night before I was to leave. I reluctantly agreed to meet Sorina there. She was full of beans on the phone at how successful her skirts and bags had become and was lining up meetings with local stores to stock some of her work.

I promised myself I wouldn't burden her with my miserable dramas when we met; she had enough real dramas herself, feeling insecure in a country she called home. I needed perspective, however difficult it was.

Billabong boy wasn't there – there was a new barman with the face of a twelve-year-old. There was a new girl behind the bar, youthful and very pretty, French pretty, with big eyes and dramatic makeup, blood-red pouting lips and a petite build. I hated her the minute I heard the barman call her Suzette.

Lionel Ritchie sang 'All Night Long' in the background and I could feel tears welling up. I hated myself again.

I was a strong Black woman with a great career and I was in Paris. What the hell was I doing crying to Lionel Ritchie?

I looked at the ceiling as if I'd never seen it before, but I had, dozens of times. I tilted my head upwards and read the range of famous quotes, hoping the tears would run back into their ducts.

'Born to be wild', 'Africa is the future', '*Je hais les resignes*', which I knew meant 'I hate the resigned'. I hated Jake right then. He had resigned himself to being with the wrong woman. If Billabong boy were there, he would've given me some chalk to write on the ceiling, 'Jake is a complete idiot!' and then in French, '*Jake est un idiot total!*'

'*Bonsoir*, Libby,' Sorina surprised me out of my thoughts.

'*Bonsoir*,' I said, sadly. 'What is wrong?'

Oh god, I didn't want to go through it all again and I wondered if I should've just posted an Instagram story saying, 'Jake and I are over, he is an idiot and I am back on the man-fast' so everyone knew the story at the same time and no repetition was required. Against my will, I told Sorina as much as I could stomach without falling into a miserable heap at the bar.

'I think maybe it's my own fault. Karma for all the terrible things I've done and said in my life to date. Or maybe I deserve it because I keep choosing the same kind of men – bastards!'

'My friend, you are such a kind, giving and generous woman.' Sorina smiled warmly and put her hand on mine. 'Look what you have done to support me, my career and most importantly, my life here. It has not only helped me, but my family also.'

'Thanks, Sorina.' I tried to sound grateful. 'I know you are trying to make me feel better, but I can't feel better. I am too angry with Jake and with myself. Maybe my time away with Judith in Barcelona will make me feel better about everything, about life.'

'I think you are right,' she nodded. 'And especially some time away from the office and the chances of seeing Jake.'

I was drunk when I got back to my apartment and was glad that I was never one to do the drunk dial. I logged onto my computer to check that my departure time for the next morning hadn't changed, and to send a quick note to Judith.

There were messages from Lauren, Bec and Caro asking why I hadn't been in touch. I still didn't want to tell them the latest disaster for the woman who didn't want to meet men anyway. I was embarrassed, especially after calling Lauren about Ames when I was drunk. I needed to appease them though, so I sent a brief message.

Hi girls, Sorry been quiet, been flat out and taking some time off to chill. Will write more later. Love you loads and hope everyone's healthy and happy xx

Just before I logged off, I realised there was a new email from Jake I had missed.

This is not what I want. I want us to be friends. Why won't you talk to me?

Because you're a fucking idiot! is what I wanted to write, but the embassy firewall wouldn't let it through anyway. I was surprised that he'd used the company email to send something so personal, but then I remembered I had blocked him on all my socials. So I typed something I knew would pass.

Choose whichever one of the following you like the most:

- If you've got nothing nice to say, say nothing.
- The quickest way to get over a man is in the arms of another.
- If you love something let it go, if it comes back, it's yours, if it doesn't, track it down and shoot it!

I hit the 'send' button and passed out.

Chapter 24

Au revoir, Jake

I didn't know how I was ever going to pull it off. I rested my head on the handle of my cabin bag, exhausted and emotionally drained. I waited for my case to appear on the baggage carousel and wondered how I could feign happiness to Judith, who was waiting for me through the Spanish customs doors.

With extra effort, I dragged my bag off the conveyor belt and headed towards the frosted glass. I took a deep breath as the doors opened and I saw Judith there, right in the middle of the crowd of others waiting for family and friends.

The minute she saw me, she smiled, waved her arms and jumped slightly. It was like a bolt of sunshine went right through me and instantly I felt better. The power of female friendship had never felt so remarkable.

'It's good to see you,' Judith said, hugging me tightly. 'You look good.'

I knew then she was lying; I looked terrible, having spent the last few days crying more than sleeping.

'Thanks for letting me come to visit. I really need a break, a holiday.' It wasn't a lie. I did need a break.

The driver lifted my case into the boot of a cab and we both climbed in the back seat. Judith gave him directions as I stared out the window.

'I like having visitors. I'm still making friends here so I'm glad you came.' Judith seemed genuinely pleased to see me, which also lifted my mood. 'We're going to get some Catalan culture and caring into you. And we don't have to talk about you-know-who at all, unless you want to.'

'I'm sorry I didn't tell you. We didn't think it was a good idea for staff to know.'

I felt weird being with Judith then, because she had known Jake longer than I had and, as far as I knew, she never had a clue about Jake and me.

'Libby, I knew about you two the whole time.' Judith looked kindly at me.

'How?' I was totally surprised. 'Did he tell you?'

'He didn't need to. He always beamed when you were in the room, or when your name was mentioned. Personally, I don't think he was a happy man until he met you. I actually thought he was gay!'

We both laughed. 'Clearly I was wrong.'

Already I felt Judith and Barcelona were going to be food for my soul. I noticed then that the elegant burgundy stripes in her blonde bob had been changed to green and that they matched her green-framed glasses. Being a translator in

Catalunya was less stifling to the personality than working for the Australian government in Paris, it seemed.

The cab pulled up outside Judith's building in the La Ribera district of the upmarket El Born area.

Judith chatted away as we exited the cab and I half-listened.

'There are designer outlets next door, including Hugo Boss, but I don't even look in his windows. You know, he was a member of the Nazi party and a supplier of uniforms for the SS and Hitler Youth?' Judith was always full of trivia that I needed to know but didn't.

'And across the road is a nineteenth-century market-place, so it's pretty noisy during the day. But the Basilica de Santa Maria del Mar and the Museu Picasso are only minutes walking distance away, so there's plenty for you to do locally.'

Judith was talking a lot and I didn't know if it was because she was talking for both of us or because she had been without company just a tad too long.

We took the lift to the second floor, stopping right outside Judith's door. Her enormous flat had tiled floors, ornate ceilings and pale yellow walls covered with an eclectic mix of paintings and prints. There were three bedrooms, a bathroom door held closed by a chopstick and a kitchen painted blue.

She took me straight to my room at the back of the apartment with a small balcony facing another residential block. The place was full of light and I felt welcomed immediately.

'I got these stripy sheets and a new bathmat just to mark your visit,' she said, handing me new towels as well.

'Just for me?' I was surprised and embarrassed by her unnecessary effort.

'Just for you. It's a treat for me to have you here.'

'Really?' I couldn't imagine having a misery guts in your house as something of a treat.

'Yes, I'm missing Paris and Australia and you bring a little of both.' Judith hugged me. 'Now, I have a meeting at the Centre de Cultura Contemporània de Barcelona, or the CCCB for short, but here's your key and there's a guidebook there,' she pointed to the desk in my room, 'if you feel like going out. Or else you can just chill here. I'll be back in about three hours and we'll have a tinto de verano. It's a red wine spritzer.'

I wasn't sure what I wanted at that point and said nothing.

'If you go out, be sure and hold on to your handbag like this.' She tucked her own bag right under her arm. 'Bag snatches happen all the time, sometimes they have knives. If you've got a good grip, they'll probably leave you alone.'

'Shit!' I was shocked and scared.

'It's never happened to me, I'm just giving the warnings that everyone gets, okay?'

Judith shut the massive medieval door behind her and I just lay flat on the bed and closed my eyes. I felt the weakest I'd ever felt, with no energy and no desire to move at all.

'Wake up to yourself,' I said out loud and pulled myself up off the bed.

I unpacked my toiletries and put on a fresh face of makeup to make myself feel better. I didn't want to turn Judith's home into another misery den, simply relocated from Paris. I looked around the bedroom and thought how emancipating it was to have so much space. Judith's apartment was four times the size of my place back in Le Marais.

I slowly descended the eighty-two stairs down to the street, hoping for just a little exercise and to start exploring Judith's town. I liked her new home: it was a busy little village inside the big city of Barcelona.

I walked for a while and found a place called Carrer de la Princesa.

I smiled for no reason, other than the fact I liked the name.

I accidentally found the Picasso museum and like every other tourist there, I paid my entry fee and spent the afternoon taking in the genius of the renowned artist. The gallery space and works helped to ground me, as visual art always had, and I thought about Lauren and how much she would've appreciated the opportunity to visit.

It was a gentle reminder of how lucky I was in the big scheme of things and that love was only one part – albeit an often-painful part – of life. I was back to remembering that the best relationship I'd ever had was with my work.

As I walked through the museum shop, I compared the size, layout and stock with that of the NAG, and I started to get homesick. It was the first time that I'd felt that way since meeting Jake. He had filled the void of home and since he had left that void was now large enough to be seen from space.

For the next few days, Judith was busy at work in her new job as a literary translator for local Catalan writers and cultural organisations, so I jumped on the Spanish version of the open-roofed tour bus.

It was cold, sitting in the January weather, but I needed the fresh air. It helped to clear my head, and I didn't have the energy to walk like I did when I first arrived in Paris. I put on the audio guide headphones but didn't really listen to the commentary as I feigned interest in the Gaudi architecture that was typical in the city.

Barcelona was as big as Paris and densely populated. I was zombie-like as we cruised past various cultural and historically significant buildings: the Barcelona FC Football Stadium, the Olympic Stadium, the Barcelona Cathedral, a monument to Christopher Columbus, the Barcelona Palace and the Miró museum.

I wanted to check it all out but I just couldn't focus. All I could think about was Jake. The pain of missing him was only heightened by the knowledge that 'she' had probably arrived in Paris. As he fell back into the marital bed, I fell deeper and deeper into a pit of despair. If this was true love then I never wanted to love again.

I got off the bus at La Sagrada Familia, in need of a spiritual injection. I went into the iconic church and lit a candle, trying to remember the last time I had said a prayer. It was overwhelming in size and I was enveloped by a sense of peace that only a house of prayer could bring. I momentarily thought I should consider going to mass sometime.

The days were long in Barcelona, and each felt like it would never end. I was enjoying playing tourist but I was lonely for Jake. Each day I sat for hours in Plaza Catalunya, the most famous square in Barcelona. I spent the time watching people come and go. They would sit, talk, drink coffee and catch up with friends. I had never felt so alone in my life.

I walked around Judith's local park, back along the harbour up to La Rambla – where tourists flooded the famous walkway – and around some backstreets, trying to remember which direction Judith's apartment was in. I walked with purpose: to beat the heartache, to take control of my mind and focus on my project: to get Jake out of my system and to start planning my return to Australia.

I felt empty; the loss greater because I'd taken a chance with Jake, even after Ames. I had believed he was different, that he was honest, that he wouldn't abandon me like the others. I saw a woman across the street who looked like Lauren and I felt another pang of homesickness.

I started thinking about going home, seeing my tiddas, losing myself in my work at the NAG. I just wanted to get back to Bonnie and Clyde, to Braddon, where I hoped I would never see Jake again.

In my depressive state, I walked around the Parc de la Ciutadella across the road from Judith's. It was the best thing I could have done. I needed some green space even if I couldn't have my favourite gum trees. I felt like I was in an oasis with its lake and fountain and palm trees.

I was as interested in the museums bordering the park and the Catalan Parliament building in the centre as I was in the people. One man in jeans and a black jacket sat on a bench playing the guitar for himself and anyone who walked past. He wasn't busking, just enjoying his craft, singing in what I assumed was Catalan but I really couldn't tell the difference between that and Spanish. It sounded more folksy than anything else, and as I smiled when I passed him he nodded in appreciation that I enjoyed his craft.

His voice faded as I continued to walk and focused on a jogger climbing the stairs of the Cascada fountain. Then I heard yelling and looked to my left to see a couple arguing in the rotunda. I stopped to make sure it was just a verbal, and felt pain imagining they were breaking up. Within seconds, they were hugging and kissing. The joy of making up, right in front of my eyes.

I sat on a bench and thought of life going on around me in this microcosm of the world: someone loving music and words, someone loving the joy of health, a couple loving each other.

I closed my eyes and smiled at the faintest hint of the sun hitting my lids. Winter is less harsh when you can find a spot out of the wind with a bit of sun. That thought carried me back to the opera house steps with Jake and tears escaped again.

I stood up, sniffled, shook my head and said to myself, 'I will survive.'

As I walked on, I heard Gloria Gaynor in my head belting out that defiant anthem that so many women sing at karaoke. Then Mariah Carey started with 'I Can't Live' and I had images of Bridget Jones singing into a vodka bottle and hitting the floor. I didn't know if I wanted to laugh or cry.

When I opened the door, Judith sang out. 'I'm in the kitchen.'

I walked in.

'It's happy hour,' she said, pouring me a glass of sparkling cava wine.

'Clearly,' I said, happy to be having a drink and a home-cooked meal. 'What can I do?'

'You can slice these.'

She passed me the reddest tomatoes I'd ever seen. It was nice to do something normal like prepare a meal with a friend.

'How was your walk?'

'It was fine until Gloria Gaynor invaded my headspace.'

'What?'

'Slap me!' I demanded.

'What?' She almost spat her cava across the table, laughing. 'I want you to slap me out of my misery, please.'

Judith laughed harder. 'You are hilarious!'

'I'm serious. Really. I want you to slap me hard!' I was almost begging Judith. 'I need to wake up to myself.'

'You don't need a slap,' Judith said softly, moving in to hug me. 'You need to have faith in rational thought. I'm not taking sides at all, but I will say that Jake was rational in all his work; let's just hope he can be rational now.'

'It's too late for me, Judith.' I shook my head and felt a wave of sadness come over me. 'He made a choice the minute he left my flat that night. He's an idiot. She's an idiot. They are perfect for each other. They can have their idiot life back now.'

'Okay, sounds like *you* need some rational thought, my friend.'

Judith sat down.

'Why aren't I rational?' I was annoyed. 'I had a great life before I met him. I was happy. I loved my family, my friends, my job, my life in Paris. I didn't want a boyfriend. I didn't go looking for a man. I actively stayed away but I took a chance on him. When I got the job at the embassy I was thrilled about the project. I was happy . . . did I say that already?'

'Yes, you did.' Judith sat there listening intently.

'And then he came along and fucked it all up, and took my happiness away.' I was crying again.

Judith handed me a box of tissues.

'Why don't you make a list of all the wonderful things in your life right now?' Judith reached across the table, grabbing a notepad and pen. 'You are, after all, the girl of lists, as I remember.'

I wiped my face and blew my nose. 'The sad thing is, I used to tell Lauren that the quickest way to get over a man is in the arms of another, because I wanted her to move on from Adam, but now I see what ridiculous advice it was. Another man is only going to cause me more pain.'

'Forget the man, let's make the list.' Judith was pragmatic.

I began the list of wonderful things as Judith checked the food on the stove.

- I am in Barcelona.
- I've been in Paris for six months – and I love everything about the city.
- I've just overseen a successful international exhibition at the Musée du Quai Branly.
- I'm working on an amazing First Nations arts initiative across Western Europe for the Australian embassy.
- I have deadly tiddas in Canberra, Paris and Spain.

I handed her my draft.

'This is a great list, and once you add that you are beautiful, healthy and intelligent, with a keen eye for fashion,' she winked, 'there will be absolutely no need to worry about Jake or any man at all, according to the list anyway.'

'The thing is, Judith, I think Jake might be the love of my life.'

I couldn't believe I had just said it out loud. Jake *was* the love of my life. I knew it, but it was too late.

'Then there may be a problem.' Judith sighed.

'Oh, you think?' I was being sarcastic.

'My grandmother once told me that most women don't marry the loves of their lives.'

'Really?'

'No. Most women marry men who will be a good husband, a good provider. That's probably why Suzanne wants Jake back. I don't know much about her, but my guess is she knows he will always take care of her. He's not the love of her life, obviously; she wouldn't have left him in the first place if that were the case. And she certainly wouldn't have let him leave the country without her.'

I nodded. 'That's what I tried to tell him, but he didn't listen. And I don't need him to "provide for me" – I don't need him in a practical sense. I want him. I love him.'

It was true: I really loved him. But he'd come in, Miley Cyrus style, and ruined my life like a wrecking ball. It hurt so much because I loved him so intensely, but that realisation only served to upset me even more and I sobbed again.

I knew Judith was treading carefully with me and had caution in her voice.

'Darl, you need to understand that the difference between you and her – apart from her being a bitch and you being wonderful – is that she makes Jake feel needed. And as ridiculous as it sounds, some men want to feel needed. It gives them a greater purpose in the relationship.'

'Oh, for fucksake. They are more complicated than we are.' I poured out another huge glass of cava.

'I'll toast to that.' Judith lifted her glass in the air and then sipped.

I looked at her wanting more answers. 'Is it because of all this wisdom that you're not married then? I mean, there's some pretty hunky Spaniards in this town.'

'I've got my fair share of men in my life, Libby. But my lifestyle is different to yours. I have different men to give me different things. Some give me great intellectual conversation, some I talk literature with, some I philosophise with, and one or two pop around for sex. It's all I want right now. And I love them all in different ways and, most importantly, we all want the same thing from each other – and that includes respect.'

'Do you ever think about getting married and having children?' I was learning about a side of Judith I hadn't seen in Paris, and I was a little surprised.

'Not really,' she said matter-of-factly. 'I'm a bit of a nomad, in the true sense of the word. I'll probably just move around Europe forever.'

I just looked at Judith. She had it all sorted and was happy with her life.

'What about you? Do you want kids?' she asked with interest. 'You never mentioned kids in any capacity when we were at the embassy together.'

I pondered the question, then answered, unsure. 'I didn't think I did. I love my career and I now want to travel a lot more. And I'd never thought about children seriously until I met Jake. I'd be happy being a family just with him, no kids. You can be a family of two, can't you?'

'Of course, you could've been a family of two.'

I tried to ignore the past tense in Judith's comment.

I woke early and knew that if I lay in bed I'd just think about Jake and weep. I had to call Mum anyway to let her know I was alive, so I got up and headed out. Judith was still sleeping, having worked till all hours translating an essay for a philosophy professor friend of hers.

I pulled the heavy door closed behind me as gently as I could so I wouldn't wake her, but the builders were already drilling and welding noisily at the marketplace across the road anyway.

I found a quiet spot to call Mum – she always kept her mobile turned off, so I figured my best chance was on the landline. I should've called sooner, she'd be worried if she found out from someone else that I was in another country.

'Iris speaking.'

Mum answered the phone like she always did, and she sounded so close it made me homesick. I started to cry before I could speak.

'Iris speaking,' she said louder.

I took a deep breath.

'I don't know who it is.' She was talking to someone in the house with her. 'They're not saying anything.'

'It's me, Mum,' I said with a scratchy, patchy voice. 'Libby. I'm in Barcelona.'

I could hear the joy in her voice. 'Dear girl, it has been

so long. How are you? What are you doing in *Barthelona*?' she said with the Spanish lisp, as if she knew the lingo. It made me laugh.

'I'm visiting a friend here called Judith. She's the woman from Melbourne who was my boss at the embassy.'

I watched a kid on a bike cruise past and held my handbag tighter.

'The one with the funny hair?' Mum asked with a laugh.

'Yes, Mum, this week it's got green stripes, but it suits her.'

'What colour is yours then?'

I touched my hair and felt the frizz that needed cutting and colouring as soon as I got back to Paris.

'It's the same, Mum.'

'Is that man with you too? The one with the thin lips?'

'He's not here, it's over.' I couldn't say anything else and started to cry again.

'Dear girl, don't cry, come home. We love you, we miss you.' I could hear the concern in Mum's voice and I hated myself for causing her worry.

'No, Mum, I can't and that's not the answer. But I miss you too, you know that.'

I was trying to hold the phone and blow my nose at the same time.

'Mum, I don't know what to do about Jake. I love him,' I blurted out, then looked around to check that no-one had heard me.

'Did you tell him?'

'Not exactly.' I sniffled.

'Dear girl, the one thing I regret about my time with your father is that I never told him enough that I loved him. It was always he who told me. He was the romantic one. I was the practical one. I think you are too much like me sometimes.'

While Mum talked the tears just kept falling down my cheeks.

'Except when it comes to line dancing, because we both know you're not very good at that,' Mum said seriously, but she made me laugh. I didn't want to be good at line dancing but I said nothing.

Mum continued, 'Men need to feel loved, needed. A man who feels that way will never leave you.'

'But Dad left us.' I had finally said what I'd been bottling up inside all these years.

'Your father died, Libby.' Mum's tone made me feel like I was a teenager being pulled into line. 'He didn't leave you. He didn't leave *me*. He had a terrible addiction. I just wish I'd harped on about the smoking more. He would've listened if I nagged him enough, he always did. But it's too late now, and you need to stop blaming your father for dying.'

I said nothing. Mum was right. Until this moment, I had never been able to accept the truth that Dad died because of his own addiction. His desire to smoke was stronger than his will to live.

'If you love this Jake fella, tell him,' Mum said gently. 'Fight for him.'

'But . . .'

'You're not in Moree, Libs. You're not eighteen. This fella isn't Peter Dickhead Dreamboat.'

I couldn't believe Mum remembered Peter, or that she had said dickhead. Mum never swore.

'Maybe you're right,' I sighed.

'I am your mother. I am *always* right when it comes to what's best for you. And I know that when you talked about this Jake fella, I felt it in my waters. You two are meant to be together, but maybe you won't be because sometimes the timing is all wrong, but it doesn't mean you're not perfect for each other.

'But either way, dear girl, you will be fine. You come from a long line of strong Gamilaroi women who know how to live their lives without relying on men to be happy. And only when you are happy yourself will you be truly happy with someone else.'

'Are you happy, Mum?'

Mum laughed. 'Of course. I've got all my kids and grannies and my daughter is in *Barthelona* being a flash Black and is making me real proud.'

I hesitated. 'Are you ever going to have another boyfriend, Mum?'

'Don't be ridiculous, I'm still married to your father.'

She *was* still married to my father and he'd been dead for over twenty-five years. That was a love I couldn't imagine. It made me think of the line in *Moulin Rouge*: the greatest thing in life you'll ever learn is to love and to be loved in return. I wondered if Mum had seen the movie.

With some hope in my voice, I said goodbye. 'I better go, Mum, I love you.'

'I love you too, dear girl.'

I walked back to Judith's with a greater sense of control over my emotions, if nothing else. It was the first time Mum had ever really talked about her love for Dad. With so much experience under her belt, perhaps she was right about Jake. Maybe he just needed to hear that I loved him, that I needed him in my life, that he made me happy. Maybe that was the other difference with 'her': she said the things Jake wanted to hear.

On my last morning in Barcelona, Judith took me to her favourite marketplace, the Mercat de Santa Caterina. The streets were quiet at 9 am because the Catalans were still sleeping; late nights meant late mornings here.

My brain was forcing thoughts of Jake to the front of my mind while Judith gave me commentary about the local buildings and architecture.

As we arrived at the freshly painted market building, I saw an explosion of colour through the fruit and vege-table displays and inhaled a strong yet unusually pleasant smell of fish.

I was amazed at the variety of everything and couldn't believe there were so many types of olives and eggs. I saw some ostrich eggs that reminded me of the carved emu egg I gave Mum for Christmas some years ago. That memory triggered an idea about getting an egg carver to Paris for an exhibition in the future. I pulled out my Moleskine and added it to my 'When I return to Paris: TO-DO LIST!'.

Judith had a favourite fishmonger called Jordi – a flirtatious fifty-year-old who winked at all his female customers – and we stopped to buy calamari and monkfish. Everything was so fresh that the crabs were still moving. It was unnerving.

As we bought mushrooms, old men stared at me and a young man said, '*Hola.*'

I knew that would've made Jake jealous, he always got funny when other men flirted with me. I liked the attention, but it took me back to the reason I was in Barcelona in the first place.

Judith ordered her vegetables in Catalan with ease and I admired her ability with languages. I stepped back a minute and just looked around, watching the sellers and buyers exchange words and foods and euros.

Before long, the market was buzzing with life. I stood still and felt a lump forming in my throat, and I forced myself to swallow hard. I am in Barcelona. I am in the Mercat de Santa Caterina. I am among *pescado*, *ensalada*, olives and breads. No-one was going to have sympathy for me while I was in such good hands in such a wonderful country.

As Judith went to a supermarket nearby, I propped myself up at Bar Joan (pronounced 'juarn') and ordered an iced coffee and a coca de vidre, a local Catalan pastry, sweet with pine nuts.

There was an old couple sitting next to me. The woman was so tiny her shopping trolley was almost the same size as her, and the Catalan tomato bread she chewed on was almost as big as her head. The husband talked with an animated face as he played with the coins he would use to pay for their coffees.

I was inspired by the longevity of what I imagined their love to be. It reminded me of Mum still being married to Dad. That thought made me smile and have some hope for Jake and me.

As the Uber pulled into a drop-off bay at the airport, I was exhausted from thinking and crying and I was emotionally drained. I needed my energy back in order to finish my project at the embassy. The job was the one thing I could look forward to.

I had felt like Judith had given up trying to make me happy as she put me in a cab to the airport and handed me a card.

'Open it on board,' she said, and hugged me tight. 'Everything is going to be all right.'

I nodded and felt overwhelmed by the friendship she had offered me the past days.

'You are going to be fine,' she said through the cab window.

Fastening my seatbelt on my Qantas flight from Barcelona, I was surprised to see the plane only half-full, with about sixty other passengers heading to Paris. I guessed most travelled with the local airline, Iberia. I opened the card from Judith.

It simply read: 'Have faith in rational thought.'

By the time we landed in Paris, I felt stronger. I had decided that my tidda was right. I needed to have faith in rational thought: if not in Jake's, then at least in my own. And especially in Mum's.

I wasn't sure when or how I was going to do it, but I needed to let Jake know I loved him. That I had been missing him desperately, that losing him – us – had been the hardest thing I'd ever had to deal with since Dad's death.

Maybe he wouldn't take me back. I wanted to move into the future and get on with life, but I had to know that I had done my best with Jake. I now knew I hadn't. I would meet with Canelle and Sorina and fill them in and see if Jake was free for dinner.

You are going to be absolutely fine, I told myself, as I sat in the Uber on the way back to the 4th and rain drizzled down the window. I remembered the strength of my mum over the years, having to raise us kids without Dad to help her. I was like Mum: I was strong, and I would take on her wise ways too.

Chapter 25

I'll be fine with or without him

As the Uber driver put my case on the footpath, my phone rang. It was Lauren, furious she hadn't heard from me. I couldn't remember the last time she'd been in such a filthy mood.

'Can you cause people any more concern? No-one's heard from you for ten days, why haven't you answered our messages? People are worried. I'm worried.'

I was a little surprised at how angry she was with me. I felt like a chastised child.

'Apart from causing everyone concern, it's also out of character. And, it's rude of you not to return messages.'

While she took a breath I said, 'I've been in Barcelona, just landed in Paris. I'll call you back in five minutes, okay?'

She perked up. 'Barcelona?'

I could tell Lauren was already appeased at the thought of me having a holiday, without knowing the drama behind the trip.

'Speak in five,' I said quickly.

The call ended and I climbed the stairs, stopping at Dom and Catherine's along the way to let them know I was back. They greeted me like parents who had missed their only daughter.

'It's good to be home,' I said meaningfully.

I called Lauren and summarised the past few weeks. It was a painful exercise, but I had to get it all out, and she had to know.

'What are you going to do now?' she asked.

'I need to tell him how much I love him. That I want to be with him.' I was adamant. 'I just hope he wants to be with me.'

'Of course he wants to be with you, you're Libby Cutmore.'

'But I'll survive even if he doesn't. Let's face it,' I said confidently, 'I've got a pretty extraordinary life, and I am capable of great things. I was absolutely fine before I met him, and I'll be fine without him.'

'Yes, yes, yes,' Lauren said impatiently. 'Now get off the phone and call him.'

I laughed. 'Yep, you're right, I'll call him right now, while I'm full of Cutmore courage.' I felt stronger having talked to Lauren.

'And good luck, sis.'

'Thanks.'

'And when you're all finished loving each other up, try sending me a message, okay?' Libby laughed.

'I promise!'

I dialled Jake's number and got his voicemail. I hung up like a nervous teenager. I didn't want to leave an unscripted longwinded message. I caught my breath, wrote some dot points and dialled again. When the phone went to voicemail for a second time, I left a positive-sounding message.

'Jake, it's Libby. I'm back in Paris and I'd like to see you. I need to see you. Can we have dinner tonight?'

I then called Canelle and Sorina, and asked them to meet me in an hour on rue du Champ de Mars for coffee. I had to get some final support for what I needed to do.

I showered, changed and raced to the Métro, desperate to see my friends and bring the day closer to the night, when I hoped to see Jake. I took the train to Bir-Hakeim by mistake – on autopilot to work – but didn't mind. The extra walk gave me more thinking time.

But as I crossed rue Jean Rey I looked to the right and saw Jake standing next to a cab. There was a woman with him. It had to be Suzanne. She was much chunkier than I thought she'd be – for a yoga instructor – and her long mousy hair was straggly and in need of a good cut and colour. I knew I was being judgemental but it made me feel better about myself. Then he hugged her. I felt sick.

I turned and ran, hailing the first cab I saw, totally forgetting Sorina and Canelle.

I raced up the stairs at home, hoping Dom and Catherine weren't in my path along the way. I collapsed on my bed and screamed into the pillow for two minutes at the top of my lungs after throwing cushions around the room. I didn't think I had any more tears left, but they fell like waterfalls of sadness.

I ran to the bathroom and dry-retched over the toilet bowl, sick in the knowledge that I wasn't even going to get the chance to tell Jake how I felt now. I couldn't, not after seeing him happy with another woman. I had failed.

Then my buzzer went. *Fuck! Dom heard me screaming*, I thought.

'Hello?' I said softly.

I wanted to pretend I had just woken from my sleep and a bad dream. That at least could explain why I was such a physical wreck.

'It's Jake.'

I felt nauseous.

'What are you doing here?' I said, angrily.

'I got your phone message.'

'Was that before or after you were completely wrapped around *your wife* on the street?' I yelled, hoping that I wouldn't throw up while on the intercom.

'What?'

'I saw you at work.' I said accusingly. 'Bastard.' I couldn't help myself.

'Can I come up, please?' he pleaded.

I pressed the buzzer and let him in. I couldn't see the point in turning him away: there was nothing more he could do to hurt me now. But when he walked through my door, I thought my heart would break all over again. I had missed him so much.

'What's all this about being wrapped around someone on the street?' Jake looked completely confused.

'Well, I saw her. I saw you.'

I poked him so hard in the chest I nearly broke my finger.

'I saw the hug. I saw you being the "happy couple",' I said with venom as I made air quotes. 'That was her, wasn't it?'

He said nothing.

'Why are you shaking your head at me? Are you going to lie to my face now about it? For fucksake, I saw you!' I screamed.

'It was Suzanne,' he said, calmly.

'So, where's your wife now?' I looked out the window to see if there was a car waiting downstairs.

'On the way to the airport. She just dropped by work to give me these.' He held up an envelope. 'She signed the papers.'

'I don't care what she did.'

They were probably fake anyway, he probably just wanted to have her one more time.

I tried not to look at him. I wanted him to know I loved him, but I also wanted him to know how much I was hurting. How wrong I thought he had been.

I picked up my handbag and pretended to search for something. He took it from my hands and placed it on the floor. He put his arms around my waist and pulled me into him, looking into my eyes.

'Please stop being angry with me, I've missed you every nanosecond, Libby.'

Angry? I was furious. 'Oh, I'm sure. Every second you weren't in bed with her, right? Or at dinner with her, or walking in parks.'

My heart started aching again and I cried, hating myself for not keeping it together.

'I didn't sleep with her, we didn't . . .' he said, looking straight into my eyes.

'Yeah, right.' I pushed him away.

'Hear me out please, Libby, I have been desperate all this time you've been away. When she first arrived I just picked her up and took her to a hotel. She didn't come anywhere near my bed. She never even came to the residence.'

Jake looked at me like a child desperate for their parents' trust.

'Why?' I asked, disbelieving.

Jake held my face in his hands.

'Because I didn't want her at my place,' he said gently. 'You are the only woman I've had there, the only woman I wanted there.'

I could imagine how pissed off she must have been if this was the truth.

'I bet she wasn't happy about that.'

'I don't know, she didn't say. She just seemed happy to be in Paris.'

Something suddenly occurred to me. 'Oh fuck, did you pay for her and her yoga mat to come here?'

He was silent.

It was pathetic.

'You really are a doormat for her, aren't you? More money than brains.' I walked away from him.

He shook his head. 'Not anymore.' He walked towards me. 'I could hardly look at her without thinking of you. I hated her for tearing us apart. But I hated myself more for allowing her to.'

I could feel myself weaken at the thought that maybe he'd missed me as well.

'You let me get on a plane to Spain with a shattered heart and self-esteem.'

'I've been an idiot, Libby,' he said, wiping my tears with his thumbs.

'Yes, you have.'

'And I am filled with self-loathing for what I have put you through. Put us both through.'

'So you should be.' I was starting to feel slightly better.

'It's not *all* my fault, Libby,' he said cautiously.

'What? Are you saying it's my fault?' I could hear my voice rising again.

'You've never said you loved me. I had no idea where I stood.' I felt guilty.

'All this time, I'm the only one who said it. I was seeing you, and we were together, and I was happy, but I never knew if you loved me. You've never told me.'

Jake searched out my eyes, still looking for the answer I was desperate to give him.

'I would never have walked out that night if I knew that you really wanted me, but you let me go without saying it.'

'Of course I love you,' I said, taking his face in my hands. 'You are the love of my life. I thought you'd be the last man I'd ever love.'

Jake beamed. 'That's all I needed to know.' He kissed me gently. 'If you never say it again, it doesn't matter. I just needed to hear it.'

He hugged me so tight, he nearly squeezed the breath right out of me. I didn't care. I never wanted him to let go. 'What now?' I asked.

'I want to write a new chapter in my life.' He kissed me again and I could feel myself melt inside. 'And I want you to help me finish the book.'

'Okay,' I said, sniffling and wiping my face with the palm of my hand.

'Come with me.'

He took my hand, leading me towards the door to the stairway.

'It's wet out. Let's just stay here. I'll make some tea.'

'Please,' his eyes pleading with me, 'it's important.'

I followed him downstairs and he hailed a cab.

'The Pont des Arts,' he instructed the driver.

As we headed the short distance along the Seine and the place he first told me he loved me, my phone beeped. It was a message from Canelle.

Where are you?

I knew exactly what to reply.

I am exactly where I should be, where my eyes sparkle.

Acknowledgements

People talk about the process of writing as a solitary one. I have never felt that way. All my books require spending time with a great cast of real-life characters I like to call 'research assistants'. And in the case of *Paris Dreaming*, we had a lot of fun in a number of cities.

Firstly, for inspiring the visual arts element of this work, I acknowledge the individual artists showcased in my novel, and the curators of the Australian Indigenous Art Commission at the Musée du Quai Branly – Hetti Perkins and Brenda L Croft – who also introduced me to the name the Musée du Crème Brûlée.

I am grateful for assistance from the Musée, notably Philippe Peltier, and the generosity of spirit of Tom Menadue and Harriet O'Malley at the Australian Embassy in Paris. Your time back in 2010 was invaluable.

I'm deeply thankful to those who took on the role of 'assistant researchers' with passion, trudging through the streets of Paris for days and nights on end. *Merci beaucoup* to my local *parisienne* guide and reader Aline Gargar-Belmont and to friends Estelle Castro, Lora Fountain, Carol Aghajanian, David Martin, Susan Spooner and David Wright.

In Spain, I thank my tidda Julie Wark for hosting me, introducing me to Catalan culture and reading drafts over a glass or two of cava!

To my research team in Canberra – Kirsten Bartlett and Rachel Clarke – your dedication to my *Dreaming* titles still does not go unnoticed.

My thanks to the Moree Mademoiselles, Cathy Craigie and Miah Wright, for advice on their hometown. And to the Deniliquin Darlings, Steven Ross and Carlee Rundell-Gordon, much gratitude for introducing Libby and me to the Deni ute muster.

For aiding research, reading drafts and offering suggestions I took on board for the original ms, I thank Emily McDaniel, Caroline Verge, Anne Cranny-Francis, Bernardine Knorr and Michelle Crawford.

Thank you to the professional women who guide my career and sit and talk as friends also: my agent Tara Wynne (Curtis Brown), my Simon & Schuster publisher Cass Di Bello, and my incredible publicist Anna O'Grady. Thank you also to my editor Elizabeth King and all the team at S&S for making my writing dreams come true with this new edition of *Paris Dreaming*.

And to those I love the most, my family, thank you for always being there.

If you enjoyed *Paris Dreaming*, you'll love . . .

More fiction from Anita Heiss